COMPLETE.

JACK OF WARWICK
OR THE
Cowboy of Texas

EDWIN J. BRETT, LIMITED,
Harkaway House, C, West Harding Street,
London, E.C. and all Booksellers.

JACK OF WARWICK;

OR,

THE COWBOY OF TEXAS.

BEAUTIFULLY ILLUSTRATED.

COMPLETE.

LONDON :
"BOYS OF ENGLAND" OFFICE, 173, FLEET STREET, E.C.,
AND ALL BOOKSELLERS.

JACK OF WARWICK.

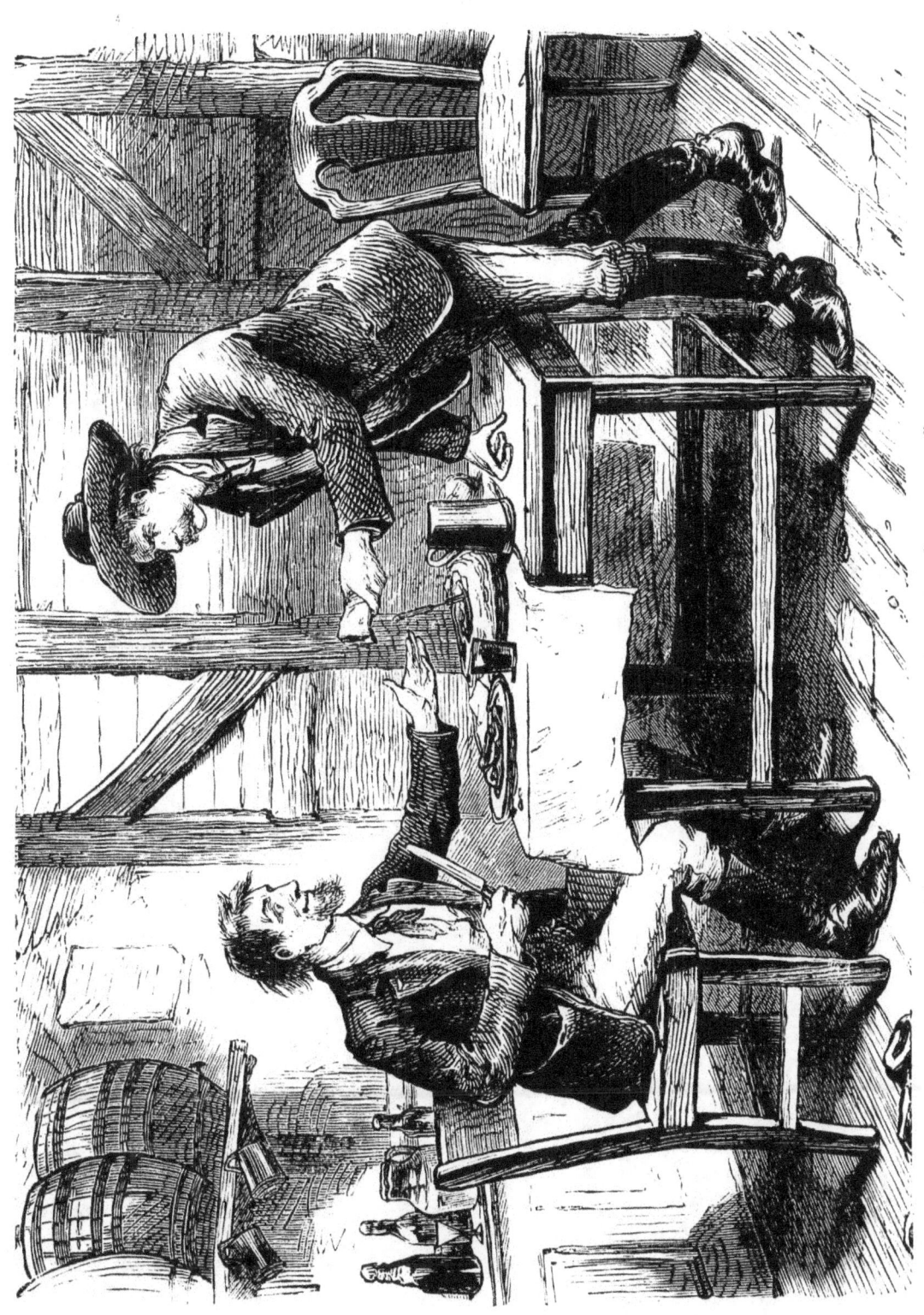

"'HERE IS A THIRD FOR YOUR SHARE,' AS AGREED."

JACK OF WARWICK;

OR,

THE COWBOY OF TEXAS.

CHAPTER I.

"TROUBLE AT HOME DIVIDES PEOPLE ABROAD."

A FEW miles from the ancient and historical city of Warwick stands an old Norman building known as Kenilworth Hall.

It is the ancestral home of the Barons of Melbury, a name which has figured in English history since the days of John of Gaunt and the Plantagenet kings.

Warwick and the surrounding neighbourhood is full of suggestive memories, conjuring up the gallant Earl Grey, the Earl of Leicester, and the immortal Shakespeare, who first saw the light at Stratford-on-Avon, close by.

It was early springtime.

The flat, well-wooded park of Lord Melbury was a scene of perfect beauty. Flowers innumerable dotted the grass; the antlered deer browsed in the fern; the swans swam on the lake amidst the water-lilies; and the rooks cawed over their nests of young in the patriarchal elm trees.

In one of these trees, up which he had climbed with wonderful nerve and cleverness, a boy could be seen.

His age was fifteen; he was fair, handsome, stoutly built, and muscular. That he was strong anybody could see at a glance, and a daring spirit flashed from his hazel eyes.

This was Jack Hardwick, called by the boys of adjacent villages, Jack of Warwick.

Jack's father kept a library and stationer's shop in the High Street in Warwick, and was well-to-do.

He had no other children.

The one great mistake of his life had been to marry a second wife when Jack's mother died.

She was a terrible shrew.

Hating Jack with all the proverbial spite of a stepmother, she led him and her husband as thoroughly detestable and unpleasant lives as their worst enemies could have wished them.

Jack often felt weary of existence at home.

Though he was trespassing, he was not in the least afraid.

No keeper would have said anything to him.

This was the reason—

He was the foster-brother of Lord Melbury's son and heir, Osmond.

Jack's mother, owing to Lady Melbury's delicate health, had nursed both her own son and the young heir.

Osmond was very much attached to Jack of Warwick.

They had always played together, and been friends and companions, until Osmond was sent to Eton College.

Then they only met in the holidays.

Osmond had given orders to the keepers that Jack of Warwick should do what he liked on the estate.

Our hero's father was very partial to a pie made of young rooks, and, it being the time to kill them, Jack of Warwick started out to get some for him.

He certainly risked his neck in climbing the high elms.

That, however, was a secondary consideration with Jack.

If he wanted anything he did not stop to think of the risk he ran in getting it.

As he threw down a plump young rook he had killed, he said—

"Thirteen—a baker's dozen. That will be enough for a pie."

Suddenly there was a loud cry.

The dead rook had struck somebody under the trees.

"Hallo, down there!" cried Jack. "Anyone hurt?"

"Hallo, you up there! Who are you?" was the reply.

"I am myself, and myself is my father's son, if you wish to know."

"Don't be impertinent."

"I can't help it," answered Jack of Warwick; "it is born in me, and so comes natural."

"You deserve a good thrashing."

"What for?"

"Throwing rooks at people. You will have to come down some time, and I'll wait for you, if it takes me all day."

"Will you? All right. I'm comfortable enough."

Jack seated himself straddle-legged on a bough, with his back against the trunk.

The dizzy height did not affect him.

"How dare you kill my rooks?" continued the person below.

"Yours?" laughed Jack.

"Yes—mine!"

"That's a good joke! Who do you think you are?"

"I am Lord Melbury's son, and if anyone has a right to speak on this property, I have."

In a moment Jack Hardwick changed his attitude.

"By Jove!" he muttered, "I fancied I knew the voice; but he ought to be at school. What has happened? Something up!"

Dropping like a monkey from branch to branch, he soon reached the ground.

The boys, who were of the same age, faced one another.

Osmond was tall and thin, with curly black hair, and a frank smile.

"Why, Jack!" he exclaimed; "I hadn't the remotest idea it was you."

"And how should I suppose it was you?" said Jack of Warwick.

"Give me your hand, old boy."

They shook hands cordially.

"Father wanted a rook pie," said Jack, "so I thought I would come to your place and get some birds."

"You are welcome to all you require."

"I know that without being told."

"Mind you don't break your neck some day climbing these high trees."

"Not likely. I'm an old hand at it. But, I say, how is it you are at home?"

"I have had a row at Eton with the headmaster, and I have had a row at home with my father."

"That's bad."

"Yes; I seem to live in an atmosphere of rows."

"What is it all about?"

"I couldn't do my Latin verses. I hate Latin and Greek; so they wanted to flog me, and I wouldn't stand it. The result was I have been sent away from college."

"Expelled?"

"Exactly," replied Osmond, gloomily, "and my father declares that he won't shelter me. I must go back—that is the ultimatum. Lord Melbury says he was seven years at Eton, and went through the same thing himself, and consequently he cannot make any allowance for me."

"Are you going back?"

"No."

"I admire your pluck. I know very well I would not if I were in your place. But what are you going to do?"

"Leave the country."

"Never!"

Jack drew a deep breath.

This intelligence fairly startled him.

He could see that Osmond was desperately in earnest.

There was a look of fierce determination in his eyes.

"I have a little money," said Osmond. "My mother always kept me tolerably well supplied, though I never got much from my father. It is only about thirty pounds, yet it is enough for my purpose at present."

"That won't carry you far."

"Perhaps not."

"Where are you going?"

"To the United States," replied Osmond. "I shall walk into Warwick, and take a ticket to Liverpool."

"What shall you do in America?"

"Heaven only knows! I must chance

that. Providence tempers the wind to the shorn lamb. I have hands and legs. Cannot I work as well as anyone else?"

"You have not any trade."

"I can learn one."

"The trade of being a poor gentleman is not much of a lookout. You can't dig; you will be ashamed to beg," said Jack. "Living on your wits is out of the question with a man like you. Take my advice, and do not go."

"I must," replied Osmond. "Never will I return to Eton to be whipped like a dog."

"The other boys put up with it."

"Let them—I will not."

"But your father?"

"Struck me just now with a cane, and I cannot forgive him for it. I'm off, so it's no use trying to persuade me to stay."

Jack looked troubled.

"I am really very sorry to hear all this," he exclaimed. "You will have to rough it."

"No matter. I shall see the world, and preserve my independence and my honour, both of which I cherish dearly."

Osmond was an impulsive and high-spirited boy—too much so, in fact, for his own comfort and well-being

He could not brook restraint, and, prospective heir to a peerage though he was, he despised conventionalities.

Jack put his hand into his pocket and drew out a sovereign.

"It is all I have got in the world," he said, "and that I saved up to buy a new bat and a set of stumps; but if it is of any use to you, take it."

"A thousand thanks," Osmond replied; "but I have all I require. It is my intention to go steerage over the Atlantic."

"You, a lord's son, travel like that!"

"I mean to drop the swell."

"An Eton boy, too! I cannot believe it."

"Fact, my dear fellow," said Osmond. "When my father has got over his temper in a few years, I shall come back. I was always of a roving disposition. Don't fret about me; I am sure to come out all right. Good-bye."

Osmond wrung his hand.

Before Jack of Warwick had time to make any reply, his friend had darted between the trees.

The next moment he was lost to sight.

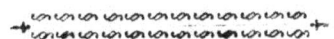

CHAPTER II.

JACK OF WARWICK HAS A LITTLE TROUBLE ON HIS OWN ACCOUNT.

Picking up the dead rooks, Jack tied a piece of string round their necks, and started for home.

He was intensely surprised at the course which his foster-brother had chosen to adopt.

It seemed madness; yet he determined to say nothing about what he had just heard, for, after all, it was no business of his, and no doubt Osmond Melbury knew what he was about.

He was very sorry to part with him, for Osmond had always been his best friend.

"In time he will come to his senses," he said to himself; "and if he should want money, he has only to write for it. All will be forgiven and forgotten."

Here honest Jack made a mistake.

Osmond would rather have starved than have asked either his father or mother for assistance.

He was too proud for that.

A quick walk brought Jack into Warwick.

He entered the house by the private door, and went into the kitchen.

His stepmother was engaged in cooking something, but she looked up angrily and spitefully.

"Where's father?" he asked.

"Serving in the shop," she replied. "Where do you suppose he is? Do you want me to be here, getting the dinner ready, and there too? How can I be in half-a-dozen places at once?"

"Who said you could or ought to be?"

"Don't speak like that to me," cried Mrs. Hardwick, "or I'll give you something you won't like. What have you got there?"

"Some young rooks. Father told me he wanted some for a pie, so I went over to Kenilworth Park, swarmed the trees, and got a few."

"Did I tell you to do it?"

"No."

"The fact is, you think more of your father than you do of me?"

"Why shouldn't I?"

"I am not going to pluck the birds," said Mrs. Hardwick, angrily, "so you can take them away again, or I'll throw them in the fire."

"You can do that if you like, of course," said Jack, "though it is rather hard on me, when I have had the trouble of getting them; besides, it is foolish."

"Go in the back-yard and pluck them yourself."

"I'll do that; I like to be busy."

"Yes, you do, in your own way. You ought to have been here to take out the books and papers."

"We have a boy."

"That is no reason why you should not help him. I tell you what it is, you are a lazy good-for-nothing fellow."

"No, I am not."

"You will come to a bad end."

"Not because you say so," retorted Jack.

"Go away."

Jack picked up the birds and went towards the door.

"You have no right to talk to me like that," he said.

"Why not?"

"Because you are not my mother."

"I'm your stepmother, your father's lawfully-wedded wife."

"Yes, that is true enough, unfortunately."

"What?"

"A nice life you lead the pair of us. I wish father had never married you," answered Jack.

Mrs. Hardwick was tall, gaunt, and angular; her arms were long, and her hands large and red.

She knew how to use them, too.

"Bring those birds back!" she screamed.

"What for?" he enquired.

"You are not going to pluck them, you scamp. I can see it in your eyes; you are intending to sell them."

"Indeed I never thought of such a thing."

"I want them."

"Then you want what you will not have."

Mrs. Hardwick's thin, pinched face grew purple with rage.

Snatching up a broom which stood in a corner, she rushed at Jack, and before he could open the door she dealt him a blow in the face.

Seeing that she was preparing to strike him again—not at all an uncommon occurrence in his experience—he flung the rooks at her.

They were propelled with all his force.

Catching her in the face, they sent her reeling back until she measured her length on the floor.

"Help! Murder! Help!" she yelled.

Hearing this dreadful noise, Mr. Hardwick ran in from the shop.

"What on earth is the matter, my dear?" he asked.

"That dreadful boy is killing me!"

"Did you knock her down, Jack?"

"I brought the rooks home, as you requested me, and because I went out she began at me," replied Jack.

"Oh, I see."

"I was going to take the feathers off, but she struck me across the face with the broom."

"Yes, yes—the same old business."

"So in self-defence I threw the birds at her."

"I don't blame you, my boy."

Hearing this reply, Mrs. Hardwick rose to her feet. She was not at all hurt; all she wanted was sympathy.

Finding she did not get any from her husband, she waxed furious.

The virago seized the broom again, and made a wild rush upon Jack.

"Get out!" cried his father.

Jack did not hesitate to take this advice; he dodged the blow she aimed at him, and made his escape into the street.

"You always take that boy's part," said Mrs. Hardwick, "and it is not at all creditable to you."

"He is my child," was the reply.

"I ought to be first in your affections. Oh, dear! what a miserable life mine is, to be sure! Why did I marry? Oh, why?"

Bursting out crying, she sank into a chair.

"Don't give way," Mr. Hardwick said.

"I can't hel—help it!" she sobbed.

"Calm yourself, my love."

"No, no. Don't ask me. It is all your fault. Send him away. Let him go to sea. If he stays in the house I won't!"

"But consider—"

"He must—he shall go! I'll persecute him until he does."

"Really I do not think it will take much more of your temper and ill-feeling to make him go. It is for me he stays."

"Well I know it. The little brute hates me."

There was a noise in the shop, which communicated with the passage that led into the kitchen by a small door.

"Some customer!" Mr. Hardwick exclaimed.

"Don't leave me," screamed his better-half.

"There is no one to mind the shop."

"Leave it alone. I'm going to faint."

"Then you must."

"Heartless man! Oh, why did you marry me?"

"Blessed if I know. Because I was a fool, I suppose."

Saying this, Mr. Hardwick ran to the shop.

His better-half did not faint.

She satisfied herself that he was really out of sight, and, going to a cupboard, which she unlocked with a small private key she took from her dress-pocket, produced a bottle of gin.

From this she helped herself to a wine-glassful.

She smacked her lips with satisfaction.

"I'll give it him when he comes back for his dinner," she murmured, with a ghastly grin.

At that moment a loud cry was heard in the shop.

Steps sounded in the passage, and Mr. Hardwick appeared in the kitchen.

He was tearing his hair.

"Woman," he yelled, "do you want to ruin me?"

"What is the matter now?"

"You quarrelled with my son. There was no one to mind the shop. I came here, and in my absence thieves broke in."

"Did they steal anything?" Mrs. Hardwick asked, anxiously.

She had a keen interest for money.

"When I counted the till last there was in it seven, sixteen, and some odd ha'pence."

"Seven pounds sixteen shillings?"

"Yes, ma'am. All gone, through your folly."

"Gone?"

"Every farthing!"

"Serve you right," Mrs. Hardwick said, spitefully. "If you had kept that precious boy of yours, of whom you are so fond, at home, instead of sending him out to steal rooks, this would not have happened."

"He did not steal them."

"I say he did."

"Allow me to beg your pardon. Lord Melbury's son and he are foster-brothers—I may add, friends. They were nursed at the same breast—my first wife's—and I—"

"Oh, if you are going to talk about your first wife, I may as well go out in the street."

"My dear—"

"Get your dinner yourself. See how you will like it," said the shrew.

"Will you listen?"

"I dare say she was a great deal better than I am."

"My love—"

"A perfect lady! I'm not, you know."

"Do be quiet," said Mr. Hardwick, imploringly.

"No. I am going out, and, what is more, I don't know when I shall come back."

There was another noise in the shop.

"Oh, lord, they are at it again!" cried Mr. Hardwick.

"Let them take the whole stock," replied his wife.

"You don't care."

"Nothing. You will have to keep me all the same."

"Will you be quiet?"

"No, I won't."

"Do you want to drive me mad?"

"Yes. I should get rid of you then, and carry on the business myself. I don't want you."

"Haven't you found me good and kind to you?"

"For your own sake. Don't I stay at home and cook your dinners?"

"It is no more than you ought to do."

"Your son's a gentleman," she replied, in an irritating tone, "and the foster-brother of a young man who will be a nobleman."

"What of that?"

"It is awfully grand, isn't it?"

Mr. Hardwick put his fingers in his ears and rushed away.

"Oh, that the law allowed a man to hit a woman—a masculine virago!" he moaned; "but it don't. The shop's been robbed again, I know. While she was talking to me, perhaps they have taken a ream of paper, or at the least new books and publications. Oh, dear! what a thing it is to marry the wrong woman. Guy, Earl of Warwick, killed the dragon; why can't he come to life again, and settle mine?"

The wretched man sighed deeply, and re-entered the shop.

This time it was not thieves.

Is was a small boy.

He was amusing himself by alternately kicking the counter and stamping on the floor in a most vigorous manner.

This proceeding he varied by putting his hand to his mouth, so as to form a trumpet, and halloaing at the top of his voice—

"Hi, yi, hi! Shop! yi, shop, shop! Yi, hi, yi!"

Mr. Hardwick went up and slapped him on the shoulder.

"Stop it," he said; "you'll hurt yourself if you go on like that."

"All right, guv'nor," replied the boy.

"What do you want?"

"I've got important news for you, sir. You said you'd pay a shilling to anyone who would bring news."

"Yes, I did."

The reason why Mr. Hardwick had made this offer was this: he had lately started a small local bi-weekly penny paper, called the *Warwick Welcome*, which he had printed at an office a few doors down the street.

His name appeared on it as editor, and as it was doing pretty well, both in sale and advertisements, he was proud of it.

He made it essentially a newspaper, and for items of news he was only too glad to pay.

"Well, sir," the boy went on, "I've got a shilling's worth for you."

"Let me see, to-day is Tuesday," replied Mr. Hardwick; "we publish to-morrow morning. I'm afraid your news is too late for this issue, whatever it may be, and perhaps it will be stale by Saturday, when we publish again."

"It's very important, sir."

"Who are you?"

"Little Johnny Tatur, they call me, sir. I'm the gardener's son up at Kenilworth Hall."

"Oh, indeed! I know your father well, Johnny; he is a customer of mine. Now, what's your news?"

"Lord Melbury's dead, sir."

Mr. Hardwick turned pale. This way startling intelligence.

"How—when did he die?" asked Hardwick.

"This morning, about twelve o'clock," answered Johnny Tatur. "The housekeeper told father that Master Osmond came back from Eton last night—expelled; to-day Lord Melbury had a row with Master Osmond, who ran away, swearing he would never come back."

"Ah, a family quarrel. Go on."

"Lady Melbury then went on at her husband, who fell down in an apple-pie fit."

"Apoplectic," corrected the stationer.

"Yes, sir; an applebeckit fit, and before the doctor came his lordship died."

"You are quite sure? I don't want any cock-and-bull story to hoax the public with."

"You ain't got none, sir."

"I'll be off to the printing-office at once. If the formes are locked up and on the machine, they must be lifted—that's all. Mind the shop, Johnny; I'll be back directly."

"Yes, sir."

"Dear, dear! fancy Lord Melbury going off like that," Mr. Hardwick muttered, as he hastened away. "He owed me a bill of about ten pounds. I think I'll double the amount. The executor will never know, and must pay it. I am sorry, poor man! Perhaps I'd best make my bill thirty pounds. Dear me! Isn't it sad and sudden! 'In the midst of life we are in death.' The parson will preach from that text next Sunday—see if he does not."

Scarcely had he gone than Jack entered the shop, and Johnny Tatur, who was full of his news, told it him.

Jack could scarcely believe it.

It seemed incredible that a man in full health and strength should have gone off at a moment's notice, as it were.

His foster-brother was now Lord Melbury, and the owner of a fine estate and ten thousand a year.

Having a doting, indulgent mother, he would be able to do as he liked.

But where was he?

Would he hear of his good, yet bad news? for though he had come into a title and a fortune he had lost a father.

Osmond was not much of a reader; politics he detested, and ordinary news had no interest for him.

It was a rare occurrence for him to take up a newspaper.

He would rather be fishing in the lake, shooting in the coverts, or over the stubble and turnips, or on horseback.

Confinement in the house, reading, schoolwork, were all distasteful to him.

Presently Mr. Hardwick returned from the printing-office, where he had arranged to bring out a special edition of his newspaper, the *Warwick Welcome*.

"Heard the news, Jack?" he asked.

"Yes, little Johnny Tatur has just told me. Very startling, isn't it?" Jack replied.

"It ought to be a good thing for you, as you are so friendly with his lordship."

"I doubt whether it will be."

"Why so? He might make you his private secretary, or get you some good paying position."

"Yes, I know; but he's gone, and there is no telling when he will come back, if he ever does," said Jack.

"But he is sure to see his luck in the papers."

"He never reads them."

"But he must take up a journal sometimes."

"The papers are not going to keep on advertising his father's death all the time. There will be a notice to-morrow, and that's all."

"He'll see that, maybe."

"No, he won't," said Jack, decisively.

"Why not?" asked his father.

"Because he will be at sea, crossing St. George's Channel to Queenstown, on his way to America."

Mr. Hardwick stared at his son in surprise.

"How do you know that?" he enquired.

"I met Osmond this morning and he told me so. He is now in the train on his way to Liverpool."

"Hadn't you better go after him?" said Mr. Hardwick.

"What's the use? How could I find him in Liverpool? Might as well look for a needle in a bottle of hay."

"But you might get the police to search the ships that sail to-morrow. There can't be very many of them."

"If I found him he would not come back; he is going to have his fling. I know him better than you," said Jack.

"Perhaps so. Let us see about dinner; my inner man cries cupboard, but whether or not your stepmother will give us any is a question."

"If she cuts up in her tantrums, I'll go to the cook-shop," said Jack. "What is the use of worrying about trifles?"

Mr. Hardwick gave little Johnny Tatur a shilling, and locking the shop door went with his son into the kitchen.

His amiable spouse was not there.

She had declared she would go out, and there was no doubt she had carried her threat into execution.

Something else had gone out, too.

This was the dinner.

Finding the saucepan was not on the stove they looked out of the window, and saw it in the yard.

In her temper she had thrown it away.

A hungry cat was greedily eating the savoury contents.

"What a woman she is, to be sure," remarked the stationer and bookseller.

"Do you know what the dinner was?" asked Jack.

"A couple of rabbits stewed with parsley and onions—my favourite dinner. No matter; we must put up with a sirloin of bread-and-cheese."

They made a frugal meal, and immediately returned to the shop.

Here they were busy serving behind the counter for a couple of hours.

Then the side-door opened.

Mrs. Hardwick appeared on the

threshold. Her face was red and her lips twitched spitefully.

Raising her hand, she threw a stone at Jack.

It struck him on the forehead, cutting it open.

Then she ran into the parlour, and promptly went into hysterics.

"Are you hurt?" Mr. Hardwick enquired.

"Yes," replied Jack, savagely. "I won't stand much more of this."

"It is not for me to ask you to stay. I will give you money, though it will grieve me to the heart to part with you."

"I'll go."

"Where?"

"Anywhere to get out of this. Let me have time to think it out," said Jack.

"Look after the shop," continued his father. "I must go to your stepmother, or she'll raise the street."

While he was gone, a tall lanky man came into the shop. He was well dressed and closely shaven, though he had a thick dark moustache. His complexion was sallow, and his cheek-bones were high.

He wore a heavy watch-chain, and a diamond ring sparkled on his finger.

"Have you a guide to Warwick?" he asked, speaking with a strong Yankee twang. "I am an American travelling in England. Just come from Stratford, where the Lord Shakespeare was born, and I guess I want to see your blamed old castle."

"Yes, sir," replied Jack, handing the American what he required. "Price one shilling. It contains every information."

The man paid for it, put it in his pocket, and then looked at Jack.

"How did you hurt yourself?" he demanded. "What's the trouble?"

"Nothing much," answered Jack, smiling. "I am suffering from a severe attack of stepmother—that's all."

"Father married a second time, eh?"

"Exactly."

"Hates you like poison? I see how the cat jumps. That's just the way with them. Why don't you skip?"

"What's that, sir?"

"Get away. That's the only thing to do. You will never have any peace as long as you stay here."

"I have been thinking of that."

"Don't think—cut. Here's my card. I'm staying at the "Swan" Hotel. Come and see me any time after six this evening."

Jack took the card.

On it he read : "Hiram T. Bunyard, Cattle Raiser, Mowbray's Ranche, near Nacogdochee, on the Trinity River, Texas, U.S.A."

"Thank you, sir. I will have the pleasure of calling on you," he said.

"What's your name?"

"Jack Hardwick. Commonly called Jack of Warwick."

"Why?"

"Because I can thrash all the boys in the villages round here."

"Bully for you!" exclaimed Mr. Bunyard. "I like a fighter. Can you ride well?"

"Anything."

"Good. Are you the son of the boss of this store?"

"The only child."

"Will he part with you?"

"Yes, he told me so just now. I must go somewhere. If I have much more stepmother, it will finish me," replied Jack.

"I'll make a cowboy of you if you are willing, for I like the look of you."

"What's that—a cowboy?"

"What you call a herdsman—a chap that tends to the cattle. I've got five thousand head at Mowbray's Ranche. Come and see me, Jack of Warwick. Good day."

Giving him a nod, Mr. Hiram T. Bunyard took his departure, leaving Jack with his heart in a flutter.

Here was a chance for him!

Texas—a land of romance! Mowbray's Ranche, near the quaint, hard-to-pronounce Indian-named place!

What a vista of adventure it opened up to him !

There did not seem to be much dignity attached to the position of a cowboy, but he had to learn that it required skill, nerve, and pluck.

The cattle range over scores of square miles of prairie land to graze.

They have to be carefully looked after, and in the winter-time, when snow falls, and the cowboys ride in the teeth of a blizzard, the task is not an easy one.

Presently Mr. Hardwick returned.

"I've got her to bed," he said; "we shall be quiet now."

"For a time," replied Jack.

"Have you thought any more about going away?"

Jack gave him Mr. Bunyard's card, and told him what the stock-raiser had said.

"It looks like a good opening," remarked Hardwick, "if you can stand the hardships you will have to encounter."

"I can rough it. Some day I may be a cattle-owner myself. I can't be worse off there than I am here with stepmother."

"It is hard to lose you!"

"Perhaps it is cowardly of me to talk of going: you will have to fight your battle alone."

"She will be better without you, because you are the bone of contention."

"That settles the question," said Jack. "I will see Mr. Bunyard—queer name, isn't it?—this evening, and sign articles."

"Very well. God bless you, my boy! I shall think of and pray for you, wherever you are. Write often. If you want money, ask for it. I have a few hundreds in the bank."

Jack was about to reply, when a footman in blue and silver livery entered the shop.

"You do printing, I think?" he enquired.

"Yes; any kind," answered Hardwick.

"I am from Kenilworth Hall. Lord Melbury is dead—sudden affair! Master Osmond has left home. Lady Melbury fears he will not return, and has sent me to tell you to print a thousand copies of this bill, and have them posted all over the country."

He handed Hardwick a sheet of paper. On it was written—

"£1,000 REWARD!

"WHEREAS, Osmond, Lord Melbury, has disappeared from his home. This is to give notice that the above sum of one thousand pounds will be paid to any person giving information of his whereabouts, or restoring him to his friends at Kenilworth Hall, Warwickshire."

"I will see to it at once," Hardwick said.

The footman in the gorgeous livery withdrew.

"That is a nice little sum for whoever gets it," observed Jack.

"It may fall to your lot," replied his father.

"How so?"

"You told me he was going to the United States. You are going also, and may run across him."

"True. More unlikely things than that have happened in this strange world."

"It is not very likely, though, when I come to think of it," Mr. Hardwick continued. "The territory is so large. However, you have my best wishes."

Nothing more was said.

The afternoon passed very slowly for Jack. He was glad when the time came for him to call on Mr. Bunyard.

That gentleman had enjoyed a good dinner, and was smoking a cigar in the coffee-room when Jack entered.

"Ha, my young friend," exclaimed the stock-raiser; "you are in time. Nothing like punctuality if you want to get on in the world."

"I am never late for business or dinner," answered Jack.

"Have you spoken to your father about my offer?"

"Yes, sir."

"How is it—a go, or no go?"

"Decidedly a go."

"Very good! I shall not make you sign any agreement. If you don't like me and my work after a fair trial, you can leave me and tackle something else; but my boys always stick to me through thick and thin; they say I am the right sort of a boss."

"When shall I be ready, sir?"

"To-night; I'm off to-morrow. All that this country has to show I've seen, and I own up that for ruins our United States can't beat you. We're not in it for ruins, though we are great on prairies, and some on mountains. You can't touch one side of our Rockies, our Alleghanies, or Sierras; your hills in Wales and Scotland are only mole-hills."

"Perhaps so, sir."

"Your beef ain't up to the mark of Texas beef; your oysters can't touch our Blue Points and Saddle Rocks. Ours is a great country. Wait and see. The

American Eagle is boss; let the old bird flap her wings and scream."

Jack was inclined to argue the point, but a moment's reflection made him think better of it.

"Now," continued Mr. Bunyard, "we shall take the steam-cars to Southampton, and there embark for Galveston, which is our principal port in Texas. Grand state Texas—finest in the Union."

"So I have heard, sir."

"Capable of immense development. Only in its infancy. Grow up with it, and make a fortune."

"I should like to," replied Jack.

"Do it. You have it within your grasp. Well, from Galveston we shall train to Hewston. It is spelt Houston on the map, but we pronounce it Hewston. From there we go to Austin, and then on to Nacogdochee, when we sha'n't be far off Mowbray's Ranche, which is my territory," said Mr. Bunyard. "Now, do you drink?"

"No, sir."

"Smoke?"

"Neither one nor the other."

"So much the better for you. A young man beginning life should have no vices. I do both, but I've made my pile. Good night; be here at ten sharp to-morrow with your baggage. Don't take much; you can get along with two suits of clothes, and a couple of shirts; boots, hat, and gaiters I'll find you in Nacogdochee."

Jack thanked him, they shook hands, and the boy went home with his head in a whirl.

No wonder at it.

A quick change had taken place in his life.

What the future would bring forth he did not stop to think.

It was enough for him that he was going to get away from his stepmother, perhaps find the wandering Osmond, now Lord Melbury, and last, but by no means least, see the world.

CHAPTER III.

MOWBRAY'S RANCHE—THE "DUN COW" SALOON—REPORTS OF ROAD-AGENTS—
TREACHERY.

THE little settlement called Mowbray's Ranche was not much of a place.

There were not a dozen houses in it.

The principal building was the saloon, called the "Dun Cow," kept by an old man named Snell. It was a public-house, a general store, and the post-office.

Next in importance came the dwelling of Mr. MacTavish, a canny Scotchman and widower, who was Mr. Hiram T. Bunyard's agent and sole manager.

He had one daughter, Helen, a sweetly pretty girl of eighteen.

Being a bachelor, Mr. Bunyard lodged and boarded with them.

Helen was the pet of everyone who came in contact with her.

Mowbray, who founded the little place and kept cattle, had been shot six years ago by a desperado.

Hearing of this in Austin, Mr. Bun-yard had come out and bought the property from his widow.

That is how Bunyard came to own Mowbray's Ranche.

The place did not grow; there was nothing to make it grow. No gold, no oil—nothing but Bunyard and his cow-boys, with an occasional loafer, on whom Snell, the saloon-keeper, and his wife, lived parasitically.

Twice a week the pony-post came in from Nacogdochee—Wednesdays and Saturdays.

It was Wednesday morning.

MacTavish rose early, and going to the kitchen, built up a fire, while his pretty daughter Helen laid the breakfast-things.

"I've got an idea," said MacTavish, "that we shall have a line from the boss to-day."

"Shouldn't be at all surprised," replied Helen. "He said in his last that he was tired of his European tour, and would be back soon."

"He'll have nothing to grumble at, I ken. The cattle are all sound. We haven't lost a head."

"Heigho!" sighed Helen.

"What is the matter with you?" asked MacTavish--"eh, lass?"

"I was only thinking of the old country," she replied. "It is years since we emigrated. I was only a little girl when we came to Texas, and poor mother died of the fever; but weel I remember bonnie Scotland, and weel I'd like to be on the blue heather again in Kincardine."

"We're doing o'er weel in this country," said MacTavish. "It's meat we get wi' our parritch, and there is always a wee drap of whisky coming my way when I want it."

"There is a charm about home," said Helen, with a far away look in her eyes.

"This is your home, and will have to be. If you set your cap at Mr. Bunyard he'd have you, and you would be mistress of the ranche."

"Oh, father!"

"He's bound to do."

"I wouldn't have him if he was worth millions of dollars!"

"Hoot—toot! who do you want, then?"

"I have not seen the man yet I like well enough to marry. Wait till he comes along and I'll tell you."

"Mr. Bunyard's got the gold."

"What does that matter? Burns sings, 'The gold is but the guinea stamp—a man's a man for a' that.'"

"If I were a bonnie lassie I'd like to ha'e the siller," exclaimed MacTavish.

After breakfast, MacTavish felt ready for a day's work.

He drank his third cup of coffee, and rose from the table.

"I'll go over to the 'Dun Cow' and see if the mail has come in," he said.

It was seven o'clock.

"If the boss is coming, maybe there will be a cablegram," replied Helen. "Should it be so, I'd like to know so as to get the bed aired."

"I'll come back before I ride out, dinna fear."

Putting on his broad-brimmed slouch hat, MacTavish walked to Snell's store.

The pony postman, as the letter-carrier was called, rode all night, and always arrived in the morning.

His name was Sam Sim, and being very thin, he was nicknamed Slim Sam Sim.

Snell was sweeping out his store, and greeted the Scotchman in a cheery manner.

In a corner near the stove, seated in a chair, was a tall, robust man of about thirty-five years of age.

He was fast asleep.

His face was handsome, but there was a daring, reckless expression about it, even in his slumber.

He was dark as a raven, his moustache long and drooping, and his dress that of a man who had worn his clothes for some time, and had travelled far.

"Who's that?" asked MacTavish.

"Stranger," replied Snell; "arrived an hour ago, just as I was opening the sheebang, called for a milk-punch of Santa Cruz rum, drank it; called for a second, drank it; called for a third, put it away; smoked the best Key West cigar I'd got, at fifty cents, curled himself up in the chair, and dozed off."

"Is that all you know about him?"

"Nothing more."

"I'll bet he's nae good. Gie me a drap of whisky; it keeps out the malaria. An ounce of prevantion, my friend, is better than a pound of cure."

"You're right there."

"Has the express come in? Ye know what I mean—the pony-post."

"Slim Sam Sim? Not yet. He won't be long, I reckon."

Snell supplied MacTavish with some of the liquor which is so dear to a Scotchman's heart.

"You'll be expecting the boss, I reckon," he said.

"Yes; every day," was the reply.

"The coach from Nacogdochee, through here to Brazos, is due to-day; he might come by that."

"He cannot come any other way, unless he rides horseback; but I don't know aboot his coming to-day in the absence of advices."

The coach Snell spoke about was the only means of conveyance of passengers and freight to Mowbray's Ranche.

It ran once a week.

Suddenly they heard the sound of hoofs.

They ran out into the road.

It was Slim Sam Sim on his pony.

The postman had his bag slung over his back; he dismounted and shook hands with Snell and MacTavish.

"Not sorry to touch bottom—eh?" exclaimed Snell.

"You bet," replied Slim Sam Sim.

"Any letter or dispatch for me?" asked MacTavish.

"A letter only. Wait a bit, though. I've had a scare; the letter is for Warner, the cowboy."

"Hech, mon! What's that?"

"Road-agents. They are at it in this section. The Brazos coach has been stopped, the driver shot, passengers robbed, and all the specie stolen, horses hamstrung, and the travellers left helpless."

"That's bad news! Whereabouts?"

"Fifteen miles from here. I saw the coach, and spoke to the people. There are six for Brazos, and two for here."

"Two for here! Who are they?" enquired MacTavish.

"Your boss, Mr. Bunyard, and a youngster," said Slim Sam Sim.

"Humph! Never wrote," muttered MacTavish; "thought to catch me napping—that's mean. Come in and have some refreshment at my—that is, at the landlord's expense."

MacTavish never spent a coin, unless it was on himself.

They all entered the saloon, and Snell handed some refreshment to the pony-postman.

"This road-agent business is becoming serious," said Snell. "I read in the papers that they boarded a train between Austin and Hewston."

"There was only one in this affair," answered the postman.

"One man stopped the coach?"

"So they say."

"He must be a daring fellow."

"Such men always are. They hold their lives in their hands, and take all risks like a fire insurance company."

The man who was sleeping in the chair moved uneasily.

"Who have you there?" asked Slim Sam Sim.

"Stranger in town."

"Ugly-looking customer; I don't like the cut of his jib, as the sailors say."

"He ordered drinks and paid for them.

I noticed he had a pile of greenbacks."

"Counterfeit, possibly."

"What he gave me wasn't. I changed a ten-dollar bill for him. Wish I had a hatful like it," answered Snell.

"Excuse me," said MacTavish, "I must go and tell my daughter the news. It won't take Mr. Bunyard and his young friend, whoever he may be, verra lang to walk fifteen miles, and we may expect them here in an hour or two; he might have written or telegraphed. I dinna like it."

MacTavish went to the counter where there was a mull or horn, and took a prodigious pinch of snuff.

"Whenever I'm vexed," he observed, "I must ha'e some sneezin'."

The stranger in the chair still slumbered, but it wasn't an easy sleep; he jerked his limbs and muttered to himself.

"Would the folks in the coach know the robber again?" enquired Snell.

"They say not," replied Slim Sam Sim.

"Wherefore?"

"He had his features concealed by a black mask made of crape. How can you tell what a man is like when you can only see two eyes glaring at you through two holes?"

"Oh, that alters the case," said Snell.

"I hope the authorities will find the rascal," exclaimed MacTavish. "There is nae security for life or property while sic fellows are aboot. If you are going to stand a glass, Sim, I'll ha'e a drink wi' you for the sake of old times."

"Why, certainly," answered Slim Sam Sim; "you are as welcome as the flowers in May. You can have as many drinks at my expense as there are stripes on our star-spangled banner."

"Hech, mon! If you talk like that people will think you robbed the coach yourself."

"I do such a thing, MacTavish! You are joking, sure," cried the pony-postman.

"You should not talk of spending money sac freely, my laddie. I'll drink to your health, however, and after taking another pinch of sneezin', I'll be off hame."

MacTavish did as he said, and left

Snell alone with Sim and the mysterious stranger.

It was Sim's custom to have something to eat when he arrived at the ranche, sleep during the day, and start again at night with his post-bag.

He did not have a clear, unbroken ride. There were lots of farms and little settlements in out-of-the-way places he had to visit.

Slim Sam Sim was the only connecting link between them and the busy outside world.

Some cold meat, bread, and a toby of ale were put before him.

"I'll take your pony into the yard and stall him," said Snell, "while you are filling up the cavities."

"Thank you," replied Sim; adding, "I don't half like the way MacTavish spoke to me."

"Pshaw! It is his way; he did not mean any offence."

"Fancy taking me for a road-agent, or having any connection with such people! Ha, ha!"

"Very good, isn't it? Ha, ha!" laughed Snell. "Eat your fill, and if any customers come in, call me out of the window."

"Right; I'll see to it."

When Snell had gone away, and Sim was alone with the stranger, the pony-postman rose cautiously.

The stranger, who had apparently been fast asleep, did the same thing.

They advanced to one another and shook hands. Then Sim resumed his seat.

"Did you make a good haul, Felton?" he asked.

"Thanks to the information you gave me, I did," replied the man addressed as Felton. "I took ten thousand dollars out of the coach, and here is a third of it for your share, as agreed."

He handed him a roll of bills.

"It's right enough. I counted it out as I came along," he added.

"Oh, I can take your word for more than that," answered Slim Sam Sim. "Where are you going next?"

"I shall lay off for a while at my cave in the Devil's Gap," answered Felton. "You pass close by it; give me a look up."

"Who's there?"

"Only the English boy I picked up starving in New Orleans a few weeks ago. You know, I told you about him. Run away from home; says his name is Tom Jones—that's all I can get out of him; but he's handy. I'm bringing him up to my business."

Slim Sam Sim grinned.

"They'll give him a short shrift and a long rope some of these days," he remarked.

"That is as it may be."

"What do you want me to do for you?"

"Just this: My next stroke will be aimed at the train which runs from Nacogdochee to Austin. I have certain information that a very large sum of money is to be expressed by Wells, Fargo, and Company; my idea is to stop the train and seize the treasure. Now, if you will find out and tell me what train this money will travel by, I'll pay you handsomely."

"It is a bargain."

"You will find me at the Gap, with the boy."

"I understand. Enough said."

Slim Sam Sim went on with his breakfast, and Felton curled himself up in the chair and went to sleep again as unconcernedly as if nothing had happened.

Felton was one of the cleverest and most notorious swindlers, bank robbers, and road-agents in the Southern States.

Up to the present time he had succeeded in baffling the detective police.

When he had made money, he would go to some city and live like a gentleman at first-class hotels.

The money gone, he would return to his old haunts and commit some fresh outrage.

No one had the slightest suspicion that he was in league with the pony-postman.

After eating all that he required, the latter went upstairs to bed, richer by three thousand and some odd dollars than he had been before.

Felton slept on.

It was fully twelve o'clock in the day when a party of men, tired, dusty, hungry-looking, arrived at Mowbray's Ranche.

They steered straight for the "Dun Cow" saloon.

This deplorable party consisted of the

travellers in the coach which had been robbed.

Mr. Bunyard walked first with Jack of Warwick, who had soon found out what roughing it meant.

They had enjoyed a quick and pleasant passage across the Atlantic to Galveston, whence they took train to Nacogdochee, and there secured a passage in the coach for the ranche.

"Welcome, gentlemen!" exclaimed Snell. "We have been expecting you, for we heard all about your mishap from Slim Sam Sim."

"If we had not been a lot of cowards," replied Mr. Bunyard, "one man would not have robbed us."

"He played it rather low down on you."

"Give me something to eat and drink. Is all well?"

"Excellent."

In a few minutes MacTavish ran in breathless, having heard of the arrival of his employer.

"It's good for sair eyes to see your face again," he cried. "We ha'e missed you mair than words can tell. The cattle are all well; and we have no bad luck to report."

"I have, though. That confounded road-agent eased me of close on five thousand dollars. If I could meet him I'd shoot him on sight."

"Ha, ha! that's brave talk."

These words came from another part of the room.

The stranger was awake.

"Did you speak, sir?" asked Bunyard.

"Yes, I did," replied Felton. "I heard your conversation, and I have always noticed that people blow most after the occurrence of an event such as you have described."

"I mean what I say."

"Why didn't you do your shooting at the time?" asked Felton.

"What business is it of yours?"

"Oh, none at all if it comes to that."

Saying this Felton appeared to go off to sleep once more.

Bunyard looked angrily at him.

"We don't want any loafers here," he exclaimed after a moment's pause. "This ranche is mine. I keep law and order here, unless anything gets so bad that I have to send to the sheriff of the county."

"He's no tramp," said Snell. "He's got the chips. I saw him handle a roll of bills."

"Anyway, we have no use for him. He ain't come to trade in cattle, has he?" demanded Bunyard.

"No, that's a sure thing; he'd have mentioned it if he'd been on that racket," replied Snell.

"He's no good."

"Not worth a red cent."

"Verra weel, let us bounce him," said MacTavish. "These strangers may do mischief."

"Stop!" cried Bunyard. "We'll ask him to give an account of himself, and if it is not satisfactory he shall be sent farther."

"That's an excellent idea," remarked MacTavish.

"Then go and wake him up, and put him through the ordeal."

MacTavish was nonplussed. The cautious Scotchman did not at all relish a task like this.

It had elements of danger in it.

Strangers in wild parts of Texas, as a rule, carried pistols about them, and what is more, they did not scruple to use them.

"I'd rather be excused," he answered. "There is an uncanny look about the chiel. He might have a six-shooter in his clothes."

"Are you afraid?"

"No, sir. I'd have you to know that a MacTavish does not know what fear is; but at the same time a mon should ken sufficient not to put his hand out farther than he could draw it back again."

Bunyard burst out laughing.

"It's a cold day when you are left, Mac," he said. "Never mind; I'm not afraid of filling an early grave, so I'll attend to this galoot all by myself."

Jack looked on excitedly, wondering what was coming now.

Snell retreated behind the counter, so as to be able to duck his head if there was any shooting, while MacTavish opened the door, as if he expected pressing business to call him into the street at any moment.

Hiram T. Bunyard's courage was well known.

"HAVE A CARE! I WILL NOT BE RIDICULED BY SUCH AS YOU,' CRIED JACK OF WARWICK."

He was considered to be brave as a lion, and as he was a dead shot, the most ruthless hesitated to interfere with him.

Felton pretended to sleep on, but in reality he was wide awake, and had been listening to the conversation.

Bunyard shook him by the arm, causing him to start up.

"What yer up to?" he growled. "Can't yer let a man alone?"

"See here, stranger," replied Bunyard, "we don't like you, and we've concluded that you must make tracks; so you'd best go at once to save any further unpleasantness."

"I can go, though it is tarnation hard to be turned out of town for nothing."

"It ain't what you've done, but what you might do."

"All the same, I tell you it's rough."

"We won't argufy the point. You've got to skip, and mighty quick, too, or I'll make you acquainted with the business end of my boot."

"Will you, by thunder!"

Felton scowled at Bunyard, who did not flinch.

"We'll have no loafers here. Off you go. March!" cried the latter.

He extended his arm towards the door.

Felton gave him a snake-like look, and took a few steps in the direction indicated.

Then he stopped, and was about to put his hand behind him.

This movement in the West is pretty generally understood to mean that a man is going to produce a pistol from his trousers-pocket.

So Bunyard interpreted it on the present occasion.

Quick as lightning he presented his revolver at the road-agent.

He had artfully concealed it up his sleeve, to be ready for use at a moment's notice.

Owing to this, he was able to forestall the ruffian.

"Would you?" cried Bunyard.

"I didn't mean nothing, boss," replied Felton.

Again Bunyard waved his arm.

Seeing that there was every probability of a conflict, the other passengers by the coach to Brazos, who had come into the saloon, ran into an inner room.

They did not want to risk their lives.

Already they had lost and suffered enough.

Slinking along sideways, Felton soon reached the door where MacTavish was standing.

He passed out into the street.

Regaining his courage, the Scotchman gave the departing bravo a kick, which accelerated his pace.

"You hound!" exclaimed Felton. "I've shot a man for less than that."

"That's what you look like," answered MacTavish. "I should say you were a Rob Roy kind of freebooter, who would never adorn anything so well as a gallows."

A second time the savage, murderous look crossed Felton's features, which had become pale as death.

He was no doubt inclined to shoot, but he controlled himself by the exercise of a supreme effort.

The odds against him were too great.

Burning with rage, the man retreated to a clump of trees, beyond which stretched the interminable prairie.

Disappearing behind them, Felton unhitched from a bough a beautiful black horse, which was already saddled and bridled.

The animal neighed joyfully as he saw his master, who sprang lightly on to the back of his Kentucky thoroughbred.

Instead of riding away, Felton trotted round in full view of those who were now outside the saloon.

Great was their surprise when he drew his pistol and fired boldly at them.

The bullet whistled past MacTavish's head.

"Hoot toot!" cried the Scotchman, "he'll do some mischief."

Bunyard and Snell promptly returned the shot.

With a wild, defiant laugh, the robber rode off unhurt.

"I'd give fifty dollars if I was mounted," said Bunyard; "the villain should repent shooting at us. Have you got a rifle?"

"It's upstairs," answered Snell, "and he'd be gone before I could get it."

"Hang the luck!" said Bunyard, in a tone of vexation, as he bit his nether-lip.

Just as they were in despair of catching the man, or in any way punishing his audacity, an incident occurred which entirely altered the aspect of affairs.

Another character appeared on the scene.

Up to this time Felton had enjoyed his triumph.

He had started to gallop over the prairie, when a young man, mounted on a strong mustang, appeared.

"By thunder!" cried Bunyard, "there is one of my boys. It's Tanner. Hi!"

"Hallo!" replied the cowboy.

"Head him off! Capture him!"

"I'll see to it," shouted Tanner.

"He'll do it," muttered Bunyard, confidently.

Felton turned his head to look.

He saw the cowboy in full pursuit of him, and not far behind.

They were both well mounted, being about equally matched in that respect.

Felton quickened his pace; so did the cowboy.

The latter had a Mexican lasso tied to his saddle, and this he rapidly uncoiled.

Adjusting the noose, he whirled the rope around him and cast it at the fugitive.

The aim was unerring.

The noose fell over Felton's head and down to his waist.

Then the cowboy stopped his horse suddenly.

The jerk caused Felton to fall from his saddle with a terrific thud.

It seemed as if every bone in his body was broken.

He was horribly jarred, and for a moment rendered unconscious.

His horse, a perfectly trained animal, remained quite motionless.

Tanner rapidly dismounted, and ran towards the fallen man.

A loud shout of satisfaction emanated from Bunyard and his companions, who were delighted at the brilliant feat.

"Glorious!" said Bunyard. "My boys can do it. Bully for Tanner! He's the prince of cowboys! We will teach this loafer a lesson. I'll take his shooting-iron away and cowhide him out of the ranche."

In this expectation he was disappointed.

The road-agent had a frame as hard as iron.

Quickly recovering from the shock he had experienced in being so rudely dragged from his horse, he sat up.

Tanner was approaching.

With a dexterity born of the urgency of the moment, Felton got out his pistol, and levelling the weapon as well as his trembling hand would allow him, fired.

There was a sharp crack on the clear, crisp air.

The cowboy put his hand to his side, tottered, and fell on his knees.

"Oh, God, I'm shot!" he cried.

Convulsively clutching with both hands at the grass, the cowboy sank forward.

"Ha, ha! not this time!" yelled Felton, dashing to his horse as he let the lasso slip off at his feet.

With the quickness of thought he was in the saddle.

"On, on, beauty!" he whispered. "On for life and liberty!"

The beautiful animal bounded into the air, and was soon careering over the prairie at racing speed.

"Well, I want to know," said Hiram T. Bunyard, "if that isn't just about the smartest bit of business ever I saw."

"He's plugged a hole in poor Tanner," remarked Snell.

"That's a sure thing, and I'm real sorry for it, as Tanner was the best cowboy I had."

"A better fellow never lived. He was a harmless chiel," replied MacTavish, "though not desirable as a boarder, as he was always ready to eat. Sakes! what that carle could put away—meat, bread, or parritch!"

Bunyard and Jack of Warwick hastened to the spot where the unfortunate cowboy was soaking the ground with his gore.

They found him sinking fast.

"Are you much hurt?" asked his employer.

"I'm going home," replied the dying cowboy, faintly. "I've got to hand in my chips, boss."

"It makes me hopping mad to think of it! That stranger's a bad egg. He was on to you like a whip-snake. Is there anything I can do for you?"

"I've got a mother, a widow, living in Tenth-street, in Austin. You might send her the bit of money that's coming to me for wages."

"I'll do it."

"Tell her I spoke of her with my last

breath, and it wasn't through fighting **or** drinking I came to my end."

"No, I'll swear it wasn't. You were only obeying orders."

"Doing my duty, boss."

"I guess that's so, and you always have done it, Tanner, ever since I hired you."

"So long as you're satisfied with me—"

"I am," interrupted Bunyard. "Don't let that prey on your mind. A better man I never had. It's hard to part with you."

"A more cowardly murder I never saw," observed Snell, who now came up with MacTavish.

"Will you bury me where I fell?" asked Tanner.

"We will."

"Keep my grave green. I'd like Warner to hev my clothes and my pipe."

"I'll see to it. It's a pity we've no parson and no doctor within hail. I don't know no prayer."

"It's sae long since I was in a kirk," said MacTavish, "that I've forgotten all I learnt."

"I've got a prayer-book in my pocket, if you'd like to read anything," said Jack.

"You read it," answered Bunyard, wiping away a tear.

Jack opened the prayer-book, and began to read. The three rough men, with uncovered heads, stood round the dying cowboy.

A smile came to Tanner's face, which was very pale and wan. His eyes closed, and his thoughts seemed to be far away.

"It is verra affecting," MacTavish said. "I canna help thinking that it might ha'e been my fate. The villain wanted to work his spite off on me."

"Who are you more than anybody else?" asked Snell, who thought that the Scotchman esteemed himself too highly.

"I belong to the clan MacTavish. We ha'e fought wi' Bruce and Wallace, and we never dispensed bad whisky, as is your custom, my friend."

"Perhaps your family had an illicit still in the Highlands."

"If so, they made gude stuff."

"Hush! I'll have no quarrelling at such a time as this," said Bunyard.

"What did the Yankee sneer at me for?" asked MacTavish.

"You take too much on yourself," replied Snell. "I guess I don't like a man who puts on frills."

"Ain't I your best customer?"

"Yes, when anybody will pay for your drinks; and I may say you ruin me in snuff."

"The sneezin' is always free. I never heard of any publican charging for the use of the snuff-mull."

"Silence!" cried Bunyard, in a voice of authority. "Will you two be quiet? I'll have no more of this!"

"I never did see such a cantankerous Scotchman," replied Snell. "He's for everlastingly snarling."

"And you are the best of all the insolent, self-sufficient Yankees," retorted MacTavish.

"Anyone would think that you were brought up in a palace, ate off gold, and drank out of silver."

"I'm a MacTavish of that ilk, but I'll say no more to a puir ignorant creature like yourself."

The Scotchman drew himself up proudly, produced his snuff-box, and took a pinch of "sneezin'," as he called it.

"Now," exclaimed Bunyard, who had been examining Tanner, "this poor soul's gone. It's a clear case of murder, and the first chance we get, that stranger shall be lynched, all the same as if he was a horse-thief."

This was a singular remark to make, but in that part of Texas they thought it a worse crime to steal a horse than to kill a man.

People in a newly-settled community are very particular about having the rights of property protected.

"Yes," replied Snell, "we'll hang him, sure pop, if ever we have the good luck to catch him!"

"The body can lie here," continued Bunyard, "till the boys have dug a grave."

"It won't hurt, I reckon. There's one sure thing—it can't run away."

Snell grinned at his ghastly joke.

"We can't do any more than we have done," said Bunyard. "Let's go to dinner."

"That's the talk," replied Snell.

"I won't say but what ma appetite

isn't inclined that way!" exclaimed MacTavish. "Puir Tanner! he owes me a month's board, which, I reckon, I shall have to forego, for the sake of his mither, but it's a melancholy consolation to know that he's taken his last meal."

They retraced their steps to the saloon, where they indulged in more than one drink.

Bunyard said he would have to send two of his cowboys to the place where the coach had been stopped by the road-agents for his and Jack's baggage.

He had only three of his old cowboys left now Tanner was dead, but Jack of Warwick made a fourth.

The remaining ones were Warner, White, and Dawes.

White was steady, but of a sullen demeanour, making friends with nobody.

Warner was a fine, good-natured, excellent fellow, and Dawes was a drunken bully, with whom nobody liked or cared to associate for his own sake.

Fear of his vile, unconquerable temper alone made people in the least degree civil to him.

Finding that all was quiet, the passengers emerged from their places of concealment, and besieged Jack with questions.

While answering these, the saloon-keeper did a good trade.

MacTavish went to his house to apprise his daughter Helen of what had happened, and in a few minutes Bunyard and Jack followed him.

CHAPTER IV.

HELEN MACTAVISH—JACK'S INTRODUCTION TO THE COWBOYS—HE MAKES AN ENEMY, AND SECURES A FRIEND.

THE house in which Mr. MacTavish, manager to the great cattle and stock raiser, Hiram T. Bunyard, lived, was built of wooden boards.

It was capacious, and well but plainly furnished.

Helen managed her father's house, with the help of a coloured woman of about fifty years of age, named Mauma.

The latter was a thoroughbred negress, and had been a slave before the war.

During that fearful contest between the North and the South, her husband, two brothers, and three sons had been shot.

She was now alone in the world, and had centred all her affection upon Helen MacTavish.

For her she would have died cheerfully.

"Helen!" cried the MacTavish of that ilk, from the parlour, "here's the laird coming wi' the new English cowboy. Let the dinner bide a wee, and come hither."

"I'm coming, father," replied a bright, cheery voice.

"Take off your cooking-apron and put your hair straight, lassie."

"What will I be ashamed of? I'm doing the work. Do you want me to be a fine leddy, and lie all day on the sofa novel-reading, father?"

"Nae, nae. Here they come!"

Helen made her appearance in the parlour just as Bunyard and Jack entered the house.

"Welcome!" said MacTavish. "The hoose is nae sae elegant as it might be, but we're in the wilds. This is Jack of Warwick, Helen. My daughter Helen, Master Jack."

Helen shook hands with Mr. Bunyard first.

"I thought you were never coming back," she exclaimed; "the place is quite lonesome without you. I missed you quite as much as I did father when he went to Galveston for a month, about shipping cattle."

Bunyard looked displeased, as if he expected to hear something more than that.

In reality he liked the girl, but she never regarded him save as another father or a kind friend.

Having spoken to Bunyard, she turned to Jack.

"I am very glad to see anyone from the Old Country, whether English or Scotch," she continued. "You will have to work here. We all try to get as much work into the twenty-four hours as we can, and we are all the better for it."

Jack thought that Helen was the prettiest, best made, and nicest girl that he had ever met in his life.

He took quite a fancy to her at once.

So did she to him, as a matter of fact, for she thought it would be a relief to have a gentlemanly young man to talk to in the evening, as the cowboys and her father always left her alone, preferring to spend their spare time at Snell's, playing cards and drinking.

Jack felt a little nervous and bashful, scarcely knowing what to say.

"I hope we shall be good friends," he replied. "If you want anything done, Miss MacTavish—"

"Call me Helen—it's all Christian-names here," she interrupted. "But come into the kitchen if you want to talk to me; I'm busy. Father and Mr. Bunyard will have plenty to speak to one another about."

Jack followed her into the kitchen.

Mauma was stirring some soup one moment, and basting some roast beef the next.

"Here's our new cowboy from England," exclaimed Helen.

"Sakes alive!" replied Mauma, "he don't look much like one. I'd guess he belonged to one of the best families in Virginia."

"Do you drink and play cards?" asked Helen.

"No," said Jack; "I like to stay at home and read or talk."

"Oh, that is jolly! What a good time we shall have!"

"They'll soon teach him," remarked Mauma. "He's struck a rough crowd here, honey, and don't you forget it."

"That's so," answered Helen. "A stranger has just shot Tanner dead, so father told me."

"Mercy! what'll happen next? I'm afraid of my life to go outdoors; they's fearful wicked in these parts, miss."

"Jack," exclaimed Helen, "do you know where Snell's is? What's the use of asking, though; that's the first place sure they'd take you to. The cowboys will be having a cocktail there by this time; do you mind going and telling them dinner will be ready in fifteen minutes by the clock, and if they are late, I sha'n't wait for them."

"With pleasure," rejoined Jack; "anything I can do for you I will."

Mauma burst out laughing.

"Yah, yah!" she said. "Hope I may never eat coon-meat again if that don't take the cake. You ask him, Miss Helen, to stand on his head. Jehoshaphat! I'd like to see that."

Jack looked angrily at the negress, which only made her laugh all the more.

"I'm not an acrobat," he replied.

"Jerusalem the golden!" answered Mauma. "You'll have to be more than that if you intend to be a cowboy."

"Why so?"

"You'll have to be a whole circus, I tell you—acrobat, clown, ring-master, and elephant, too. Yah, yah!"

"Never mind, I daresay I'll get licked into shape in time," responded Jack.

"They'll teach you to take a tumble."

"Mauma," said Helen, "hold your tongue."

"I'm dumb, miss, as an oyster."

"Jack of Warwick," continued Helen, "I want to warn you."

"What of?" asked Jack.

"Poor little Tanner, who is dead, wasn't a bad sort, though I didn't cotton much to him. White is tolerable —that's all. Dawes is a loud-voiced, hard-drinking caution of a bully. Warner is a real nice fellow, and if you want a friend in this section, I'd advise you to cultivate him."

Jack looked curiously at her.

"Do you like Warner so much as all that?" he enquired.

Mauma clapped her hands.

"Lor' sakes!" she exclaimed, "if he ain't jealous. I do believe he has fallen right in love already. Yah, yah!"

Helen laughed, too, and Jack blushed up to the eyes.

"Will you be quiet, Mauma," said Helen. "I only like Warner as a brother. Run along, Jack. Hurry up. Do what I have asked you."

Jack went off at once.

It was enough for him to know that Helen regarded Warner only as a brother.

He felt that he could do anything to

gain the approbation of this beautiful prairie-flower.

As Helen had predicted, the cowboys had stabled their horses, and gone to the saloon to get a cocktail before dinner.

Here they heard the news of their comrade's death, at which they were furiously indignant.

With many an oath and angry exclamation, they vowed vengeance on the perpetrator of the outrage.

Warner, White, and Dawes had elbowed their way to the counter, driving the coach passengers to the table.

As Jack of Warwick entered they looked at him inquisitively.

He bore their searching scrutiny without betraying any nervousness.

"If you please," he exclaimed, "is Warner here ? "

"That's this child," replied Warner.

"And I'm Dawes," said that individual. "Now, who in thunder are you ? "

"They call me Jack of Warwick. I have just arrived here with Mr. Bunyard from England," answered Jack.

"Just aroved ! " cried Dawes. "Say, boys, this is the new cowboy we have heard about."

"I guess you are about right," remarked White.

"He'll have to pay his footing," continued Dawes. "What are you going to stand, youngster ? "

"Dinner is nearly ready. I don't drink, and I sha'n't stand anything," was Jack's firm but somewhat injudicious reply.

It was not calculated to please the cowboys at all.

"You won't set up the drinks when I tell you ? " said Dawes.

His eyes blazed, and his short-cut black moustache fairly bristled with rage.

"I'll stand you a glass of water."

"Jeemanetti ! " cried Dawes. "He offers me a glass of water ! "

"You'd better take it a teaspoonful at a time, till you kinder get used to the taste of it," said White.

"Ha, ha ! that's good. I shouldn't think of taking it any other way."

"I've come here to work, not to drink," exclaimed Jack.

"Work ! " repeated Dawes, with intense scorn. "You work ? "

"Yes. I don't see why I shouldn't work as well as any of you as soon as I know the ropes."

"They won't get any work, I reckon, out of a tenderfoot like you," sneered Dawes.

"That's all you know," retorted Jack.

"The kind of thing you'd like to be put on would be to wind up an eight-day clock—ha, ha ! "

"Ha, ha ! " laughed White and Warner.

"Have a care ! I will not be ridiculed by such as you," cried Jack, with flashing eyes.

"What do you do when your dander's riz," asked Dawes, "and you feel real mad ? "

"Fight," answered Jack, laconically.

"So do I. It's kinder strange that you and I should agree on one point, ain't it, don'tcherknow, my lardyda, played-out-old-country swell ? I guess I can lick any Britisher of my size and weight, and you don't come up to within two stone."

This was true, for Dawes was much heavier, taller, and older than Jack.

"I don't mind tackling you after dinner," replied our hero. "I think I could get away with a half-bred bull-puncher like you."

"Don't give me no back-talk," said Dawes. "Are you game for a fair up-and-down, rough-and-tumble, give-and-take mill, or not ? "

"After dinner, I say."

"I can't fight when I'm full of beef and puddin', nor you either ; you want to back out."

"Honestly, I do not."

"Pshaw ! You are about as honest as a thief in State's Prison. Do you want me to give you the coward's blow ? "

"You can if you like," answered Jack, quietly. "I'm not running."

He kept his eye on Dawes, however, watching closely his every movement.

The enraged cowboy struck out at our hero, who very cleverly ducked his head.

The blow missed him, but struck White on the cheek.

"Jeeroosh ! What yer up to, you big lummux ! " cried White.

"I ask your pardon—" began Dawes.

He had no time to say any more.

Jack was an accomplished wrestler as well as a fighter.

He seized Dawes in an anaconda-like hug, which squeezed all the breath out of his body and nearly choked him.

Then he gripped him under the left leg, gave him a mighty heave, and cast him like a log of wood over his shoulder.

The cowboy fell heavily on the floor in front of the stage-coach passengers, who recoiled with fear.

Blood gushed from his mouth and nose, and for a time he did not move.

White rushed to the side of his friend and lifted his head on to his knee.

"I think I'll go to dinner now," exclaimed Jack, in his calmest manner.

"You're a cool fish, by gosh!" said Warner. "But I like you all the better for not blowing. If you will let me, I'll be your friend?"

"Let me see, you are Warner. Miss Helen likes you, and I would rather have you for a chum than anyone else."

"Well said. Is it a go?"

"Call it a bargain. I shall want a friend, since I have made an enemy of Dawes."

"You must watch him," replied Warner; "he's treacherous when he's in his ugly moods. I believe you have half killed him."

"No; he moves. Look!" said Jack. "Snell is bringing him some whisky. He opens his eyes."

"Then we will skip to the ranche."

Together Warner and Jack quitted the saloon, and wended their way to MacTavish's house, from which escaped a savoury smell of roast beef.

Presently Dawes spoke.

"What was it? Earthquake?" he asked.

"No," replied White.

"What hit me? Was it the side of the house?"

"The new cowboy threw you."

"Great Scott! how did he do it?" enquired Dawes.

"He got his arm round your throat somehow," said White, "and then he put his hand under your leg, gave a heave, and you went flying through the air like a comet; presently you comes down in a heap, kerchunk—whop! I thought, sure pop, you'd have busted the floor in, and kinder dug your own grave."

"I'm disgraced," hissed Dawes, between his clenched teeth; "but I'll be revenged, you bet!"

"There's nothing to be ashamed of," observed Snell. "The galoot tuk you by surprise, sonny, and played it low down on yer, with a new style of wrestling you wasn't acquainted with."

"Oh, wrestlin', was it? I never was no great shakes at wrestlin'," replied Dawes; "but he's got my Ebenezer up, and I'm bound to pay him sooner or later. Help me up. Jiggered if I ain't sore all over! Blow wrestlin'! I don't want no more of it. Give me a fair stand-up fist fight."

Snell and White assisted him to his feet, and he limped towards the bar.

"Give me some more of that old rye," he went on.

In about ten minutes, with the aid of nearly as many drinks, he felt himself again, and, in company with White, went to dinner.

MacTavish was carving a splendid sirloin of beef, which weighed at least fifteen pounds.

Bunyard, Helen, Jack, and Warner were seated, and Mauma was waiting at the table.

"Come, come, boys, you are late!" exclaimed Bunyard. "Set to."

"We'll make up for that, boss," replied Dawes. "There was a bit of a ruction in the saloon, and we had to see it out."

"Anyone hurt?"

"Not worth a cent."

Jack smiled and looked at Helen, to whom he had related what had occurred before the dinner was served.

"Have you spoken to your new comrade?" asked Bunyard.

"Oh, yes; we have made acquaintance," answered Dawes.

"I hope it will be a lasting one. You can give Jack a mount on Tanner's mustang, and show him around this afternoon. My boys work in pairs, Jack, and we divide the herd between them. Dawes and White will chip in together; you can travel with Warner. It's play in summer, but it's mighty hard in winter."

"We must take it as it comes, sir," replied our hero.

"I'll show Jack what there is to be done," said Warner. "If he is to be under my charge, we had best start together."

"That's so. MacTavish and I will dig a grave for Tanner, and you can all be present at the funeral when you come back to supper. Slim Sam Sim will be off presently; he will send on another coach-driver to take the passengers to Brazos, and apprise the sheriff of the robbery; also of the death of Tanner, which I hope will result in an arrest."

"Mebbe," observed MacTavish, "the chappie who killed Tanner was the road-agent himself."

"By thunder!" cried Bunyard. "What a fool I was not to think of that! We ought to have made him a prisoner."

The dinner was soon over, and the cowboys went off to saddle their horses.

"Let Jack of Warwick look out for himself when I get a chance to pay him," Helen heard Dawes say.

"I'm with you," replied White, to whom he was speaking. "You know you can rely on me."

She called Jack to her side.

"For Heaven's sake!" she whispered, "beware of Dawes. I have taken more than a passing interest in you."

Jack smiled.

"Although this part of the world is strange to me, I know how to defend myself," he replied.

"But he is a terrible fellow, and already hates you."

"That makes no difference. I shall be all right," said Jack.

"Good-bye till supper-time!" Helen exclaimed.

In a few minutes Jack had joined the other cowboys in the stable-yard.

Dawes and White, who were already mounted, cantered off.

Warner was waiting for Jack.

Bunyard and MacTavish were smoking and drinking, while they rested and talked business.

Jack was soon in the saddle and cantering over the prairie in a direction where a herd of long-horned cattle could be discerned, leisurely cropping the grass.

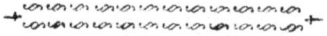

CHAPTER V.

THE DEVIL'S GAP—IN THE HIDING CAVE OF THE ROAD-AGENT—TOM JONES—THE ATTACK ON THE TRAIN AND ROBBERY OF THE EXPRESS CAR.

About half a day's journey from Mowbray's Ranche, in the direction of Nacogdochee, was a long range of sandhills, where no grass or trees would grow.

These sandhills were at least ten square miles in extent. In some parts they were of a rocky formation, and it was said that Indians lurked there in caves in the early days of the settlement of Texas by the Spaniards, who were superseded by the more enterprising Americans.

So inhospitable was this track of land that even the rattlesnake, the prairie-dog, and the owl avoided it.

Only the long-tailed grey sand-squirrels were to be met with, and they were not a numerous colony.

In a cave in this locality, Felton, the road-agent, had made himself a temporary home.

When he got away from Mowbray's Ranche he galloped to the sandhills.

Dismounting from his horse on arriving at his destination, he concealed the saddle and bridle under an overhanging rock, and turned the animal loose.

The horse rubbed his nose affectionately against his master's cheek.

"Don't stray far, Dick; I may want you soon—I can't tell when," said Felton, patting its neck.

The horse neighed, as if he fully comprehended what was said.

"Poor Dick!" muttered Felton, as he picked his way over the sandhills, "I wonder if he would love me so much did he know who and what I am?"

His feet sank deep in the sand as he proceeded.

There was a slight breeze blowing, and a myriad of minute, gritty particles assailed his face, getting into his mouth, irritating his eyes and nose, and penetrating down his back.

"A plague on these sand-dunes!" he muttered. "I shall be glad of a bottle of wine to wash this grit out of my throat."

He was not long in reaching the vicinity of the cave which he had selected for his hiding-place.

Putting his fingers to his mouth, he gave a shrill whistle.

It was evidently a preconcerted signal.

A boy of fifteen, or thereabouts, came out of the cave and stood at the entrance.

The road-agent strode towards the lad who had so promptly made his appearance, but stopped short suddenly, and had good reason to do so.

In front of him was a deep and horrible chasm.

Some convulsion of Nature had riven the subterranean rocks asunder, and an abyss had been formed which seemed to have no bottom.

It was called the Devil's Gap.

Behind the cave the rocks rose high, and as the chasm curved round it, no one could approach save from the front.

If Feltom had taken another step he would have been precipitated into the fathomless gulf.

But he knew his danger.

"Shoot the plank over, Tommy," he exclaimed.

The boy took up a long plank, and exerting all his strength, managed to steady it across.

"Good enough. I'm coming," continued Felton, who, balancing himself carefully on the narrow pathway, crossed over.

One false step, and his career would have been ended then and there.

Dashed from side to side of the abyss, he would have fallen, a lifeless, mangled, unrecognisable mass of humanity, somewhere in the bowels of the earth.

The boy shook him by the hand.

They went into the cave together, after removing the plank.

There were some wooden stools to sit on; a large flat rock served as a table; light flowed in from the entrance.

Felton went to a corner where there was a case of wine, knocked the head off a bottle, and drank some of the contents out of the broken vessel.

"You are back earlier than I expected you," remarked the boy.

"What has that to do with you?" replied Felton, who had an irritable temper. "I come and go as I please."

"Certainly."

"Look here, Tom Jones, which you say your name is, I don't mean to be dictated to by you. I want you to know that you are my help. That was the bargain between us—wasn't it?"

"Yes, I admit that, and I have done everything you told me since."

"Even to helping me attack the Brazos stage last night," replied Felton, with a hyena-like grin.

"I held the horses after you had shot the driver, and kept on holding them, while you robbed the passengers."

"Exactly, and that's where I have got you."

"I wasn't the robber."

"You were an accomplice, so you needn't be so high-toned. The authorities would hang you as high as they would me."

The boy was sitting down; he bowed his head, and looked very miserable.

"I did not think you would try to get a hold over me like that," he said; "I fancied you were a respectable man when I first met you."

"You know what I am now."

"Yes—a robber and murderer."

"Quite correct, and you are my accomplice. We shall do more robber's work together."

"Never. I didn't know your purpose yesterday, or I would not have come with you. I have been deceived, but you shall not deceive me further."

Felton laughed lightly.

"Come," he said, "don't get up in the stirrups. I met you a week ago in New Orleans. Is not that so?"

"Yes; I had landed there. I came from Liverpool. A sailor robbed me of all my money. I was homeless, friendless, starving, in a cotton shed on the Levee."

"Go on," cried Felton, nodding his head approvingly.

"You came along, and asked me what the trouble was. I told you, and you took me to your hotel, engaging me as your clerk. You brought me to Austin, and from there to this place."

"True. Now tell me all about yourself. I've been good to you, and should like to know your history."

Tom Jones was not in a communicative mood.

"I ran away from my home in England," he replied.

"What was that for?" inquired Felton.

"Reasons of my own; it does not concern you."

"Yes, it does. You may say that I have adopted you. What's your real name?"

"I have told you—Tom Jones."

"That is not good enough for a gentlemanly chap like you. I am going to make a road-agent of you. Yesterday you made your first start in your new profession by robbing the coach; in a short time we shall stop the train and rob the express-car. You can't go back. If you have any foolishness with me, I shall put the police on your track. You are in my power now, my fine young fellow."

Tom Jones bit his lip with vexation.

He saw the force of Felton's reasoning.

"You will get a good bit of money if you are successful in stopping the train," he said, thoughtfully.

"Some thousands," was the reply.

"Then what will you do?"

"Go to some city and live like a gentleman until it is all spent. You shall come with me. When it is gone we will go on the road again and make some more. It's a jolly life, though a trifle risky."

"Have you ever been in prison?" asked Tom.

"Hallo! it appears it is your turn to question. Well, I will answer you frankly. I have. It was some time ago," said Felton. "I got three years for a bank robbery in New York, and served the time in Sing-Sing Gaol, on the Hudson River."

"Suppose you get caught again, and I with you?"

"In that case you will be sent up as well as me," replied Felton with a grin.

"Not a very pleasant prospect. I think I would rather be back in New Orleans, starving on the wharf, and take my chance."

"Too late! I've got my grip on you," Felton said, shaking his head.

"Let me go."

"No! If you bolt I'll follow you up. I don't mind getting locked up too, so long as I have my revenge on you for leaving me. I want company, and you suit me."

Tom sighed deeply.

He could see that if he ran away he would be in danger any moment of being denounced, exposed, and arrested.

Felton was indubitably his master, and intended to rule him with a rod of iron.

No more was said.

For the next week Felton did nothing but smoke, drink, and sleep; he called this laying off, and indulged his vicious propensities regardless of everything else.

Tom used to get his meals ready for him, and he listened to the stories he told him of many crimes attempted and committed.

For hours he would sit outside the cave and throw pieces of red sandstone down the Devil's Gap.

It must have been very deep, for he never heard one touch the bottom.

Felton was waiting for the promised visit from Slim Sam Sim, the pony-postman.

Until he came with information respecting the gold which was to be dispatched by Wells, Fargo and Co., he could do nothing.

At last the pony-postman made his appearance in the afternoon.

"Ha, Sim," cried Felton, "the sight of you is very welcome. I'm rusting in this accursed corner, and have to get drunk twice a day to prevent softening of the brain or acute madness. Have you got a mouth on you?"

"Try me and see," replied the postman.

Felton handed him a bottle and a glass; a gurgling sound indicated that the gift was appreciated.

"That's good," said Slim Sam Sim. "It just touched the spot. It's awful hot outside, and I had a thirst on me a yard long."

Suddenly he noticed Tom.

"Say," he added, "who's that?"

"My boy," answered Felton. "I found him down to New Orleans. He's only a runner yet, but I mean to make a man of him before I've done. He was with me when I robbed the stage. I tell you he's got grit in him, and should get to the top of the profession."

"He is sure to under your tuition, unless, by ill-luck, he gets his neck broken."

"What news do you bring?"

"The train will pass a spot about thirty miles from here, to which I will conduct you, to-night at one o'clock," said Slim Sam Sim. "In the express-car is a box containing a large sum in gold."

"To-night—so soon? We must brace up and start without delay. Let us lay our plans and map this thing out," replied Felton.

Instantly he threw off his lethargic air, and was the sharp man of business again.

A long discussion ensued between him and the pony-postman.

It was arranged that they should leave the cave in an hour's time, and travel to the railroad.

Sim had his pony on the prairie.

Tom could ride behind Felton.

There were only three of them, but they considered themselves quite sufficient to rob the train, which Sam stated would consist of only two passenger-carriages and the express-car.

When they got possession of the specie, Sim was to go on to Nacogdochee, getting his share of the plunder on a future occasion; and the two others would return to the cave and remain there until the hue and cry had ceased.

The storm would soon blow over.

When opportunity offered, Felton and Tom would go to San Francisco, and enjoy themselves in that gay city on the Pacific.

Accordingly they loaded their pistols, of which each had three, all six-shooters, and, crossing the Devil's Gap, walked through the sand to the prairie.

As if by some instinct he knew that he was wanted, Felton's horse was standing by the picketed pony of the postman.

With their pistols stuck in their belts ready for instant use, the marauders mounted.

"Now, Tom, jump up behind!" exclaimed Felton. "You can hang on to my waist, and you won't come to any grief."

"I don't want to go," replied Tom; "let me stay in the cave. What do you want to drag me into a thing like this for?"

"You've got to do as I tell you. If I get off my horse, I'll thrash you within an inch of your life."

"I don't wish to be a road-agent."

"Put a bullet in the young cub's leg," cried Sim. "I wouldn't stand any fooling, and we can't afford to lose time."

"That's the idea. Are you coming? I sha'n't ask twice."

With these words Felton pointed a pistol at Tom, his eyes sparkling like diamonds.

"All right; don't shoot," replied Tom.

To avoid having his leg broken, the boy took a spring, and vaulted on to the back of the horse.

"Off, and away!" said Felton, who was soon galloping over the plain, closely followed by Slim Sam Sim.

They did not draw bridle until they had gone fifteen miles, which was half the distance they had to travel.

A small stream enabled them to water the horses, and they refreshed themselves out of their whisky-flasks.

By this time the sun was setting, and they resumed their journey at a more leisurely pace.

It soon grew dark. There was no moon, but the stars gave an uncertain light, now bright, now flickering, which enabled them to see whither they were going.

It was the same undulating, monotonous prairie.

Here and there were a few patches of sage-brush and chaparral, from which a jack-rabbit would now and again pop out, stand on its hind legs, erect its long ears, and peer curiously at them.

At length the line of railroad, which was a single track, was reached.

"Here's the spot where I reckon to do the trick," exclaimed Sim, reining in his panting pony, whose coat was flecked with foam.

"Why here in particular?" asked Felton.

"Because I have prospected, and found that there is no station, no ranche, no chance of even a section man."

Felton looked at his watch.

"Half-past midnight. We shall not have long to wait," he said. "Where is the danger-signal?"

Slim Sam Sim unfastened the flap of his mail-bag, which he carried at his saddle-bow, and produced a lamp.

It had a large red bull's-eye.

"Here you are, take it and light it," he replied; "it is a regulation-lamp which I found at the depôt. I may add that it was found before it was lost, and the man it belonged to wasn't looking."

"Bully for you!" cried Felton; "you deserve to make a fortune quickly, and live long to enjoy it afterwards."

"When you have stopped the train, what are you going to do?" asked Sim. "It is just as well to have everything cut and dried."

They all dismounted, and hitched the horses to a rail in an old fence.

Felton took three black masks from his pocket, and gave one to each of his companions.

He donned the third one himself.

These crape face coverings made them look singularly hideous and repulsive.

They were calculated to inspire the beholder with awe.

"You must go to one passenger-car," said Felton, "and Tom to another, to keep the travellers quiet. If necessary, shoot. I shall settle the driver, the stoker, and the express-agent. The box of gold we will carry to the side of the line, and put on my horse. You will have to take Tom behind you. I shall dash off and wait for no one."

"Good. Hark! I think I hear her coming."

Putting his hand to his ear, Felton listened attentively.

His sense of hearing was well-attuned to all sorts of sounds.

"Right you are," he cried. "The old en-gyne's a-comin'. Be spry, boys. It's a fortune or nothing."

In a moment he was gone, and it was with difficulty that they could distinguish the dark outline of his figure on the line.

Tom's heart beat so wildly that he could scarcely breathe.

A mist came over his eyes, and he felt as if he were going to faint.

"Brace up," whispered Sim. "Have some style about you! It's nervous work.

Kinder neck-or-nothing business. Have a nip of this."

He handed him his flask. Tom drank, and his brain seemed to be set on fire.

"Feel better?"

"Yes, thank you."

"There is no drawing back now. F. will shoot you if you show the white feather—ay, if he has to hunt these United States through for you. I know him."

The train was now heard distinctly as it tore along the track.

Tom shuddered and shivered as if it were cold, though it was a calm, warm night.

He knew that he was engaged in an awfully perilous enterprise.

There was little time for reflection, however.

The programme was carried out to the letter.

Felton stood on the line in the centre of the track, and as the train approached he waved the red light over his head.

On rounding a slight curve the driver saw the signal, which he thought was intended to warn him of danger.

Instantly he whistled "down brakes," and shut off steam.

The brakesman applied the air-brake, and the train came to a standstill within a few yards of Felton, who jumped upon the engine.

There were two sharp reports, the bullets rattling against the iron-work of the car as Felton fired.

"That is only to show you what I can do, boys," he cried. "There are ten of us in this gang. We don't want to hurt you if you have sense. What we are after is the money in the express-car. Jump off and lie low for a quarter of an hour, and you won't be hurt. What's the use of all the world to a man when his wife's a widow?"

"You bet," answered the driver.

He was only too glad to be given the chance of getting off the engine, and did so with alacrity.

His mate had already gone.

Felton now went to the express-car, at the door of which the agent was standing, wondering what was the matter.

He was not left long in doubt.

Sim and Tom were in the cars, threatening the passengers with their pistols, and keeping them in a state of terrified quietness, each one having been ordered to hold his hands up.

This effectually prevented them from getting at their weapons, if they carried any.

The clerk flashed his lamp upon Felton, and recoiled on seeing the black mask.

Well he knew this symbol of lawlessness, robbery, and murder.

"Who are you?" he asked, in a shaky tone of voice.

"Hands up!" shouted Felton.

The young man had been seeking his pistol-pocket, but he at once obeyed the injunction.

"We are road-agents," said Felton. "You are all surrounded. It is useless to resist. Show me the gold consigned by Wells, Fargo, and Co."

"We—haven't—got—any," the clerk stammered.

"You lie—my information is positive. Speak or die!"

The clerk pointed to an ordinary deal box in the corner of the car, hard by where he was standing.

Felton seized it, and exerting all his strength, bore it away.

The clerk did not dare to fire, because he could not tell how many robbers there might be about.

He had been told the train was surrounded.

And the idea of three men robbing a train full of passengers savoured of the impossible.

In this instance it was the very audacity of the proceeding which ensured its success.

When Felton had got the box on the saddle, and was in the stirrups, he blew shrilly on a silver whistle.

This was the signal of recall, and both Slim Sam Sim and Tom quitted the cars hurriedly.

They were side by side when they reached the pony.

Felton was a little way ahead.

This Tom distinctly saw by the starlight and the faint glimmer cast by the lights in the train.

Suddenly the sharp crack of a pistol rang out.

Slim Sam Sim put his hand to his side, uttered a sobbing cry, and fell to the ground.

He was shot through the heart.

Tom noticed a puff of smoke curling up from where Felton was sitting on his horse.

The shot had come from that direction, not from the train.

Sick at heart, and wishing this night of horrors were over, Tom got on the pony.

To stay by Slim Sam Sim would have been to invite capture.

"Off, off!" cried Felton.

He put his horse to its utmost speed, and Tom followed him, not knowing what else to do.

Not a friend had he in that part of the world; nowhere could he go.

On that boundless prairie he would starve if he remained behind.

His heart was filled with a nameless horror.

What kind of a man was this fellow Felton?

Surely a fiend in human shape.

He had shot and killed his friend and accomplice, cowardly, basely, like an assassin.

Without any warning he had sent him to his long account.

Tom's blood ran cold.

Whose turn would it be next?

Perhaps his own.

The day broke serenely, and as the sun rose the white mist was dispelled as if by magic before its golden rays.

It was with difficulty that Tom kept up with the road-agent, who occasionally slackened his pace to enable the boy to recover lost ground.

At length Felton drew rein, for there was now no danger of pursuit.

"Ha, ha!" he laughed, as Tom drew alongside of him, "our fortune is assured for the next twelve months. We need run no risks so long as the money lasts, but I have a playful knack of making the golden dollars fly."

"You ought to buy a business," Tom remarked, "and settle down on your capital. Take an hotel."

"Pshaw! I should drink myself out of it in six months; besides, I am too restless and volatile for a tradesman's life."

Tom did not pursue the subject any further.

He was thinking of the cruel, treacherous, and awfully sudden death of Slim Sam Sim.

Felton noticed his dejected air, and immediately guessed the cause of it.

"Sim went off sudden, didn't he?" observed the road-agent.

"Very much so," replied Tom, laconically. "What made you do it? I know it was you, for I could tell where the ball came from owing to the smoke rising in your direction."

"Oh, you were smart enough to see that," cried Felton. "You are not such a fool as you look, Master Tom Jones, or whatever your name is. Anybody who picks you up for that might as well lay hold of a rock snake and think the reptile won't bite. I must watch you closely."

"I fancied you and Sim were friends," said Tom, who considered himself highly complimented.

"There is no friendship in business," answered Felton.

"What do you mean?"

"Sim had the bulge on me. It was this way. He put up the coach robbery and the train job. He could betray me any time, so I thought I would cut all risks and get his share of the plunder by plugging him with a bullet. He is out of my way now. I sha'n't want him any more, for I shall leave this section of Texas to-day and go elsewhere. This part is worked out, sonny."

"Where are you going next?"

"That is telling. You will find out in time. Serve me well, and I will treat you like a brother."

"My fate may be the counterpart of Sim's," remarked Tom.

"It may be," returned Felton, callously; "I can't say. I'm a peculiar fellow, and have my moods. Offend me or try to give me the slip, and you will find me as bitter an enemy as the world ever contained. I'd get locked up myself so as to have you in gaol, too."

"You must be fond of prison life," replied Tom, with a half sneer.

"Not so much of that, either," answered Felton; "but I'll back myself to get out of any of these western or southern gaols in less than a month."

"How would you do it?"

"By using the golden key. Every warder has his price. Here we are at the sand-dunes. Hurrah!"

They were approaching their hiding cave. Of this they were glad, for they were both tired and hungry.

Tom was especially fatigued, owing to the excitement he had gone through. His nerves were greatly overstrained, and he felt so low-spirited he could have shed tears had he given way.

When the limit of the prairie was reached, and the sandy tract began, Felton dismounted, hid his saddle and bridle, turning his horse loose as usual.

"Good old Dick!" he said, patting the handsome creature's neck. "Don't go far. I reckon I shall want you again before the day is out."

The horse rubbed his nose against his master's shoulder, and with a neigh of pleasure trotted off towards a patch of alfalfa-grass, which had grown up on the prairie.

"Get out of that saddle!" exclaimed Felton. "We'll have to put the box of specie on the pony. Look alive! To see you sitting there anyone would think you were the gentleman and I was the nigger."

Tom was on the ground in a moment, and helped to place the treasure on the pony.

They steadied it, one on each side, and started over the sand for the cave.

"Shall I have to take the pony back, and turn him loose on the prairie?"

Felton burst out laughing.

"What are you laughing at?" asked Tom.

"You'd make a hermit laugh," replied Felton. "I opined just now that you were mighty smart; but I begin to think you must be an idiot!"

"Why so?"

"To ask a question like that! My word! if some cowboy was to find Sim's pony near here wouldn't it complicate matters for me! My horse don't matter; there's very few that knows him; but the pony-post has been all over the country. You will see what I mean doing with him directly."

"You're right," said Tom; "I did not think of that. You know I have not had so much experience in the ways of the wicked world as you have."

"Who says the world is wicked?"

"I think it must be since I have known you," Tom coolly replied.

The other looked at him queerly.

"IN VAIN HE TRIED TO SCRAMBLE OUT."

No. 3.

"Boy," cried Felton, "don't irritate me! My temper is uncertain. I don't want to hurt you; I'd rather have you for my friend and companion—make a sorter son of you, dress you, feed you well, and take you around—that is, if you will give me a show."

"I ought to be grateful; but I'm not," replied Tom.

"Why shouldn't you be?"

"That's what I can't make out. You act well towards me; you promise well; yet I don't like you."

"It's singular," said Felton, reflectively. "You are not the only one; nobody seems to like me, neither men nor women. I have never been able to keep a friend; but it does not matter; I can live alone. If I want company I can always find it in a city."

During the discussion they had walked up to the Devil's Gap.

The plank was across the chasm as they had left it.

With a great deal of care the box of gold was taken from the pony's back, and placed on the plank.

Tom went first, sitting astride the plank, and pulling the box, while Felton, in the same position, pushed it.

At last it was landed safely across the abyss.

"Bully for us!" said Felton. "Now I'll settle the postman's pony, and you can get breakfast. I'll make something of you before I've done with you. At present all the wit you've got is to catch a blind horse, and then I don't believe you'd hold him."

"Perhaps I have more in me than a fellow like you thinks for," replied Tom.

"Hallo! showing your teeth again!"

"Yes, I am."

"You have done that more than once lately. What is the meaning of it?"

"I'm the son of a gentleman, and one myself by birth, position, and education. More than that, I— But you may find out some day. I'm thankful to you for what you did for me in New Orleans, yet if I had known what you were, I would have starved before I went with you."

"There's a mystery about you, my bonny boy, and I must fathom it."

"If you can," replied Tom, quietly.

"You may think yourself clever," cried Felton, "but if I don't double discount you, I'm not here."

Shaking his head, Felton recrossed the plank, and went up to the pony.

It was a gentle creature that Slim Sam Sim had ridden for years.

Taking a red bandanna handkerchief from his pocket, the road-agent bound it round the pony's eyes.

"This way," he said, hypocritically patting the horse's neck. "Come along, old girl, to your oats."

The animal backed and kicked out as if it did not exactly understand what was going to happen.

It was not the accustomed voice of the master she had been used to in the heat of summer and frost of winter.

"Steady, lass, steady!" continued Felton. "Easy does it. Come to your stable. Gently over the stones. So!"

Still the horse would not go forward.

It neighed piteously, as if fearing some awful calamity.

Felton, generally brutal, never gentle, lost his temper, and picking up a stone, turned the pony round, and hammered its forehead.

"Back, confound you!" he cried. "What in thunder do you want to give me all this trouble for?"

Frightened, the creature backed, and fell over the edge of the Devil's Gap. It tried desperately to hold on with its front legs.

In its struggle the handkerchief came off, and Felton saw the big eyes nearly starting from the head.

With a wild screech of terror the pony lost its grip, and sank like a lump of lead into the abyss.

Down, down, ever down into a vast profundity it went.

Not a sound arose, and after listening for a while, Felton crossed the plank and entered the cave.

After witnessing the fate of the pony, Tom had preceded him, and was getting the breakfast ready.

"I make a clean sweep, don't I?" asked Felton. "A man who holds his life, or at least his liberty, in his hand, should never give a chance away; the least oversight may betray him to his doom."

While Tom was preparing the repast, Felton broke open the express-box, and looked at its contents, which consisted of a quantity of twenty-five dollar gold pieces.

They were wrapped in paper rolls, each roll holding fifty.

Around his waist he wore a leather belt.

Taking it off, he packed the gold in it, and again fastened it on.

This did not exhaust the supply, so he put the remainder in his capacious pockets.

"Jerusalem!" he remarked. "I should not like to ride a race carrying this weight. I'll have to change it into dollar bills the first chance I get, you bet!"

"Have you obtained as much as you expected?" asked Tom.

"More. We'll enjoy ourselves now. I'll treat you well. What is the use of living if you've got no money?"

"Work for it. That is the best way to get on."

"Rubbish!" answered Felton, beginning to eat. "Any man can work, but it takes a clever fellow to scheme. I don't belong to the working division— no, sir; not me!"

"You'll come to a bad end. If you are not hanged, they will make you work in prison."

"Stop your croaking. If I want to hear a sermon I'll go to church or chapel for it. Give me some claret!" said Felton. "And look here, if I hear another word of that kind out of your mouth, you'll regret it. Be advised, and take a back seat."

Tom was silent at this threat.

He did not like the look of the man, and after Sam's death, he was more than ever afraid of him.

Handing him some claret, he sat down on the floor of the cave, for there was no furniture, and the two ate a hearty breakfast.

Then sleep came upon them—all absorbing, irresistible.

"I'm off!" cried Felton, with a yawn, as he rolled on his back with a blanket for a pillow. "Can't even give it up to smoke a cigar! Did you draw the plank over the gap?"

"No; but I will," answered Tom.

"That's right; make the cave safe."

Felton closed his eyes, and was soon snoring like a humming-top; but Tom did not follow his example.

Wild thoughts were surging in his mind.

To continue to live with the road-agent any longer would be to submit to a hateful thraldom.

He would be dragged deeper into crime at every step.

He reflected for a brief space, and then determined to run away, though he had neither money nor friends in America.

Seeing that Felton was in a deep slumber, he stole out of the cave, crossed the plank, and drew it over to the other side of the Devil's Gap.

That would not keep Felton a prisoner, because he could climb over the cave, and escape by the back way.

It would, however, hinder him considerably, and allow Tom more time to get away.

His future might be hard; he might starve on the boundless prairie; but that would be better than to be linked to a deep-dyed criminal such as the merciless road-agent had shown himself to be.

Tom hastened over the sand-hills. Tired though he was, his spirit kept him up.

At last he reached the prairie.

Not a house, a tree, or even a bullock or sheep was to be seen.

On all sides was the undulating prairie, so wearying to the eye.

On, on, he trudged, having only one wish, one hope—to distance pursuit on the part of Felton.

For miles he walked. In time he became so exhausted that he could scarcely drag one foot after the other.

Suddenly he saw a clump of trees, and his heart beat quicker.

His strength returned. He pressed on, and came to a well of pure spring water, which had evidently been dug for the use of cattle, and planted round with shade trees for protection from the heat.

The footprints of cattle could be seen all round.

With a sigh of relief, such as the thirsty traveller in an African desert breathes when he comes to an oasis, Tom sank on his knees and drank.

Then he lay on the grass and fell fast asleep.

He could bear no more.

CHAPTER VI.

JACK OF WARWICK AND WARNER MAKE A DISCOVERY WHILE HERDING.

It was seven o'clock, and breakfast-time at MacTavish's house, at Mowbray's Ranche, and everyone was at the table.

All at once Snell burst into the room, his face all aglow with excitement.

"Pretty doings!" he exclaimed. "We shall be all murdered in our beds if we don't look out!"

"Eh, mon!" cried MacTavish. "What's to do now? You look for all the world as if a swarm of bees had settled on your hair!"

"A new postman has come. Sim has been shot dead. He and some others stopped the train, and robbed the express-car of a large sum of money, with which the thieves got clear off."

"I am surprised," said Bunyard. "Sim was the last man I should have suspected of being in league with road-agents!"

"Aweel! you never know anybody now," replied MacTavish. "The warld is becoming vera wicked."

"It is because everybody wants to get rich in a hurry, and people won't work as they used to," said Bunyard. "But you have some more news, Snell? I see you have. Out with it, man!"

"The new pony-post reports that the authorities have received information from certain cowboys that a party of Comanche Indians are on the war-path, scalping, raiding, and burning."

"That's bad news."

"A troop of United States cavalry have been asked for to put them down. They have come from the Indian territory, where they were thought safe on their reservation. They are going to hold some of their old-fashioned rites at what they call the Sacred Tree."

"Why, that is not thirty miles from Mowbray's Ranche. I have seen it," cried Bunyard. "They will be round our ears like hornets."

A painful silence ensued.

What with the proximity of road-agents and Red Indians the position was not an enviable one.

The Indian territory or reserve lay between Texas, Arkansas, New Mexico, and Kansas.

A reputation for daring and ferocity had always attached to the Comanches, who were dead shots and splendid riders.

As picturesque savages at a distance they might be admired, but as neighbours they were undesirable.

"We must be on the alert," exclaimed Bunyard. "I fear troublesome times are in store for us."

"Helen," said MacTavish, "I forbid you going far from this house."

"Do not fear for me, father," she rejoined; "I will be very careful. The skulking rascals shall not easily catch me."

Breakfast was soon over.

MacTavish took several pinches of "sneezin'" from his mull, or box, made of cow's horn.

The cowboys went to the stable and saddled their horses, preparatory to starting out to look after their cattle, which, if not herded, would stray to long distances, and get mixed up with other herds.

"We shall have a storm of some kind to-day," remarked Warner. "You don't know what our Texas storms are, Jack."

"Regular hair-raisers," said Dawes. "The English tenderfoot will weaken, I guess, if he meets one."

"Not I," replied Jack. "If it won't hurt me, I can stand it."

"You can blow," continued Dawes, with an ill-concealed sneer; "but I don't think you have much grit in you, after all. England's played out, and so is everything in it."

Dawes was about to mount his mustang, when Jack seized him by the leg, hauled him down, and gave him a blow which sent him spinning.

He went round and round like a tee-totum several times, till finally he measured his length on the grass.

"Ha, ha!" laughed Warner; "that just served you right!"

"Do you still think the British are played out?" asked Jack.

White helped his friend to rise.

"I—I didn't mean anything!" said Dawes. "You are so hasty. Can't you take a joke? It's a blow with you first, and a word afterwards."

"That's my style, and you ought to know it by this time. Keep a civil tongue in your head."

"I wish you were dead!" hissed Dawes. "How I hate you!"

"What's your friendship worth?" asked Jack. "You and I were born to be enemies, and if you try to injure me I'll strike back, bear that in mind, you big, raw-boned, red-faced bully!"

"My time will come," answered Dawes, with a snarl. "You shall pay for that blow with your life!"

He again mounted, and, accompanied by White, whipped up his horse viciously, and galloped over the rolling prairie.

Jack and Warner rode off in a more leisurely manner in another direction.

"I should not take any notice of that fellow," said Warner. "Contemptuous indifference would be my plan, and a sort of severely let him alone. He'll do you an injury if he can."

"That's all very well in theory, but not in practice," replied Jack. "I have met men like him before. He's a bully and a coward. I must make him afraid of me, or I could not live at all—he would make my life so miserable."

"Perhaps he does not mean to let you live."

"I'll watch that," said Jack, with a confident smile.

After riding some miles, they came to the cattle, which numbered two thousand head, all fine long-horned Texas steers, branded with the letter B to denote their ownership.

Their first care was to ride amongst them, slashing their long whips, and count them, Jack taking one side, Warner the other.

The result of the census was that they found about a score were missing.

This often happened, as cattle will stray, and they had to look them up at once, and drive them, when discovered, back to the herd.

Warner carried, slung over his shoulder, a first-class binocular glass, which enabled him to sweep the prairie for miles.

He looked to all points of the com-

pass, and at last an exclamation escaped him.

"I think I see them!" he exclaimed.

"It may be the Comanches," said Jack.

"Hope not. I don't want no Comanches near me," answered Warner; "but, anyway, it is difficult to tell at this distance."

"What shall you do?"

"Go and see, of course," said the cowboy.

They started, going due east.

The perspiration ran in streams down their faces, for it was scorchingly hot.

Not a breath of air stirred the heat-laden atmosphere.

Jack's head ached till it seemed to threaten to burst, for he suffered more than Warner, owing to not being acclimatised.

Flashes of lightning shot athwart the sky, and the distant rumblings of thunder were distinctly audible.

A sulphurous smell assailed their nostrils.

Grasshoppers were silent, prairie-dogs went into their burrows, the rattlesnakes forgot to hiss, as the horses dashed past them.

In short, there was an awful hush on the face of Nature.

This foretold an impending convulsion.

A smart ride of half-an-hour enabled the cowboys to see that the objects Warner had distinguished were in reality the lost cattle.

They were running as if instinct had told them to seek some shelter.

"There are the beasts," cried Warner. "No Comanches this time, thank goodness!"

The clouds, which were of a grey hue, dropped lower every moment.

A deep, solemn stillness brooded over the vast solitude.

"What is going to happen?" asked Jack, who drew his breath with difficulty.

"I can't tell yet," replied Warner. "We shall have fun of some sort before long. Let us press on and head off those cattle. If they are lost, we may be days finding them."

They urged on their panting steeds, who were as much under the influence of the weather as their masters.

After a time they overtook the cattle

and whipped them round, causing them to go back towards the herd.

Suddenly a white cloud collected in a south-westerly direction, and came directly in their path.

It advanced, each moment growing larger.

Dust rose round the cowboys, the clouds grew denser, the lightning more vivid, and the wind began to moan.

"Down—down!" shouted Warner.

"What is it?" queried Jack.

"Ask no questions—do as I do."

Warner dismounted with the utmost alacrity; Jack did the same.

The horses, trained to a life on the prairie, sank upon the grass, rolling on to their sides at a word from Warner, and turned their heads away from the cloud.

This constantly grew larger and denser.

Warner cast himself under the protection of his horse's body, which made a kind of wall for him, and Jack imitated him.

"It's the sandstorm!" cried Warner, hoarsely. "Shut your mouth and eyes; it don't last long."

Yes, it was the dreaded pampero, as the Mexicans call it; the sirocco of Africa; the simoom of India.

On it came, covering the boys and horses with thin particles of hot, burning sand.

Its rush and its roar were fearful.

To breathe, for a brief space, was next to an impossibility, and Jack thought he would be suffocated.

After a time, which seemed an age, the air cleared; the pampero had passed over them.

Warner rose and shook the sand off his body—he was thickly covered with it—and drew a deep inspiration.

In a moment Jack was by his side.

"Do you have this often?" he asked.

"Pretty frequently," replied the cowboy. "It ain't half as bad as a blizzard in winter, though. The snow blinds you, and the cold gets into your bones. You've got to be one of the toughs to stand Texas."

As if they knew that all danger was over, the mustangs rose from their recumbent position and snorted their satisfaction.

To Warner's vexation, the cattle had turned round and faced the pampero, tearing and bellowing through it.

They were careering eastward like mad creatures.

"Look!" said Warner. "The brutes are off again, and we must follow. No dinner for us to-day."

"Why not?" asked Jack.

"If we don't pursue, we shall lose them."

Getting astride their horses, they once more went after the lost cattle, finding it difficult to overtake them, though they kept them well in sight.

After the pampero came the thunderstorm, which had been threatening all day.

The lightning flashed, the thunder crashed, and the heavy rain fell from the surcharged clouds with tropical fury.

In less than five minutes the cowboys were drenched to the skin.

Then the furious storm rolled over southwards, the glad sun streamed out, the air became cool as if by magic, and the prairie-hens flew about among the soft bush; the grasshoppers chirped; the owls and the prairie-dogs came out, blinking and barking.

Nature was rejoiced at the relief from the recent strain.

All at once a clump of trees appeared on the verge of the horizon, looking dwarfed and ghostly.

The cattle were heading towards this spot.

"Say," said Warner, "this is bully. The stock are going to the well. I thought the animiles knew their book. They are pretty well choked up with sand, and knew enough to go somewhere for a drink."

"What well is that?" asked Jack.

"One of ours. We have had several dug in different places. This is one we seldom use, as the pasture is not particularly good, owing to its being so close to the sand-hills. It will be nice to have a rest and a wash there, and I guess we shall be able to get back to the ranche for dinner, after all."

They eased their horses and trotted towards the well.

A thick steam was rising from the ground.

The sun was raising the moisture which had just fallen.

"I've a little drop of old Snell's

whisky in my flask," said Warner, "which I always carry in case of accidents. After the pampero, we want something to wash our mouths out."

"I'm grit all over," replied Jack. "It is making my skin itch terribly; it makes one wish there was such a thing as a scratching-machine."

The cowboy laughed.

Coming up to the oasis, they dismounted, loosed the bridles, left the animals to feed on the rich grass, and threading the trees, came to the well.

The bullocks had done drinking, and were tearing down some of the lower boughs of the trees.

"A nice dance you've led us!" said Warner, twisting the tail of one of them.

"Hallo!" he added, as a figure lying on the ground caught his eye; "somebody camping out. What does this mean? I own up I didn't bargain to meet strangers."

Jack of Warwick was by his side in the twinkling of an eye.

"Why," said he, "someone is either dead or asleep. Who can it be? I'll wake him if he is alive."

It was a boy of his own age, lying on the ground with his face on his arm.

A shake roused him. He turned over, opened his eyes, and yawned.

"Good heaven!" cried Jack, "it is my friend Osmond."

He was so amazed he could say no more.

Warner looked on in silent astonishment.

The boy on the grouned jumped to his feet, and caught Jack of Warwick by the hand.

"Thank God!" he exclaimed, "I have met a friend at last."

"Osmond—"

"I am known as Tom Jones," interrupted the boy. "Keep my secret, for I am in deadly peril. My life is in danger. You will tremble when you hear my sad story; but, first, tell me how you came here, in the wilds of Texas?"

Jack related his adventures in a few words, for they had not been very startling hitherto.

"This is Warner, my friend," he added; "we are both cowboys, and work for Mr. Bunyard. You can speak freely before him."

Tom, for it was the boy of mystery whom Felton had picked up in New Orleans—in reality Osmond, now Lord Melbury, of Kenilworth Hall—had slept soundly for several hours, so exhausted was he.

So soundly, indeed, that neither the pampero nor the thunderstorm had disturbed him.

"Oh, Jack," said Osmond, "I have had such a fearful time of it here."

"Your troubles are all over now," answered Jack. "Providence must have brought us together, old friend, for your good."

Osmond shook his head.

"I am a fly in a web," he rejoined; "never can I tell when the hideous spider will pounce upon me."

"Have you heard from England?"

"Not a line."

"I have news for you."

"Good or bad?" asked Osmond, breathlessly.

"Both. Your father is dead; you are Lord Melbury. Your mother has offered a thousand pounds for your recovery."

Osmond looked as if he had been struck by a bullet.

"Father dead!" he repeated. "How — when?"

Jack told him.

"Ha!" continued Osmond, sorrowfully, "I behaved badly—my conduct killed him. There is a malediction on me. Well I know it!"

"Nonsense!"

"No, no; it has begun to work already. I shall never enjoy my proper position as Lord Melbury—never—never —never!"

He sank to the ground and covered his face with his hands.

The cause of his grief was an enigma to Jack.

He could not make anything of it.

Naturally he thought he would be delighted to hear that he had come into the title and estates, however much he might grieve at the sudden death of his father.

It was a strange meeting altogether.

"The malediction is on me," continued Osmond. "I will fight against its evil influence as I may, and you, Jack, will help me; but I fear it will prevail."

Jack urged him to tell him and Warner all that had happened since his arrival in America.

They carried some lunch with them, to partake of which he was very glad.

He was depressed and nervous. While he was narrating his adventures he trembled as he spoke of Felton.

Jack and Warner were profoundly interested in the startling narration.

CHAPTER VII.

OSMOND FINDS FRIENDS AT THE CATTLE RANCHE, BUT HE FALLS UNDER THE SPELL, AND IS HELD IN THRALL AGAIN.

WHEN Jack of Warwick and Osmond, the young Lord Melbury, had finished exchanging confidences, and thoroughly knew what each had been doing since they parted in Kenilworth Park, Jack endeavoured to persuade his friend that he was distressing himself without reason.

Osmond, however, was not to be shaken in his belief.

He argued that he had run away from home after quarrelling with his father, who, in consequence of his conduct, had a fit, and died.

For Lord Melbury's death he held himself responsible.

"I must bear my punishment as well as I am able," exclaimed Osmond. "Some day the curse which I know and feel is on me may be removed; but, mark my words, not so long as Felton lives."

"He is an outlaw," remarked Warner, "and if anyone shot him no jury would convict the slayer."

"You don't know the man," said Osmond. "There is magic in his eye; he can wither you with a glance. One day I thought of escaping from my thraldom by stabbing him; he caught my eye, and my arm fell to my side as if paralysed."

"That is a nervous fancy," laughed Jack.

"Call it so if you like. I am under a spell when in his sight—indeed, when I can't see him I can feel that he is somewhere near."

"He would not frighten me in that way."

"If he were outside this belt of trees I should have to go to him, urged by irresistible attraction."

"You must be very weak."

"I only state a fact; how to account for it I do not know. Felton dominates me by his will," replied Osmond.

Jack reflected a moment.

"We shall not have time to go to the ranche for dinner, and must make up for it at tea-time," he said. "I will introduce you to Mr. Bunyard; he is a boy short, and will no doubt take you on. In the meantime we will try to catch this road-agent; he will have bad luck with me, for I shall not hesitate to shoot him as I would a coyote."

"Beware! he is a desperate man."

"Pshaw! we are three to one," cried Warner.

"Where is the cave in the sand-hills?" asked Jack.

"I can show you; but you will not let him make me his slave again?" said Osmond, piteously.

"Fear not; you shall enjoy your own and live as an English nobleman."

"That day, I am afraid, will never come," sighed Osmond.

"Don't give way."

"I cannot help it. You do not know that man. Yet I will go with you, for I should like to see him killed like a poisonous reptile; he is not fit to live."

Without further parley, the three started across the prairie for the gap in the hills, leaving their horses at the wells.

Jack could see that Osmond was thoroughly unnerved, also that Felton had established a singular influence over him.

It might be by some mesmeric power, or the magic of a strong will over an organisation too feeble to resist.

However caused, it existed, and that, too, in a remarkable degree.

It was a wonder to Osmond, when he came to reflect upon the matter, how he had been able to summon up sufficient courage to leave the cave.

At times he was sorry he had done so, because he was oppressed to the heart by a sickening, haunting dread that Felton would pounce upon him at any moment.

He started at the least sound.

A shadow made him shake like a leaf.

When the sand-hills were reached, and they approached the Devil's Gap, his tremulousness increased till he felt faint.

If it had not been for his companions' firm bravery he would not have gone another step.

Their example encouraged him somewhat.

He would have given half his fortune to be at Kenilworth Hall by his mother's side, though even there he would have dreaded Felton's coming.

"Look out!" he whispered. "There is the gap just as I described it to you, and on the other side is the entrance to the cave."

The plank was lying on the sand just as he had left it.

Jack took it up and threw it across the yawning chasm.

"Now for it, boys!" he cried. "I'll lead the van, Warner next, and as you are so terrified at this road-agent, Osmond, you may come last."

"I guess we'll kill the fox in his hole," observed Warner.

Advancing carefully, with a pistol in one hand and a knife in the other, Jack approached the cave and looked in.

There was nobody to be seen.

He stepped boldly inside and scrutinised every corner, but it was clear that the bird had flown.

Felton, no doubt, on awakening, had instantly discovered Osmond's flight, and argued that the boy would relate his adventures to the first person he met.

This would put people on the road-agent's track, rendering the cave insecure as a residence.

Consequently he had removed to safer quarters.

Yet there was every possibility that he was lurking about the neighbourhood.

"This fellow, Felton, is no slouch," exclaimed Warner. "He has slipped us, but we must be on our guard."

"There is a way of escape at the back," said Osmond. "It can be got at by climbing up the rock."

"Quite a snug, well-arranged hiding-cave," remarked Jack, looking round. "The Devil's Gap is just made to throw bodies down."

"Say," cried Warner, "what kind of a chap is this Felton to look at?"

Osmond described him as well as he was able.

"By gum!" continued the cowboy. "I'll bet it's the same rooster that shot our chum, Tanner."

"No doubt of it," replied Jack. "He came on to the ranche after stopping and robbing the stage. There is no doubt that he is a daring man."

"Would you like some of his wine?" asked Osmond. "We have plenty here, also something to eat—sardines, salmon, lobster, biscuits."

"You bet!" answered Warner. "Bring it on. I never refuse a good thing. Champagne and lobster is what I could enjoy till further orders. Set it up, and believe in the gratitude of yours truly."

Osmond knew where everything was kept, and speedily laid out an excellent repast.

There was some champagne left in the basket.

Giving Warner and Jack a horn each, Osmond popped the cork, and poured out the sparkling vintage.

"Ah," said Warner, drawing a deep breath of satisfaction, "that goes down good, as the nigger observed when he was making a dinner of crow-meat."

"It touches the spot," replied Jack.

Scarcely had the words escaped his lips when the entrance to the cavern was darkened.

A form appeared at a little distance from the threshold.

Over the face was a mask of black crape.

The eyes glared through the holes like live coals.

Warner and Jack were standing with their backs to the apparition, but Osmond was facing it.

He was holding out the champagne bottle in order to replenish the horns.

Directly he saw the black mask he began to tremble violently.

A startled cry escaped his lips, which went livid.

The cowboys turned round sharply to see what was the matter.

As they did so, the stranger fired his revolver into the cave.

The bullet narrowly missed Warner, striking the bottle in Osmond's hand, and shivering it to fragments.

In a moment the cowboys recovered from their surprise, and fired back.

They were too late.

With a mocking laugh the figure stepped briskly on one side and disappeared.

Uttering an oath, Warner dashed after him.

"I knew what would come," exclaimed Osmond, faintly.

He staggered, and would have fallen had not Jack placed his arm round him.

"Courage," replied our hero. "No bones are broken. Who was it?"

"Felton. I could swear to his mask."

Two more shots were heard outside.

Then Warner returned out of breath, his eyes glaring and his hand clenched.

"Confound him!" he cried; "he has got away."

"How?" asked Jack.

"I followed him to the top of the cave. He was well down at the bottom, running like a hare. I gave him two shots, but he dodged and doubled so I couldn't hit him. Was it our road-agent?"

"You have guessed correctly."

"Let us get out into the open plain," continued Warner. "We are in greater danger here than we should be there. Hang the food and the liquor. One's life is too dear a price to pay for it."

"Well said—march," answered Jack.

"I dreaded that he was lurking near," said Osmond.

"I think I have to thank him for aiming that shot at me. Well, I shall have the honour of squaring accounts with him some day," observed Warner.

"Did I exaggerate when I called him a terrible man?"

"Not in the least."

Jack supported Osmond out of the cave.

Snatching up two bottles of wine, Warner put them in his pocket.

"To drink on the prairie," he remarked.

They crossed the Gap, and made their way over the sand without being interfered with further.

On gaining the edge of the prairie they thought they could discern a horseman galloping in the distance.

Of this they could not be sure.

It was extremely probable, however, that it was the retreating form of the road-agent.

When half-way between the sand-hills and the well they halted to drink the wine Warner had appropriated.

He declared that the bottles were burning holes in his pockets.

"Would Felton know you and Warner?" enquired Osmond of his friend.

"If it is he who killed Tanner, as we suspect, most undoubtedly he would," rejoined Jack.

"Then I shall not be safe at your ranche; he will know where to look for me."

"Go back to England. Mr. Bunyard will lend you the money if you tell who you are, and I vouch for the truth of your story."

"Perhaps that will be best," said Osmond. "Fancy going through all I have, after being used to a good home and respectable surroundings! It would drive some fellows mad."

"Keep your end up," said Warner; "we'll see you through."

"Thank you. I know you are both my friends," answered Osmond.

Presently they made a move to the well.

Jack let Osmond mount behind him on his mustang.

The strayed cattle were driven back to the herd, who were all watered and left for the night.

It was about six o'clock on a warm, oppressive evening when they arrived at home, and put up their horses.

They had to pass Snell's saloon on their way to MacTavish's.

Hearing a noise, Warner suggested that they should go in.

They did so.

To their astonishment they saw a Red Indian standing in front of the bar, talking to Snell in a rather animated manner.

MacTavish was seated at a table, drinking his favourite Scotch whisky, and taking copious pinches of snuff.

The Indian wore beaded moccasins, and, from the collar of bears' claws round his neck, and the eagles' feathers in his hair, seemed to be a chief.

His face was covered with red paint, and his scalp-lock hung defiantly over his high forehead.

He had been drinking, for his voice was thick and heavy, and his gait somewhat unsteady.

"Give Indian drink," cried the redskin. "Me pay. See—dollar bill. Drink him all up."

"Do you want to turn yourself into a walking whisky-keg," asked Snell, "and then take that old tomahawk out of your wampum belt, and raise Cain in this village?"

"Me make no muss," rejoined the Indian. "Quiet 'nuff if give drink quick."

Snell had enjoyed experience of Indians before this, and knew that when intoxicated they became mad.

All the savage in their nature came to the surface.

No fear of consequences served to restrain their wild beast-like thirst for blood.

"Well," he exclaimed, "you won't have no more to drink here. If you want to imbibe still further, I'll sell you a dollar's worth of tanglefoot, but you must go out on the prairie and drink it."

"No, boss—drink here," was the stolid reply.

"Then I'm done with you—all except bouncing, if it comes to that."

"Me big Indian. No use to try to shake me—can't."

"I've got a club, and don't you forget it," said Snell, angrily. "Sit down and sober up, or take yourself off."

He took up his club, and brought it down with a bang on the counter.

It made the glasses ring.

"Or-right; me go to sleep," replied the Indian.

He retired to a chair, sat down, but did not close his eyes.

"Aweel," exclaimed MacTavish, "I am very glad the carle did not raise a rumpus."

"Was I not right to refuse to serve him?" asked Snell.

"Quite. When the whisky's in the wit's out with these sons of Belial. Ah, Warner! ah, Jack! who have you with you?"

His attention had been so taken up with the redskin that he had not hitherto noticed the cowboys.

"An old friend of mine, sir," replied Jack. "We met in the most extraordinary manner on the prairie."

"Aweel, that is verra strange."

"I have to ask you to take him under your protection, and after supper will tell you all about his wanderings."

"That is reasonable. He shall be welcome on your recommendation, for he could not have a better sponsor. You are a gude lad," said MacTavish.

The Scotchman nodded his head approvingly.

Pointing to the mull on the counter, he added—

"I'll thank you for the sneezin'."

It was a point of economy with the Scotchman never to use his own snuff when he could get that of the saloon-keeper for nothing.

Jack went over and got the snuff, but as he was conveying it to MacTavish he abstracted a quantity.

This he concealed in the hollow of his hand.

Giving the mull to the Scotchman, he stole up to the Indian, who had apparently gone off to sleep, with his head leaning on the back of the chair.

His eyes were closed, his legs were stretched out, and his arms hung listlessly by his side.

The only weapon of the redskin was the tomahawk, which was stuck in his belt.

With a dexterous movement, Jack gently removed the tomahawk.

Then he let the snuff fall on the Indian's chin.

Neither Snell nor MacTavish had observed this little bit of pantomime.

Warner had been watching him, though, and expressed his delight by a series of violent winks.

Coming to his side, Jack whispered—

"How is that?"

"First class. I took it all in, sonny," replied the cowboy.

"What will he do?"

"He'll sneeze his head off, I guess."

The Indian could not help inhaling the snuff, and began to shake his head and move his feet uneasily.

"Sneezin'," remarked MacTavish, as he filled his nose, "is a verra agreeable compound. I like it much, and—"

His words were brought to an abrupt conclusion.

The Indian suddenly threw up his arms wildly, and sprang to his feet.

His features became convulsed in the most hideous manner.

Lowering his head, he gave vent to one of the most powerful sneezes that ever proceeded from a human being.

"Hech, mon!" shouted MacTavish; "the poor callant is going clean daft."

He had no time to say any more.

Up went the redskin's arms, and down went his head in obedience to the irresistible law of nature which governs sneezing.

Again he delivered himself of a stupendous "at-chew-chew-chew!"

He stamped his feet on the floor, seized the back of the chair, and, with streaming eyes, gasped for breath.

MacTavish could not make it out at all.

His opinion was that the redskin had suddenly gone out of his mind.

Dreadfully alarmed, he retreated behind the stove, and taking up a chair, prepared to defend himself.

"Keep off!" yelled the Scotchman. "I'll not be murdered by a wild Indian!"

Snell perceived the joke when he saw the cowboys laughing.

"This is some of your doing!" he cried.

"The red's got a bad cold in his head," replied Jack. "It's kind of draughty on the prairie!"

"You bet," remarked Warner, "that he'll be so mad presently, he'll get on the war-path."

The Indian had to sneeze a third time.

It was impossible for him to help it.

This was the last time, however, and, wiping his eyes with the back of his hand, he looked up.

"Ugh!" he exclaimed, with a guttural grunt. "Something make bad medicine for Indian's nose—bad—very bad!"

"Ha, ha!" laughed Warner. "You'd do to hire out to a waxwork show."

The Indian strode over to the cowboy and seized him by the ear.

"Wugh!" he said. "What white boy laugh for?"

"Leave go of my ear!" cried Warner. "I want you to quit!"

"Pull ear hard—so."

"Quit, I tell you! Do you hear me? Oh, say, won't someone drive off this varmint?"

Snell came from behind his bar, and gave the redskin a blow on the head.

He reeled a few paces, then stopped and sought in his belt for his tomahawk.

It was gone, as Snell knew, having been taken by Jack.

"Somebody fool Indian," said the redskin, with a scowl. "Perhaps the fool-killer come around soon."

"Clear out of here!" exclaimed Snell. "I told you we did not want you. Can't you see your room's better than your company?"

"Me got bad head—heap bad. Go now. Come back; plenty Indian then."

"Is that a threat?"

"Scalp—burn."

"Who are you?" asked Snell.

The Indian drew himself up to his full height, which was over six feet.

He was powerfully built.

"Me Stormcloud, chief of the Comanches," he said, proudly. "Me have blood before one more moon."

Casting a deeply malignant look upon those assembled, he opened the door, and stalked away.

A dead silence reigned for a minute.

Snell looked blankly at MacTavish.

"I'm afraid this will turn out to be a bad business," remarked Snell. "If I'd known it was Stormcloud, I'm darned if I'd have given him that crack on the nut; it all comes, though, of the boys larking."

"How do you mean?" enquired MacTavish.

"They primed the Comanche with snuff. Lord! it was funny. I thought he'd have sneezed his head off his shoulders. Didn't he look scared!"

"It was altogether wrong for a savage and a heathen to be subjected to the civilising custom of snuff-taking," replied MacTavish. "The puir de'ils dinna ken snuff from sand. I'll thank ye for the mull."

"Where is it?"

"I have drappit the thing on the floor, I reckon."

It was found, and given to him.

Under its soothing influence he became less excited.

"A wee drap muir of the dew off Ben Nevis, as we ca' it in Scotland, if you please," he added.

"There'll be trouble with the Indian," remarked Snell, as he served him.

"I hope not" said Jack. "If so, it will be my fault, for I played the snuff trick on him; but before that you were not too civil to the chief."

"Let us hope that they will go away soon," exclaimed MacTavish. "They have come to perform some sort of a ceremony at their sacred tree, with their heathen rites. If they lift a steer or two it can't be helped."

It was getting on towards tea-time, and the cowboys repaired to MacTavish's house.

Tea in the West is always called supper, and Helen was busy getting it ready in the kitchen.

In a corner was a large trough made of wood, and full of dough, for she was going to bake in the morning.

The cowboys walked into the kitchen, wishing her good evening, as was their custom on their return from their daily work on the prairie.

Her quick eye at once detected the presence of a stranger.

"Sakes!" she said, "who have you got there? I did not know there was a new boy coming to the ranche."

"An old friend of mine," replied Jack; "lately from England. We met accidentally."

"Is he going to work for us?"

"No; he's had enough of this country already, and wants to go back, don't you, Osmond?" asked Jack.

"I wish I had never come," answered Osmond. "There is no place like home, though a fellow does not always think so. It takes experience to open one's eyes."

"Did you think you could pick up gold on the prairie?" Helen inquired, with a merry laugh.

"Something of that kind, I suppose," he rejoined, sheepishly. "I wish, though, I could see a few trees on these prairies of yours, Miss MacTavish."

"What do we want with them? We could not graze our cattle on trees. We require grass, and we've got it in plenty."

"There are trees all over England, and yet we raise stock."

While he was speaking, Dawes and White came in.

They stared insolently at Osmond, especially the former.

"What's that about England?" he demanded. "Have we got another Britisher here?"

"Yes," replied Jack of Warwick, taking up the cudgels on his friend's behalf.

"We're all surrounded."

"Don't you like it?"

"No; that's flat!" said Dawes. "You may just as well hear it first as last, my boy!"

Dawes was indulging the vulgar habit of chewing tobacco, which was a favourite pastime of his.

He did not care where he exuded his saliva, and he did so purposely on Osmond's boot.

This was unmistakably an intentional insult.

As such Ormond was justified in regarding it.

"What do you mean by that?" he asked, indignantly.

"Find out," was the laconic reply.

"I demand an instant apology."

"You won't get it."

Osmond felt the blood of the Melburys mounting to his head.

He clenched his hand, and walked up to the overgrown cowboy.

"You cad!" he said. "If you do not beg my pardon, I'll thrash you within an inch of your life."

"Spell 'able' first. Don't get excited and drop your 'h's,' as most Britishers do until they have been long enough in this country to learn their own language," sneered Dawes.

Osmond replied to his taunts by standing on his toes and looking him full in the face.

To this the cowboy retaliated by knocking him clean off his legs.

Helen screamed loudly.

"Ha, ha!" laughed Dawes, "I guess I can knock spots out of a Britisher when I once get on my mark."

His triumph was not of long duration.

Jack threw his arms round his burly

form, and giving him a Cornish hug, raised him off his legs.

His ribs threatened to crack under the pressure.

The next moment Jack gave his favourite throw over his shoulders, and Dawes went flying across the room.

He descended into the huge trough of dough.

In vain he tried to scramble out.

The more he struggled the farther he got in, and the harder he stuck.

Everyone present burst into a fit of boisterous laughter.

"Confound it!" said Dawes. "Won't somebody lend me a hand? I don't want to lie here, a regular laughing-stock."

"You have only yourself to thank for it," replied Helen. "Why don't you let people alone? You are nothing but a fire-brand."

"I can't abear Britishers, and your father is filling the shanty with them."

"We are as good as the Yankees, or better, I'd have you to know," replied Jack of Warwick.

"Help me out, and I won't say no more."

Nobody moved to assist him.

"Skip lively," continued Dawes. "Hurry up, or the dough will be my shroud. I'm half choking."

"If so," returned our hero, "we'll put you in the oven and bake you; it will be a novelty—baked cowboy, with the crust on. Who'll have some? Quite a delicacy for anybody with a cannibal instinct!"

"Don't chaff. Pull me out."

"Will you promise to behave yourself?"

"Yes, yes!"

Jack gave him his hand, Warner did the same, and White lifted him by his hair.

Between them their exertions sufficed to extricate him from his unpleasant predicament.

"Oh, dear!" sighed Helen, "there's all my bread spoiled—nearly half a barrel of flour gone to waste."

Dawes was literally coated with dough.

Loud and prolonged merriment greeted his appearance as he stood up.

"Perdition!" he cried, savagely. "I hate you all worse than ever, especially this man from Warwick."

"How about your promise of amendment?" asked Jack.

"That is all pretence—I didn't mean it. Wait and see what I'm made of. I ain't no man of straw."

Saying this, he stalked sullenly into the yard, followed by his chum White, who was always ready to condole with him.

Although the latter tried to scrape him with a spade, it was of no use.

He had to put on another suit of clothes, which he kept for Sundays and for outings.

"Did the ruffian hurt you much?" asked Helen, kindly, of Osmond.

"He's loosened my teeth and cut my mouth," replied the latter.

"Ah, he's a hard case; we have a deal of trouble with him," said Helen. "Go into the parlour; I'll bring the supper in. Mr. Bunyard's out with his gun after prairie-hens and wild turkeys. I don't expect him in till dark."

Jack and Warner went into the parlour and sat down, but Osmond stood in the porch to get rid of the blood which had collected in his mouth after the blow he had received from Dawes's powerful fist.

In front of him was a narrow strip of flower-garden, divided by a path, at the end of which was the road, lined on each side with black walnut, chestnut, and other trees of young growth.

Suddenly he heard a slight cough.

Looking up, he saw, standing only a few yards from him, a face and figure he knew too well.

It was the dreaded road-agent.

Felton had dared to venture alone into the heart of Mowbray's Ranche.

A terrible fear took possession of Osmond.

He trembled violently, and though he strove to cry out, his tongue clove to the roof of his mouth.

The fierce, glaring eyes of Felton fascinated him.

Seeing that he had established an influence over him, the villain beckoned to Osmond with his hand.

Slowly he walked backwards towards the road.

Osmond felt himself constrained to follow him, and did so, with bowed head and tottering limbs.

If he could only have uttered one

word his friends would have rushed to his assistance immediately.

But it was not to be.

He was utterly incapable of speech at that time, and Jack and Warner, being tired, had not remarked his absence.

Under the trees stood the road-agent's horse.

To this spot Osmond was irresistibly attracted by the peculiar power exercised over him.

Grasping him by the waist, Felton slung him on to the horse's back, and sprang up after, holding him tight.

"Away—away!" he cried, patting the animal's neck.

Instantly the horse bounded down the street.

A minute sufficed to bring him on the prairie, over which he flew with the wings of the wind.

Osmond's absence did not long remain unnoticed by his late companions, who were far from guessing what had happened.

The clatter of the horse's hoofs fell upon their ears as it cleared the street.

"Someone's about," cried Warner. "The boys are all in. It must be a stranger in town."

"Where is Osmond?" asked Jack.

"I don't know."

They rose in alarm.

He was not to be seen in the front, nor was he in the back.

Going into the road they looked around them.

The prints of the horse's hoofs were distinctly visible in the soft sandy dirt.

MacTavish came out of Snell's, and walked towards them.

In vain they questioned him.

He had seen no one.

All at once Jack's quick eyes caught sight of a sheet of note-paper, which had been stuck on the broken branch of one of the trees.

He ran to it, and read the following, hastily scribbled in pencil by a bold hand—

"I have taken away the boy who was

with me in the cave. Let those who interfere between him and me again beware! I am not to be trifled with, as anyone will tell you who knows

"FELTON, THE ROAD-AGENT."

"Come here, quick!" exclaimed Jack. "Read this. The mystery is explained—we have been outwitted."

MacTavish and Warner hastened to his side.

"Hech!" said the Scotchman, when he had read it. "What with reevers and what with redskins, we are likely to have a good time of it, I'll go bail!"

"Poor fellow!" observed Warner; "he knew it was coming."

"Who was the little carle, anyway?" asked MacTavish.

"My foster-brother," replied Jack. "He ran away from home before I left Warwickshire, owing to a disagreement with his father."

"What is his name?"

"His father died the very day he left, and he is Lord Melbury, of Kenilworth Park."

"Hoot, toot, mon!"

"There is a reward offered by his mother of a thousand pounds for information of his whereabouts."

MacTavish held up his hands, while his face assumed a dolorous expression comical to witness.

"The Lord help us!" he groaned, "and we ha'e lost the siller."

"I meant to have told you before," said Jack.

"It would ha'e been gude if you had. I'd ha'e locked him up in the coal-bunk till we could ha'e communicated wi' his puir mither. And now to think he's gone! Well, boys, it canna be helpit—let's take our supper."

With which philosophical reflection he led the way into the house.

Sorrowfully the cowboys followed him.

Jack was nearly heartbroken at losing his old friend.

The future was dark and uncertain. What would become of Osmond?

"'GREAT SCOTT!' CRIED THE MAN, 'AIN'T YOU A GHOST?'"

CHAPTER VIII.

THE SACRED TREE.

THE moon, now at its full, was riding high in the heavens when Felton drew rein, after a furious ride of many miles.

His horse was breathing heavily; its head drooped, and its flanks were flecked with patches of white foam.

The double burden had fatigued it greatly.

Osmond, overcome with excitement, had fainted in his captor's arms.

Though he had plenty of spirit ordinarily, he was not strongly built, and recent events had unnerved him greatly.

When his steed came to a standstill, Felton looked around him.

He uttered a cry of joy at what he saw.

On his right were some trees which encircled a ruined wooden house, that was fast falling into decay.

In the garden corn was growing wild and rank, and weeds flourished everywhere, especially in the vicinity of a well.

Standing alone, some yards from the house, was a very aged tree, which had not a leaf on its withered branches.

It had been struck by lightning.

Felton alighted, and deposited the senseless body of Osmond on the grass-covered ground.

Then he removed the saddle and bridle from his horse, and led him to the well.

The windlass and bucket were still there, in a fair state of preservation, and drawing some water, he found it fresh and good.

Giving the horse as much as he thought it prudent to allow him to drink in his heated condition, he patted his neck, and told him to wander whither he pleased.

Master and horse thoroughly understood one another.

The latter neighed affectionately, and trotted off.

Felton was unconcerned, for he knew that a few notes on his whistle would recall him at any time.

From the holsters he took some whisky, tobacco, cheese, and biscuits, which he placed on the ground, as well as a cup to drink out of.

The saddle and bridle he carried to the old house.

The door had fallen from the hinges, and the moonlight streamed through holes in the roof.

It was utterly destitute of furniture, save a couple of three-legged stools and an aged rickety table.

There was but one storey to it, which was divided into a common or living-room and two bedrooms.

The floor was nothing but earth, with stones trampled or knocked into it, and grass was growing through the interstices.

Felton was a close examiner, and liked to pry into everything.

The chimney was intact, and, to his surprise, he saw on the hearth the ashes of wood, which had been recently burnt.

There were some rib-bones, too, lying about, which looked like those of an antelope.

He went into the bedrooms; one had been empty of furniture and undisturbed for a number of years.

Cobwebs hung everywhere, thick and black, and an owl flew with a startling "whirr" out of the broken casement.

The other room showed signs of having been recently tenanted, for there was a comfortable bed of dry grass in a corner.

The broken window had been plugged up with the same material, as had the leaky roof.

"Humph!" muttered Felton, "this is a nest; but where's the bird?"

Having gratified his curiosity, he returned to the tree, the circumference of whose trunk was considerable.

He noticed that about four feet up, there was a large hole, big enough to admit of the passage of a man's body.

Going closer, he looked in.

The trunk was hollow to the ground, and capable of holding half-a-dozen men.

"Now for a little supper, and to wake the boy," said Felton.

Osmond was moving uneasily.

"Mother—mother!" he moaned.

"Oh, heaven, take this curse away from me!"

Felton looked at him contemptuously.

"The fool," he muttered; "he's calling to his mother. I'm the curse, I guess. That's not very complimentary. Wonder who and what he is? I heard the English cowboy call him Osmond—that ain't no common name; it ain't got rooted in these United States."

He went to the well and mixed himself a strong horn of whisky-and-water, after which he prepared another for the boy.

"Here, Osmond," he said, coming back.

"Who calls?" asked Osmond, faintly.

"Your old boss—I've toted you off from the ranche."

A repulsive shudder ran through the boy's frame.

"Oh, yes," he replied; "I recollect now. Where are we?"

"Darned if I know—somewhere on the plains. I've got the dollars, and I'm going to work my way up to Little Rock in Arkansaw, and indulge in some gambling at faro. You bet, I'm a dandy faro-player."

"Are you?"

"My word, yes; I can bet on the ace and copper the Jack as well as any man in the United States."

This was unintelligible to Osmond, who had never heard of a faro-table.

"And I'm just boss at keeno," added Felton. "But drink this; you're kinder low."

Osmond did as he was bidden, and the fiery spirit put new life into his stagnant blood.

He got up and felt like a man again. Some biscuits and cheese appeased his hunger.

"We are together again," remarked Felton, in his kindest manner, which did not amount to much, as he was always hard and cold. "Aren't you pleased to think of it?"

"No," answered Osmond, honestly.

"By Jove!" laughed the road-agent, "I like that. You've got a little hatchet about you somewhere, haven't you?"

"Indeed I have not. Why do you ask?"

"Oh, I thought you were like young George Washington, and could not tell a lie. But see here, we shall camp out to-night. I ain't got no blankets. There's an old shanty hard by, in ruins 'most. I saw a grass bed there. We'll sleep together, and if you try to slip me again, by the heaven above us, I'll kill you—mind that! When I sleep it's like a darned little weasel, with one eye open."

"Not always."

"Wal, I'll allow you bested me in the cave in the sand-hills, but I was dog-tired, and full as a goat of wine and whisky."

"Get me a little more of the same stuff; I'm faint still," said Osmond.

The road-agent stared at him.

"Say!" he exclaimed, "when did your nigger die?"

"Excuse me, but I have always had servants to wait on me, and just now I'm not strong."

"You blow your own horn. Who are you?"

"That's my secret, and I am not going to disclose it to anyone; least of all to you."

"All right!" exclaimed Felton, eyeing him closely. "Be a boy of mystery if you want to. You might, though, oblige me by getting into that old tree and seeing what is inside."

"A nest of snakes, perhaps?"

"No, siree. They wouldn't nest there like a lot of clams on Coney Island. I looked in, and thought I saw something shining. Come, git, or I'll have to welt you with a hickory-stick."

Osmond did not dare to disobey him; he had no more will of his own when with this man than a little child.

He walked up to the tree, and Felton gave him a lift up.

He threw his leg over and dropped into the hollow.

It was just possible for him to touch the bottom of the opening with his hands.

"Is there anything at the bottom?" cried Felton.

"Lumps of gold, glass beads of different colours, and a lot of claws of some animal," was the reply.

"Bear's, perhaps. I'll tell you what it is—we've struck the sacred tree of the Indians. In the old days, before the Government sent the reds on the reservation, it was thought a sight of by the critters."

Osmond hauled himself up, and alighted on the ground with some beads and claws in his hand.

These he handed to Felton, who examined them carefully.

"Yes," he remarked, "these are Indian offerings to the sacred tree, which they call Galichoo. They think a spirit dwells within it, which watches over the destinies of their nation."

"That is a curious belief."

"It's good enough for them. What are they but Pagans?"

"Are there many of them?" asked Osmond.

"Not now. Once the Comanches were a very powerful nation. They made their power felt, not only in Texas and Arkansaw, but lorded it in Arizona, so, you see, they were known both sides of the Rocky Mountains; but the whites have wiped out considerable of them. Their born foes, the Apaches, have accounted for thousands, while bad whisky, and smallpox, hard winters, short rations, and grasping agents have done the rest. No, there are not many Comanches left, boy."

The picture he drew of this formerly magnificent Indian people was strictly true.

Incapable of being civilised, like the Cherokees, they were each year becoming smaller in number.

The presence of the paleface in their midst did not agree with them.

"What do you say to having some sleep?" enquired Felton. "I reckon you are not made of cast-iron material any more than I am."

"I wish I could go to sleep and never wake again," answered Osmond, in a gloomy manner.

"You won't think that way when we get to Little Rock, put up at a fashionable hotel, with board at four dollars a day, eat and drink of the best, take drives, and go to the theaytre. I sha'n't ask you to join in any more robberies for months. We'll live fast while our money holds out; and I may win gambling—as I usually do. Fact is, I like you, and shall call you my son. It will give me an air of respectability, make me high-toned, for you're gentlemanly; besides, you will be a companion. Tumble?"

"I suppose I must do as you wish, because I can't help myself."

"That's the sensible way to look at it."

"If you would send me back to England, I would give you a thousand pounds."

"You!"

Felton looked at him in a searching manner as if he would read his heart.

"You—you," he repeated, "give me what is equivalent to five thousand dollars in our money?"

"Yes; double that."

"Where will you get it from?"

"I—I," stammered Osmond, seeing he had made a mistake—"I can't tell you."

"Are you lying to me?"

"No, indeed. I have a great deal of money in England."

"I guess you're a crank, and trying to play it low down on me, sonny. Come on to bed. The dry grass will hold the pair of us.

"Plague take me," he added, in an undertone, "if I can understand why he left his country, if he had the shekels he talks so big about. Oh, pshaw! it's a ghost story."

He was about to lead the way into the ruined house, where he intended to pass the night, when he paused abruptly.

A startling sight presented itself to him.

The moon made everything nearly as bright as day.

The print of a newspaper could have been easily deciphered by its luminous aid.

Coming across the prairie he beheld a band of mounted Indians.

They were riding at full speed.

As well as he could hastily compute, their number was about a score.

"The Comanches!" cried Felton. "Perdition! what do they want to come here for, this night in particular?"

"What is it?" asked Osmond, excitedly.

"The redskins. That's the what is it."

They were in the shadow cast by the broad proportions of the sacred tree.

If they ran across the space intervening between the tree and the house, they would infallibly be seen.

To be seen, in all probability, would mean torture or death, perhaps both.

"There's no end to my trouble," said Osmond; "but I think I would rather trust to an Indian than to you."

Felton grew furious with rage.

"Ungrateful cub!" he cried, seizing him by the leg. "In you go mighty quick!"

He lifted him, and dropped him into the hollow tree.

"Not a word," he hissed, "or I'll stab you to the heart! I'm coming. You'll have to lie low. D'ye hear?"

"Yes," replied Osmond.

The next moment Felton was beside him.

There was ample accommodation for both of them in the trunk.

The moonlight, streaming into the hole through which they had entered, enabled them to see one another.

It was a bold move on the part of the road-agent, but was the only course he could have taken under the circumstances to avoid being captured.

Still he was far from being at ease.

He concluded that the Comanches were about to visit the sacred tree to perform some heathenish rite.

He might be discovered, and then—

It was not at all pleasant to speculate what might happen afterwards.

To put his head out of the tree would be dangerous, because he would attract attention.

Yet, he wanted to see, as well as hear, what would be going on, and, drawing his knife, he began to bore a hole about three feet up.

Kneeling, he could easily see through this.

The wood and bark being rotten, he did not find it a difficult task, and by the time the Indians came to the spot, he had accomplished his purpose.

A round hole through which he could put three fingers enabled him to see well on one side.

To his satisfaction the Indians halted on that side.

He was not mistaken in supposing that the tree was the sacred Galichoo, and that they were coming to it; nor had he erred in guessing they were Comanches.

No better riders were to be found on the plains, and their splendid physique showed that they belonged to a once commanding race.

They dismounted, unsaddled and unbridled their horses, and each put a long rope, like a halter, round the neck of his animal, and staked the other end in the ground.

Two Indians went to the well to draw water for their beasts, and themselves, and companions.

Felton counted the Indians, and estimated their number at twenty-five.

This was a formidable force to encounter.

The Comanches did not appear to have come from a long distance, for the horses showed no signs of fatigue.

Possibly they had been camping on the prairie.

"Take a look at the varmints!" whispered Felton; "and be careful. If they spot us, they'll raise our hair, sure!"

Osmond applied his eye to the extemporised peephole.

One Indian was walking about giving orders; he was evidently the chief. Three others were standing together, each having an air of authority.

"I say," exclaimed Osmond, "I saw the big Indian at Mowbray's Ranche in the afternoon. He made a row in the saloon, and vowed to be revenged when he was kicked out. His name, he said, was Stormcloud, chief of the Comanches."

"Is that so?" replied Felton.

"I cannot be mistaken in my man."

"Not likely. When he left the ranche, he had his horse close handy, you bet. A Comanche never walks. Oh, my! won't there be a how-de-do if they find us in this blessed tree!" whispered Felton.

"If we keep quiet there cannot be any danger."

"I opinion not, unless the medicine-man pokes his 'tarnal head in the tree-hole."

"Would you shoot?"

"No; I'd try another and a better game than that."

"What?" asked Osmond.

"Wait and see. I'm all there, and if I don't best these scalp-merchants, call me a fool," replied Felton.

He smiled grimly.

Osmond became silent, and waited the

course of events with an external calmness which belied what he felt in his mind.

There was danger ahead.

He knew this as well as Felton, but he did not betray any anxiety, for he did not think the Indians would dare to kill him.

If they made him a prisoner, it would be no worse than being dragged to a prison by Felton, as he knew he would be in the end.

He preferred a life with the Comanches to being the helpless tool of the road-agent.

Scarcely venturing to breathe, they waited.

Felton never took his eye from the peephole.

He could see all that was going on.

The subsequent proceedings interested him greatly.

What they were will be seen very shortly.

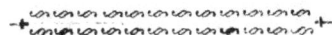

CHAPTER IX.

THE INDIAN RITES, AND WHAT FOLLOWED THEM.

FOUR of the Indians gathered in front of the trees, while the remainder, wrapped in their blankets, squatted on the ground.

The four were Stormcloud, Running Deer, and Death's Head, great chiefs of the Comanche nation, and Matchi, the medicine - man, or sorcerer of the tribe.

After a brief conversation among themselves, Stormcloud faced the Indians, and raised his hand.

Immediately every eye was fixed upon him.

"Braves of the Comanches," he exclaimed, "we have journeyed many miles to visit Gaichoo, the aged tree, which, generations ago, was sacred in the eyes of our ancestors. The white men have taken our land from us, and we are starved in a country we are compelled to dwell in. It is our purpose to-night to ask the spirit that hovers about Galichoo if we shall have any success in fighting against the palefaces, in order to regain our land. Matchi will summon the spirit. We will be guided by what he tells us. Is it well?"

A unanimous chorus of approval followed thee words.

There was not a dissentient voice amongst the Indians.

Matchi was an elderly man, whose hair was grey; he had a keen though hollow eye, his cheeks were sunken, but the expression of his face denoted deep thought and sense.

He knew well enough that to undertake a war against the white men was madness.

It could only result in defeat; but he was compelled to sanction the journey to the sacred tree, on account of the impetuosity of the young braves.

Their agent on the reservation, to basely enrich himself, had, during the past winter, robbed them of their food and blankets.

The United States Government allowed them an ample supply.

Yet, they did not get what they were entitled to in exchange for the land and hunting rights taken from them.

The winter had been unusually cold and severe.

Their sufferings had been acute and manifold.

Many of the weaker squaws and papooses had perished during the inclement weather.

The Indians' hearts were sad and heavy. They burned for revenge and freedom.

Matchi knew well that no spirit dwelt in the tree, but he would have been no medicine-man if he had not pretended that he held intercourse with an unseen world.

The Comanches had a blind, superstitious faith in his power.

It was his intention to dissuade them from their warlike purpose, and induce them to return to their reservation.

A few raids on isolated ranches, and some cattle-stealing, he had no objection to, but he did not mean to advise them to go on the war-path.

"The pride of the Comanches is lowered," continued Stormcloud ; "their glory has departed from them. White men swarm on their land like bees in spring. The buffalo has been driven away. Game is scarce. The palefaces treat the red men like dirt under their feet. The spirit of Galichoo will tell us if we are to endure our slavery any longer. I have spoken !"

He sat down, and Running Deer took up the parable, speaking very much in the same strain.

The party visiting the tree, he said, were a picked lot of braves, but five hundred men of the tribe remained behind, on the reservation, ready to sally forth at a word.

If the hatchet were dug up, they would carry death and desolation into Texas.

Once more the Indian would roam free and unmolested on the prairie, or perish, tomahawk in hand.

This tall talk was also much applauded, for it was pitched in a way calculated to please his audience.

Death's Head, whose name must have been given him on account of his extreme ugliness and cadaverous appearance, also spoke to the point.

The three chiefs sat in a line together, in front of their followers.

Matchi slowly advanced to the sacred tree.

He halted within a few yards of it, and, producing a powder from a bag he carried in his hand, placed it on a flat stone.

Rubbing two dry sticks briskly together, he kindled some sparks, which lighted the powder.

A dense smoke arose.

Dancing up and down, enveloped in the fumes, which had a strong smell like that of incense, he muttered an incantation in a singing tone.

Every moment his contortions became more grotesque and violent, while his voice grew louder.

The Indians watched him with rapt attention.

As the smoke died away, he lowered his voice, and when the vapour disappeared, he ceased.

He then cast himself on the ground,

face downward, and remained perfectly motionless, like one in a trance.

Felton had watched this eccentric performance with a sensation the reverse of agreeable.

What was to come next?

He was not kept more than five minutes in suspense.

Matchi rose, and, bowing to the north, west, south, and east, walked to the sacred tree.

The medicine-man again had recourse to his bag.

This time he took out three lumps of virgin gold, which he poised in his hand, and threw one after the other into the hole.

This was an offering, intended to propitiate the spirit.

Not that the cunning rascal intended to part with his gold.

When the ceremony was over and the Indians were asleep, he meant to get it back.

"What generosity !" exclaimed Stormcloud.

"It is worthy of a great nation like the historical Comanches," Running Deer said.

"Galichoo will like that," remarked Death's Head.

Matchi waved his hand.

"Silence !" he cried. "I have not done yet."

A third time he put his hand into his bag.

It was not powder or gold that he brought out, but something totally different.

His movements were curiously watched by the Indians.

Facing them and turning his back on the sacred tree, he held up a live prairie hen, the neck of which he twisted.

Tearing open its breast with his fingers, he plucked out the quivering heart.

This he held aloft for a moment.

Then, after muttering some wild incantations over it, he faced the tree and dropped the heart into it.

"O Great Spirit," he said, in a chanting voice—"O Galichoo, the protector of the Comanches, is it well for us to dig up the buried hatchet and go on the war-path against the paleface, or shall we smoke the calumet of peace and remain in our lodges?"

There was a pause.

He placed his hand to his ear, and, bending forward, listened.

A reply was what he was supposed to be waiting for.

This, of course, he would pretend was only audible to himself.

He intended it should be in the negative.

The nerves of the Comanches were strained to their utmost capacity of tension.

It required all their stolid immobility to keep them quiet.

This moonlit scene was weird in the extreme.

"Hush!" he continued; "the spirit of Galichoo speaks!"

It did speak, sure enough, but in a very different way from that which he had expected.

Felton was becoming terribly alarmed for his safety.

He was also somewhat enraged.

The three lumps of gold cast into the tree by Matchi, had hit him on the head.

Nor was this all.

The heart of the bird, reeking with blood, had fallen on his face, causing him a feeling of nausea.

"I'll give them a taste of Galichoo," he muttered.

Sinking his voice to his chest, he spoke loudly in a deep bass tone, which came from the tree with a hollow, cavernous sound.

"Comanches!" he exclaimed, "I am the spirit; listen to the words of Galichoo: It is not well for you to fight the white men. They are as the sands of the seashore. Go to your reservation, or dire vengeance will overtake you. Go —leave— fly at once! I have spoken."

The effect of this speech upon the Indians was almost indescribable.

They trembled violently, and rose to their feet.

"Away—away!" shouted Stormcloud; "the spirit has spoken."

A rush was made towards the spot where the horses were coralled.

Matchi was sorely puzzled.

Yet he was not at all frightened.

"Something wrong in this," he said, shaking his head. "The spirit never spoke before, though I said it did speak."

The old rogue had played for years on the superstitious fears of his tribe.

He was not going to allow anyone to play on him, however.

In this he displayed more courage than anyone would have given him credit for.

Stepping close to the tree, he put his head into the hollow.

He could see nothing, however.

"Who's in there?" he asked.

Felton was equal to the occasion.

He got hold of the medicine-man by his long, prominent ears, and tugged at them.

The effect was surprising, but not altogether unexpected.

Matchi was dragged into the tree head first.

Meanwhile the Indians were off in a desperate hurry.

They did not stay to look for Matchi.

Getting on their horses, they galloped over the prairie at top speed, as if the Father of Evil were at their heels.

Osmond was sitting on the ground.

Felton was kneeling, and as Matchi was dragged into the hollow tree, the road-agent fumbled in his pocket.

The next moment something warm spurted over Osmond's face, and the Indian rolled in a heap upon him.

"Ugh!" uttered Matchi faintly, "I am dying!"

Felton's arm moved again, and the redskin was silent—for ever!

He had been stabbed at close quarters, and the second thrust of the knife had entered his heart.

Struggling to his feet, Osmond looked wildly at the road-agent; he was filled with horror, for he knew that a dreadful deed had been committed.

The pale moonlight played upon Felton's face.

A smile curled his lips, and he appeared to be well satisfied.

"What have you done?" Osmond asked.

"Let the daylight into that son of a gun who pretended to talk to the spirit. Aha! he got taken in. The kinder spirit he wanted doesn't use a sharp bowie-knife."

"Have you killed him?"

"You bet. What d'ye take me for— a sardine?"

"He did not bargain for that, poor fellow!"

"Bah!" cried Felton, "don't give

me any of that sentimental humbug! Who's going to shed tears over a red-skin?"

"He is a man and a brother," Osmond answered, who had peculiar ideas about the noble savage.

"Is he?" sneered Felton. "Try him. There is an amazing amount of brother-hood about a redskin. The odds are, we should have been tomahawked by this time if I had not used my wits."

"Are we to stop here all night?"

"By no means. The reds are so badly scared that they have vamoosed the ranche. The medicine chap is settled. The Comanches won't come here again yet awhile, and we will luxuriate in the shanty over the way."

Felton was about to rise from his knees, when he heard a voice singing close by—

"'Way down on the Sawance river, far, far away."

"Hist!" he whispered; "I must look out. That's United States; there's no Comanche about that."

He got up, and slipped on his black crape mask.

Peeping out of the hollow trunk, he was very ghost-like and awe-inspiring as the moonlight played upon him.

With astonishment he saw an elderly man standing between him and the ruined house.

He had grey hair, and beard of the same hue, and was dressed like a miner.

Stooping, the man turned over a large stone, disclosing a hole, from which he took a bottle, which he raised to his lips.

Some kind of liquor could be heard gurgling down his throat.

"Here's to those in our arms we love in our hearts," he said, clasping the bottle.

He took another strong draught.

"Good old whisky!" he added. "Drink her down, down, down!"

He replaced the bottle in the hole, and, looking at the sacred tree for the first time, noticed Felton.

The face of the road-agent, concealed by the hideous mask, startled him.

It was like a picture framed in the tree-bark.

"Snakes alive!" cried the man. "Wh —what's that?"

Felton wagged his head to and fro, rolling his eyes as he did so.

"Oh, Lord! it moves—it's alive!"

"Ha, ha, ha!" laughed Felton, in an unearthly manner.

The old man sank to his knees, keep-ing his eyes fixed on the black mask, as if fascinated by it.

"I don't mind humans, but I bar ghosts," he said, his teeth chattering. "Oh, dear, this is a solemn warning!"

Seeing that he was a harmless creature, easily frightened, and alone, Felton told Osmond to follow him, and emerged from his place of concealment.

He was glad to do so, as his limbs were getting cramped by confinement.

"Well, neighbour!" he exclaimed, "what's the matter with you?"

He removed his mask as he spoke.

"Great Scott!" replied the man, "ain't you a ghost?"

"No more than you are. I've been hiding, with my young friend, from the reds."

"They been here?"

"Yes; a score or more of mounted Comanches, but I gave them a kind of fright. You see, this is their sacred tree."

"I've heard something about that. Are you on the tramp?"

Felton nodded.

"So am I. I sleep in the old house sometimes. I'm Old Dave Crasker, the placer-miner; for years I've been seekin' my fortin', and I ain't found it yet."

"Don't you ever strike it rich?"

"Sometimes I pick up a few goodish lumps of gold, and then I hev ter git to a city and make the rocks fly. Oh, I'm a bully spender, you bet; it's always a feast or a famine with me."

"Same here, Dave; they call me Wild Bill. I guess you are going to sleep in the shanty? Have you any objection to us as bedfellows?"

"Not I. Do you know where you are?"

"Not the least bit in the world?"

"It's haunted ground, and that's what give me such a bad scare when you began masqueradin' in the holler tree."

"What d'ye mean?"

"It's called Hanging Man's Holding, and 'tis said the ghost walks reg'ler, though I've never seen it."

"Give us a drop of your rye, and tell us your story," exclaimed Felton.

Dave laughed, explaining that he kept

certain stores in a *cache,* for fear some-one might find them, and very gene-rously gave the bottle to his new acquaintance.

"You see," exclaimed Dave, "as I've heard tell by some of the cowboys, this claim belonged to a chap who had bad luck. First his wife and child died, then his cattle took the disease and died, too; so one day he went into his wood-shed and hanged himself."

"He wasn't much good after that," grinned Felton.

"No, unless it is to scare folks. Three or four parties have tried to settle here, but they've been haunted right clean out of it."

"You don't mean that?"

"Fact, stranger. The skeleton is lying in the shed now, with the rotting rope round the neck. Step around, and I'll show it yer."

Felton nodded, and Dave conducted him and Osmond to the back of the old house.

The door of the shed was open.

Moonlight streamed in, and revealed the ghastly spectacle of a man's skeleton lying full length and perfect on the floor.

"Bah!" exclaimed Felton; "I don't like the look of it. Shut it up. I'm not a carrion-crow."

He sometimes had a strong opinion that his indignant fellow-citizens would some day or other hang him.

He naturally enough shuddered at the idea.

Old Dave closed the door, and they sought the interior of the house.

"I've had a queer feeling lately," said the placer-miner, "that I sha'n't be long before I am lying alongside them there mouldering bones."

"Anything wrong with your internal organisation?" asked Felton.

"I'm as sound as a roach."

"You shouldn't think of such a thing, then."

"I can't help worriting. Some voice says to me of a night, 'Dave, you old sinner, you're doomed'; and I've come to believe that I've got to pass in my checks."

"Bah! You're a fool."

Saying this, Felton threw himself on the grass-bed, his example being fol-lowed by Osmond and Dave.

They were soon fast asleep. Felton snored, and started at intervals; Dave talked to himself; and even Osmond kicked, and threw his arms about.

The minds of all three were over-strained.

In an hour the moon declined, dark clouds swept up before the rising wind, and darkness reigned on the earth.

Old Dave, as will be seen presently, had cause for apprehension.

He was really nearer his end than he or anyone else expected.

CHAPTER X.

THE RETURN OF THE INDIANS.

WHEN day broke, Felton awoke and got up, having more than one reason for doing so.

When engaged in what he was pleased, by a perversion of terms, to call business, his brain was far too active to let him indulge in sloth.

He had a raging thirst, which impelled him towards the well, and he meant to water his horse.

Long before the sun was high in the heavens he intended to be on the way.

He hoped by good treatment to win Osmond's confidence.

Until he got his secret out of him he could not rest.

Osmond had inflamed his curiosity by stating that he had an unlimited com-mand of money.

Thinking over the pleasures that awaited him when he reached the city of Little Rock, Felton arrived at the well.

He swung down the bucket, took a deep draught of the cold water, and was about to whistle for his horse.

But he checked himself.

He had good reason to do so.

He saw a sight which was well calculated to startle him.

The Indians were returning to Hanging Man's Holding.

In a compact body, with Stormcloud at their head, the Comanches were swiftly riding over the prairie.

Only a quarter of a mile separated them from the ruined house.

They had evidently recovered from their alarm, and having missed Matchi, had come back to look for him.

Their religious belief included good and evil spirits.

Perhaps they feared that he had fallen a prey to one of the latter, as Galichoo was displeased with them.

It was not until they had got a considerable distance that they missed the medicine-man.

Death's Head had then remarked that his horse was galloping with them, riderless.

He communicated this fear to the chief.

Stormcloud called a halt.

A brief palaver was held, and it was decided to return to the sacred tree and investigate.

Felton was, for a moment, at a loss how to act.

He did not wish to abandon Osmond to the rage of the Comanches, which would be intense when they discovered the dead body of Matchi.

If he could have given the alarm to Dave and Osmond, he would gladly have done so.

This, however, would have been ruinous to himself.

While he was running to the house to rouse them, he would stand the chance of being surrounded and captured.

If he whistled or shouted, the same thing would result.

There was not a moment to be lost.

He had a large sum of money in his pockets and belt, the result of the robberies of the stage and the train.

With this he had proposed to enjoy himself for a year at least, and he was not to be thwarted by wandering Indians.

He ran to his horse.

" Dick ! Dick !" he cried.

The horse neighed, and cantered to meet him.

In a moment Felton sprang on to his back.

" Away !" cried the road-agent; " my life depends on you."

The horse seemed to understand his master ; for, throwing back his ears, he started at railroad speed.

His feet seemed to scarcely touch the ground.

The Comanches saw the horse and rider in a moment.

Loud cries arose, rifles were raised, and shots fired, but Felton's luck adhered to him.

He escaped untouched.

The Comanches reined in their horses at the word of command from Stormcloud.

They dismounted and grouped themselves together, some talking, some watching the rapidly-vanishing form of Felton, others looking for trails on the grass.

The chief did not think it worth while to pursue Felton.

Stormcloud walked to the sacred tree, and ventured to look in.

The chief started, and uttered an exclamation of surprise.

In a moment, Running Deer and Death's Head were at his side.

" What have you seen ?" Running Deer asked ; " your face is full of grief."

" Look !" replied the chief. " I can see the form of Matchi ; he moves not."

" The spirit of Galichoo has killed him with his lightning power," said Death's Head.

" Not so ; white men have been here."

With these words, Stormcloud put his long arms into the hollow, and taking a firm hold of the body, dragged it out.

Two gaping wounds showed that Matchi had met his death through the instrumentality of a knife.

The dead body was stretched out on the grass, and the Indians, murmuring loudly, crowded round.

" Brothers," said Stormcloud, bowing his head, " this is not the work of Galichoo; we have been fooled by the palefaces. Matchi is dead ! One paleface has escaped. We saw him flying on the wings of the wind, but there may be more of our enemies lurking here. If so—if we find them—what punishment do they deserve ?"

" Death !" was the unanimous reply.

" Yes; we will deal with them as they have dealt with Matchi."

"Torture! the stake! death!" cried the Comanches.

They had had time to reflect, and they were clever enough to see that a trick had been played upon them.

This they did not relish.

Their savage hearts burned for revenge.

At a sign from Stormcloud, Death's Head began to run about like a dog looking for signs.

He soon struck a trail.

"Ugh!" he ejaculated. "Come."

The chief followed him; the other Indians grasped their rifles and waited for orders.

Stormcloud and Death's Head entered the old house.

The trail to the bedroom was easy to find.

Through the open door, which, like all the rest, hung on a rusty hinge, they beheld old Dave and Osmond asleep.

In his eagerness to get at the sleepers, Stormcloud knocked against the door.

It fell with a loud crash.

This awakened the two sleepers, who sprang to their feet.

"Indians!" cried Dave, drawing a pistol from his belt.

He presented it at Stormcloud's head.

The Comanche had his tomahawk in his hand, but he recoiled when he saw the weapon of death.

Well he knew its fatal power.

"One bold bid for life!" continued Dave. "There's lead in this, and you are going to have it."

He fired.

Osmond, actuated by some indefinable influence, took upon himself to save the chief's life.

He seized Dave's arm as he pulled the trigger.

The bullet flew harmlessly through the ceiling.

Stormcloud now threw himself on the old miner and bore him to the ground, when he was disarmed by Death's Head.

The chief glared with ferocious satisfaction at the prostrate miner.

"I guess you're boss," exclaimed Dave. "I knew it was coming. Finish me off as quick as you like. I ain't afraid to go, and I ain't sorry for trying to plug a hole in you; but I don't see why the boy should have interfered; he ain't Injun-born, nor yet Injun-bred."

He cast a reproachful glance upon Osmond.

"The Indians have done us no harm," replied Osmond. "Why should you try to kill them like vermin?"

"They'll do harm enough yet, you bet. They're p'ison," said Dave, bitterly.

Stormcloud placed his hand kindly on Osmond's shoulder.

"You save Indian—me grateful," he exclaimed. "None of my young men will hurt you. You shall be my son. Speak! Who kill medicine-man and put in tree of Galichoo—him?"

He pointed to Dave, who was still lying on his back.

"No," answered Osmond.

"Ugh! This prisoner try to kill me," continued Stormcloud. "Now we kill him. Tie him to stake, burn! Bad white man! See what Indian do."

Old Dave did not plead for mercy.

He had encountered Indians before, and was thoroughly acquainted with their natures.

To beg any favour at their hands would have only excited ridicule.

His fate was settled, and he knew it.

"Don't hurt him," cried Osmond. "Let him go free."

"No. Stand back!" Stormcloud replied. "He shall die. If you say too much—make it bad for you."

Osmond deemed it prudent to keep silent.

If he could not help Dave he need not endanger his own life.

One comfort he had—Felton was gone; and if the Indians were his masters, he preferred them of the two.

With regard to Dave, he thought he had acted rightly.

If the miner had killed Stormcloud before being called upon to defend himself, both he and Osmond would have been murdered.

Death's Head procured a lariat, and bound old Dave hand and foot.

The Indians were not yet ready to amuse themselves with him.

Hardy as they were and accustomed to fatigue and hunger, they could not exist without sleep and food.

Those two essentials of life they had been without for some time.

"Follow me," said Stormcloud. "You are my son. I will teach you to ride, to take scalps, and to shoot bears. You shall become a mighty chief."

Osmond inclined his head.

The chiefs left the house, and he followed them.

The prospect offered him was not an alluring one, especially for a rich English nobleman, but he did not dare to say nay to the offer.

His life was safe, and he was freed from Felton's thraldom.

But for how long?

A few words from Stormcloud explained to the braves what had happened.

It was arranged that old Dave should be tortured and burnt at the stake after the Indians had taken food and rest.

One man was to keep guard, and see that Osmond did not try to escape.

The Indians had a supply of meat, and this with well-water sufficed to appease their hunger.

Osmond pretended to sleep, though he was wide awake.

Death's Head was the sentinel.

Gradually all the Comanches were resting on the ground.

An hour passed. The sky became duller and heavier. The wind moaned in fitful gusts over the prairie.

Death's Head was only human, and after a while he too slept.

Seeing this, Osmond determined to try and save the old miner from the fate that threatened him.

Though nervous and sometimes weak, Osmond was far from being a coward.

The warlike blood of his ancestors coursed in his veins.

Looking round him he saw that the Comanches were all motionless.

Crawling on his hands and knees, he made his way to the house.

He was fully aware of the great risk he ran.

Even the friendship of Stormcloud was not likely to ensure him against punishment for liberating a captive, if he were found out.

Reaching the old house, he went into the bedroom.

Dave was lying on his back perfectly helpless.

"Ha!" he said, "have you come to kill me?"

"Hush!" replied Osmond, "not so loud."

"Why should I be silent?"

"The Indians are all asleep. I am here to set you free."

"Is that so, boy? Then God bless you! Cut these thongs. I'll soon be making tracks."

Osmond took out his knife and severed the cords.

In a moment old Dave was on his feet.

"No time for talk," he whispered, as he wrung the boy's hand cordially, "but you've made a friend of me, I tell you."

"Away!" cried Osmond. "We shall be caught."

"I've suffered the pangs of death in anticipation this last hour. I told you I thought I was booked."

"Yes."

"Well, it came partly true. Have they got your friend—Wild Bill he called himself?"

"He has escaped. Do go," urged Osmond.

"Won't you go with me?"

"I prefer to stay. The Indians are all right with me. Go! it is you who endanger both of us."

"True. I'm a volunteer for liberty. Good-bye, lad; here's for off."

Dave quitted the house through the window, and Osmond crawled back to the camp.

His heart was almost in his mouth.

Until he regained his former position he could scarcely breathe.

His absence had not been discovered.

This time when he tried to go to sleep, he found no difficulty in doing so.

How long he slept he did not know, but he was roused by a chorus of voices.

The Comanches were running to and fro in an excited manner.

Not being acquainted with their language, he was unable to understand what they were making all the fuss about.

He could guess, though.

Death's Head had apparently roused himself before the others, and made a visit to the house.

He, of course, found that Dave had by some mysterious means escaped.

This discovery he announced to Stormcloud, who roused the rest.

Hence the commotion of which Osmond was the centre.

A council was promptly held, and,

scouts were sent out in all directions to search for Dave.

In an hour's time they returned, announcing that their efforts had been futile.

No sign of the fugitive could be found.

Dave, doubtless, had his hiding-places on the prairie, which were unknown to the Indians.

It was about midday, and after a long confabulation, Stormcloud ordered his followers to mount.

The horse which had belonged to Matchi, the chief presented to Osmond.

" Can my brother ride? " he asked.

Osmond had been afraid that the chief would suspect him of having had a hand in old Dave's escape.

His kind manner entirely dissipated this idea, and his mind was relieved.

" Yes," replied Osmond. " I have been used to horses since I was a child."

" Good! We are going on the war-path. Is my brother armed? Can he fight? "

" I have only a knife; and I am not a warrior."

The chief looked at Osmond, as if trying to remember where he had seen him before.

Clear as his memory was generally, he could not recall the time and place, though Osmond recollected full well that they had met in Snell's saloon at Mowbray's Ranche, when Jack of Warwick had given the sleeping Indian a dose of snuff, and Stormcloud had been ignominiously turned out.

This secret he discreetly kept to himself.

Stormcloud asked him, after a pause, where he came from, and what he was doing on the prairie.

The question puzzled him not a little. He did not know how to answer it.

At last he said—

" Great chief, I am the son of a settler, many miles away from here. I ran away from home to see what life on the prairie was like, and a few days ago I met the captive who has escaped."

" Did he kill the medicine-man of the Comanches? "

" No. When we came to this spot all was still. I will swear that."

" It is well. My brother is too young to lie. I see it in his face."

" Where are you going? " enquired Osmond.

" To attack some white men who live near here. If my brother is no fighting-man, he can stay with the horses."

" I cannot fight against my own race."

" You have spoken well. The blood of the palefaces shall not be on your hands," answered the chief.

He led Osmond to the horse he had presented him with.

In another minute all were mounted, and, at a word, commenced galloping over the vast plain.

Although the prairie very much resembles the sea in being alike on all sides, Osmond had been long enough on it to know the points of the compass.

He was soon sure that the Comanches were heading in the direction of Mowbray's Ranche.

He recollected vividly that Stormcloud had vowed to be revenged for the indignities put upon him by Snell and Jack of Warwick.

An Indian never forgets, and rarely forgives.

If his suspicions were correct he was to be made to assist, or at least look on, the butchery of his friends.

This was a terrible reflection.

How he longed to be able to get in advance and warn them of their danger!

It was maddening to think that he was powerless to act in the matter.

If he attempted to leave his new friends, he would be shot.

After some hard riding, Stormcloud halted his men, and caused them to dismount.

The horses were carefully staked, being allowed the length of their lariats to graze.

It was about three o'clock in the afternoon, and the sun was already declining in its western course.

The dark clouds which had threatened rain had been swept away by the wind, rendering the sky clear.

A few miles off, Osmond could distinguish trees and houses, the shape of which put him in mind of Mowbray's Ranche.

He felt certain that that was the objective point of the Indians.

The chief detailed half-a-dozen braves to remain with the horses, as a sufficient protection against the cowboys if they should come that way.

Death's Head, Running Deer, and the remainder were to accompany him.

"Will my white brother stay," asked Stormcloud, "or come on the war-path?"

Osmond made a sudden resolution.

"I will come," he replied.

"Good! Here is a tomahawk. May it soon be red with the blood of the palefaces, who have taken the red man's land."

Receiving the weapon, Osmond placed it in his belt.

Not that he had any intention of fighting against his own race.

He fancied that the nearer he got to the scene of action, the more useful he might be to the unfortunates who were to be attacked.

The war-party started on foot, carrying their rifles at the trail.

A profound silence reigned amongst them as they marched in Indian file.

Stormcloud led the van, Osmond being placed immediately after him.

All possibility of escape seemed to be precluded.

Yet Osmond did not lose heart.

He firmly hoped that some chance of warning the whites would, by a merciful Providence, be given him.

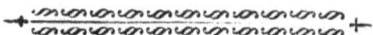

CHAPTER XI.

FIGHTING ON MOWBRAY'S RANCHE.

A BETTER occasion for a raid on the cattle-ranche could not have been chosen by the discontented and bloodthirsty savages.

It was MacTavish's birthday.

After twelve o'clock it was made a holiday, and the cowboys rode in.

Snell shut up his saloon, and came with his wife to the manager's house.

Helen and the old coloured woman, Mauma, were busy cooking wild turkeys and beef; a plum pudding boiled in the pot; a keg of beer was tapped.

There was plenty of whisky, and, in fact, a feast worthy the event was prepared.

Little did the revellers imagine that they were in danger.

Mr. Bunyard, however, had been low-spirited all the morning.

While the cowboys, who for once had agreed to forget their differences, were drinking and talking in the parlour, the cattle-raiser called MacTavish and Snell into his private room.

He placed a sheet of paper before them.

With much surprise they saw that it was headed—

"The last will and testament of Hiram T. Bunyard."

"Hech, mon alive!" MacTavish exclaimed. "What is this?"

"I have been making my will," replied Bunyard. "Lately I have been depressed. If anything happened to me, my property would go to my brother in Galveston, with whom I quarrelled years ago—that is to say, if I died intestate."

"Dinna talk of dying."

"We never know when our end is near. My brother is rich, he does not want money. There are those who do; among the needy ones I class your daughter."

"Helen is a gude girl," remarked MacTavish, with a father's partiality for his first and only one.

"Read the will. I have left all I possess to her. It is only for you and Snell to witness the document, and then put it in your pocket. I have signed it. The paper is a printed form. I have filled in the details; it is quite legal."

MacTavish lost no time in appending his signature, and Snell followed his example.

Of a sudden they were startled by the sound of a horse's hoofs galloping in the street.

They stopped outside the house.

The cowboys rushed out, and were followed by their elders.

"THE MISSILE OF DEATH FLEW WIDE OF THE MARK."

A United States cavalryman, mounted on a strong bay horse, had drawn rein at the garden gate.

"Hallo!" he cried. "Are you all dead in this one-horse place?"

"We are very much alive," replied Bunyard.

"Call it a town! Why, there are only two houses in it."

"We don't stable our cattle in houses."

"Well, you'll excuse me," said the soldier, "but I'm sent from the main body to scout."

"Don't apologise. There is no need."

"I have been knocking at the door of a saloon here, kept, as the painted sign tells me, by a mutton-headed clam called Snell. No one came. I shouted myself hoarse. If I'm any judge, he should be called Snail."

"Take it easy," exclaimed the saloon-keeper. "I'm not much troubled with custom unless travellers come along."

"How do you live? Perhaps you could retire on a fortune to-morrow."

"Maybe. However, you see this is a birthday, and we are celebrating the event."

"Ah," remarked the soldier, "I see. You'll be singing 'When Johnny comes marching home' directly. But, say, can you give me some refreshment for man and beast; and, after that, a little information?"

"Why, certainly. One thing at a time. Step down and step in," answered Bunyard.

"I'm a thousand times obliged, but I can't dismount; time's valuable."

"Please yourself. What shall we get you?"

"Water for my horse, food and anything in the shape of drink you like to part with for me."

"Dawes," cried Bunyard, "get a pail of water. Jack, a plate of beef, cut from the outside. Warner, the whisky bottle. White, glass of water. Hurry up!"

The cowboys dispersed to obey these orders.

A conversation ensued between the soldier and Mr. Bunyard, occasionally joined in by MacTavish and Snell.

It appeared that news had reached the Fort, near Nacogdochee, where the soldiers were quartered, that a road-agent was committing atrocities, and that the Comanche Indians had quitted their reservation without leave.

The authorities were afraid the reds would raid on the white settlers.

Also they apprehended that the robber would commit more crimes.

Captain Sinclair, in command of a troop of eighteen men, had been sent out to punish the Indians and secure the road-agent.

Captain Sinclair had halted about twenty miles east of Mowbray's Ranche, and had sent out the trooper, whose name was Snape, to see if he could collect any information.

"You have come to the right shop," said Bunyard. "Felton, the road-agent, was here a couple of days ago, and so was Stormcloud."

He related the circumstances attending their coming.

"That is good news," replied the soldier.

"They cannot be far off," added Bunyard.

"No; I shall return at once to our camp and tell the captain."

"Say," exclaimed Snell, with an eye to business, "couldn't you persuade your officer to make this ranche his headquarters?"

"Well thought of."

"You see, this could be the base of operations. In the eating and drinking line I have plenty to sell."

"And we have money to buy. Consider it done. Our captain shall move on here. We will settle the Indians and the road-agent."

"Bully for you," said Snell; "I'll promise you a good time."

"When do you think you will be likely to come?" asked Bunyard.

"To-night, perhaps," rejoined the soldier; "but more probably to-morrow."

The cowboys now brought him what he had asked for.

He satisfied his appetite, and thanking the ranchmen for their favours, put spurs to his horse.

Soon he was but a speck in the distance, returning by the route he had traversed in coming.

"It will do me good to have the soldiers here," remarked Snell.

"Ay," replied MacTavish, "and be a protection, too."

"It is always dangerous," Bunyard said, "when those redskins escape from their reservation. But come, Helen is calling us. The good fare MacTavish has provided for our delectation is ready."

"May excellent digestion wait on appetite," cried MacTavish. "Aweel, I'm fifty, but I dinna feel forty."

The seniors led the way to the dining-room, where Helen and Mauma had spread the banquet.

It was truly an ample and a luxurious dinner, which did them great credit.

As the cowboys followed their leaders, they smacked their lips in anticipation of the treat in store.

MacTavish was in high good-humour. He chuckled to himself as he thought of the will he had in his pocket.

In the event of Mr. Bunyard's death —which, be it understood, he was far from wishing for—it gave Helen a fortune.

"We'll a' get fou to-day," he muttered. "No one shall spare the liquor, if I have to pay the piper."

This was something extraordinary for him to say.

As a rule he was extremely parsimonious, not to say niggardly.

The clock struck one, and all sat down, MacTavish at the head of the table to carve the two turkeys, Bunyard facing him to dispense the beef, and Snell at one side with a fine ham before him.

Everybody did justice to the dinner, and expectation rose high when the pudding was put on the table.

If there is anything a cowboy can enjoy it is a plum-pudding.

MacTavish poured a tumbler of brandy over it, setting it on fire in true Christmas fashion.

But, alas! for human wishes, it was not destined to be cut that day.

"That's a prime pudding, miss," said Dawes.

"Yes, Ben," replied Helen. "You will think so when you taste it. I made it—English style."

"Is that what you have in the Old Country?"

"Always at Christmas-time and on birthdays, don't we, Jack?"

"Yes," answered Jack. "The turkey would not be much without the pudding."

MacTavish was about to plunge the knife into it, when a quick footstep was heard in the garden.

Everyone listened attentively.

"Someone comes!" Mr. Bunyard ejaculated. "What now?"

The window was open.

A boy appeared before it with a white face and starting eyeballs.

It was no other than Osmond.

"Arm! arm!" he cried. "The Indians are here!"

He sank half-fainting on the window-sill.

Bunyard ran to the spot and lifted him into the room, while the others rose to their feet.

The cowboys looked blankly at one another.

"Speak plainly," said Bunyard. "What is it we have to dread?"

"The Comanches!" replied Osmond. "I have no time to tell how they captured me; it is enough that they are hiding in the clump of trees near Snell's; some have broken into the saloon, and are drinking. I gave them the slip to warn you, they will be here directly. For God's sake do something!"

He could say no more.

Trembling and nerveless he sank into a chair.

The utmost confusion prevailed, and no wonder, for the direful news was totally unexpected.

They were altogether unprepared.

Fortunately, Mr. Bunyard did not lose his head.

He was just the man for a crisis like this.

"Boys," he exclaimed, "listen to me. Jack and Warner, shut, bolt, and bar all doors and windows. Dawes and White, get the rifles, pistols, and cartridges."

The cowboys were off at once.

In view of such an event as was about to occur, the doors had been provided with bolts and bars of iron, as well as the wooden shutters of the windows.

A plentiful supply of arms was kept handy, with ammunition.

For some time the Indians had been quiet.

Yet, it was never known when they might take it into their heads to leave their reservations.

"I will help," said Helen, bravely.

"No," replied Mr. Bunyard. "You and Mauma will retire to the store-room, where you will be safe from bullets."

He led them both gently and firmly to a room between the parlour and the kitchen, and which had no windows.

A lamp afforded them sufficient light to see one another.

"Keep cool," he added. "All is not lost. Thanks to Osmond's timely warning, we may keep the wretches at bay."

"Heaven help us!" sighed Helen.

He left the women, who were joined, a moment after, by Mrs. Snell, an elderly lady, bold and courageous, who required a good deal of persuasion from her husband to induce her to hide.

Rapidly the house was barricaded.

Snell, Dawes, and White went into the kitchen. Mr. Bunyard, Warner, and MacTavish stood, one in the passage, the two others in the front room.

Jack roused Osmond, and went upstairs, to go from room to room, in the order of light skirmishers.

All were fully armed.

Holes had been bored in the shutters and doors, to fire through and reconnoitre the enemy.

No precaution was neglected.

Had it not been for Osmond's warning, the whole company would have been surprised at the dinner-table.

An awful massacre must have ensued.

As it was, the ranchemen would at least be able to have a fight for their lives.

"How did you escape from Felton, and fall into the hands of the reds?" asked Jack.

Osmond told him briefly.

"How I got away just now," added he, "I scarcely know. It was sheer luck. The Indians glided like snakes up to the clump of trees. Running Deer went forward to reconnoitre. He found no one about. With his tomahawk he broke into Snell's saloon. When the others saw there was drink to be had, they joined him, only a few being restrained by Stormcloud. The eagerness to obtain drink was so great, that they took their eyes off me. Knowing the ground, I bolted. You know the rest."

His remarks were cut short by the hideous war-whoop of the Indians.

Jack put his eye to a hole in a window-shutter, and looked out.

He saw the Indians running down the street, shouting and yelling, waving their rifles, and brandishing their tomahawks.

They had by this time all partaken of enough drink to madden them, or, at least, to work them up to a high pitch of excitement.

It was an awful, terrifying sight.

At the head of the howling savages was Death's Head, whose ugly countenance was more repulsive and forbidding than ever.

All at once Death's Head came to a halt.

He saw that the house was barricaded.

The occupants were prepared, and the dwelling could not be carried by a *coup-de-main*.

The others also paused in their headlong career.

Jack saw his opportunity, and putting a rifle through a hole in the shutter, took deliberate aim at the chief.

Rather nervously he fired. It was the first time he had raised a weapon of a deadly nature against a human being.

The bullet sped on its errand of death.

It struck Death's Head in the body, and with a horrid yell he sank on his knees, clutching frantically at the sand in the road.

His race on earth was run.

At the same time Bunyard and MacTavish fired also.

Two more Indians fell.

This effectually checked the advance of the Comanches, who, had they not anticipated the achievement of an easy victory, would have much preferred a night attack.

Stormcloud ordered a retreat.

Before they went, however, they poured a volley obliquely into the house, and, with defiant cries and gestures, vanished.

It was easy to see that they went to the saloon.

This was to procure more drink, and deliberate.

Their dead they left where they had fallen.

Hearing cries and groans below, Jack left Osmond, telling him to keep a good lookout, and descended to see what had occurred.

He hoped nothing serious had happened.

Nevertheless, he feared the worst.

A couple of bullets had entered the bedroom to which he and Osmond had gone, going over his head and lodging in the ceiling.

They passed easily through the soft wood of the shutters.

Had the Indians been able to see any-one to aim at, they would have done considerable mischief.

As it was, they had to fire at random.

Those in the kitchen had not left their posts. The women were still huddled together in the store-room.

Going into the front room, Jack was horrified to behold Mr. Bunyard lying on his back, with MacTavish and Warner bending over him.

Blood was flowing from a wound in his lungs, he groaned as if in great pain, and drew his breath with difficulty.

"It's a sad sorrow," MacTavish ex-claimed ; "but every bullet has its billet."

He took a pinch of his usual comforter.

"Is the governor badly hurt ?" asked Jack.

"Hard hit. It's consolin', vara con-solin', as a body may say, to think that he had the guid sense to make his will when he did."

Jack was inclined to smile at the smug hypocrisy and selfishness of the thrifty and canny Scot.

Who else would have thought of profit at such a time ?

"We never know what may happen," remarked Jack.

"True, John," said MacTavish. "We are cut down like a frost-killed flower in the night. He must be worth ten thou-sand p'un's English."

"That is a deal of money for Helen to come into," Jack replied.

"Hoot! I've reckoned wrangly. It's mair nor that, taking the cattle and next year's calving into consideration."

Bunyard moved his blood-stained lips, and feebly asked for water.

Silently Warner went to procure some, and communicated the sad news to those in the kitchen.

Who could tell whose turn it would be next ?

The Comanches were not driven off; they were only repulsed for a time.

In a little while they would return to the attack.

The unequal struggle would recom-mence, with a dire desire for vengeance egging the relentless savages on.

The dying man, for such he was, could not speak much. When he tried to use his voice, he was half-choked with the rushing blood.

It was strange that he should have had a presentiment of coming evil; yet, it was well for Helen.

"This is a sorry birthday," observed MacTavish. "There's sma' chance of us gettin' fou the night, boys."

Bunyard moved his hand to his waist-coat, and looked at Jack affectionately.

"Jack Hardwick !" he muttered, feebly.

"Yes, sir."

"My watch and chain for you."

"I hope you will live to wear it for long years."

"No; my work is done," replied the stock-raiser, sadly.

Suddenly a dog, which was kept chained in the yard, began to bark furiously.

He was a quiet animal, and would not have barked so without provocation.

Fresh danger was at hand.

"The Indians are at the back !" cried MacTavish. "Go, Jack, and tell Snell to be careful. Now comes the tug-o'-war. We must fight for our lives !"

"To the last drop of our blood," Jack answered.

"Right. I have the spirit of Wallace and Bruce in me !"

"Mind you show it," said Jack, who had not a very high opinion of the Scotchman's courage.

Passing the store-room, he heard the old coloured woman crying.

"Lor' sakes ! Miss Helen," sobbed she, "it is cruel to have to die at the hands of Injuns, for they always muss your hair so in scalping !"

Seeing that under her cap she only had about a dozen hairs, this need not have troubled her much.

"We must pray for our deliverance," replied Helen. "Join me."

"Don't ask me, miss; I couldn't think of a prayer if it were ever so, nor a hymn tune," answered Mauma.

"Nor I," said Mrs. Snell. "Try a drop of the ginger-brandy cordial; it'll give you strength to hold up a bit."

"Now you's talkin' !" exclaimed the coloured cook. "I ain't gwine ter despise prayin', but it kinder goes against the grain; my mind is so upset like."

Jack went on, thinking it best to leave them alone, though he pitied Helen from the bottom of his heart, and wanted to comfort her.

A stern sense of duty called him elsewhere.

As he entered the kitchen, he saw Snell, Dawes, and White crouching on the floor, under the shelter of a wall.

"Look out!" cried Snell. "The yard's jes' full of the varmints. They've killed the dog. I saw it done with a tomahawk!"

"Why don't you fire at them?" Jack enquired.

"I was waiting for an order from MacTavish."

"Take it from me, then."

Before they could rise, a storm of bullets crashed through the shutters, hissing past Jack on all sides.

How he escaped unhurt was a wonder.

"Down!" said Snell, hoarsely, "unless you want to be shot."

Disregarding this advice, Jack put his rifle in a hole and fired, directly afterwards dropping on his knees.

He knew the Indians, after the discharge, would have to reload, and that was his opportunity.

It was satisfactory to hear a despairing shriek, which changed into a death-wail.

Another Indian had gone to the happy hunting-grounds.

With shouts of fury the Comanches retaliated, but all within being sheltered by the wall, they did no harm, except smashing the crockery on the dresser-shelves.

"Up!" exclaimed Jack. "Now's our time."

Four rifles this time dealt death and destruction among the Indians.

Then came a pause.

There was a scampering of feet, and by looking out, Jack saw that the foe were going to the right side.

No windows were there. Merely the weather-boards of which the house was built, it being entirely of wood.

"Bravo! They are beaten off. Hurrah!" cried Jack, wild with the delirium that warfare brings with it.

"Bully for our side!" said Dawes.

Their triumph was short-lived.

A new cause of apprehension arose.

The Indians, as they retreated, had to pass the woodshed, and Jack saw each of them take with him a bundle of faggots, dry as chips, which were used for kindling wood.

The crafty savages intended to burn them out.

There could be no doubt that this was their fell purpose.

Unless the besieged made a sortie they could not get at the enemy now.

The Comanches had lost several of their number, and were picked off so successfully, that they were chary of showing themselves.

Jack lost no time in informing Mac-Tavish of this change in front on the part of the Indians.

"What are we to do now?" he asked.

"I'm sair perplexed," replied the Scotchman. "It's hard to dee; but that's what it is coming to. Aweel! it's a pity a puir soul canna take his money with him when he has to go to the next world."

"For shame to think of money!" cried Jack. "Shall we rush out and have a hand-to-hand fight for our lives?"

"Don't get sae excited."

"I won't be smothered like a rat!"

"Bide awee," answered the cautious Scot; "something may turn up. There's a cellar; perhaps I might hide in there till it's a' over."

Jack walked away disgusted.

MacTavish, in this awful moment, thought only of himself.

He did not spare a word even for his daughter Helen.

By this time Bunyard was at his last gasp.

Jack could stand the confinement and suspense no longer.

He boldly unbarred the front door, and looked out.

The street was entirely deserted.

Creeping along by the wall, he looked round the corner.

He saw the Indians busily piling up the faggots against the wood.

One had got some hay at the bottom, and was striking two flints together to ignite the pile.

CHAPTER XII.

THE DEFEAT OF THE REDSKINS, AND PURSUIT OF THE ROAD-AGENT.

THE situation was a very critical one.

Jack felt his flesh creep with horror when he saw the preparations for a conflagration which were being made by the incendiaries.

The Indians were chanting a wild death-song.

Already they fancied they saw their victims perishing in the flames, or rushing out to fall before the bullet or the tomahawk.

Running Deer was dancing, under the influence of Snell's whisky, very much in the manner of an Eastern dervish.

He waved his tomahawk and rifle, and whooped like a maniac, as if confident of a speedy victory.

It was a tempting shot, and Jack could not resist it.

One savage the less would not make much difference, but still the death of this howling redskin would be a satisfaction.

He drew his pistol from his belt, and fired at him.

Running Deer did not want to do any more dancing; he fell with a loud shriek to the earth, and began to think of the happy hunting-grounds.

He was rapidly travelling in that direction.

Fearful yells arose from the Indians, who rushed round the corner.

Jack was too quick for them.

He darted into the house, shutting and barring the door again.

The Comanches emptied their rifles against the door and shutters, but did no harm.

Furious with rage, they retired to complete their foul work.

In the front room Jack found only Warner, who was looking in a melancholy manner at the corpse of Mr. Bunyard.

MacTavish was nowhere to be seen.

The women in the store-room, terribly alarmed at the last fusillade, were sobbing and crying.

"The boss is dead," exclaimed Warner, "and I can't tell where Mac has gone

"Shot, perhaps," replied Jack.

"Not here, or I'd have seen him fall."

"It will all be over soon," said Jack.

"What do you mean?"

"I've been outside to prospect, and the reds are preparing to set fire to the house."

"Why can't we run?" asked Warner.

"What's the good? They would overtake us; and we should be shot down. I don't see any chance of escape."

Jack paced the room impatiently.

His mind was sorely troubled.

"If it wasn't for Helen, I shouldn't care so much," he exclaimed. "Poor girl! she is young to die."

Suddenly Osmond came into the room.

He was very pale, but a smile sat on his face.

"Help is at hand!" he cried.

Warner and Jack looked at him as if he had taken leave of his senses.

They could not imagine where any help was coming from.

"I looked through one of the shot-holes in the window," continued Osmond, "and I saw some mounted men riding down the street."

"Are you sure?" asked Jack, his eyes brightening.

"Well, I wasn't dreaming."

"The soldiers! Hurrah!" Warner cried.

Jack rushed to the door and ventured to open it.

He saw in a moment that Osmond had not deceived him.

A troop of United States cavalry were trotting along the road.

They were evidently coming towards the house, but so leisurely were their movements that they did not know there was any danger.

The trooper who had visited the ranche that morning had said that they would come.

Their arrival was much quicker than had been anticipated.

Though they knew it not, they

came just in time to save precious lives.

Jack ran out through the garden.

"The Indians are here!" he shouted. "They are going to burn us out!"

Captain Sinclair, who was in command of the troop, reined in his horse.

"What do you say?" he demanded. "Indians here! I see none! Where are they?"

"Round the corner! Look! here they come!"

As Jack spoke, the Indians, who had been roused by the voices, made their appearance.

They had succeeded in lighting the pile of faggots, and a dense smoke arose, accompanied by a crackling sound.

Directly the Comanches saw the troopers, they discharged their rifles.

Three saddles were emptied, the soldiers falling heavily to the dust, while their horses galloped away, neighing in terror.

Retribution was swift.

"Charge!" cried the captain. "Give no quarter! Cut them down!"

The soldiers set upon the Indians, who in vain tried to escape.

They were hunted like deer, and cut down remorselessly.

Some placed their backs against a tree or a wall, and fought bravely until they were killed.

Others, panic-stricken, ran like frightened sheep, only to fall before the heavy cavalry-sword.

In a few minutes not one Indian was left alive.

While this terrible war of extermination was going on, Jack and Warner seized poles, and scattered the burning faggots.

The fire had not yet caught the boards of the house.

Dawes came out to see what was going on, and noticed that Jack was hard at work.

He thought no one was looking at him.

Levelling his pistol, he aimed at his enemy, thinking that, if he killed him, his death would be put down to the Indians.

Shots were being fired, for the soldiers used their revolvers as well as their sabres.

A stray bullet might strike anybody.

Dawes pulled the trigger, grating his teeth viciously.

As he did so, his arm was knocked up. The missile of death flew wide of the mark.

Turning round, Dawes saw Osmond at his shoulder.

"Perdition take you!" he yelled. "What did you do that for? Wasn't I trying to kill an Indian?"

"No, coward!" replied Osmond.

"What then?"

"You fired at Jack of Warwick, you hound; and I have a good mind to put a bullet through your heart! I don't know why I withstand the temptation."

"Is he your friend?"

"The best I have in the world."

"Well, all I can say is, I fired at a red. You are mistaken, and I defy you to prove it."

"I shall try."

"Oh, give me a rest. Who will believe you? Get out, or I'll knock spots out of you!" shouted the cowboy.

Osmond received a push, which made him fall back, and Dawes ran up the street to watch the soldiers.

When all was over with the Indians, the soldiers stabled their horses; the captain arranged to make Snell's saloon his headquarters for the night, and as the cavalry paid for all they had, the proprietor was glad to accommodate them.

Five troopers had been killed.

These, with Mr. Bunyard, were placed in a shed to await burial on the morrow.

As soon as Jack saw there was no danger of fire, he hastened to the store-room, and assured the women that the peril was over.

It was a great relief to them to hear this.

They had begun to abandon hope.

Mrs. Snell went back to her house.

Mauma, with the aid of Warner and White, took the shutters down.

Osmond remained in the road, watching Dawes, and Jack led Helen into the parlour.

"Oh, Jack," she said, "this has been an awful afternoon. I gave up hope at one time. Thank heaven you are unhurt!"

"Do you really take so much interest in me?" he asked.

She blushed up to the eyes.

"I will not answer your question," she replied. "Your heart ought to tell you that—that I look upon you as a dear friend."

"No more than that?"

"As a very dear friend. Will that suit you?"

"Yes," said Jack, kissing her. "I am satisfied; and you know that the feeling is returned. My word! Helen, it is lucky the detachment of cavalry came this way when they did, or we should not have been talking now."

"Was the danger so imminent?"

"The reds were about to set fire to the house."

"Is anybody hurt?"

"Mr. Bunyard is killed. That is our only casualty, as far as I know. The body has been removed. Some soldiers have been shot, and I guess all the Comanches are wiped out. Look through the window."

Helen did so.

Dead Indians were lying about in all directions, and a fatigue party of soldiers were engaged in removing the bodies.

"I am so sorry about Mr. Bunyard," said Helen. "He was always a good friend to us."

"You don't know how good yet," said Jack.

"What do you mean?"

"I heard your father say that he had made his will in your favour."

"In mine! Why?"

"I don't know. You are heiress to all his property."

"What a noble, splendid man!" cried Helen. "I was afraid, at his death, we should have to quit the ranche. At father's age he does not want to go about begging for work."

"I say!" suddenly exclaimed Jack, "where is Mr. MacTavish? I have not seen him for a good half-hour."

"It is impossible for me to tell, as I was shut up in the store-room," Helen answered. "Do please look for him. If anything has happened to him it will be a terrible blow to me!"

"Wait here. I will go."

Jack searched the house from top to bottom.

No trace whatever was to be discovered of MacTavish.

Had he madly rushed on his fate, and been slaughtered by the Indians?

This question forced itself on Jack's attention, and, leaving the house, he went into the street.

There was just a chance that MacTavish might have gone to Snell's saloon for a pinch of "sneezin'."

This was generally his excuse to his daughter when he wanted to go out for something stronger than water.

Jack quickly arrived at the saloon, which was patrolled outside by a sentry.

Inside, the soldiers had made themselves at home, by loosening their accoutrements, lighting their pipes, and drinking.

Snell was as busy as he could be, attending to the bar, which had not suffered much depletion of stock at the hands of the Indians.

His wife was cooking steaks and chops in obedience to eager demands on the part of the hungry men.

Captain Sinclair was smoking a cigar, and drinking a bottle of wine with his orderly officer.

"Hallo!" exclaimed Snell, in an excited manner, when he saw Jack of Warwick. "How goes it? What a time we're having!"

He was thinking that the custom of the soldiers would recoup him for the loss he had sustained by the Indian raid.

"How long do the cavalry stay?" asked Jack.

"To-night only; they're off to-morrow morning."

"So soon! What for?"

"They have orders to capture Felton, the road-agent, and take him to Nacogdochee to be tried for his life; if he shows fight, he is to be shot."

"That is good business."

"The captain said just now he should ask for a cowboy to volunteer to show him the way over the prairie."

"Osmond is the boy for that work, and I will go with him," replied Jack.

He had an idea that Felton was not far off.

It was more than likely that he was haunting the neighbourhood in search of Osmond.

"I will tell the captain what you say!" exclaimed Snell, "and I have no doubt he will accept your services."

"Thank you; work it round for me; but, I say—"

"What now?"

"Do you know anything of MacTavish? He can't be found anywhere."

"Not me," rejoined Snell. "He left me alone in the front room, with the remark that he was going to see what he could do."

"The Indians must have killed him," said Jack. "But it is very singular that I can find no trace of him. This will be a great blow for Helen."

"She's got the dollars," observed Snell, with a knowing wink. "Stick up to her; she'll make you manager of the farm, for I can see she is sweet in your direction, and in a few years you can marry her, and be boss."

"Don't talk such nonsense," said Jack, pretending to be offended.

In reality, he was highly delighted.

"Ain't I seen you kiss her, and ain't my wife told me that the girl takes a lot of stock in you?"

"That may be so—I hope it is," replied Jack; "but I must go back and look after MacTavish."

"What a shock to a birthday party!" exclaimed Snell. "I don't want to keep mine if any more friends like these darned Comanches are coming to visit us."

"It will be a lesson to all the tribes!" exclaimed Jack: "Sioux, Apaches, Crows, Cherokees, Piutes, and the rest."

"You bet," replied Snell, emphatically.

Some soldiers, crowding round the bar, engaged the attention of the landlord, and Jack went away to pursue his search for MacTavish.

In the road he met Osmond.

"I was looking for you, Jack," said the young Lord Melbury, "and I am glad I have found you."

"What for?" asked Jack.

"You have an enemy."

"I am perfectly aware of that fact. You mean Dawes, my fellow cowboy."

"Exactly; that is the one I want to warn you against."

"Has the villain been doing anything lately?"

"He tried to shoot you just now, when the soldiers were charging and cutting down the Indians, and you and Warner were putting out the fire."

"The treacherous hound!" exclaimed Jack.

"He would have killed you if I had not knocked his arm up."

"I'll make him pay dearly for it," cried Jack; "there will be some changes on this ranche soon, I reckon, and if Mister Dawes does not skip, I shall."

"He means you no good."

"I do not fear him. Come into the house. I am not master, but I can hold my own."

"I will join you presently," answered Osmond. "I want to have a look at the dead Indians."

"Curious fancy."

"No, it isn't, when you come to think of it. The soldiers have laid the redskins on their backs, all of a row, on a bank by the roadside. It is a picture I may never have a chance of seeing again."

Jack nodded, and they separated.

He would have been very much annoyed at Dawes's infamous behaviour if he had had the time to think about it.

As it was, his mind was filled with doubts and fears as to the fate which had befallen MacTavish.

Helen met him in the passage, looking up anxiously in his face, where she saw nothing to encourage her.

"I can hear no tidings of your father," he said; "but as no one has seen his body, we may hope that he is alive."

"He is of a cautious disposition, and may be hiding," replied Helen.

"Ah!" cried Jack, "that is a good idea; let us look in the cellar."

This was built underground, being approached through a trap-door in the centre of the passage.

An iron ring enabled Jack to pull up the door.

All was dark and silent.

"Below!" exclaimed Jack. "Is there anyone there?"

He was rewarded by hearing a deep groan.

"Oh, good Mister Indian," said a voice, which was undoubtedly that of the lost Scotchman, "dinna fash yourself about me; I'm a' richt."

Jack turned to Helen with a smile.

"It is your father, safe enough," he said, "but he seems to have rather confused ideas of things in general."

"He keeps his whisky in the cellar," replied Helen, "and no doubt he has been keeping his courage up until his mind is rather clouded. I am so glad he is found. Shall I procure a light?"

"Not yet."

"There is a ladder to go up and down by."

"He thinks I am an Indian. I'll act one."

MacTavish had indeed been solacing himself with whisky; he was, as the sailors say, half seas over.

His excited imagination made him believe that the Indians had captured the house, and killed all except himself.

It was his turn now, and he trembled at being discovered in his gloomy retreat.

"All gone!" he muttered—"Mr. Bunyard, my poor dear daughter, the cowboys, and that Warwickshire lout, Jack Hardwick. I'm the next. Aweel, what's the good of living? I—oh, dear! listen to that!"

"Ugh!" Jack said, in guttural tones.

"Spare a puir Scotchman," cried MacTavish, "and I'll give you a drap o' ma whisky, and some sneeshin'."

"As the leaves fall in winter, so has the white man to die."

"Dinna say that. I have not paid my last quarter's life insurance, and the policy will not hold gude."

"Will the paleface die by the cord?" asked Jack.

"Na, na!" said MacTavish; "I'm against being hang't."

"By fire? He shall have his choice."

"Na; mabbe I'll have eneuch of that in the ither warld."

"The bullet is quick, the tomahawk is speedy."

"Leave me here," replied MacTavish. "I'll prefer to die of whisky, which I reckon is the proper death for a Heilander."

Jack burst out laughing, as did Helen. They could not contain themselves any longer.

"Who's that laughing and speering?" asked MacTavish. "It sounds like my lassie and that Warwick lout. Ah, Jack, if you have been deceiving me, I'll tan that hide of thine, as sure as I'm on my back in this wee bit cellar."

"You must forgive me this time, sir."

"It's vara bad form to make fun of your elders and betters."

"I could not resist the temptation."

"Have the Indians gone? Is the hoose safe frae the burning?"

"Perfectly. The cavalry arrived in the nick of time; not a Comanche remains alive."

"Praise be to the Lord! I think I'll come oot of this."

MacTavish scrambled to his feet with alacrity, but speedily rolled back into a recumbent position.

"Hoot, toot!" he exclaimed; "the worriting of this day has completely overcome me!"

"Will you stay there till the effect has worn off?"

"Do you mean to insinuate that I, Sandy MacTavish, am drunk?" the Scotchman demanded, indignantly.

"Not at all, sir," answered Jack.

"It's gude for you! I am a sober character. When I lived in Glasgow, I was never carried home more than twa times in one week. Leave me; I will be amang you anon."

Jack left the cellar-flap open so that he could obtain plenty of air.

In a short time he was snoring loudly.

All Helen's cheerfulness returned now, for she was deeply attached to her father, who, with all his faults, was very fond of her.

No more danger was to be apprehended from the Indans.

Life on the farm would go on as usual.

While Helen went to the kitchen to assist Mauma in preparing tea, Jack sought Osmond.

He had scarcely joined him by the side of the road, when Captain Sinclair came up.

The American officer was a bronzed veteran of fifty, who had spent years in the various forts on the plain.

"I guess," he exclaimed, "that you two are cowboys on this ranche, and perhaps you can give me some information I require."

"With pleasure," replied Jack.

"It is about this road-agent," continued Captain Sinclair. "He is well-known to the authorities as a desperate character, and I have orders from the governor of the State to capture him. Where was Felton seen last?"

"I can answer that question," said Osmond; "for I was the last to see him, at a place called Hanging Man's Holding."

"Where and what is that?"

"An old ruined house, some miles from here."

"What were you doing there?"

Jack looked warningly at Osmond.

The glance was to inform him that it would not be prudent to let the captain know his secret.

Sinclair would think Osmond in league with Felton.

Probably he would hold him as a witness as to the robbery of the railroad express.

"My comrade was looking for stray cattle, sir," said Jack, "when the Indians made him a prisoner, and brought him here."

"That is a strange story."

"He made his escape from the Comanches, and warned us of our danger."

"What was Felton doing there?" continued Captain Sinclair. "And how did this boy know him?"

"Felton had been here," replied Jack. 'He killed a cowboy. When my comrade saw him at Hanging Man's Holding, he was no doubt hiding."

The captain looked curiously at them.

"It seems to me that you are all mixed up together," he exclaimed. "If I am trifled with, beware!"

"Who is trifling with you?"

"I don't assert that you are, but understand this: I won't stand any nonsense. Mark me well, I shall take this boy as a guide."

"Very well," answered Osmond; "I am willing."

"I volunteer for the service also," said Jack.

"Good. You can have a couple of our empty saddles to ride there on, but you will have to walk back."

"If you catch the road-agent, shall you hang him?"

"I have no power to do so."

"What then?"

"He will be hanged without doubt; but my duty is to deliver the rascal to the sheriff at Nacogdochee, who will place him in the gaol to await his trial."

"Suppose he shows fight?" suggested Jack.

"Ah! that is different. In self-defence we should shoot him. Now, I shall count on you two."

"When, and at what time?"

"Daybreak to-morrow. You will be roused by the sound of the bugle."

The captain turned on his heel, and returned to the saloon, where dinner awaited him.

Although they knew it not, Dawes, concealed behind a tree, had been listening to this conversation.

"Ha, ha!" he muttered; "I shall be riding that way to-morrow, and I may meet you on the way home. If so, look out!"

In a self-satisfied way he forgot himself so far as to laugh aloud.

Jack heard the sound.

He darted to the spot, and seized the cowboy by the collar.

"Spy!" he cried, "what are you doing here?"

"Let go!" shouted Dawes. "I suppose I can stand behind a tree if I choose to do so?"

"I am told that you fired at me to-day."

"It is a lie," returned Dawes. "Who says so?"

"Osmond, who is my chum, and too hard-headed to fancy such a thing."

"I deny it. When I fired it was at a redskin. What did the English fool want to interfere for?"

"To save my life. Here's an earnest of what I shall do if you attempt it again!"

So saying, Jack gave a heave and a twist, and the cowboy flew into the air.

His progress was arrested by the branch of a tree, to which he clung with grim tenacity.

By dint of considerable exertion, he contrived to get astride the bough.

There he sat, bruised, panting, furious.

"I'll make you swallow a bitter pill before long," he hissed.

"What kind of one?"

"One of Dawes's patent lead pellets. Worth a guinea a box."

"That's a threat."

"Of course it is. You are not in Warwick now. You are out West, where we cowboys, when we say a thing, mean business."

"Thank you," said Jack, with his quiet, provoking smile. "I'm going to prescribe some of my pills for you."

"What are they?"

"Stone pills, such as you see lying in the roadway. Pick up some, Osmond, and pelt him," cried Jack.

With alacrity Osmond obeyed.

"That's mean," exclaimed Dawes, becoming alarmed.

"You ought to be a judge of meanness. However, I'm going to do it. Look out!"

As he spoke, Jack threw a stone.

It went with such precision that it hit the cowboy in the back.

Osmond directly afterwards struck him on the shoulder.

"Oh! ouch! oh!"

The missiles came upon him thick and fast.

Unable to stand the attack, he slipped down the trunk and ran away as fast as his legs would carry him.

"Ha, ha!" laughed Jack. "I soon stopped his crowing."

"Do you think it wise to irritate a fellow like that?" asked Osmond.

"Bah! I don't care whether he is a friend or a foe. He does not like me, and I don't suppose he would ever alter."

"I know why he dislikes you."

"It is more than I have been able to fathom. Perhaps you won't mind enlightening me on the subject."

"He is in love with Helen MacTavish, and feels mad because she favours you," said Osmond.

Jack seemed surprised at his revelation.

He had never remarked or suspected that the cowboy was fond of Helen; but he could easily believe it.

The thing was quite natural, for anyone would be likely to love her, not only on account of her beauty, but for her sweet disposition.

"I'll lower his pride and presumption!" exclaimed Jack.

A silvery voice was heard at his elbow.

"Who are you talking about?" asked Helen.

She had tripped out to ask them to come in and have a cup of tea.

"Why, you were the subject of our remarks," replied Jack. "Osmond says Dawes is in love with you."

"Is that all?"

"It is enough, I think."

"Don't be jealous," said Helen. "I have known for some time that Dawes admires me. But I don't like him, so you need not be in the least degree uneasy. Come in to tea."

Jack was mollified, and entered the house.

MacTavish came out of the cellar, and Captain Sinclair paid them a visit.

The Scotsman brewed a large bowl of whisky-toddy, and contrived to celebrate his birthday, after all.

There was no singing, though, or attempt at merriment.

The sad death of Mr. Bunyard had cast a gloom over the company, who had known him long enough to appreciate his sterling qualities.

It was late when they went to bed, and Jack awoke with a headache, due to the punch, when he heard the sound of the bugle.

Dressing quickly, he walked to the stable, where he was joined by Osmond.

Both were ready for the adventure which was before them.

They expected a good deal to result from it.

Jack was firmly of opinion that Felton would not leave Texas until he had made a last effort to find Osmond.

That he would return to, and lurk about, Hanging Man's Holding was more than probable.

A couple of horses, belonging to troopers shot the day before, were given to the boys, who mounted and rode in advance of the cavalry.

Jack did not know the way, never having been in that direction, but Osmond did.

They had not gone more than a hundred yards before Captain Sinclair called a halt.

During the past evening a grave had been dug for the soldiers who fell in the affair with the Indians.

The bodies had been placed in it, and covered over.

Now the troop was halted to pay a parting tribute of respect to their dead comrades.

This took the shape of three volleys, which were fired, on horseback, from their carbines in quick succession.

This melancholy service being performed, the troopers again started at a trot.

They looked very martial in the rising sunshine, which glinted on their arms and accoutrements.

Jack looked over his shoulder.

Helen and her father were at an upper window.

The former waved a handkerchief,

and an encouraging smile sat on her lips.

In the street our hero saw Snell, and in the stable-yard Dawes was mounted, while White and Warner were putting the saddles on their mustangs.

Little did brave Jack of Warwick dream of the awful peril that was threatening him.

CHAPTER XIII.

FELTON IS RUN TO EARTH—IN AN IRON GRIP—DAWES IS DRIVEN FROM THE RANCHE—STARTLING NEWS.

IT was midday when the troopers arrived at Hanging Man's Holding.

They were fatigued by the heat of the blazing sun.

A prospect of rest and water was very agreeable to them.

The trees, which grew in patches round the house, offered a tempting and welcome shade.

Galichoo, or the sacred tree, reared its withered head in a forbidding manner.

"Halt! Form line!" cried the captain. "Rear rank, take close order—halt, dress, dismount!"

In a minute each man, having obeyed these orders, was standing at his horse's head.

Suddenly a form sprang up from the grass.

He had been sleeping near the foot of the sacred tree.

Looking wildly around him, he seemed to be utterly bewildered.

"Felton!" shouted Osmond. "The road-agent!"

It was clear that the ruffian had returned to the spot, and had fallen asleep.

He had been run to earth by his intended victim.

His horse was grazing fifty yards off.

Putting his whistle to his lips, he blew it shrilly.

Too late!

One of the troopers headed off his horse, subsequently catching it.

Captain Sinclair drew his sword, and rode up to Felton, who, like a stag driven to bay, prepared to fight.

He presented a revolver at the captain.

"Stand back!" he cried, hoarsely, "or your blood will be on your own head!"

"Fool!" replied the officer. "I call upon you to surrender in the name of the law."

"On what charge?"

"Murder and robbery. Resistance is useless. You will be riddled with balls if you show fight, for you are wanted, dead or alive."

Felton laughed maniacally.

"Death before capture!" he cried.

At the same moment he fired.

Fortunately for Captain Sinclair, his charger, which was a mettlesome animal, reared at that precise juncture.

This action saved his rider's life.

Two shots, fired in quick succession, entered the horse's chest.

It rolled over, throwing the captain heavily.

Seeing the robber's determination to shoot, Private Snape, whom we have seen before at Mowbray's Ranche, set spurs to his horse.

He dashed upon Felton.

Before the latter could fire a third time, Snape had struck him on the head with the flat of his sabre.

With a heavy groan, the road-agent sank to the grass.

Instantly Jack and Osmond ran forward and held the villain down.

Snape dismounted, and taking off his horse's curb chain, bound Felton's hands together with it.

This rendered him as harmless as if he had been handcuffed.

He was in safe keeping now, struggle how he would.

Disengaging his feet from the stirrups, Captain Sinclair got away from his dying horse, and approached the spot.

"Well done, Snape!" he said. "Bravo, boys! I had a narrow shave, but all's well that ends well."

"I thought you were done for, sir," remarked Jack.

"I've been under a hotter fire than that during the Civil War, and escaped. Are you sure he is our man?"

"Perfectly," answered Osmond.

"So am I," said Jack. "That is the villain who shot the cowboy."

"I don't want to make any foolish mistake. You boys will be summoned on the trial, I guess, to identify him," continued the captain.

"Shall we?" asked Osmond, somewhat crestfallen.

He did not very much relish this prospect, for it would bring out prominently his peculiar connection with the road-agent.

"Those in the saloon at your ranche who saw him before he killed the cowboy, will also be of use, but as he always wore a black mask when stopping the stage or the train, the passengers could not identify him."

The road-agent soon recovered consciousness, and opened his eyes.

"So," he said, glaring at Osmond, vindictively, "I am caught, and you are going to swear against me. You ought to be in the dock with me, for you were my accomplice in the robberies."

Captain Sinclair looked enquiringly at Osmond.

"What does he mean?" he asked.

Osmond turned deathly pale, and made no reply.

He did not for the life of him know what to say.

Luckily Jack's presence of mind enabled him to come to the rescue.

"The man raves!" he exclaimed.

"No, I don't, either," answered Felton, his eyes gleaming maliciously; "and he can't deny it."

How those basilisk eyes pierced through Osmond and made him tremble!

The fateful orbs exercised a mesmeric influence over him.

"I can answer for my friend," said Jack. "We both come from the same part of England, and we shall not fail to be forthcoming at the trial."

Felton struggled to his feet, foaming at the mouth with rage.

"Aren't you going to take him, too?" he demanded.

"What for?" asked Captain Sinclair.

"I allege that he has been my accomplice."

"Oh, then you admit that you are the man wanted? You have criminated yourself. All you say will be used in evidence against you."

Felton bit his lip with vexation.

In his fierce desire to drag Osmond down in his disgrace, he had revealed what it would have taken trouble to prove.

"You have given yourself away nicely," said Jack, with a sneer. "I should advise you to keep your mouth closed in future."

Captain Sinclair waved his hand.

"It is needless to say more," he exclaimed. "I have no authority for the boy's arrest, and certainly shall not take him to Nacogdochee on this man's unsupported testimony."

"That settles it," cried Jack.

"Does it?" hissed Felton. "I'll be revenged on both of you yet. There isn't a gaol in these United States that can hold me."

"An idle boast," remarked Captain Sinclair.

"No, it isn't, either. Ask them at Orleans; ask them at Galveston; ask—"

"Be silent for your own sake. I shall have to repeat all this."

"I don't care. Give me a cup of water, and start for Nacogdochee as soon as you like. I'm not weakening."

"See to his wants, Snape, and guard him closely."

"Yes, sir," replied the trooper.

"We shall rest here to recruit the men and the horses, for a couple of hours."

The captain walked away to have a look at the old house, and smoke a quiet cigar.

Osmond stood, shivering like a leaf in the wind, before the road-agent.

"Come away!" said Jack.

"Bah!" cried Felton. "Don't think you have done with me."

He raised his chained hands, endeavouring to dash them in Osmond's face.

"Come, none of that!" said Snape.

He laid his heavy hand on the prisoner's arm and restrained his violence.

Snape beckoned to the boys to go, for the prisoner was getting frantic, stamping his feet and biting his lip till the blood came.

"DAWES ROLLED ON THE GROUND WRITHING IN AGONY."

No. 6.

Jack led Osmond away towards the well, where they joined the troopers, who were quenching their thirst.

"It's no use his kicking," observed Jack. "He's caged right enough."

"I shall have no peace till he is dead," answered Osmond.

"Take my advice."

"What is it?"

"Get off to England as quick as you can. The stage from Brazos to Nacogdochee will pass through Mowbray's Ranche to-morrow."

"Will it?" asked Osmond, hopefully.

"Yes," rejoined Jack. "Well, there's your chance. Take the train from Nacogdochee to Galveston, and rejoin your mother. Take your place as Lord Melbury. You will hear no more of Felton, except that he is dead."

"And you, my dear old friend?"

"I shall stay here until I marry Helen, and even then I don't know that I shall go back to the Old Country, unless it is for a trip."

"What shall I do without you?" asked Osmond.

"Come and see us. You know your way now. I like this country. Why, I don't know; but it is growing upon me," replied Jack.

A couple of hours passed by quickly.

Captain Sinclair thanked the boys for their service, and said they would hear from the sheriff when they would be wanted at the trial.

Felton was placed on a horse between two troopers.

His attitude was erect and defiant.

Not in the least cowed did he appear in his hour of calamity.

When the cavalrymen rode off, the boys started on their homeward track.

Osmond decided to act upon the advice Jack had given him.

The latter declared that there would be ample evidence to hang Felton, if they could only prove against him the murder of Tanner, the cowboy.

Justice was not likely to let so notorious a criminal slip through her fingers.

It was a long way back to the ranche, but they reckoned to do it in about six hours.

If they had brought their rifles with them they could have had some good sport.

Wild turkeys and prairie hens were continually springing up in their path.

When two-thirds of the distance had been traversed, they came in sight of a herd of cattle.

It had belonged to Mr. Bunyard, and, of course, by his will was now the property of Helen MacTavish.

Another similar herd grazed in the same locality.

One was tended by White, the other by Dawes.

Whether this particular one was that of Dawes or not, they could not tell until they drew nearer.

"These are some of our cattle," Jack exclaimed. "I can see our brand on that steer over there."

"For heaven's sake, look out for Dawes!" said Osmond. "You remember what he threatened yesterday?"

"We've got our pistols," replied Jack; "isn't that good enough?"

Going a little nearer they saw Dawes sitting on his mustang.

The recognition was mutual.

"Hallo!" he cried, "how have you thief-takers got on to-day?"

He dismounted, leaving the mustang to crop the grass, and advanced with his hands in his pockets.

"Do not pretend friendship," said Jack; "there is bad blood on your side against me. The fact is, you hate me because a friendship has sprung up between Miss Helen and myself."

Dawes became livid with rage.

"Perdition!" he cried, "didn't I know her before you did?"

"Has that anything to do with it?"

"What did you want to come here at all for?"

"Because it suited me."

"It would have been better for you if you had stayed in your own country. Go back where you belong, Johnny Bull."

"I will when it suits me," replied Jack.

"I hate the pair of you!" exclaimed Dawes, who was beside himself with a passion he did not try to check.

The blood rushed to his head, and his eyes burned so that he could scarcely see. Like a lightning flash he snatched out a pistol, pointed it at Jack, and fired.

Osmond sprang forward, receiving the

ball in his right arm, thereby, in all probability, saving the life of his friend.

"That's for one," cried Dawes; "now for the other."

Before he could fire again, Jack knocked him down, and, falling on the wretch, disarmed him.

A couple of blows with the butt end of the revolver caused the cowboy to see many stars.

His attempt at wholesale murder was happily frustrated.

"Mercy!" whined Dawes. "I didn't mean nothing. Mercy!"

"It's more than you deserve," said Jack; "but you are as harmless as a dead snake now, and I don't wish to stain my hands with your vile blood."

"Lemme go, and keep dark about this."

"Go where?"

"I dunno," said Dawes. "It's clear I can't return to the ranche after this. None of you would have me. I'll go somewhere and get a living, you bet, and you'll see no more of me."

Jack searched the villain's clothing.

He only had a knife. Of this he deprived him.

"Lie there," he exclaimed. "I'll attend to you presently. If you move I'll shoot you like a dog."

"All right, boss," replied Dawes.

He was quiet and humble enough now, like all cowards when they are conquered.

Walking to Osmond our hero saw that he was sitting on the grass, his handsome features convulsed with pain.

His right arm hung helplessly by his side.

"My poor friend," said he, "are you seriously hurt? I hope not."

Blood trickled down the wounded arm, staining Osmond's shirt-cuff and running over his hand.

"The pain is in my arm," answered the young earl. "I don't think the ball has entered my body. Whatever it is, I rejoice at it, for Dawes meant to kill you, and I have saved your life."

"Come, let us have your jacket off and turn up your shirt-sleeve. A doctor can't tell what's the matter till he has seen the wound."

"Do as you like."

At length the arm was bared up to the shoulder.

As he had raised it to protect his friend, the bullet had passed right through the fleshy part above the elbow without touching his body.

The blood was flowing from two holes.

A gentle pressure by the fingers convinced Jack that the bone was not broken.

Tying a handkerchief tightly round the wound he stopped the bleeding.

"You will be all right soon," he cried. "We will ride home on Dawes's mustang. I can hold you. It is a nuisance, though, for you will not be able to start for England to-morrow."

"Shall I be obliged to lie in bed?" asked Osmond.

"For a few days. No longer, I hope. Now I'll attend to Dawes. He must not leave without my giving him something to remember us by."

A long-lashed whip, such as cowboys use, had fallen from the Texan's hand when he dismounted.

Picking it up, Jack cracked it in the air, and advanced to Dawes, who was standing up with an anxious face.

"Can I skip now?" he enquired.

"When I've done cowhiding you," was the reply. "I want to teach you a lesson."

"We may meet again," said Dawes, in a menacing tone; "and if we do, and I've got the whip-hand, I'll have your life."

"Pshaw!" retorted Jack. "I fear not your threats."

Raising his whip, he lashed out at Dawes, who in vain tried to ward off the blows with his hands.

The cuts fell thick and fast.

At length he uttered wild yells, mingled with appeals for mercy, and rolled on the ground writhing in agony.

Jack relentlessly continued his punishment.

"Get up," he said, when his arm ached. "I reckon we are quits."

Dawes rose, looking perfectly demoniacal.

"I'm a-going," he hissed; "but if you have washed your hands of me, I haven't mine of you."

"Bah! What you've got is only your deserts. Clear out, or I'll repeat the dose."

Dawes saw him raise the cowhide again, and deeming it prudent to beat a retreat, started off at a shambling gait across the prairie.

Bitter thoughts surged through his mind.

A fierce undying desire for vengeance burned in his heart.

"Look here," shouted Jack; "if you dare to show your face again at Mowbray's Ranche, I'll hand you over to the sheriff."

Dawes paused.

"Won't you call it square?" he said. "You might let me come back and say nothing about my share in the shooting."

"Can't be done," Jack replied, shaking his head.

"I guess I'll starve on the prairie, as I've got no gun."

"Starve, then."

"A man must live."

"There is no good and valid reason why you should. Your fate, whatever it may be, is of your own making."

Dawes again trudged on.

Nothing was to be expected in the way of clemency from his conqueror.

He had to take his chance on the solitary plain.

Gradually his form dwindled to a speck, and disappeared in the distance.

While writhing on the ground, he had dropped his flask, which Jack picked up, giving some of the contents to Osmond, which refreshed him greatly.

With difficulty our hero got his friend in front of himself on the mustang, and at a walking pace, to avoid jolting, he started for the ranche.

The sun was setting when they arrived, and went to the stables.

A dead silence hung over the place; not a sound was heard.

With the help of White and Warner, MacTavish and Snell had lain Mr. Bunyard in his last resting-place.

The dead Indians had been placed in a trench, and the whites, who had been so providentially spared, were grouped in MacTavish's parlour.

They rose eagerly as Jack and Osmond entered, MacTavish being cut short in a eulogy he was pronouncing on his deceased employer.

"Hech, but he war a gude mon to us," he was saying.

"Here's Jack of Warwick," exclaimed Helen. "How did you succeed? What is wrong with Osmond?"

"It's a long story," replied Jack, accommodating his friend with a chair.

Osmond looked faint, and was decidedly feverish.

A hectic spot burnt on each cheek, and his lips were parched and livid.

Jack related circumstantially all that had happened on that eventful day.

Everybody was astonished.

Felton a captive, Osmond wounded, Dawes a fugitive, with the brand of a would-be assassin on his brow!

General satisfaction was expressed at the capture of Felton, who was regarded as a pest as bad as the Comanches.

Everyone sympathised with Osmomd, who was put to bed by Jack, the latter volunteering to sit up at night as nurse.

Though the loss of Dawes made MacTavish short-handed, neither he nor anyone else was sorry at the loss.

Towards morning Osmond developed a high fever; which, however, somewhat diminished during the day.

As Jack had to attend to his duties, Helen and Mauma, by turns, waited upon the invalid.

It looked as if his journey to England would, of necessity, be postponed for a long time.

There was no absolute danger, but when the fever left him, and his wound healed, he would remain weak.

Travelling would be impossible until his strength was restored.

Jack told everyone at the ranche who Osmond really was, and did not scruple to say how he had met Felton, and how cruelly he had been coerced by him into participating in the raids upon the stage and the express-car.

Not one of them blamed him—how could they?

He received their sympathy; for he had been the innocent tool in the hands of a villainous man.

A fortnight passed, but no news arrived from Nacogdochee.

Certainly, they heard that Felton had been lodged in gaol by Captain Sinclair and his troopers.

But that was all.

The day for the trial had not been fixed, and the sheriff had not sent any summonses for those at the ranche to attend.

Osmond was able to get up, to sit

about the house, or lounge under the trees in the garden.

His illness had reduced him to a state of attenuation, but he gradually began to put on flesh, through the liberal diet supplied him by Helen's kindness.

Jack and the other cowboys were very busy, as it was the season for branding the calves with Bunyard's mark.

It was impossible to prevent cattle straying occasionally, and joining other herds.

At stated times the owners of herds, within a considerable extent of territory, held what is called a round-out.

A place was selected, to which every cattle owner drove his beasts, and each one searched among the lot for any stray cows or steers he had lost.

These were easily distinguished by the brand on the hide.

By this means each recovered his own, and so things went on for another year, when a fresh round-out was held.

The calm that reigned at Mowbray's Ranche was not to continue long.

On a Sunday morning, the only day of rest the hard-worked cowboys were able to enjoy, Jack was sitting outside Snell's with Warner.

They were waiting for the stage to Brazos, which they expected about eleven.

They anticipated some intelligence respecting Felton's trial.

It was about time the case was set down for hearing.

At the usual time, the stage drove up, and the driver, throwing the reins on his horses' backs, began to look up his cases and parcels.

There were some dry-goods for Helen, a case of whisky for MacTavish, and a variety of articles for Snell.

The stage contained only one passenger, a middle-aged man, rather grey, close-shaven, thin, short, with a cunning face like a weasel's.

His manner was consequential, he spoke quickly, and was dressed in a black suit, with a tightly-buttoned frock coat, and a high silk hat, both rather the worse for wear.

"This is Mowbray's Ranche, I presume?" he exclaimed, addressing Jack.

"Yes, all there is of it at present," replied Jack.

"Small place—eh?"

"Very. But we hope to grow larger in time."

"My name is Perks, sir," said the little man—"Perks, the lawyer. I have come all the way from Warwick, England, on a very special mission."

"Indeed!" cried Jack, in surprise. "I am from that town."

"What name, may I enquire?"

"Hardwick, son of the stationer in High Street."

"Ha!" said Perks, as his countenance fell, "I have heard of you. Bad boy! ran away, like young Lord Melbury."

"Are you after him?"

"Hush! Reward! One thousand pounds! Hope to get it, and expenses paid by his mother."

"Too late, Mr. Perks," answered Jack. "I have found him. The reward is mine."

The lawyer opened his mouth and gasped for breath.

"Halves!" he stammered.

"Not a shilling! Lord Melbury is in my care now, and would have been on his way home had he not met with an accident."

"Anything serious?"

"No, he is recovering. But how did you track him here?" asked Jack.

"Most curious thing out," replied Perks. "Lady Melbury sent for me, and put the case in my hands unreservedly. I traced the boy to Liverpool, and from there to New Orleans. There I lost him."

"Well?"

"I was advised to take a tour through the cattle-raising region of north-east Texas, as there was a rage among English youths to be cowboys. Strange taste for a young nobleman; but here I am."

"Then you did not know Osmond was here?"

"No more than Adam; came on spec," replied Perks.

"You've struck it without much trouble."

"Thank the Lord! Beastly country! Want to go home. I shall take his lordship with me."

"Certainly; but the reward must be paid to me."

"Humph! Give me a third. I ought to have a third."

"No; get what you can out of the mother."

"I'll fight you in the law courts, as sure as I'm a lawyer—smother me, if I don't!" cried Perks.

"His lordship is my friend," said Jack, "and will protect my interests."

"Pshaw! What do you know about law? But the inner man cries 'Cupboard!' Where can I get refreshments?"

"In the saloon."

"Humph! name of Snell. Keeps the 'Dun Cow.' Good sign. I'll go in."

The lawyer entered the saloon just as Snell was coming out, and was informed that he would be attended to directly Snell had exchanged a few words with the driver of the stage.

"Mornin', boss!" exclaimed the driver. "Heard any news?"

"Not an item, Sam," was the reply.

"I did not know but what the post might have brought it, but s'pose not, as it only happened night before last."

"What is it—president dead?"

"No, sirree; worse nor that. The darned hard-shelled road-agent's broke gaol."

"Felton!"

"That's the skunk's name; he's scooted with three convicts, after killing four of the warders."

"Did all get off?"

"Yes; Felton and a Spaniard named Lourada, who murdered a woman, in for life; Eddowes, bank robber, in for fifteen years; and Claxton, forger, in for ten. Nobody knows where they have gone—no trace, no sign."

"Jerusalem! that's bad news," replied Snell. "I'd as soon have heard tell of an earthquake."

Jack and Warner held their breath with amazement.

Felton at large with other desperadoes!

The air was full of danger again.

CHAPTER XIV.

COWBOYS AT THEIR PRANKS—PERKS, THE LAWYER, SHOWS THE INNOCENCE OF HIS DISPOSITION.

WHEN Snell had heard the startling news which Sam, the stage-driver, had to tell him, he conducted Mr. Perks, the lawyer, into his saloon to give him such creature comforts as he was able to supply at short notice.

Mr. Perks, who was a thorough man of business, and sharp at driving a bargain, arranged for board and lodging during his stay at Mowbray's Ranche.

Jack and Warner returned to Mac-Tavish's house to impart the intelligence respecting Perk's arrival and the escape of Felton and the other desperadoes.

MacTavish and Helen were sitting in the parlour, looking over the stockbook, as they had determined to send a thousand head of cattle to market next week.

There was a demand for steers for export, and good prices could be realised.

Helen was quite a woman of business.

She knew as well as her father how to take advantage of a turn in the market.

Osmond, with his arm in a sling, was seated at the window.

He looked dreamily out at the flower-spangled garden.

Suddenly Jack rushed into the room.

"News!" he cried. "Such news!"

"Out with it," said MacTavish, helping himself to a pinch of "sneezin'."

"Felton has escaped from prison."

At this announcement a look of blank dismay stole over every face.

"Hoot, toot!" growled MacTavish. "I'm sorry for that."

Osmond turned deathly pale.

He seemed in danger of falling, for he grasped the back of a chair with his trembling hand.

His enemy was at large once more, when he had fancied that he was doomed to expiate his offences on the scaffold.

The only man he feared and hated in the world was free, and would, perhaps, persecute him again.

With an almost breathless interest he listened to hear further particulars.

Jack went on to say that Felton had three accomplices in his gaol-breaking, who had helped him to murder the warders.

Whither those four had gone was entirely a matter of conjecture.

Still there was a strong likelihood of their lurking somewhere on the prairie between Nacogdochee and Mowbray's Ranche.

This was a terrible contingency to contemplate.

When captured, Felton was, of course, deprived of all the money he had upon his person.

Being destitute, he would be driven to his old courses to obtain a living.

"Heaven preserve us!" said Helen. "I shall always be in a state of terror now. What with Dawes being a destitute fugitive, and Felton being at large, I shall never have any peace. Can't we sell out and go East, father?"

"No," replied MacTavish.

"We really are not safe here."

"We must stand our ground."

In spite of her fears, Helen could not refrain from laughing.

"You might seek safety in the cellar," she hazarded.

"Come, come, that's too bad," cried MacTavish. "I'm a man for a' that, and no one shall hurt my chiel."

As he spoke, the Scotchman kissed her affectionately.

"Wake up, Osmond!" exclaimed Jack. "I have some news for you, in addition to what you have heard."

"Indeed! I hope it is good," the young lord replied.

"Your mother, Lady Melbury, has sent a lawyer after you."

"How do you know?"

"He is here; I have just left him."

"At this ranche?"

"Yes, he is having some lunch at Snell's. You will see him shortly; he tracked you to New Orleans, and travelled in this direction on spec. We got into conversation, and I told him you were here; so you will have to go back with Mr. Perks, as he calls himself."

Osmond shuddered.

"Perhaps he is an agent of Felton's," he remarked.

"Impossible; Felton does not know

who you are. Be brave, and dismiss this ruffianly robber and murderer from your mind."

"I cannot."

"This is moral cowardice. You never used to be like it in England."

"Then I had no such person as Felton to terrify me. My head swims. I am going to be ill again."

His face became ghastly white.

If Jack had not caught him he would have fallen.

The corners of his mouth twitched nervously, and he gasped for breath.

"Why did you tell him?" asked Helen.

"It was foolish. I did not stop to think," replied Jack.

At this moment Mr. Perks made his appearance at the door.

"Good day to all," he exclaimed. "Name of Perks, a lawyer."

"Guid morning to you," answered MacTavish. "Jack has told us a' aboot you."

"May I venture to enter without fear of an action for trespass?"

"Freely, mon, freely."

"I thank you. Will you present me to the lady?"

"Wi' pleasure. The liddy is ma daughter, Helen MacTavish. That little chap there is Lord Melbury, of whom you are in search, I hear."

"True. Your servant, madam. What is the matter with the young lord of Kenilworth Hall?"

"Hearing of your coming, from me," replied Jack, "he grew excited, and is about to have a relapse, I fear."

"From what does he suffer?"

"Shot through the arm; it was owing to a quarrel with a cowboy on the prairie."

"Dear heart!" cried Mr. Perks, "dreadful fellows, these cowboys!"

"Not all of them."

"Lord Melbury's is a valuable life. Worth ten thousand a year. He should not be allowed to fight."

"It wasn't his fault."

"I shall make him a ward in Chancery, and get myself appointed guardian by the court," said Mr. Perks, "smother me if I don't."

By this time Osmond was in a dead faint.

With Warner's assistance, Jack carried

him to his bedroom, and laid him down.

They sat by his side until he recovered.

"Leave me here," he said. "I am all right, and shall see you at dinnertime. I only feel weak and dizzy."

"You will not be able to go with the lawyer just yet," remarked Jack.

"Not at present," sighed Osmond.

"To travel in the weak state you are in would kill you. As your friend, I shall not allow it, old fellow."

"Can't you go back with me?"

"I have told you I cannot," answered Jack. "The Old Country will not see me again till I hear of the decease of my stepmother."

"But I will give you the run of my mansion, and a good income as my private secretary."

"A thousand thanks! But I can't accept your offer."

"There is much more attraction here," laughed Warner.

"Helen MacTavish."

"Ah, yes; I see," said Osmond, with a smile, while Jack flushed up to the roots of his hair. "Well, she's a sweet girl. Anyone could love her."

"Dawes did, passionately," observed Warner.

"Confound Dawes!" exclaimed Jack, angrily. "I have settled him. He, at least, will not show his face at this ranche again."

"Don't be so sure of that."

"Bah! who cares for a fellow like that?" observed Osmond. "He is not in the running with Jack. But, I say, old fellow, you will stick to me?"

"Yes."

"I can rely on your support?"

"To the death of one of us."

Osmond held out his emaciated hand, which his foster-brother shook in the warmest manner.

Leaving the invalid, the cowboys returned to the parlour.

Helen had gone to the kitchen to superintend the dinner.

"Jack," exclaimed MacTavish, "it is clear that the young laird canna go on a journey."

"Not for a fortnight, sir," replied Jack.

"That is my opinion, so I have asked Mr. Perks to stay as my guest for the time."

"Very good, sir."

"He need not waste his siller at Snell's. Though if he likes to pay for my glass in return for the puir hospitalitee I can show him, I will na say him nay."

"Whenever you like," replied Perks, cheerily; "I have plenty of money."

"Jack Hardwick!" exclaimed MacTavish.

"Yes, sir."

"Will you please show this gentleman around? And mind to bring him home to dinner at five. We dine at five, Mr. Perks, because of the heat, I wish you to know."

With a polite bow, which would not have disgraced a courtier, MacTavish quitted the room to indulge in a sleep in a hammock, which he had slung under the verandah.

"I want to see all I can, boys," said Perks.

"We're the ones to oblige you, sir," replied Jack.

"Can't find our equals in Texas," remarked Warner.

Mr. Perks smiled blandly.

"Treat me well, and I will reward you handsomely," he said.

"It is a ticklish country, sir," Jack answered, "but we know the ropes. Sit down and help yourself to the governor's whisky while we go and get you a gun."

"What for?" enquired the lawyer.

"Shooting. A gun isn't to toast muffins with."

"No; I am aware of that."

"Leave all to me."

"But, I say—"

"Didn't Mr. MacTavish put you in our hands to show you around?"

"Certainly; but, smother me—"

"Keep quiet and wait; we'll show you fun. Antelope-shooting and—"

"Ah! that's good. Let me kill one. I'm going to write a book about my adventures in Texas."

"We'll keep you posted up to date," said Jack.

"Can't we find the gentleman a ring-tailed screamer?" asked Warner.

"Certainly. We'll try."

"What's that?" enquired Perks.

"A kind of wild cat, sir; very much like the domestic species, but awfully fierce," answered Jack.

"Humph! don't mind the antelope, yet the screamer sounds dangerous; however, I will leave it all to you."

Jack nodded to Warner, and they left the room together.

Mr. Perks was very anxious to see what sport on the prairie was like.

He intended to write a series of sketches, which he would contribute to the *Warwick Mercury* on his return home.

Jack had determined to play him all the tricks he could, for he had taken a dislike to the fussy, consequential lawyer.

This resolve he communicated to Warner, who was in high glee at the prospect.

"We'll take him for a walk," said Jack, "and give him an eye-opener."

"How are you going to begin?"

"We'll start with wild cat shooting," replied Jack, "and then make war on the antelopes."

"But we have neither the one nor the other about here."

"Yes, we have. In the passage is a stuffed antelope. Take it to the clump of trees back of Snell's."

"Oh, I see; and how about the cat?" laughed Warner.

"I can see Miss Helen's in the road, playing with a dead chipmunk."

"If you kill the animal there will be a row."

"Who talked about killing?" asked Jack. "You know everything, don't you?"

"No; I'm only just boiling over with a desire for information."

"Simmer down, then. I shall put blank cartridges in the lawyer's gun. Now, cut along."

Jack took up a single-barrelled breech-loader which had belonged to Mr. Bunyard.

He broke a cartridge in halves, throwing away the shot, and inserted the powder only in the breech.

Then he rejoined Mr. Perks, who took the gun, examined it as critically as he would have done a writ issued from the High Court of Justice, and expressed himself ready to start.

"Remember, I want to see and know all!" he exclaimed.

"You are as bad as the Census, but I'll see you through," Jack replied.

They walked through the garden into the road.

Helen MacTavish's pet cat, a fine, large, sandy-coloured creature, was under a tree, where it had killed a red squirrel or chipmunk.

"There, sir!" whispered Jack, "there's your chance!"

The lawyer looked up at the sky.

"Where?" he demanded.

"A wild cat, sir. Under that tree."

"Am I loaded?"

"The gun is if you aren't. Aim low and fire straight," said Jack.

"Sup—suppose I miss?" stammered Perks.

"Then you must run for it, or you are lost!"

With considerable misgiving as to the result of his shot, Perks presented the gun.

He looked at the cat, and the cat looked at him, as if wondering what he was going to do.

Nervously he pulled the trigger.

The discharge frightened the animal, who darted across the road.

She wanted to seek shelter in the house.

"Run!" shouted Jack.

The cat was, of course, unhurt, but Perks thought he could see the blood dripping, and bolted for his life.

Up the road he ran, not halting till he reached Snell's.

In his wild flight he had thrown down the gun, which Jack picked up, and restored to him.

He took off his hat, and mopped his perspiring brow with a large bandanna handkerchief.

"Better luck next time, sir!" exclaimed Jack. "You peppered the creature finely."

"It is my first try at a wild cat," replied Perks. "Of course allowance must be made."

"They are very hard to kill."

"Is—is—the beast gone?" enquired Perks, anxiously.

"Yes, sir; I saw it scooting over the prairie as if it were a lightning express on an air line."

"I wish I had bagged the brute, because I would have had it stuffed to take to Warwick."

"You may have better luck with the antelopes."

"Ah, yes; lead the way. Bring on your antelopes. I long to shoot one of those creatures."

Jack conducted him to the clump of trees, near which Felton had shot the unfortunate cowboy, Tanner.

Warner immediately made his appearance.

"Oh, here you are!" he said. "I was looking everywhere for you. Was it you who shot just now?"

"Mr. Perks shot at a wild cat," Jack answered, slipping a cartridge into the gun.

"Kill anything?"

"Not quite, but the cat went off hopping mad. Mr. Perks is an elegant shot."

"He can try his 'prentice hand on an antelope. I saw one grazing back of the clump," exclaimed Warner.

"Is that so?"

"You bet! This way, boss; I'll show you."

Warner led the way cautiously.

Every now and then he stopped and held up his hand; then he would sink on his hands and knees, peer over the long grass, and pretend to listen.

"What shall I aim at?" asked the lawyer.

"At the deer, of course," replied Jack; "you don't want to hit a tree."

"Yes, yes," answered Perks, testily, "I know that. You fellows want to be too smart."

"Hit where you like; antelopes are easily killed. Fire directly you have covered your quarry," said Jack.

"Right; I'll do the trick this time."

Warner at last led Perks to the spot where he had placed the stuffed antelope.

It was standing erect.

"Ha! good!" ejaculated the lawyer.

"Now's your time!" cried Jack. "Chip in, sir."

"I fully intend to do so, my dear boy."

"He's got his back turned, and can't see you."

"Leave me alone; I'll whip a summons into him, and sign judgment in less than no time."

"Bravo! You can do it."

"Trust me; it will be a case of execution immediately and no appeal. Look out!"

Perks fired, and as the mimic antelope was only a few yards off, he could not help hitting it.

The charge of shot knocked it over.

"Dead for a ducat!" shouted Perks. "I'm the man to do it; there isn't even a kick left in him. I will secure my prize."

"Let Warner do that," replied Jack.

"Very well. Take it to the house, my boy. We will have antelope steaks for supper, like real prairie hunters."

Perks was very well satisfied with his exploit, which he flattered himself would make a sensation in Warwick.

Already he fancied he saw it in print, in the colums of the local paper.

Suddenly he heard a peculiar rattling noise in the grass not far from where he stood.

"Look out!" said Jack, "that is a rattlesnake."

"Great Cæsar!" cried the lawyer. "Do you encourage such horrid things?"

"The prairie swarms with them. This one is just warning you to keep out of his way."

"Will they hurt?"

"Their bite is certain death. They strike at the legs."

"Hadn't we better retreat?" asked the lawyer.

"Wouldn't you like to kill this joker first? If so, ply a few shots into him, and blow his head off, or break his back!"

"Right! give me the gun," replied Perks, excitedly.

Giving him the gun, as requested, Jack threw a stone at the snake.

The reptile erected itself in its wrath.

Louder than ever sounded its rattle.

Mr. Perks trembled slightly, but contrived to cover the snake.

He fired, and literally blew its head to pieces.

The body immediately seemed to be transformed into a piece of animated cord, trying to tie itself into knots, and then untie them.

The muscular contortions were singular and terrible to witness.

"There's a lot of life in that snake yet," remarked Jack. "Though its head is gone, it wants to fight. It will die here, but not till the sun goes down."

"Is that a fact?" said Perks, taking out his note-book.

"I have always found it so. This evening I will cut the rattle off for you as a curiosity."

"Do so. Hallo! what's that?"

He saw something in the grass moving to and fro. Levelling his gun, he fired.

Jack ran forward, looked, and burst out laughing.

"What is it?" asked the lawyer.

"I thought it was a prairie dog," Jack answered; "but I see it is a prairie hen, which was sitting on a nest of eggs."

"Have I killed?"

"You have blown the hen and the eggs to smithereens."

"Ah! I'm improving," said Perks, with a smile of satisfaction.

"Considering it was a pot shot, you couldn't very well miss," replied Jack. "Would you like a wing to put in your hat?"

"Well, yes; it will look sportsman-like."

Jack handed him one, which he put in the band of his deerstalker.

"What's the next thing you have in view for me?" continued Perks. "There is plenty of time between this and dinner, you know."

"Suppose you have a cow ride?"

"A what?"

"It's the fashion out here. Everybody rides cows. Come this way."

Just round a corner of the clump a cow was tethered, being kept there for milking purposes.

Jack took the halter off her neck, and told Perks to mount.

"Where's the saddle and bridle?" asked Perks.

"We always ride bare-backed; tuck your feet under the animal, and hang on by the horns."

"That seems curious."

"Ah, many things seem curious in Texas to a stranger, but this is a trained cow."

"It has long horns, and looks somewhat fierce," said Perks, hesitatingly.

"She's as quiet as a lamb, warranted sound, and has no vice. Miss Helen rides her," replied Jack.

"Give me a leg-up. This is quite a novelty, but I'll show you what I can do. Fancy, cows to ride—ah, ah! Queer people these Texans!"

"You'll get on in time, sir."

With Jack's assistance, Mr. Perks did get on, but he very soon came off.

The cow, ordinarily good-natured and docile, resisted the liberty taken with her by a stranger.

She lowered Perks, who rolled off on to the grass.

"Hang the beast!" he cried; "what did she do that for?"

"It's her playful way, sir," answered Jack.

"I don't like such games, but I am not going to be beaten. Push me up again.

"All right; up you go."

This time the lawyer got a firm grip of each horn.

He stuck his knees into the animal's sides, and tried his hardest to hold on.

The cow swished her tail as if a legion of flies had attacked her; she bucked and jumped.

It was all of no avail.

The lawyer had effected an entry, as it were, and obstinately refused to be ejected.

Finding that she was mastered, the cow got frightened, and started off in the direction of MacTavish's back garden.

It was here that Helen milked her.

Jack tore down a bough from a maple tree, and began to belabour the animal's flanks.

"Hi, hi!" he shouted. "Off and away. Hi!"

The cow grew maddened at this strange treatment, which was different from anything she had been accustomed to.

The garden-gate was open.

Smarting under Jack's blows, the animal dashed into the garden, prancing about, and playing sad havoc.

The most promising vegetables were trampled under foot.

Mr. Perks was becoming alarmed.

He would have jumped off, only he was afraid he might hurt himself.

Warner heard the noise, and joined in the chase.

MacTavish and Helen ran into the yard.

Mauma, the coloured woman, was baking a huge sirloin of beef, and came to the open window of the kitchen with a big spoon in her hand.

"La sakes!" cried Mauma, "here's a man running away with one of our cows."

Jack and Warner dashed into the corn-patch, and hid themselves.

They abandoned the lawyer to his fate.

He rushed upon his doom.

"Hey, mon alive, where are you coming to?" cried MacTavish.

"I don't know, smother me if I do!" replied Perks.

"Stop at once, you fule!"

"I can't; wish I could."

"The man's gone clean daft," cried MacTavish.

Like Johnny Gilpin, the lawyer continued his wild career.

To the consternation of old woolly-headed Mauma, the cow went direct towards the kitchen-window.

"Keep off!" she exclaimed. "I don't want no cows here!"

Perks tugged at the horns, but with no result.

The cow plunged through the window, knocking Mauma down, and Mr. Perks was shot on to the table.

A pudding and sundry other things were upset, the table rolled over, and the lawyer was pinned between it and the wall.

"Help!" shrieked Perks. "Police! Murder! Help!"

"Lor' a mussy!" cried Mauma; "the world's coming to an end, I guess."

The cow was the only sensible one in the party.

Feeling that it was rid of its burden, it got up, and looked round.

It gave vent to a prolonged "moo."

Then it darted towards the window, to return to its verdant pastures.

Unfortunately for himself MacTavish was coming in by the same way.

He and the cow met.

As a matter of course, MacTavish got the worst of the encounter.

He went down, and the cow went over him.

When the animal had disappeared round the corner of the yard, tail erect, and head down, MacTavish was a very considerably trampled upon kind of man.

The lawyer had got up and was standing with his back against the wall,

He drew his breath with difficulty.

MacTavish advanced towards him fiercely, shaking his fist.

The overturned table was between the irate Scotchman and the English lawyer.

That alone prevented a breach of the peace.

"Now, sir," exclaimed MacTavish, "will you have the kindness to explain to me what this means?"

"It isn't my fault," replied the lawyer. "I assure you I am not to be blamed in this affair."

"What on earth did you want to ride the coo for?" roared MacTavish. "It makes me wax wroth!"

"Isn't it the custom of the country?"

"Custom be bothered! We raise cows, sir; we don't ride them in Texas!"

"Dear me! Jack of Warwick told me you did."

"He was fooling you, mon," replied MacTavish, "and a mon of your years should have known it."

"I apologise. It sha'n't occur again, smother me if it shall!"

"If it does there'll be a sick man in Mowbray's Ranche, so I tell you. I can't stand too much of this sort of thing."

"My dear sir, take a pinch of snuff."

"Not of your offering. Go to Snell's and have your dinner. I want no more of you."

"Nor I of you. I can be quite as independent as you, Mr. MacTavish!"

"Get out, or I'll help you!"

"Take care, sir; I'm a lawyer. Lay a finger on me, and I'll bring an action for assault in the court at Nacogdochee."

"You mean hound! I'll—"

"Forbear! I'm peacefully inclined. Let me go. I have no desire to stay. You shall not be troubled with me again, unless I come to see young Lord Melbury, whom I am going to take home with me as soon as he is well enough," said Perks.

"You are welcome to the boy. I do not want him."

"Then I will say good day, and thank you for your hospitality."

Bowing low and smiling sarcastically, Perks edged round the table, and went out by the door.

Outside the garden-gate he found Jack and Warner waiting for him.

The other cowboy, White, was spending his time in Snell's saloon, making himself happy, after a fashion, with bad whisky and worse tobacco.

"You rascals!" cried the lawyer,

" you have been enjoying yourselves at my expense ! "

" The cow ran away with you, sir," replied Jack. " It is a very high-spirited animal."

" So I should think, when it is goaded. However, I forgive you ; but don't do it again."

" No, sir."

" I want to see life on the plains."

" Aren't we showing it you ? "

" Well, yes; frankly, I must admit you are, but that cow-ride was going a little too far, smother me if it wasn't ! "

" Come right out on the prairie."

" That's just what I want to do. Lead the way; I'll follow. MacTavish will have no more to do with me. I shall have to stay at the saloon till Osmond, Lord Melbury, gets well."

" He's an awfully mean man," said Warner. " Don't vex yourself about him."

" I don't, but I have not been treated well," replied the lawyer. " He has insulted me."

" Oh, pshaw ! He'd do that to any-one to save the price of the victuals," rejoined Warner.

Jack gave the lawyer the gun, and they walked on to the prairie, going by Snell's and the clump of trees.

As they got to the clump Jack called a halt.

" I guess," he said, " we had better take some light refreshments with us ; a chap soon gets thirsty on the prairie."

He went away, and procuring an empty catawba wine bottle, filled it with vinegar and water, adding a little salt.

Some slices of dry, hard bread completed his preparations.

Helen saw what he was doing, and burst out laughing.

" You are going to play some tricks on that unhappy lawyer ! " she exclaimed; " I know you are."

" He is going to write a book about Texas," replied Jack.

" And you are supplying him with his facts."

" Exactly so. He wants to see every-thing, don't you know, smother me if he doesn't ! " said Jack, mimicking the lawyer.

" What a dislike father has taken to him."

" There isn't much to like about the fellow; he is all self. I'll tell you all about it when I come back," answered Jack.

He hastened away, and rejoined his companions.

They rounded the clump, having the boundless prairie before them.

On the left was a solitary pine tree.

Warner saw something which looked like a sheet of paper nailed to the trunk.

He called Jack's attention to it.

With a quick step and a fluttering heart our hero walked to the tree.

On the paper, written in pencil, were the words—

" Not dead yet.—-FELTON."

" What does that mean ? " asked Perks.

" Just this," answered Jack : " our lives are not safe."

" Why not ? '

" The road-agent has lost no time in coming here. Perhaps he and his com-panions are lurking somewhere about."

" There is no cover for them on the prairie," observed Warner.

" It is very serious," said Jack. " Don't say anything at the ranche, either of you."

He tore the paper down, crumpled it up, and threw it away.

A sound like mocking laughter pro-ceeded from the clump of trees.

It was easy enough for anyone to hide there.

Between the trunks was a dense jungle-like growth of cat-briars, black-berry canes, and climbing, interlacing vines.

" Did you hear that ? " asked Warner.

" What was it ? " queried Perks.

" I will soon find out," replied Jack.

Snatching the gun from the lawyer's hand, he ran to the clump, and boldly plunged into the undergrowth.

In a minute he was lost to sight.

Warner and Perks breathlessly waited to hear some sound.

All remained still as death.

Five minutes elapsed.

It seemed an age to the expectant watchers.

Suddenly there was a loud report.

" By gosh ! " cried Warner, " Jack's found something, you bet."

Presently the cracking of boughs and twigs was heard.

A human form was seen coming out of the clump.

But it was not Jack.

In a moment the figure leapt over a bush, landed on the grass, and darted away over the prairie.

"Dawes!" shouted Warner.

The cowboy, for it was he, made no answer.

He was as fleet of foot as an Indian.

Warner hesitated to give chase as he was unarmed, and Dawes soon put a considerable distance between them.

A minute later, and Jack made his appearance.

Pursuit was now hopeless.

"Confound the fellow!" he exclaimed, "he crept through the bushes like a hare, while I got stuck in a mass of vines."

"Did you see who it was?" enquired Warner.

"Not until I had fired. I saw a figure crouching, and thinking it was Felton, I let fly."

"To kill him?"

"Why, certainly. I would not hesitate to shoot that rascal outright whenever I might meet him. No jury would convict me."

"You're right. No Texas jury, anyway."

"Somehow Dawes saw the barrel of the gun gleam in the sunlight, and made a dive. I missed him; that's all there is to say," concluded Jack.

He paused and looked after the retreating figure.

The cowboy was nearly out of sight.

It was clear that Dawes had nailed the warning paper to the tree.

But how did he know of Felton's escape from gaol?

Had he met the road-agent and fraternised with him?

Or had he come to the ranche to steal food and water, and merely posted the placard out of bravado?

It might be a trick to frighten the dwellers at the ranche.

On the other hand, he might have been sent by Felton as a special messenger to strike terror to their hearts.

"He is gone at last," remarked Warner.

"Ay," replied Jack gravely; "but he may come back and bring others with him. I know not what to think."

"Someone ought to be on the watch at night."

"You and I will take it in turns," said Jack; "we need not say anything about it."

"Will this affair, which I do not understand, stop our shooting expedition on the prairie?" asked Perks.

"Not in the least. I promised to show you some sport, and I will."

"Thank you. I want to see all I can. Life in the wilds is exciting. Smother me, if I shall not be able to write a stunning book!"

"It will not be my fault if you do not."

"I have talent and power as a descriptive writer. Can't I draw up a brief or a declaration!"

Jack loaded the gun again, handed it to the lawyer, and made another start.

This time they met with no interruption.

Jack's mind, however, was filled with gloomy forebodeings.

He had a presentiment of coming evil.

Felton would, no doubt, strike a blow at Mowbray's Ranche, but how and when the blow would fall he could not tell.

He walked along with an affectation of cheerfulness.

Occasionally he whistled, but it was not for want of thought.

After going a few miles they came to a spot where a cow had died some weeks previously.

The buzzards had picked the flesh off the bones. A strange and startling sight was the skeleton to Mr. Perks, who at once took out his book and made a note of it.

"Skeleton of a buffalo, I suppose?" he asked.

"Oh yes; put it down buffalo," replied Jack.

Mr. Perks was unaware of the fact that the buffalo had long ago been driven out of the States.

They were only to be found now in small herds in the remote territories.

A couple of buzzards were sitting near the quarry.

They had been picking at pieces of the skin, which had fallen to the ground.

Hearing voices, they flapped their heavy wings.

They had a gorged and tired look about them.

"Ha, birds!" exclaimed Perks. "What are they?"

"Wild turkeys, sir," replied Jack.

"Good eating?"

"Rather! We consider them a great delicacy. Drop one! Do not let them escape!"

The birds rose lazily in the air.

Mr. Perks fired.

His prowess was rewarded, as one of the buzzards fell, badly wounded.

Jack rushed forward and dexterously seized it by the wings and head.

With a jerk he wrung its neck.

This feat was, in reality, a clever one, for a wounded buzzard will fight for life with beak and claws.

"What are we to do now?" asked the lawyer.

"Dine. Warner will get grass and sage-brush for a fire. I will pluck the bird. Then cook and eat," said Jack.

"I have long wished to taste wild turkey."

"Now's your chance; it may never occur again."

"True. I will avail myself of your kindness."

"I have a bottle of catawba wine for you, and some bread," Jack added.

"Excellent!" cried Mr. Perks.

Warner built up the fire, and Jack plucked the breast of the buzzard, which he cut off and put on the embers to cook.

"Aren't you going to have any?" asked the lawyer.

"We have it so often that we are tired of it," answered Jack, throwing away the remainder of the bird.

In a short time the meat was broiled, and presented to Perks, with a knife, as well as the stale bread, and the so-called catawba.

The flesh of the buzzard is very rank, and generally repulsive.

No man could eat it unless he were starving; and then he could not relish it.

Perks bit the tough unsavoury stuff, and made wry faces over it.

At last he put it down.

"Don't you like it, sir?" asked Jack.

"Can't go it," answered Perks, "smother me if I can! Hand me the wine, please."

The bottle was uncorked and given to him.

He put the neck of it in his mouth and took a few gulps.

"Ouch!" he cried, "what horrid wine; it's worse than the wild turkey!"

"The gentleman does not know what's good," said Warner, who with difficulty refrained from laughing.

"Don't I, by George! That's an insult, smother me if it isn't!" indignantly retorted the lawyer.

"Wild turkey and catawba wine are luxuries in Texas," Jack observed.

"You can keep them. Oh dear, how ill I feel! I—I want to go back."

"Will you have a cow-ride?" asked Jack.

"No, no; I've had enough of that. No more tricks," replied Perks. "I'll sue you for damages in the Supreme Court. Oh, how bad I feel!"

The lawyer pressed his hands to his waistcoat and groaned.

Beads of perspiration stood on his forehead.

"We'll leave you to yourself," said Jack.

"No, no; don't leave me!"

"You are only a few miles from the ranche. It is impossible to get lost."

"If he does, a night on the prairie will not hurt him," remarked Warner.

"Unfeeling rogues!" cried the lawyer; "can you abandon me to my fate?"

"Make a note of it."

"You have poisoned me."

"Put it in your book," said Jack. "You wanted points about Texas; now you've got some."

"Hardened wretches!" whined Perks.

"Good-bye, lawyer; see you later," said Warner.

Perks was now rolling on the ground in an agony he could not control.

"Would you leave me to perish in this deserted wild?" cried the lawyer. "I did not think it of you."

Jack turned a deaf ear to his supplications.

"Take up the gun," he said. "Mr. Perks won't require it; before the morning he will be dead, according to his account."

Warner shouldered the breechloader, and coolly walked off, followed by Jack.

"WITH A FEARFUL SCREAM HE PLUNGED INTO THE DARK ABYSS."

The two were anxious to get back to the ranche, owing to the unexpected appearance of Dawes.

It was incumbent upon them to be on the look-out.

At any moment a catastrophe might befall them.

As for Perks, they knew that his internal pains were only caused by the carrion flesh and the vinegar they had beguiled him into taking.

The qualms would soon pass over.

Perks rolled on the grass groaning and whining. He watched the forms of the cowboys till they became indistinct.

His head swam, and a mist came over his eyes, as if he had taken the ague.

Gradually his pains stopped, and he fell asleep.

The sun began to decline, its fierce power was ebbing away, and a gentle breeze arose, making the prairie-grass wave gracefully.

The lawyer was aroused by a strange voice saying—

"Hallo! Say, stranger, where do you hail from?"

Mr. Perks got up, rubbed his eyes, and recognised the man he had seen escape from the clump at Mowbray's Ranche.

"You're called Dawes, aren't you?" he asked.

"Never mind what my name is," replied the cowboy. "I suppose you have heard about me, but you can call me Smith or Jones, if you like. The question is, have you any money in your clothes?"

"Money!"

"Yes. Didn't I speak plain enough?"

"I never travel with money."

"Bosh! You can't travel without it. Turn out your pockets."

"Are you a—a robber?"

"Something of that sort. See here, I've got a persuader in the shape of a knife."

"Do—don't kill me!" Mr. Perks cried. "Here is my purse; take it."

He reluctantly tendered Dawes his purse, which contained a substantial sum.

"What are you doing in this section?" enquired Dawes.

"Pleasuring. I'm an English gentleman, travelling for health and a knowledge of foreign countries."

Dawes put his finger to his nose.

"Too thin," he said. "You are after that boy they call Osmond, at Mac-Tavishs's. I've heard something."

"You are very intelligent. I like you," replied Perks.

"That's more than I do you."

"Alas! everybody in this country seems to have a prejudice against me!"

"Pshaw! I've been listening at the ranche, and I know you are a kind of kerbstone lawyer, with your office in your hat; and you are after Osmond."

"Suppose I am—what then?" said Perks, making a determined stand.

"Who and what is he?"

This question was a poser; for Perks did not know how far it would be safe to answer.

Dawes was undoubtedly enquiring with an object.

He drew a knife from his belt.

"Do you want to make acquaintance with this?" he asked.

"No, no! Don't do anything desperate," replied the lawyer.

"Speak out, then. Who is this boy?"

"Don't you really know?"

"If I did I should not ask."

"Well, it's a great secret; he's the young Lord Melbury, who has run away from home."

"Has he got money?"

"Heaps of it. There is a thousand pounds reward offered to anyone who will take him to his mother, in Warwick, England."

Dawes smiled.

"I suppose you think you are going to have that?" he asked.

"Certainly. I have come out here after him, and luckily found him, so the reward is fairly mine."

"You said it would be paid to anyone who took him back?"

"Yes; that is so."

"If I took him home I guess I should be entitled to it as much as you."

"Eh?—what?" cried Perks. "I don't like that, smother me if I do!"

He began to fear he had said too much.

"What's to prevent me from claiming it?" asked Dawes.

"Nothing, save a sense of honour. I told you it in secrecy — strict secrecy."

"Honour don't count in this deal."

"Well, let me go home," said Perks. He made a step forward.

Dawes gave him a blow on the back of the head which stretched him on the ground.

Brandishing his knife the cowboy stood over him.

His attitude was so threatening that the lawyer feared his life was in danger.

CHAPTER XV.

A TIMELY RESCUE—THE OLD MINER—A DARK DEED.

Mr. Perks was helpless before his unscrupulous assailant.

He held up his hand, crying in a tremulous voice—

"Forbear. I am a man of peace, and have done you no harm, nor do I wish to do you any. Why should you injure me?"

"I've no use for you now," replied Dawes.

"In what way have I been of service to you?"

"By telling me about young Lord Melbury—that is to say, Osmond, up at Mowbray's Ranche. I can see my way to getting more than the thousand pounds reward offered by his mother."

"How so?"

"The boy is a mine of wealth."

"Is that why you are going to kill me?" asked the lawyer.

"Yes. You shall not have him. I can see my way to living like a gentleman out of him, after what you have told me. I'm tired of being a cowboy; it's hard work and small pay."

As he spoke these words, Dawes stooped.

Perks could see the knife raised over the region of his heart.

"Stop!" he cried. "Do not commit a crime, the memory of which may embitter your whole life."

"I want to make money out of the boy," replied Dawes; "so do you. There is not room in the scheme for both of us."

"Yes, there is."

"I can't see it."

"We'll go halves," said Perks, eagerly. "Put up that horrid-looking knife, and listen to reason."

"Not for me."

"I'll guarantee you plenty of money."

"No, no; all or none."

"Stay!" urged Perks. "Remember that Jack of Warwick knows all about Osmond."

Dawes laughed contemptuously.

"Jack!" he cried in a tone of scorn; "we will soon settle him and his friends."

"Who do you mean by 'we'?"

"That's my business," replied Dawes. "I shall put you out of the way first, and square accounts with the others later."

"Stop—forbear! There is such a thing as retribution."

"Stop talking."

"But—"

"I have no time to listen to your nonsense. Die!"

Just as the knife was about to descend a loud voice alarmed the cowboy, who trembled violently.

It came from behind him.

"Fair play!" it said. "Never strike a man when he is down. No, sirree."

Dawes turned round with the quick momentum of a teetotum.

He was confronted by an old greyhaired man, who had him fully covered with a Remington breechloader.

"No tricks," continued the man; "no fooling; drop that knife of yours, and talk business."

"Suppose I refuse?"

"Then I fire—sure pop!"

"Who are you?"

"I'm old Dave, the placer miner, pretty well known in this section as the most extraordinarily unlucky cuss that ever walked."

"I've heard of you," said Dawes.

"Very likely. One of your cowboys met me at Hanging Man's Holding, when the Comanches were about," was the reply.

"You ain't no good, and I don't want you to interfere with me."

"Drop your knife, I say, or—"

Dave cocked his rifle with an ominous click.

In a moment Dawes let his bowie-knife fall.

He knew that to refuse to do so would condemn himself at once to death.

Old Dave advanced to the spot, picked up the knife, and placed it in his belt.

"That will do," he remarked; "got anything else?"

"No," growled the cowboy.

"Nary shooter?"

"Don't I tell you I ain't heeled in any way. Darn your old thick head! if I wasn't at your mercy, I'd have shot you down!"

"Very good."

"I feel kinder mad to think I've been outwitted by an old played-out placer miner," said Dawes—"a mean white who won't work."

"Who says so?"

"Why did you leave the towns to come here and look for lumps of gold on the surface of the earth?"

"To get rich quickly."

"You haven't done it yet. Ha, ha!" sneered Dawes.

"You lie!" cried the old miner, sternly. "I found a lump to-day which will make me independent for life."

"Did you—honest?"

"I was a fool to tell you; but, you reptile, you can't do me much harm. It is true that I struck it rich this morning, soon after sunrise, and there is more where the lump I've got came from."

"More!" repeated Dawes, thoughtfully. "Where?"

"Close around Hanging Man's Holding. I'm camping out there now. It's my headquarters for the time. And now, tell me, what's your quarrel with this man? I'll be judge between you. If he's robbed you, he shall make amends; but I'll have no letting of blood."

Mr. Perks had made no remark during this colloquy.

When Dave spoke as he did, however, he sprang up.

His manner, from being despondent, was confident and hopeful.

"I've got a right to state my own case," he now exclaimed: "and, first tendering you my thanks for your timely interference, I will."

"Proceed," replied old Dave. "I guess I am master of the situation—eh, cowboy?"

"I give in," growled Dawes.

"Take a back seat, then, or take yourself off altogether."

"I can do that."

"Do it mighty quick, then, or I shall be under the painful necessity of expediting your movements."

"Perdition to you for interfering with me!" retorted Dawes; "but I'll get even with you."

"Do you dare to threaten me?"

There was no answer.

"Darn your hide! if you talk back to me, I'll drop you in your tracks. Git!"

Dawes knew that if he did not hurry away he would be shot without further notice.

Muttering to himself, the cowboy stalked across the prairie.

Old Dave now turned his attention to the English lawyer.

"Say, stranger, you're in luck," remarked the miner.

"My dear sir," replied the lawyer, "I am deeply indebted to you. In what way I can thank you I scarcely know."

"I don't want money, and I don't want help, so the mere saying of your being grateful is quite enough. I guess you hail from Mowbray's Ranche—eh?"

"I do."

"Are you going back, or will you spend the night with me at my place?"

Mr. Perks sat down on the grass and placed his hands on his waistcoat.

This movement indicated that there was a new and intense pain in that region.

"Have you been poisoned?" asked the old miner.

"I feel like it," groaned Mr. Perks. "These cowboys have done nothing but play tricks on me all day."

"Trust them for that."

"It was the wild turkey and the catawba wine they gave me that settled the business."

"What?"

Perks pointed to the bit of meat he had thrown on the ground, and to the half-empty bottle.

Old Dave carefully smelt and sampled the two.

"Well, I swar!" he cried. "Where do you hail from? You surely were not raised in this country."

"I'm from England."

"Gosh! If I didn't think you were a Britisher. You'll have to tell me your story; but I can tell you that you've been eating buzzard, and drinking vinegar and water."

"I have no particular story to relate," exclaimed the lawyer. "A boy ran away from home; his mother offered a reward, and I have found him; he is not very well just now, but when he is recovered I shall take him home, and receive the money."

"Did you let on to the cowboy about this?"

"I did, unfortunately."

"Ah! I see it all now," cried old Dave. "He wants to take the boy back to his mother, collar the money, and leave you out in the cold."

"Precisely," replied Perks.

"You are safe with me. Say which you will do—come to my place, or return to the ranche?"

Mr. Perks shook his head.

"I'm so bad," he answered, "that I do not think I can do either at present."

"Can't you crawl a few miles leaning on my arm?"

"Many thanks, my friend, but it is impossible. I am suffering from internal pains, which affect my limbs," responded the lawyer.

"That's kinder aggravating! What's to be done?"

"Leave me here. If I don't turn up by morning, Jack of Warwick is sure to look me up."

"Well," said Dave, good-naturedly, "if it's a case of camping out, I shall stay by you."

Perks endeavoured to dissuade him from his intention, but he remained obdurate, holding that there was danger to be apprehended from Dawes.

In this conjecture he was quite correct, for the cowboy had not retired to any great distance.

He had hidden himself in a patch of long, reedy grass.

From this advantageous position he could watch the movements of the two men without himself being observed.

Dave had some dried meat in his pocket, with which he appeased his hunger; a little keg slung over his shoulder contained water.

This was indispensable when making long marches on the prairie.

Perks gladly availed himself of some of this supper, and gradually the feeling of nausea passed off.

Darkness had now fallen, and it was too late to think of travelling.

"If you feel drowsy," exclaimed Dave, "don't be squeamish about saying so. I kin keep my eyes open."

"It's rather hard on you," replied Perks. "I am a perfect stranger, but if ever you come to Warwick ask for Lawyer Perks, and I'll give you a welcome that shall be a return for your kindness. If I don't, smother me—that's a fact!"

"I don't want no thanks," said Dave, "and it ain't rough on me neither, old pard."

"You like to sleep occasionally, I suppose?"

"Oh, yes; I ain't saying anything about that. No sleep ño man, as the saying is; but just now I want to sit and think."

"That is not bad business, always provided that your thoughts are of a pleasant character."

"Mine are that, you bet!" cried old Dave, whose wrinkled face was wreathed with smiles.

"I am sincerely glad to hear it. My mind is contented, too. When I get back to England I shall be some hundreds of pounds richer than when I started, and I shall have had a nice trip to boot."

"Mayhap I'll come and see you in the Old Country next fall," said the miner, thoughtfully. "You heard me brag as I'd found gold?"

"Yes. You mentioned the fact in the presence of Dawes."

"It's no idle boast of a vain old fool. There's a bit of ground not far from Hanging Man's Holding that literally swarms with nuggets and dust. My only trouble is to know how to get the gold to Nacogdochee."

"You must have a horse."

"Yes. I reckon I'll have to do a horse trade afore long. You see, stranger, I've struck it rich, and I'm afraid lest someone will come in and jump my claim."

"I won't say a word," remarked Perks.

"It ain't a man like you I should be afraid of, but those cowboy chaps might attempt to best me out of it. Great Scott! wouldn't I shoot free if I saw any galoot prospecting around my find!"

"Get all you can to a banker."

"That's my intention, boss. I'll sell my gold and bank the money. In a few months I shall be a made man."

Perks congratulated him upon his success, and, pillowing his head on his arm, went to sleep.

The miner sat up, with his rifle resting on his knees, ready for immediate use.

In his belt were a pistol and a knife, for, though he did not live in the midst of alarms, he never knew when he might be attacked.

Dave had not always been a miner.

It was only within the last few years that he had quitted the city and its busy whirl for the quiet, contemplative life of the rolling prairie.

He had a history, as such men usually have.

It was the old story of a doting husband and a faithless wife.

Dave had killed the man who destroyed his happiness. The jury had acquitted him; he plunged into a reckless course, and ultimately, half mad and wholly ruined, he bought a pick and a spade.

Going west from Baltimore, which had been his home, he came to Texas.

His toil and suffering had made him very keen as to the value of money.

Now he had found gold, the fact absorbed his whole soul.

He fancied himself travelling like a prince in Europe, and revelling in every enjoyment that money can purchase.

It was a dark night, only a few stars being visible.

Dave chuckled and talked to himself, building castles in the air.

He was all unconscious of a snake in the grass which had crept close up to him.

Taking advantage of the darkness, Dawes had approached the man without being observed.

He was determined not to let Perks return to Mowbray's Ranche.

That would have spoiled all his plans.

What these plans were we shall soon see.

Dawes had heard all that the miner had said about his finding gold, and his prospects.

Why should he not take to himself this new source of wealth?

With respect to the miner, he cared little whether or not there was one old man the less in the world.

This view extended as much to the lawyer as to the miner; but Dawes had thought better of killing the former.

When driven away by Jack of Warwick, he had walked away until he was in a fainting condition.

His staggering limbs almost refused to support his body.

At this critical moment, when he was near the Devil's Gap, he encountered a man who was on horseback.

He wore a mask of black crape.

It was Felton.

The road-agent, who had so recently escaped from gaol, asked the cowboy some questions, the replies to which let him know that Dawes was banished from the ranche, and panted for revenge; that Osmond was still there, and suffering from illness.

Placing the exhausted cowboy on his horse, Felton conveyed him to the well.

Here he was given food and water, and when he had rested, he was sent to the ranche to stick on a tree the notice which Jack had discovered.

Felton had told him to return to the well the next day, where he would meet him.

Having found out all about Mr. Perks's business in relation to Osmond, Dawes considered that it would not be a bad stroke of business to take him to Felton.

The latter could do what he liked with him.

Dawes fancied there was a fortune in the affair for the robber and himself.

But he did not know Felton's character.

Had he done so, he would have shunned him as the bulbul does the black snake.

Being an outcast, he thought it was a capital thing to throw in his lot with the road-agent.

He hoped to be revenged on Jack of Warwick, and to be able to prosecute his suit for Helen MacTavish's hand.

A man like Dawes naturally gravitated towards a ruffian like Felton.

Birds of a feather flock together, simply because they have tastes and motives in common.

All was still on the prairie.

Dawes watched the old miner by the aid of the dim starlight.

He had been deprived of his knife, and his only weapon was a large jagged stone.

Gradually Dave's head began to nod.

A soporific influence was stealing over him.

Forgetting all about his promise to Perks to sit up and watch, he rolled over onto his side.

His rifle still rested on his knees, but his hold upon the butt was only a nerveless grasp.

In short, the man slept.

It wanted about three hours to midnight.

The cowboy crept on his hands and knees to the spot where the miner was reclining.

Raising the jagged stone, he dashed it with all his force on the sleeping man's head.

Again and again he struck him, and old Dave died without being able to utter a word.

So effectually had this dark deed been done, that Mr. Perks was not roused from his slumber.

Dawes possessed himself of the rifle, the revolver, and the knife belonging to the dead man.

"Ha, ha!" he laughed. "I am a match for anyone now. I'll have his gold before long."

Some hours would have to elapse before the day would dawn.

He placed himself by the side of Perks, touching his elbow, so as to be able to feel the slightest movement.

Yet he could not sleep.

He fancied that the old miner was staring at him with lack-lustre eyes, and pointing to a gulf in the earth.

His excited imagination pictured flames and smoke issuing from this unfathomable pit.

At length, unable to rest, nervous and feverish, he got up and dragged the body of old Dave to a distance.

Tearing up grass with his hands, he covered it over.

Then he walked up and down until he was exhausted, when he again placed himself by the side of the lawyer.

Presently he dozed off, and dreamed that the stars had turned into fiery, blood-red darts, which were falling on him, piercing through his flesh, scorching and burning his heart.

He awoke with a start.

Perks, the lawyer, had got him by the arm.

It was broad daylight.

"Ha! old fellow," said Perks, "so you went to sleep, after all. I thought you would not hold out. As for me, I am like a giant refreshed; pains all gone. I can walk to the ranche, and you can go after your gold."

He paused.

"Hullo!" he added. "Bless my soul! it's—it's the cowboy!"

Dawes was wide awake by this time.

He clutched the rifle, and sprang up.

"All right, boss!" he exclaimed. "You've no call to be skeart."

"But—but where's the old miner?"

"Oh, he's cleared out. I came back while you were asleep, and made it up, for I really didn't mean any harm to either of you, so he told me to see you to MacTavish's, and—"

Perks retreated hurriedly.

"I don't believe a word of what you say," he interrupted.

"Don't you?" asked Dawes, coolly.

"You're a lying rascal!"

"Perhaps I'm not so good a hand at telling a lie as a lawyer. Just step out and follow me, or—"

"What?" gasped Perks.

Dawes levelled his pistol at him.

"I'll give you the lead, you darned old fossil!" he replied.

Mr. Perks accepted the situation at once; he was without arms, and yielded to the force of circumstances.

He was rapidly becoming well acquainted with the manners of some of the cowboys of Texas.

"All right," said Perks; "don't shoot. I am not a target, and have a strong objection to being perforated."

"What's that?" asked Dawes.

"Having a hole made in me. Don't you understand the English language?"

"We talk United States in Texas."

"You had an old schoolmaster, named

Noah Webster, who wrote a dictionary for you, and—"

Dawes stamped his foot angrily.

"Stop your fooling," he cried, "and put yourself alongside of me. If you get my mad up I'll plug you!"

"I am willing to go where you like, if you will only spare my life," said Perks. "I have friends at Mowbray's Ranche, and if you injure me—"

"Pshaw! I know all about them.

Come along, or I'll send you to join the miner."

This threat had the desired effect.

Perks shuddered, held his tongue, and walked quietly by the side of the murderous cowboy.

He began to tremble for his life.

He made a vow that, if he got out of this scrape, he would at once quit Texas, and leave Osmond to get back to England the best way he could.

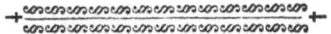

CHAPTER XVI.

THE ROBBER'S CAVE.

PERKS had not gone many yards before he was startled by falling over something.

"Hold up, there!" cried Dawes, as if talking to a horse.

"Oh, Lord! what is it?" asked the lawyer.

His hand had touched something wet.

He withdrew it, and held it up, to find that it was covered with blood.

Then he looked down, and recoiled with horror.

It was the body of the old miner he had stumbled over.

"Horrible!" muttered the lawyer.

Dawes gave him a smart kick.

"Step out!" he exclaimed; "anyone would think it was your funeral instead of the old man's. You ain't got nothing to cry for as yet."

The lawyer continued his journey, but the words "as yet" fell like ice upon his heart.

In a very dejected manner he walked along, expecting that every time the cowboy quickened his pace he intended to offer him some violence.

But he was mistaken.

It is true that Perks's life rested on a thread, but his fate was to be decided by a higher authority than that of Dawes.

A long walk under the perpendicular rays of a scorching sun brought them, about midday, to the well.

Here, according to appointment, Felton was waiting to meet Dawes.

He was lying under a tree, smoking a cigarette, with an air of nonchalance which showed that imprisonment had not subdued his spirit.

The same satanic smile played around his cold, cruel mouth.

His eyes sparkled with the daring wickedness which was always surging in his busy mind.

He sprang up as he saw the cowboy appear.

Somewhat curiously, if not suspiciously, he looked at Perks.

"Who is this person you have with you?" he asked.

"I brought him along as a witness, because I thought you would not believe my tale," replied Dawes.

"No enigmas. Who is he, I ask?"

"I'm a lawyer from England, named Perks," said that individual, promptly.

"Hold your tongue until you are spoken to," cried Felton. "Proceed with your story, Dawes."

"Since I joined your band," the cowboy exclaimed, "I've been on the lookout for a chance to do the firm good."

Felton made a gesture of impatience.

"Cut it short," he interrupted. "Did you post up my notice?"

"Yes; and had a bad scare through Jack of Warwick, who—"

"Hang your talk! What about this lawyer fellow?"

"He is over here after the boy Osmond, who is sick at the ranche."

"Ha! there's a mystery, after all," cried Felton, much interested.

"I should rather think so—a big one, boss!"

"My instincts never deceive me. Something told me not to let that boy go."

"His mother has offered a reward of one thousand pounds for him," continued Dawes.

"She is, then, rich?"

"Considering that he is Lord Melbury, an English peer, up to ten thousand a year, you may well say that."

Felton became greatly excited at this intelligence.

"Incredible!" he cried; "it does not seem possible."

"There!" said Dawes, "I knowed you wouldn't believe it, and that's why I brought old Uncle Perks along. He told me, and he can bear witness. There is money in that boy Osmond, I tell you."

"Is this true, mister?" asked Felton of the lawyer.

"Oh, yes! I'll swear to the truth of every word of the statement," replied the lawyer.

"Can anyone corroborate you?"

"The lad they call Jack of Warwick is able to do so, for Lord Melbury and he are foster-brothers."

"Very good. Inform me, if you please, why the boy came to this far-away country?"

Perks related, in a few words, how Osmond had left Eton, and been coldly received by his father; of the scene between them; Osmond's flight; and the subsequent death of the old nobleman.

He added that he should take the boy back, and claim the offered reward.

"I guess not, mister," replied the road-agent. "I am the captain of a band of robbers; my name, Felton. I shall see to Lord Melbury. You will be lucky if you live to reach England."

Perks had begun to hope.

He now recommenced to shake and tremble.

"What do you want of me?" he demanded, in considerable trepidation of spirit.

"You cannot travel without money. Where have you cashed your letter of credit?"

"In Houston City, at the Third National Bank. I have five hundred pounds there," said Perks.

"Very good indeed! The bank clerk has your signature. You have a cheque-book. You must give me a cheque for the money, except fifty pounds, which you can keep to go home with."

"Ha—hum—ho!" stammered the lawyer. "It will require pen and ink."

"You need not hum and ha; I will take you where you can find it."

"If I give you the cheque will you let me go? It is rather hard luck, smother me if it isn't!"

"Certainly. I shall not be afraid of you. My band and I are here to-day and gone to-morrow. We defy the police."

He laughed sardonically.

"Come," he added, "I will conduct you to my retreat."

"Thanks. I hope it is not far, for I am pretty well done up, smother me if I'm not!"

"An hour's tramp. Refreshment awaits you."

"Have I done well, boss?" asked Dawes, eagerly.

"Excellently well. You are worthy to belong to the band. Away to the cave! Lourada is going to Houston. He shall collect this man's money," was the reply.

Fatigued as he was, Perks was obliged to content himself with a drink of water.

After this very light refreshment, the trio trudged across the prairie to the sand-hills.

Felton, with an audacity all his own, and a peculiar assurance, had returned to his old haunt.

Very few men would have dared to do this, because the cave was well known to Osmond and Jack.

However, those latter never dreamed that the escaped prisoner would go back to a place where it was likely he would be searched for.

He and his confederates in crime were safer there than they might be elsewhere.

The three men who had escaped with him from the gaol at Nacogdochee, had been born and brought up as gentlemen.

Greatly had they fallen from their high estate.

Lourada was a Spanish marquis, having the blue blood, the pure Castilian *sangre azul* running in his veins.

A gambler, a spendthrift, followed by a father's curse, he came to the Southern States, only to sink lower, and find a home in a prison for stabbing a woman of low degree in a fit of jealousy.

He was still young and handsome, and a very pleasant fellow when sober, but a demon when under the influence of drink.

Eddowes was an elderly man, who had been a confidential clerk in a bank for many years.

Yielding to sudden temptation, he robbed the bank, was detected, and sentenced to a long term of imprisonment.

Claxton was more than middle-aged, and one of the cleverest forgers in the world. He, too, had received a long sentence.

These were the men with whom Felton had broken gaol, and was now associated.

He had led them to the cave, where, as we know, he had a stock of provisions and drink stored.

The future plans of the band were as yet undecided.

Felton did not wish to leave the Devil's Gap yet, because he wanted to get Osmond into his power once more.

Since the revelation made by Dawes, and vouched for by Perks, he was doubly determined not to lose him.

There was an idea floating in his mind that he might be able to go with Osmond to England.

No one there would know his antecedents, and Osmond would not dare to tell.

Mixing in the best society, and being well supplied with money, entirely through the young lord, the road-agent would live the life of a gentleman.

Every luxury which money could buy would be his, and he could indulge the most extravagant tastes.

This was a better prospect than being the captain of a band of robbers, however successful their operations might be.

In the long run they were sure to be hunted down by the myrmidons of the law.

Perks was very glad when the sandy region was touched, and he was informed the cave was not far off.

Even Dawes breathed a sigh of relief, for they had been walking since daybreak, and their feet ached so much that they could not have held out much longer.

When Felton came to the Devil's Gap, he put a whistle to his lips, and blew shrilly.

The blast aroused Lourada, who was sitting outside the cave, paying particular attention to a bottle of brandy.

Eddowes and Claxton were inside, playing a game at euchre.

"Welcome, captain!" Lourada exclaimed. "I see you have a captive. Is he lean or fat?"

"We shall get over two thousand dollars out of him," replied Felton. "He has to give us his signature."

"That is good. It is time we made a move."

"Are you dull?"

"Fearfully so. It would be a relief from this monotony to have a fight with somebody."

"Be patient, my dear marquis; all will come in good time. We cannot rush things."

"No, no; that would be folly, but really I want some excitement," Lourada answered.

He yawned, and threw the stump of a cigar down the gap.

"Do you not see we are waiting?" cried Felton.

"What for?"

"The plank. How can we cross this gulch without it? Do you want us to visit the interior of the earth?"

"Not yet; though you may go there unless you repent. All in good time."

"Kindly cease your jests, and put that plank across. My friend Mr. Perks is anxious to be introduced to you, and will get tired of waiting."

"A thousand pardons."

Saying this, the Marquis de Lourada jerked the plank across the yawning, cavernous depth.

Dawes crossed first, and Perks stepped on to the narrow causeway next, with some hesitation, being encouraged by Felton.

"Balance yourself well," cried the latter. "This gulf is rather treacherous. If you go down, there is no coming back."

"Ugh!" growled the lawyer; "it is worse than a Chancery suit."

"How's that?"

"You may get out of that some day."

When half-way across, Perks stumbled.

He fell on one knee, and grasped the narrow plank with both hands.

It was a moment of horror.

Pale as death, he steadied himself, and exerting all his nervous energy, crept the rest of the distance.

It was a great relief when he landed on the other side.

Felton, who was made of sterner stuff, was quickly after him.

"Bravo!" he said. "'Faint heart never won fair lady.'"

"He is doing well in this country," remarked Lourada, with a sardonic smile.

Perks drew his breath with difficulty.

His face streamed with perspiration.

The glimpse he had got of the depths below had given him a fright from which it was difficult to recover.

"The gentleman has had a bad sort of a scare," exclaimed the Marquis de Lourada, "but doubtless a tumbler of wine will revive him."

"Yes," replied the lawyer; "give me some drink."

Some burgundy was handed to him, and he recovered.

"I am not used to crossing such awful places," he said.

"If you will kindly write out the cheque for four fifty on your bank at Houston," said Felton, "you can go when you like."

"Ah yes."

"Of course, I trust to your honour not to betray our hiding-place."

"Not for worlds."

Lourada smiled again.

"What do you take the gentleman for?" he enquired. "You can see he belongs to the first rank. Do not advise him to go. I am just beginning to like him, and could enjoy his society."

"Excuse me, I must depart," said the lawyer, hurriedly.

"Refresh yourself. Eat, drink, sleep. You are welcome. I, Gonzales de Lourada, say so, on the word of a Spanish nobleman."

"Thank you; I will do what is required of me, and go," said Perks.

Tired as he was, he had an idea that he could get back to Mowbray's Ranche, catch the stage from Brazos, and reach Houston before the robbers would be able to cash his cheque.

He fully intended to betray them.

In spite of his promise, his first act would be to tell the police where the hiding-place of the robbers was.

Lourada, with a polite bow worthy of the Escurial, conducted the lawyer into the cave.

He apologised for the absence of chairs.

Pen and ink were supplied him on the top of a flat stone, which served him as a table.

With a reluctance he could not conceal, Perks took from an inner pocket a cheque-book.

Writing out a draft for the amount required, he gave it to Felton.

"There you are," he said. "I can do no more."

"You have cheaply ransomed yourself," replied the road-agent. "Will you take anything before you leave us."

"I will not trespass any more on your hospitality."

Eddowes and Claxton were so absorbed in their game that they only looked up.

They smoked incessantly, and drank brandy at intervals.

Seeing that Perks did not care to be detained, Felton showed him to the outside of the robber's cave.

"Will someone come with me to the edge of the prairie?" asked the lawyer.

"Dawes shall go," replied Felton.

"I'm dog-gone tired, boss," said the cowboy.

He looked as if he could scarcely drag one leg after the other.

"Very well. Go to sleep."

Saying this, Felton looked significantly at Lourada.

"Oh, certainly," exclaimed the latter. "I will gladly make myself of use if the gentleman will accept my escort."

"One is as good as the other." said Perks. "I only want to get out of this."

"You do not like our company?"

"Not much."

"Ha! ha!" laughed Lourada. "Some people call us jolly dogs. There is no accounting for taste."

He shrugged his shoulders, and would have crossed the plank had not Felton stopped him.

"Let the English gentleman go first," cried Felton.

"Pardon me."

"You are forgetting your manners."

"What would you have? Lately I

have been out of good society. Evil communications are corrupting."

Perks placed a foot on the plank.

"When I reach the prairie how shall I go to get to the ranche?" he enquired.

"Strike a bee line from east to west."

"How shall I know the west?"

"By the sun. It is sinking now."

Perks nodded, and stepped on the plank without further ado, which bent a little under his weight.

His courage began to revive.

He thought he would be able to outwit the robbers yet, clever as they undoubtedly fancied they were.

"I'll baffle them, smother me if I don't!" he muttered.

These were his last words on earth.

He was half-way across, looking before him, keeping his eyes averted from the dismal gulf.

Felton stooped.

Grasping the end of the plank, he gave it a sudden jerk.

The lawyer lost his balance.

With a fearful scream he plunged into the dark abyss.

Down, down, down!

The wretched man uttered no further cry.

He was lost to sight for ever.

Withdrawing the plank, Felton calmly put a cigarette in his mouth.

He did not seem in the least disconcerted.

"Will you oblige me with a light, marquis?" he asked.

"With pleasure?" answered Lourada.

Dawes shuddered, hardened as he was.

He crept into the cave.

Felton was a man who attracted others; but, at the same time, he made them afraid of him.

"Poor wretch!" ejaculated Lourada.

"The lawyer has served his last writ," replied Felton. "Curse the whole race! How I hate them!"

"*Amigo mio,*" said Lourada, "there are only two ways of doing a thing in the world."

"Well?"

"They are the right way and the wrong way, and yours is the right," Lourada answered.

"I always am right from the word 'go,'" exclaimed Felton. "Come, let us finish that brandy."

"With all my heart."

They entered the cave together.

A grave expression crossed the face of the road-agent.

"I have an idea," he said, "that events are going to march quickly with us."

"Why so?"

"That I cannot tell."

"Will it be for good or ill?" queried Lourada.

"Again I reply that I am unable to inform you. Am I a sybil to unfold the book of Fate?"

"*Caramba!*" cried the Spaniard, "what do I care? We will fight for liberty—eh?"

"To the death!" rejoined Felton, savagely.

They lapsed into silence, and the sun sank below the horizon.

Dawes was fast asleep.

The other bandits, Eddowes and Claxton, continued their play.

The gaming instinct was strong within them.

Little did they dream how soon the truth of their captain's words would be realised.

CHAPTER XVII.

A LITTLE PICNIC AND A GREAT SURPRISE.

WHEN Jack of Warwick awoke on the day following his abandonment of Perks on the prairie, he walked over to Snell's saloon, fully expecting to find the lawyer there.

Great was his astonishment when he heard that nothing had been seen of him.

He was now sorry that he had left him to his own resources.

Little did he imagine that he had been thrown down the Devil's Gap by Felton.

This idea never entered his head for a moment.

He determined to set out in search of the lawyer without a moment's delay.

Returning to MacTavish's to breakfast, he found Helen and Osmond at the table.

MacTavish, Warner, and White had already breakfasted, and ridden off to see after the cattle.

Osmond expressed himself as feeling much better, and asserted that he thought he would be able to travel to England in a few days.

"I am glad to hear you say that," exclaimed Jack, "though I shall be sorry to lose you, old fellow."

"Why not come with me?" replied Osmond.

"I have already told you I cannot do that. Helen would not let me go."

"Oh, you need not make that the excuse, and stay on my account," said Helen.

"Do you want to get rid of me?"

"If you think you can find a better sweetheart in England."

"I know I cannot. The whole world would not supply one."

"Do you think so much of me as all that?" she asked, her eyes brightening.

"Much more than I can find words to express," answered Jack, with an earnestness there was no mistaking.

Helen felt highly flattered at hearing this.

She loved Jack dearly.

"I wish you could both come and live with me at Kenilworth Hall," Osmond said.

"Your lady mother might object to the wife of a cowboy," remarked Helen.

"Not she. I'd make that all right. Where is Mr. Perks to-day?"

"That is what I cannot make out," returned Jack. "I am sorry to say that Warner and I left him on the prairie last night, after playing him a heap of tricks."

"Is he lost?"

"I fear so; and it will be my duty to go and hunt for him."

"Then you will not ride after the cattle to-day?" said Helen.

"No. The stock must take care of themselves. My first care shall be for the English lawyer."

"I will have a ride with you," Helen cried. "There will be nobody at home except Osmond, and Mauma can look after him. It is a long time since I have had a gallop. Take me with you, Jack, and let us have a little picnic all by ourselves."

"Agreed!" answered Jack.

He was only too glad to have such a fair and lovable companion.

No proposition could have pleased him better.

Helen hastened away to pack up in a neat little basket some fowl and ham and bottled lager beer.

"I wish I was well enough to go with you," exclaimed Osmond; "but I know I am not sufficiently strong to ride a horse."

"Keep house, and amuse yourself by reading," Jack replied.

"All the time you are gone to look after Perks I shall be on tenter-hooks."

"What for?"

"Fear of Felton."

"Dismiss him from your mind; he will not dare to come here."

"Who can tell? I shall sit with a pistol in front of me."

"Arm Mauma too; I would," said Jack, in a good-natured, chaffing manner.

"Don't chaff. That old woolly-headed negress is of no use."

At that moment Mauma came into the room with a dish of hot buckwheat cakes.

She looked indignant.

"Good lands!" she exclaimed, "if I has got wool on the top ob my head, is that my fault?"

"Of course not," replied Jack.

"It was de gift ob Nature, to keep de sun off."

"I see."

"Then what that sassy white boy want to go and insult me, saying I was no good?"

"He didn't mean that, Mauma," Jack tried to explain.

"All a pack ob lies."

"No, no; it's truth."

"Yoh's full ob deceit, same as all de cowboys. Take your old buckwheat cakes."

Mauma flung them angrily on the table, and bounced away to the kitchen.

"The old lady has a nice temper," laughed Osmond.

"It's the way with all old coloured

servants. They are petted and spoilt, until they become like favoured children. Good-bye, Osmond; don't be nervous."

"I can't help it."

"We shall be back soon. If you are very nervous go to Snell's; you will have company there," continued Jack; "but I guess you will have no trouble."

As Jack left the room he heard Osmond talking to himself.

The words were audible.

"Bad, bad! I dreamt all night of Felton. Bad!"

"Pshaw!" muttered Jack. "He's got that road-agent on the brain. I like him much; but I wish he was back in England. He worries me."

In ten minutes he had two mustangs saddled and bridled.

Taking them to the front door, he found Helen waiting for him, basket in hand.

Assisting her on to the side-saddle, he took charge of the picnic basket, and away they went.

When they were trotting over the soft turf, the cool breeze fanning their faces, the blue sky overhead, their spirits expanded.

"Oh, Jack," cried Helen, "isn't this jolly? When I am outside a house I feel life is worth living."

"So do I," answered Jack; "we will enjoy ourselves to-day."

They both fully made up their minds to do so.

There is an old saying, however: "Man proposes, but God disposes."

Hunting for the missing lawyer was rather a difficult affair, and they got near the well where Dawes had met Felton, after some hours' search, without finding any trace of him.

When the well was reached, Helen could not help being impressed by the quiet beauty of the scene.

Alighting from their mustangs, they let them roam at will, while they unfastened the basket, and spread out their lunch under the protection of a spreading hemlock tree.

After quenching their thirst and satisfying their hunger, they allowed their thoughts to revert to the English lawyer.

Up to the present time they had not been able to discover the faintest trace of Mr. Perks.

They had scoured the prairie to a considerable extent, but the unfortunate man had disappeared without leaving a sign behind.

"It is very strange," remarked Jack, as he lazily lounged on the grass and puffed at a Mexican cigarette.

"Poor man! I hope he will find his way to the ranche."

"Warner or White may strike his trail, though I begin to doubt it," Jack replied.

"Is it any use to search further?"

"Not the slightest. If he could have wandered as far as this it is about as much as he could accomplish."

Helen shaded her eyes with her hand.

"What is that coming along over there?" enquired she.

"I see nothing," answered Jack.

"You are looking in the wrong direction. See over there, a singular object is approaching."

"Ah, I see it!" cried Jack. "It is coming the way of the Brazos road. That is the line of country the stage travels through. Wonder what it is?"

"What a queer head it has!"

Jack stared as curiously as she did at the peculiar creature that was traversing the vast plain.

It evidently could see the trees, and thinking it would obtain shade and water, those two most desirable things on the prairie, it was coming that way.

Gradually it came nearer, walking slowly, as if weary.

Ten minutes passed in intense expectation.

Jack advanced to meet the peculiar thing.

Suddenly he burst out laughing.

It was simply a man, with his head thrust through a hole in a box of an oblong shape.

The box rested on his shoulders, and his arms were tied behind his back.

No covering was on his head. The face was that of a man of forty, thin and long, with the jaws of a Yankee.

He had once been in the possession of a black beard and whiskers; but only one side of his face was now so adorned, as someone had ruthlessly cut the hair off the other.

Helen saw what it was, and she, too, laughed heartily.

All at once Jack stopped his merriment.

He became very grave.

Written on the box with a piece of charcoal or burnt cork was the following inscription—

"Done by Felton, road-agent; present address, 'Texas.'"

The man's eyes beamed with delight at seeing Jack and Helen.

"Say, stranger," he cried, "this ain't no laffing matter. The road-agents have stopped the stage; shot the driver and three passengers. I only escaped by hiding; but they found me at last under some seats and cushions, and started me on my travels this way."

Jack promptly removed the box.

"Made me a pretty picture, I guess," continued the man. "But I'll make them suffer for it, as sure as my name is Deep, of Austin."

"How many did the band consist of?" asked Jack.

"Four. Their faces I could not see, as they wore black masks."

This number corresponded with that of Felton's band.

"It was sharp fighting," added Mr. Deep, of Austin.

"Did you take any part in it?"

"Well, no; I was under the seat. But one of the passengers dropped one robber, and the stage-driver killed another. Only two were left."

"Why didn't they shoot you?" Jack enquired.

"They got drinking champagne and gambling for the money they took from the dead men; in fact, they felt larkish; and when they found me, through a sneezing fit I had, they treated me as I have explained," answered Deep.

He looked wistfully at the viands and bottles spread on the grass.

Jack took the hint, and invited him to help himself, which he was not slow in doing.

"The best of the joke is," he went on, "that Felton did not know who I am, or he would not have let me go free."

"May I ask who you are?" enquired Jack.

Mr. Deep laid his finger alongside his nose in a very knowing manner.

"It's a secret," he replied; "but I don't mind telling you. I keep a private detective bureau in Austin, and as the Governor of the State has doubled the reward for Felton, I started out to see if I couldn't trace him to his lair."

"It was a pity that you did not take him when you had a chance."

Jack spoke with something like a sneer.

He saw that the man was an arrant coward.

"You must know I am not a fighter," said Deep. "I'm the 'nose.' I smell out things, and let the police do the fighting. I'm a detective plain and simple. And now, may I venture to ask who you are, and this young lady, who, pardon me, is as pretty as a Sharon rose?"

Jack did not refuse to gratify his curiosity, and Mr. Deep, who had a way of fishing for information, soon got to know all about affairs at Mowbray's Ranche.

He learnt the history of Jack of Warwick and Osmond.

As soon as this was divulged, he became as much interested in the young Lord Melbury as others were.

But he did not say so.

The Austin detective was far too cunning for that.

"Ha, ha!" he exclaimed. "I can't help laffing now it's all over."

"At what?" Jack asked.

"Fancy shaving half a man's face, and then starting him off with a wine-case over his shoulders!"

"I am glad you came in this direction," said Jack.

"Why so?"

"I have an idea that Felton is hiding in his old cave."

"Ah! where is that?"

"About an hour's ride from here. Now is your chance to capture the great robber."

Mr. Deep shook his head.

"As I said before," he replied, "I am a detective, and not a thief-grabber, understand that."

"There are only two of them now, according to your showing, since you were attacked by four, and two fell."

"I don't care, sonny, even if Felton was alone, and you could lead me straight to him. This dog don't fight—that's decisive."

"FELTON GAVE HIM A BLOW WHICH KNOCKED HIM TO THE VERGE OF THE ABYSS."

"All right. Will you come and reconnoitre?" asked Jack. "Just look around and see if I am correct in my supposition that Felton is hiding in his old retreat."

"You don't get me on that string either. He's a desperate man. If he caught me again he would not let me off so easily. You go and make an examination, then report to me."

Jack smiled contemptuously.

"No, Mr. Deep," he exclaimed, "I am not such a fool as to work for you."

"We'll share the reward! This young lady and I can go back to the ranche. I'll walk, if she'll show the way; and if Felton is where you think he is, I'll soon have the sheriff of Nacogdochee county down on him."

"I can see the sheriff as well as you if I have anything to tell him. I have reasons of my own for stopping the career of Felton, if I can, and if you will not aid me you cannot expect to reap a reward to which you are not entitled."

Helen looked pained and astonished at Jack's avowed determination to go in search of the road-agent.

In vain she endeavoured to dissuade him from his rash task.

"Come home with me," she said. "If Felton is lurking in the sand-hills we shall hear of him soon enough."

"I will not provoke a conflict should I find him," replied Jack.

"I am fearful of danger; it looks like running into the lion's den."

"Don't fret," smiled Jack, who was inclined to be headstrong. "If I find Felton in the cave, I shall ride on to the sheriff, so you will not see me for a few days.

"If the contrary should be the case—"

"Then you may expect me home at supper-time. Mr. Deep can accompany you, if you have no objection to his company."

"I would rather have yours," she replied, archly.

"Another time, my dear girl," said Jack. "What I am going to do is business. We are not safe at the ranche while Felton is at large."

"Retribution will overtake him," exclaimed Helen. "However, a wilful man must have his way, as father says. Be careful."

A teardrop trembled in her eye.

She was deeply affected, for she feared that he was about to expose himself to more danger than he dreamed of.

Waving his hand he sprang upon his horse and galloped off.

Presently he looked back.

Helen was mounted, and Mr. Deep was walking by her side.

At first she had a mind to follow Jack and share whatever peril he might have to encounter.

Thinking, however, that this would anger him, she forbore.

Breathing a fervent prayer for his safety, she journeyed to Mowbray's Ranche in a very melancholy mood.

Meanwhile Jack hastened towards the sand-hills.

The day was extremely hot, but he minded it not, having got acclimatised by this time.

He did not exaggerate the gravity of the situation.

Felton had shown his teeth already, with his usual daring.

What he would do next no one could anticipate with any certainty, but remembering his threats against Osmond, it was unlikely he would leave him long unmolested.

He had thrown down the gantlet by his waylaying the stage.

It was an act of defiance against the executive authorities.

There seemed to be no limit to the man's reckless daring.

Jack in due course arrived at the sandy regions, which he well recollected.

Tethering his horse with a lariat and a stake he carried for that purpose, he proceeded to the cave.

Lizards and snakes hissed warningly as he passed their hiding-places.

Swarms of mosquitoes of unusual size attacked his hands and face.

Hollow rumblings were heard among the rocks, as if predicting some seismic disturbance.

Flashes of jagged forked lightning shot out from the sky.

Everything seemed to urge him to go back and give up his perilous undertaking.

But he was obstinately determined to persevere, no matter what obstacles he would have to encounter.

At length he found himself at the Devil's Gap, at the spot facing the cavern where Felton had formerly sheltered.

All was dark and still inside.

The plank had been placed across the chasm.

No sign indicated that there was anyone dwelling in the gloomy recess of the cave.

Not a sound fell upon his listening ears.

But this was not enough for Jack.

He wanted to make certain beyond the shadow of a doubt.

"Hallo! within there!" he shouted.

There was no answer.

"Come out and surrender. You are surrounded, back and front!" he added.

Still the silence of the grave reigned everywhere.

Summouing all his courage to his aid, he determiued to cross the plank.

He dismissed his lingering fears.

Stepping on to the frail bridge he looked into the abyss.

It might have been fancy, but he thought he saw flame mingled with smoke in the depths below.

With difficulty he repressed a shudder.

Quickening his steps he was soon on the other side.

How his heart beat at that moment!

He advanced to the entrance of the cave, his right hand in his pocket grasping his revolver.

Suddenly a tall form stepped from the shadow into the sunlight.

In each hand was a six-chambered pistol, with which he covered Jack.

The latter had no time to draw.

Before him stood the redoubtable road-agent.

Around his face played the old satanic smile.

"Felton!" gasped Jack.

"I have been expecting you, Master Jack of Warwick," was the reply. "Move hand or foot, and I drop you down the gully."

The Devil's Gap was in truth just behind our hero.

Though burning with rage, Jack was passive as a lamb.

To have attempted to shoot would have been to court instant destruction.

"Dawes!" cried the Texan robber.

In obedience to his summons Dawes made his appearance with a coil of rope.

"Yes, captain," he said.

"Disarm and bind him. Remove the plank."

These commands were rapidly executed.

Jack's surprise was now complete, for he had little expected to see the cowboy at the cavern.

Dawes performed his task with a fiendish glee, chuckling to himself.

In a few moments he had tied Jack's hands tightly behind his back.

His pistol and knife were taken away, and the plank was removed

Lourada, who had evidently been drinking heavily, staggered to the front, and leant his back against the rock.

His eyes were bloodshot, the swarthy face was flushed, and his limbs were shaky.

"What now?" he asked.

"I have made an arrest," responded Felton.

"Shoot him like a dog! *Caramba!* we give no quarter! Eddowes and Claxton were killed this morning in that accursed stage affair!"

"Silence!"

"Shoot, shoot, I say!" the Spaniard cried.

"Not yet," answered Felton. "You let your tongue run too fast; go to sleep again, my good Lourada."

"*Caramba!* not bad advice. Dawes, give me some brandy, and I will e'en court the drowsy god."

He staggered back again to the cave, supported by Dawes, who supplied him with more drink.

Everything had happened so suddenly and unexpectedly that Jack seemed as if his mind was paralysed.

He thought of Helen's sage advice, and blamed his hot-headedness for not taking it.

What was his life worth now he was in Felton's hands?

Not so much as a bird's when in front of a sportsman's gun.

The bird has the chance of a miss, Jack had none at all, unless something unusual intervened.

But he determined not to show any weakness.

"What brought you here?" asked Felton.

"My legs," replied Jack.

The road-agent gave him a blow in

the face, which knocked him to the verge of the abyss.

Another foot, and he would have rolled over the ragged edge of the Devil's Gap.

"Don't sass me," cried Felton. "Give me an answer to my question."

"A man named Perks came after Osmond; he is lost, and I came to look for him."

"You will find him down there."

"Eh—what? You cannot mean—"

"I mean what I say; he is in the depths."

Felton pointed to the yawning gulf.

"Demon! fiend!" ejaculated Jack of Warwick.

"That is precisely what I am. Everyone will find me so. I am incapable of participating in the softer sentiments of humanity," answered Felton, without exhibiting any trace of annoyance at the bold speech. "My heart is dead. I know not mercy. I have no idea of pity, nor does remorse ever enter into my calculations. You will not see Perks, the lawyer, this side of the grave. Ha, ha! It is a brave thing to have the power to kill!"

He laughed maniacally.

"What made you think of coming here?" Felton went on, after a pause.

"I thought you might make for the old spot," Jack answered.

"Does anyone know of your intentions?"

Jack was silent.

His only hope of help rested upon Helen MacTavish and Mr. Deep, of Austin.

"Will you swear that no one knows that you set out to come here?" asked the road-agent.

Jack still hesitated.

He had a very keen sense of honour, and regarded an oath as being so binding, under any circumstances, that he would always despise himself for breaking it.

He would rather have accepted death than swear to a lie.

Felton's eagle eye at once detected his faltering.

"Come, come," he said, "it is best to make a clean breast of it, or—"

He paused, and tapped his revolver significantly.

"I do not wish to say anything more," replied Jack.

"Very well; take your choice. Life or death—which is it to be?"

Jack underwent a desperate mental struggle.

He wished to live for Helen's sake, and because life seemed so bright.

He felt the cold muzzle of the robber's pistol pressed against his forehead.

Oh, if he had been free, and could have seized his tormentor by the throat!

But he was as helpless as a child.

"Speak!" hissed Felton.

"I will," answered Jack, catching his breath. "Helen MacTavish knows I started for here."

"Who else?"

Again Jack struggled with himself, but he had to give in.

"A man we met. You put his head in a box, and turned him on the prairie to die."

"What! that skunk alive? Who is he?" enquired Felton, in surprise.

"A private detective from Austin, named Deep—after you for the double reward the State's Governor has offered."

"Perdition!" cried Felton. "If I'd guessed that I'd have shot him through the head. I was drunk, or I should not have been so idiotically merciful."

There was a momentary pause.

Felton was considering the situation.

"I can see what you had in your mind," he said, presently. "You heard from Deep that I robbed the stage, and reckoned I should be here."

"That was it."

"Deep was too much of a coward to come with you to spy."

"He isn't much on fighting, so he went back to the ranche with Miss MacTavish."

"Exactly," smiled Felton; "and you were estimating that they would organise a rescue-party if you did not return to-night."

Jack was silent.

The reply to the question was so obvious that he did not take the trouble to answer.

"Since I lost Eddowes and Claxton," mused Felton, "I am too short-handed to attack the ranche. Only the cowboy and I. Lourada is no good."

He looked contemptuously at the Spaniard, who was hopelessly intoxicated.

Probably he would remain helpless for days.

"How many rifles can you count on at the ranche?" asked Felton.

"We have two new stock-hands. Then there are MacTavish and his daughter, Snell and his wife, Osmond, Warner, and White."

"But the stock-hands are not there in the daytime?"

"The cowboys might be kept, knowing you are at large."

"That is so. Dawes and I could not do it alone," exclaimed Felton, thoughtfully, "unless we could take them by surprise; and that is out of the question after what you have told me. Yet I must have Lord Melbury."

Jack looked up in amazement.

"You know Osmond's name!" he cried.

"It would appear so since I have mentioned it."

"How in the world did you ascertain that?"

"Easily enough. I extracted the information from Perks, the lawyer. Of course I am all the more anxious now to get the boy in my power."

"What will you do with him?"

"Travel for the present."

"But after the crimes you have committed, you will never be safe anywhere."

Felton twisted his moustache.

"Think so?" he rejoined. "I beg to differ. Osmond will not dare to say anything. I can influence him, and I laugh at all others."

He snapped his fingers with a cynical air.

"Look here," he went on. "I don't mind telling you that it is too hot for me to stay in Texas."

"You will find it hot wherever you go," remarked Jack.

"I can disguise; but that is not the question. Lord Melbury I must have, and you must get him for me."

"How can I do it? The thing is impossible."

"I mean him no harm. You must swear to go at once to the ranche, and either bring him to me or come back yourself to be dealt with."

"To be shot?"

"Yes."

"I cannot ask Osmond to do such a thing," cried Jack; "it is monstrous and inhuman. Why should he make such a sacrifice for my sake?"

"Because he is your friend."

"Ah, but friendship has its limits."

"Not to an impulsive and romantic boy like Osmond," said Felton. "Rather than see you return to death—certain, inevitable—he will give himself up to me again."

"I have heard him say he would rather die than live as he is living."

"It is not a question of his death, but yours, my friend. That alters the case very materially."

Jack could not decide offhand.

It was a terrible situation to be placed in, and he wanted time to think.

There was a chance that, in spite of his hatred of and repugnance to Felton, Osmond would give himself up to save his friend.

It would be like placing himself in a horrible bondage.

Yet he was grand, noble, and self-sacrificing in his disposition.

But was it fair to ask him to do so?

Was it not Jack's duty to suffer death rather than expose his friend to the domination of Felton?

That was the question which Jack of Warwick had to answer to his own satisfaction.

"Give me time," he said.

"Very well," returned Felton, lighting a fresh cigarette and looking at a watch he had stolen from a stage-passenger the night before; "you shall have one hour."

"It will be enough."

"At the expiration of that time you take the oath, and either send Osmond here, or return yourself. If you refuse the oath—death!"

Jack became plunged in deepest thought.

With an anxious countenance, Felton walked moodily up and down the sandy plateau.

Dawes had dropped off to sleep, and Lourada was still in a drunken stupor from which he showed no signs of awakening.

Not a breath of air moved, and the heat was almost unbearable.

All at once Dawes woke up, rubbed his eyes, and walked over to Jack.

The latter was so absorbed that he did not notice him.

Seeing this, the cowboy prodded him

in the arm with the sharp point of his knife.

"Oh!" cried Jack. "Who is that?"

Dawes laughed quietly.

"Wake up. It's only me," he said. "You did not expect to find me here. I was kicked out by you, and had to go somewhere; fortunately I met with the captain, and now I'm one of the band."

"It won't do you much good."

"Whatever happens to me," replied Dawes, "you won't live to see it, for the boss will finish you off presently. I heard him say so. Which is it to be— go for a jump down the gap, or take a bullet? Lord! how I laughed when that lawyer chap did his jump! It's fine fun. I shall laugh more when you leap, though."

"Let me alone," said Jack, impatiently.

"Oh, no; I can do as I like. You're not boss now."

"Pshaw! you are worse than a gadfly."

Dawes had not heard Felton's remarks. He fully believed that Jack was to die shortly.

"Feel bad, don't you, to think you fell into a trap?" he went on. "I saw you coming, and told the boss; then we hid."

"Will you desist?"

"No; I like to torment you."

Jack could not use his arms, but he could his feet; and, raising his right one in the French fashion, he gave the cowboy a kick under the ear with his heavy iron-studded boot.

This stunned Dawes.

He rolled against the side of the cave, knocking his head, and falling senseless on the sandy floor.

"Reptile, lie there!" muttered our hero.

Again Jack busied himself with his thoughts, but he could not make up his mind how to act.

It was an embarrassing dilemma.

The time was quickly flying.

Presently the road-agent would ask him for his decision.

Jack turned cold and hot, his head ached, and almost in despair he breathed a silent prayer to heaven for guidance.

CHAPTER XVIII.

THE TWO FRIENDS—SELF-SACRIFICE—A NOBLE ACT.

WHEN night fell, and Jack of Warwick did not return to the ranche, Helen MacTavish began to grow very anxious.

She was in the parlour playing draughts with Osmond.

Mr. Deep was in another part of the room, near the open window, smoking and drinking whisky with MacTavish.

Both Osmond and the Scotchman had heard about Jack's bold attempt to find out whether the road-agent was in the old haunt.

Osmond and Helen were absorbed with their own thoughts, playing almost mechanically.

Yet they did not talk upon the subject which filled them with conjecture and apprehension.

Mr. Deep had been well received, and after a good dinner, felt quite at home.

He made himself familiar with Mac-Tavish, and told wonderful stories about his skill as a detective, and the cases of an intricate nature he had brought to a successful conclusion.

That he was a boaster, MacTavish had no doubt.

Nevertheless, he was amusing, and in a lonely spot, where a stranger was a novelty, he was welcome.

"You ha'e seen a deal of life, I'm thinking," remarked MacTavish, after Deep had told an improbable tale.

"You can bet your bottom dollar on that, squire, and win all the time," Deep replied.

"I should like to hear one or two more of your experiences, Mr. Deep, and that's a fact."

"You shall. I'll do it with pleasure."

"Can I offer you a pinch of 'sneezin'' first?"

"I don't care. Snuff clears the head mighty quick."

"Ay, it's gude for the understanding. I ken that fu' weel," answered Mac-Tavish.

"I have had some remarkable cases," began Deep; "the funniest one, though, was the loss of the Aztec diamond. Heard of it?"

"Yes, of the diamond—not of the story. It was found in Peru. Worth half a million. Brought to this country, and owned in Orleans."

"Correct. It was stolen. Police all baffled. Detectives at fault."

"Well?"

"Case put in my hands. I suspected a discharged clerk; traced him to Florida. He was living in poor style, and working for a man who owned an orange-grove and pineapple estate."

"Had he got the diamond?"

"You wait, old hoss. I'll tell the story in my own way."

"But how could you find the Aztec diamond in a pineapple?" MacTavish asked, who was getting mixed through the quantity of whisky he had been taking.

"Did I say anything about a pineapple?"

"Hoot, hoot, mon! Keep to your text."

"Who's running this story—you or me?" demanded Deep.

"Why, you are, only I canna get the hang of it."

"Leave me alone. Where was I?"

"In an apple-garden in Florida."

"Ah, yes. Pineapples you mean. Well, this clerk, whose name was Nixon, had a wife, and a crocodile, of which he was very fond."

"The wife?"

"No, no; the crocodile," cried Deep, who was growing annoyed at these repeated interruptions. "The wife was a little beauty, but Nixon seemed to think a plaguey sight more of his croc. than he did of his wife."

"Was it a big one?"

"Never you mind the size of it. He had a tank built for the lazy brute in his back garden, and when not at work was for everlasting watching the scaly reptile."

"Did it require watching?" asked MacTavish.

Deep brought his fist down on the table with a thump.

"There's a silly question to put!" he exclaimed. "Did it want watching, when it was shut up in a back yard, and wasn't a twelvemonth old?"

"Why didn't you say so at first, you fool?"

"Don't call me names, or you may find the diamond yourself," Mr. Deep said, helping himself to more whisky.

"You are well named; in fact, you're so deep I can't fathom you."

"Ha, ha! Good joke. Wait a bit. Where do you think that diamond was?"

"I dinna ken."

"Call yourself a canny Scotchman? Go 'long. Where was it?"

"If it's a conundrum, you can ask me an easier one."

"Now, whist! don't get excited, and I'll tell you."

"Mon, you're the longest-winded fellow I ever saw. Come to the point, or I shall make you," roared MacTavish.

"It was— Just hand me the snuff," replied Deep.

MacTavish stood up and clenched his hand.

His curiosity was stimulated, and his imagination greatly excited.

"I'll hond you nae sneeshin' till you speak up," he cried. "Where was that diamond? Are you going to tell me?"

"Well, you see, I offered to buy that croc.; but he wouldn't part with it at any fancy price."

"What the deevil has the crocodile to do with the diamond?"

"Everything, as you will see," replied Deep, who seemed in a provoking humour. "Crocs., you know, abound in the lagoons of Florida. Any nigger would get you a young one for half-a-dollar."

"Am I buying crocodiles?"

"No. Who said you were?"

"What are you quoting the prices for, then? If you dinna tell me where that diamond was, I'll hammer you wi' my fist."

The honest Scotchman's face glowed with rage.

"I stole that croc. one dark night," continued Deep, "and took it home and killed it."

"Hech, mon! What did you do that fule's trick for?"

"My detective sagacity led me to believe that I should find the diamond, and I did."

"Where—in Heaven's name, where?" shouted MacTavish.

"In the crocodile."

"What?"

"Inside the crocodile. He'd made the poor beast swallow it, and—"

MacTavish interrupted him.

"You're a fearful leear!" he yelled fiercely. "And I'll nae keep a mon in my hoose who tells lees."

"Fact, I assure you," returned Deep, with imperturbable gravity.

"I wouldn't believe you on your oath. Helen, my lassie."

"Yes, father."

"Call one of the cowboys out of the kitchen to see this loon to Snell's. I'll have no more of him."

Helen went out and summoned Warner, who was smoking his pipe and talking to White and Mauma.

Mr. Deep showed no resentment at his expulsion.

He drank some more whisky, and, taking hold of Warner's arm, moved off with an unsteady gait.

Stopping on the threshold, he said—

"If ever you should want to buy a croc—"

"Hoot! Take him away!" interrupted MacTavish.

"I'll give you my address in Austin," completed Mr. Deep. "The purchase may prove a profitable speculation."

Warner dragged him out, but not in time to save him from the Scotchman's wrath.

He received a kick in the rear which made him expedite his movements.

"Really, this is painful," he muttered as he got outside. "I'll never tell any more crocodile stories. A Scotchman can't take a joke. Which way is it to the saloon?"

"Hang on to me. I'll show you," replied Warner.

"I've been drinking tangle-foot whisky."

"You are safe with me."

"Mind I don't fall. Hold me up."

"Sure to do that," answered Warner.

"Are you certain you know your way to the saloon?"

"I ought to in the dark, for I've been there often enough."

"Don't let me get lost on the prairie."

"No, sir."

"And say," continued the detective, "when Jack returns, let me know at once. If he's found the robbers, I'll borrow one of your horses and be off to the sheriff at once. Ha, ha! I'll nail the reward, and then I will see about other things I have in view."

Warner thought he would play a joke on him, and instead of conducting him to Snell's he led him into the yard.

Here there was a pit into which manure was pitchforked, to be used for the garden.

It was only about half full.

If anybody fell in he could not quickly get out again without obtaining some assistance.

It was a dark night, though a few stars were shining,

"This way, boss," said the cowboy, leading him to the pit.

"I don't see any light."

"No custom, no light; but they'll light up soon enough when you knock."

"Ah, yes! Queer kind of place, this," remarked Deep.

"And queer people in it," answered Warner. "The boss is a peculiar chap, and is a mark on strangers."

"Don't say that, because I'm strange, and— Why, where are we? This is not the road!"

"Don't you fret. I'm the boss guide. Come on."

"But it's—it's a yard! I heard a horse neigh. Take me back. Hallo! Whoop! Jerusalem! Where am I?"

Mr. Deep had walked to the edge of the manure-pit while he was being talked to.

He saw the trap, but too late to save himself.

Warner gave him a push, and sent him headlong on to the soft wet compost below.

"You rascal!" he roared. "I'll pay you for this! How dare you do it to a person of my distinction?"

"It's a bully place to sleep," replied Warner.

"What! Moly Hoses—I mean Holy Moses!—you are not going to keep me here all night?"

"That's what's the matter."

"Rogue, thief, villain! I'll howl the place down!"

"You may shout till you're blue, and no one 'll come to you."

"I'll complain to your master," yelled

Deep; "he doesn't employ you to play tricks upon travellers."

"That's what I'm here for."

"I'll give you a dollar if you'll get me out."

"Not before morning. I'll tell Jack of Warwick where you are when he comes back."

"Is he a friend of yours?"

"He's my particular chum, and I holed you because you wanted to steal a march on him and get the reward for the capture of Felton."

"Oh, is that it? Well, look here, I won't do it. Jack of Warwick shall have all the reward if—"

"Hold on! I know you won't do it, because you can't," grinned the cowboy.

"I'll make it a five-dollar bill."

"You may raise the offer to twenty, and I won't get you out," replied Warner.

"Am I to stop here all night?"

"That's the ticket."

"Well, I'm durned!" ejaculated Mr. Deep

Hearing Warner's retreating footsteps, he gave vent to language which was more forcible than elegant.

In vain Deep grabbed at the side of the pit.

He found it utterly impossible to raise himself.

His most strenuous efforts were of no avail.

Warner had an idea that MacTavish would not be displeased to hear of what he had done.

He knew that the Austin detective had been turned out for some offence he had committed.

When he reached the parlour, Mac-Tavish, Helen, and Osmond were grouped together talking earnestly.

It need scarcely be said that Jack of Warwick's fate exercised their minds.

"I've landed the stranger," exclaimed Warner, with a subdued smile.

"Oh, Snell will make him comforable enough," said MacTavish.

"He isn't at Snell's."

"Hech! whaur have you put him, then?"

"I just dropped him in the pit, and you can bet your pile he won't get out before morning."

MacTavish laughed heartily, and gave Warner a dram of spirits.

"Take it," he exclaimed; "you've earned it. Certainly it's against the laws of hospitality to put a man in such a place; but that fellow deserved the treatment."

"All right, sir; I guessed you would not be displeased. Good-night."

"Stay a while," exclaimed MacTavish. "Jack of Warwick has not come home. We are discussing the matter. How long would it take him to go to the cave in the sand-hills, reconnoitre, and come back?"

Warner made a mental calculation.

"He ought to be back by this time," he remarked.

"I am afraid the poor fellow is captured. He has walked into the lion's den."

"I told him so!" exclaimed Helen. "Oh, why did he not take my advice?"

She hid her face in her hands, and began to cry.

"Hoot, toot!" said MacTavish, "dinna freet."

"I can't help it. If anything happened to Jack of Warwick, I shall never hold up my head again in this world."

"My puir lassie, I will not ha'e you fash yourself; there is plenty of time yet for him to come."

"Yes," chimed in Osmond; "the horse may have gone lame. I will not give up hope."

At this moment a horse was heard galloping up the road.

It stopped at the gate.

All listened attentively, and in a short time a quick footstep sounded on the garden path.

"It is Jack!" cried Helen. "I know his welcome step."

She was correct in her surmise.

The door was pushed open, and Jack of Warwick stood before them.

He was pale, haggard, and dejected.

This could not be wondered at, for, at the last moment, he had yielded to the pressure put on him by Felton.

He had taken the oath.

Everyone grasped him by the hand, congratulating him on his safe return.

"Thank heaven!" said Helen, "you are with us again."

"Jack always turns up trumps," remarked Osmond.

"Bravo! bully for you!" exclaimed Warner.

"That's all varra well," observed MacTavish. "I'm as glad to see Jack as anybody; but, my lad, tell me if you have found the robbers?"

"Yes," replied Jack, "I have, but—"

A chorus of joyous exclamations interrupted him.

"Hold on!" he cried. "I've got a sad tale to tell. Felton, and a Spaniard, and Dawes, our old cowboy, are in the cave."

"Hoot awa', mon! Dawes!" said MacTavish. "I can scarce believe it."

"It is true, nevertheless. They captured me."

"And how did you escape? It's nae so easy to get out of their clutches as it is to climb Arthur's Seat in Edinburgh, or go through the Trongate in Glasgow."

Jack quietly told the story of his capture, and his conditional release.

They listened with bated breath.

"I swore," concluded Jack, "that I would only stay here two hours."

"If you go back, what then?" asked Helen.

"I have told you. I shall be shot."

"Shot!"

"Yes, Helen, and thrown down the Devil's Gap."

Osmond was trembling violently.

He saw how the matter stood.

"Why," asked MacTavish, "should you keep such an oath to such a man?"

"My dear friend," replied Jack, "an oath is an oath, no matter how, when, or where it is taken."

"But he is a robber, murderer—everything that is bad!"

"I acknowledge that; yet it does not absolve me."

"Jack is right," observed Helen, with tears in her eyes. "It is a question of honour, of faith, of religion."

"Pshaw! I should laugh at it," answered MacTavish. "Are not we strong enough to go this night and storm his castle?"

"Father," cried Helen, "you shall not risk your life."

"Someone might be killed," replied MacTavish; "but we should corner the road-agent."

"I could not allow it," said Jack.

"Why not?"

"It would be a breach of my oath."

MacTavish helped himself to some whisky, took a pinch of snuff, and paced the room impatiently.

Up to this time Osmond had not spoken.

He had been thinking hard, though.

Advancing to Jack, he took him by the hand, and looked into his eyes affectionately.

"Jack," he said.

"Yes, old fellow," replied Jack, who returned the pressure of his hand warmly, his eyes being moist with tears.

"At school you read about the two friends, Damon and Pythias?"

"Yes, again."

"They would, and did, lay down their lives for each other."

"A third time, yes."

"I will be your Damon. Yes, Jack, I will go to Felton."

"No, no," said Jack. "I do not wish it—I do not ask you."

"It is my privilege as a friend. Felton will not kill me, but he will you. He only wants to make money out of me, if he can; but I'll escape, and track him to his doom."

"He knows who you are."

Osmond looked graver.

"Who told him?" he demanded.

"Perks, the lawyer. He knows you are Lord Melbury, and intends to play you for all you are worth."

"So much the better," remarked Osmond; "he will not kill the goose he thinks is going to lay the golden eggs."

Osmond's magnanimity was greatly admired by all.

Jack wrung his hand heartily, but he could not speak for the moment, his heart being too full for words.

A lump rose in his throat, and tears came into his eyes.

The sacrifice was more than he had a right to expect, and he doubted if he ought to accept it.

Helen took Osmond's other hand.

"Thank you," she said. "Some day I hope you will reap your reward, as you deserve."

The light had faded out of the young lord's eyes; he began to tremble, and it was clear that the dread of Felton was upon him again.

"Good-bye," he added. "You have all been very good friends to me. If I get a chance I will write to you. Come, Jack, you will see me part of the way?"

"I hate myself for letting you go," answered Jack.

"Do not say that; it is best that you should live, even if I have to suffer."

"The chiel's right," MacTavish exclaimed. "Felton will not hurt you, and, by giving him a sum of money, you may be able to buy him off. He will treat you differently now he knows your rank. I wish you luck."

Warner went out and saddled two fresh horses.

Jack and Osmond walked up the garden path.

Not a word was exchanged between them.

When the horses came up, they mounted, and waving an adieu with their hands, galloped on to the prairie.

Osmond looked like a criminal going to his execution.

He trembled very much at times, and was ghastly white.

It was only with difficulty that he retained his seat in the saddle.

Jack was also low-spirited.

They hurried on to their destination.

At length they reached some hilly ground, and pulled up to breathe their steeds.

"I should like to know what Felton will do with me," remarked Osmond, gloomily.

"Try to make money out of you," replied Jack. "My idea is he will go to England with you, and play the part of a fine gentleman."

"In that case I can put the police on to him."

"True!" exclaimed Jack; "but the English police have nothing to do with what has taken place out here. They will laugh at you, and if an American detective went across the Atlantic, Felton would turn round on you for your share in the robbery of the stage and the express."

"I did not mean to have any share in it; I was compelled."

"We all know that; yet you would have to come here and stand your trial. You would be acquitted, of course; but it would gain you an unpleasant notoriety."

"What would you advise me to do?"

"That is a difficult question to answer He will be always playing with your feelings and preying on your purse. I can't advise you. Be guided by circumstances."

"Shall I run away from him if I get the chance?"

"If you do he will follow you to England; and how are you to get there without money?"

"Granted that I could reach the coast, I would work my way in some ship. Oh, what a fix I am in with that fiend—I can't call him a man! I wish I was dead!" exclaimed Osmond, in a despairing tone of voice.

"Cheer up," said Jack.

"I can't, old fellow; only wish I could."

"It is always darkest before dawn. You will come out all right."

The ground was now more level, and they started their horses again.

Osmond's mind was in a whirl.

The only course of action he could decide upon was to escape from Felton whenever he got the chance.

He did not care about returning to England for a few years, and it mattered little to him how he got his living.

His disposition was an adventurous one; he was getting used to roughing it.

To his mother he had already written, assuring her of his safety, and he would write again to allay her anxiety.

While those thoughts were agitating his brain, Jack pulled up at the sand-hills.

"Here we are!" exclaimed our hero. "I suppose we must part. Do you recollect your way?"

"Not in the starlight," was the reply.

"Then I must perforce go with you. I believe I could find the accursed spot blindfolded."

"I dread crossing the Devil's Gap."

"Mind what you are about, or down you will go to meet Perks, the lawyer."

"What? You don't mean to say Felton cast him down there?"

"Indeed I do; he told me so himself," answered Jack.

"The double-dyed rascal!" Osmond said. "Hanging is too good for him."

They got off their horses, tethered them as usual, and began to cross the sand-hills.

Jack was well acquainted with the path they had to traverse.

Jagged pieces of granite rock arose here and there.

Suddenly a tall figure stepped forward from behind one of these.

"Stand!" cried a voice, which they knew to be Felton's.

The boys halted in a moment.

"I have brought Osmond," said Jack, "and as he has come with me to save my life, I have one favour to ask of you—treat him well."

"That will depend upon how he behaves," replied the road-agent. "If he is my willing slave—"

Osmond interrupted him, firmly but quietly.

"I will be a slave to no man," he exclaimed.

"We shall see," replied Felton. "This is not the time to discuss that matter. Come with me to the cave."

He drew the boy's arm within his own.

A smile of malignant triumph curled his lip.

The rich young Lord Melbury was in his power once more.

No sooner had Felton touched him than Osmond felt the old sensation of weakness approaching to cowardice.

His will was dominated by the man's stronger one.

"Don't hurt me, and I will do what you tell me," he said.

"That is the way to talk. Come," answered Felton; "a bird might as well try to escape from the fascination of a rock-snake as you from me."

Jack waved his hand.

"Farewell!" he exclaimed.

Thinking that he had performed his part of the compact, he was about to depart.

He was mistaken, however.

The road-agent gave a shrill whistle.

Springing up from the ground where he had been lying concealed, Dawes flew upon Jack.

Giving him a blow under the ear, which made him somewhat oblivious of things in general, he rapidly passed a rope round his arms.

"Ha, ha!" laughed Felton. "All the fools are not dead yet!"

Recovering himself, Jack looked indignantly at the road-agent.

"What does this mean?" demanded he. "It is a breach of faith. You declared, if I induced Osmond to come to you, I should be at liberty to return to the ranche."

"And you believed me?"

"I certainly did."

"More fool you, then. I have no respect for my word. I live to deceive. I am a bird of prey."

"If I could get at you," cried Jack, "I would pay you for this, you black-hearted ruffian! How I have been deceived!"

"You evidently thought you knew a great deal; but you did not."

"What is to be my fate?"

"I don't know," replied the road-agent, carelessly; "that depends entirely upon Dawes."

"How? I do not understand."

"He said he had a grudge against you, and I good-naturedly told him that if he could capture you, he might do as he liked with you; so if he chooses to plug you with a bullet, or throw you down the Gap, he is perfectly at liberty to do so."

"You mean that?" gasped Jack.

"I shall not interfere."

So saying, the road-agent marched along with Osmond.

Not for a moment had Jack imagined that Felton would play him such a dastardly trick!

The rascal had shown himself more of a scurvy knave than ever.

He did not seem to have one redeeming point about him.

"Say," exclaimed Dawes, "ain't this prime? You started me on a wild career, and now you've got to reap the fruits of it."

"Kill me at once, and have done with it," replied Jack.

"I hate you enough to do it; but I want to have fun with you first," Dawes rejoined.

"What do you mean by that?"

"Just what I say, sonny. You've got to die sooner or later, there is no discount on that; but as the boss has given you up to me, I shall take my time over the job."

Dawes gave his arms a twist which nearly wrenched them from their sockets.

With difficulty Jack suppressed a cry of anguish, for the pain was acute.

"Aren't you cornered?" laughed Dawes. "You'll never see Helen again, but I hope to."

"She knows what you are," replied Jack, provoked into answering.

"I'll burn the ranche, and carry her off somewhere.

"Villain! I wish your words would choke you."

Dawes gave him a savage kick.

"Don't you talk back, or I'll break your neck on short notice," exclaimed he. "I ain't going to take cheek from a Britisher."

Perforce Jack was silent again, though his blood pulsed like liquid fire through his veins.

The brutal cowboy made him walk to the cave, whither Felton and Osmond had preceded them.

When they reached the plank, Jack paused.

"I can't walk over," he said, "unless I have my arms loose to balance myself."

"That's so," answered Dawes.

He removed our hero's weapons from his belt, and then undid the rope which bound him.

One after the other they crossed the frail bridge.

Then, having gained the other side of the chasm, Dawes was careful to rebind his prisoner, and remove the plank.

"Into the cave!" he exclaimed. "I'm just dog-tired for sleep. You can pitch in that corner. I'll take a half hitch round your legs, and in the morning I'll—"

He paused as if to give more weight to his words.

"Go on," said Jack; "I'm not afraid."

"I'll burn you, as the Indians do their captives. If I shot you or put you down the Gap, or stabbed you, there wouldn't be much suffering, but if I burn you slowly, I guess you'll suffer some."

Jack gave him a disdainful look, walked into the cave, lay down in a corner, allowed his legs to be tied—in fact, he could not help it—and tried to forget his troubles in sleep.

"It's no good kicking, sonny," Dawes observed. "I've got you in the hollow of my hand."

Jack made no reply.

"Needn't think I'm going to lose sight of you either," added the cowboy. "I'll pitch by your side."

The grey dawn of morning was now stealing into the cavern.

This, however, did not permit objects to be distinctly perceived.

Felton and Osmond were reclining on some blankets at the end of the cave,

and Lourada was still in his drunken stupor not far off.

Osmond was wearied, physically and mentally.

He soon slept.

Jack was not more than mortal.

He, too, soon fell asleep, and from the sound that emanated from Dawes, there could be no doubt he was in the arms of the drowsy god.

Felton was wide awake.

A remarkable peculiarity of this man was that, when he wished to do so, he could dispense with sleep for thirty or forty hours at a time.

On this occasion he wanted all his faculties about him.

When he was satisfied that Dawes and Lourada were unconscious, he rose.

Touching Osmond on thè arm, he awoke him.

"What is it?" asked the boy, half frightened.

"Hush!" was the reply. "Not a word."

"But—" began Osmond.

"Follow me," interrupted Felton.

Osmond did so without any further demur, and the robber noiselessly led the way out of the cave.

The sun was rising like a ball of fire.

Its golden rays were spreading over the eastern horizon.

They crossed the plank, which Felton silently placed over the yawning chasm.

Then he quickened his pace over the sandy track.

Passively Osmond walked in his steps.

Reaching the prairie, Felton unfastened the two mustangs which Jack had tethered.

"One for you, the other for me," he said.

"Where are we going?" asked Osmond, timidly.

"To see the world."

"Will you abandon your companions in crime?"

"Bah! What do I care for them?" replied Felton, cynically. "I mean to lead the life of a gentleman. From to-day I give up robbing. Felton, the road-agent, will live at his ease."

"How can that be done without money?" Osmond ventured to enquire.

"I have saved enough to go on with from the last stage robbery. I took

Lourada's share while he was drunk; the rest I shall get from you."

"But I am penniless."

"You must telegraph to your mother," said Felton; "tell her you want five hundred pounds paid to your credit at the First National Bank of Little Rock, the city to which I am going."

"Well, what then?" asked Osmond.

"Lady Melbury will go to her banker, and tell him to communicate with Little Rock, and you will receive a message to this effect: 'The First National Bank will pay five hundred.' Mount!"

"You have no feeling for your friends. What will become of Dawes and the Spaniard?"

"They will fall into the hands of the police, I reckon, and spend a considerable number of years within four walls—that is to say, in prison."

"Will Dawes release my friend Jack?" asked Osmond.

"Don't ask me any more foolish questions," said Felton, making a gesture of impatience. "How do I know what the cowboy will do? What do I care? I have done with him. Mount!"

Osmond breathed a weary sigh.

He got on the horse.

Felton was already up, and they cantered away.

Osmond was now more over-burdened with care on Jack's account than on his own.

He was afraid that Dawes might do our hero a deadly injury.

Yet he hoped that the cowboy would not dare to hurt him during Felton's absence.

The road-agent had said no word of his intention to flit.

Lourada and Dawes were absolutely in the dark.

How much the vindictive cowboy hated Jack of Warwick, Osmond did not know, though he was aware that they were rivals for the affection of Helen.

It was a relief to him when Felton drew rein and called a halt.

This he did not do until they had reached Hanging Man's Holding, where, at least, he was sure of water.

The place was entirely deserted save by a young cow, which had strayed from the herd.

Felton went up to it, drew his pistol, and put a bullet in the beast's brain.

It fell to the ground with a low moan.

"Get some wood and build a fire," cried he. "We'll have some fresh beef for breakfast, anyway."

"It is one of Bunyard's cattle," said Osmond. "I can see his brand."

"I don't care a straw whose property it is. I'm hungry, and need food. Set to while I carve some meat off."

They were soon both at work.

After a refreshing rest, and a hearty meal, they started again in a north-easterly direction.

Felton did not dare to linger in that neighbourhood.

He was extremely anxious to get out of Texas as quickly as he possibly could.

There was danger to him in the very air.

CHAPTER XIX.

DAWES TRIES HIS HAND AT TORTURING HIS CAPTIVE—THE SPANIARD WAKES UP— A FIERCE FIGHT ENDS TO JACK'S ADVANTAGE.

THE sun was high in the heavens when Dawes roused himself.

Jack had been awake some time, pondering over the position in which he was placed, but seeing no means of extricating himself from it.

Dawes stretched his limbs, and said he "guessed he'd steer for a drink."

There was some water in a tub, warm, and of not a very good flavour, for it had been brought from a distance, and had stood for some days; large animalculæ abounded in it.

When he had taken out a cupful, he did not like the look of it.

"Reckon," he added, "this water must be adulterated with some whisky, if it is only to destroy the polly-wogs."

He accordingly made a half-and-half

drink, which, when disposed of, settled his nerves and enlivened him.

Looking round, he was unable to see Felton or Osmond, which surprised him to a great degree.

Lighting a lantern, which formed part of the stores the road-agent had accumulated in the cave, he walked all round the place.

Not finding any sign of the missing ones, he went outside, only to meet with the same result.

"The boss has gone somewhere," he muttered, "and taken that English cub with him."

He chuckled to the tune of his malevolent thoughts, and added—

"But that will not prevent me from carrying out my programme with regard to Jack of Warwick."

Going back to the cave, he drank some more whisky.

Then giving Jack a vicious kick, he told him to get up.

"How can I?" replied Jack. "Do you forget that I am bound?"

"Oh, I'll soon settle that," Dawes said, cutting the cord which bound our hero's ankles. "Don't think you can scare me. I'm no mugwump to be bulldozed by you."

"I have said nothing to raise your ire."

"No, but you have been thinking a lot, haven't you? What do you mean by thinking of me badly, and abusing me under your breath, you ugly Britisher?"

"Can a man help his thoughts?" asked Jack.

"Don't sass me, or I'll thrash the life half out of you. Where's Felton? You saw him and the boy go out."

"Indeed I did not. This is the first intimation I have had that he is not in the cave."

"Bah!" exclaimed Dawes, with a sneer, "you can't deceive me. It's clear you won't speak; but, by thunder! I'll make you, my friend."

"Why do you seek to pick a quarrel with me?" asked Jack.

"Pshaw! you are my prisoner. What would I want to quarrel with the likes of you for?"

"Perhaps you will be human enough to give me some biscuits and water. I am parched and famished."

"Nary bite! nary sup! It's too good for you," said Dawes. "I can't pity a cuss of your sort. You'd no kinder business to come over here. Why didn't you stay in your own country, you Johnny Bull? We Yankees don't come and invade you, to take the bread out of your mouths."

Jack bit his lip, refraining from making any reply.

He was suffering acutely from thirst and want of food.

But he had to endure his misery uncomplainingly.

Dawes now busied himself in making some curious preparations.

He took the rope which bound Jack's hands behind his back, and adding another piece to it, slipped it over a projecting ledge of rock.

Hauling it tight, he fastened it, and Jack stood with his back to the wall, unable to move.

This done, Dawes collected all the empty wooden boxes that had once held provisions, broke them up, and piled them round our hero's feet.

The wood was as dry as tinder, ready to kindle at a spark.

All this time Lourada had never stirred.

His burly form was stretched at full length near the entrance to the cavern.

"For heaven's sake!" cried Jack, determined to make a last effort to touch the heart of his enemy, "what are you about?"

"Making ready for a light up," was the reply.

"Have you gone mad?"

"Not a cent's worth. Oh no; I'm not crazy—no fear."

He applied himself again to the spirit-bottle, and his speech became thick, his eyes wild, and his feet unsteady.

"Hic!" he went on, "what's the matter with the master? Where's he gone—hic!—that's what I want to know?"

Suddenly his eyes lighted on a piece of paper which was fastened to the wall by the aid of a nail taken from one of the wine-cases.

On it was something written in pencil.

"By gum!" cried Dawes, sobering a little. "He means something, or I'm very much mistaken."

"'THROW THE SPANISH UPSTART DOWN THE GAP,' CRIED DAWES."

With bleared and bloodshot eyes, the cowboy read the pencilled lines—

"To all whom it may concern. This is to give notice.

"Felton, the road-agent, has gone to parts unknown.

"Let those catch him who can.

"This is my defiance to the whole world, especially Texas, which will never see me again."

Felton was fond of doing this kind of thing.

The man was gifted by nature with a large amount of vanity.

His self-conceit could not be kept down.

At the slightest provocation it came to the surface.

"Gone and left us!" ejaculated Dawes. "If that ain't real mean, I'm not standing here."

Jack was interested.

"What's that?" hs demanded in a husky voice.

"The boss has bolted!" exclaimed Dawes. "Here's a notice."

"Felton and Osmond gone?"

"That's so. I'll settle my account with you, and I guess I'll be off too."

"Let me accompany you."

"Not much! Oh no; I can't do business that way. The Spaniard can bury you—that is, what's left of you when I've done the burning; but he does not show any sign of life yet. The drink's real sodden into him."

"Why should you persecute me like this?"

"Because I hate you!"

Hissing these words through his teeth, Dawes struck a match and advanced to the pile of wood he had placed around Jack.

His intention was to light it.

Then he would gloat over his victim's dying agonies, and depart silently, as the road-agent had done.

But it was not to be.

The Fates were not yet prepared to cut the thread of Jack of Warwick's young life.

Being more than half intoxicated, Dawes made a false step and lurched over against Lourada.

Recoiling, he cannoned against the wall and fell heavily on the man, who was now thoroughly aroused.

"Thousand saints! What are you doing?" cried Lourada.

"Blessed if I know," was the reply.

Lourada sprang up and kicked him in the side.

"Give me a chance, stranger," cried Dawes.

"Get up," replied Lourado. "I'll teach you to insult a Spanish hidalgo."

Dawes rose to his feet and grinned at him like a monkey.

"Where did you get your title?" he asked. "In gaol?"

"Villain! I was born a marquis. Am I to be insulted by a cowboy?"

"I'm as good as any greaser that jumped across the Rio Grande."

"Draw your knife!" cried Lourada, "and defend yourself, for I will have your life for that insult, or lose mine in the attempt."

"Come on, then," answered Dawes. "You sha'n't take any cowardly advantage of me."

"Draw! This shall be a duel to the death."

Dawes produced a formidable-looking bowie-knife from his belt.

Lourada drew a dagger.

"Caramba! now for it!" he said. "You are not the first cowboy I have killed, and I hope you will not be the last."

For a brief space they looked at one another with concentrated fury in their eyes.

Dawes steadied himself and awaited the onslaught of the Spaniard.

It was not long in coming.

With a howl like that of a wild beast, Lourada threw himself on the cowboy, and beating down his guard, stabbed him in the arm.

Dawes retaliated with a thrust in the leg.

They continued to cut and slash at random, inflicting severe injuries on one another.

Each one panted hoarsely as he tried to reach his adversary's heart.

At length the superior strength and agility of Dawes gave him an advantage which he was not slow to take.

He had driven Lourada against the wall.

With a quick thrust he ripped his adversary's right arm open, almost to the top of the shoulder.

Yelling with pain, the Spaniard dropped his arm to his side.

In a moment Dawes plunged his knife into his body, and with a groan Lourada sank to the ground.

The knife had penetrated to his heart, killing him almost instantly.

Dawes was in a condition scarcely much better, for he was bleeding from several wounds of a severe character.

Every moment he became weaker.

"The fool!" he said. "What did he want to attack me for? He has brought his fate on himself, and left me in a queer state."

Feeling faint, he drank some brandy, and leant against the wall.

Jack had watched this furious and horrible contest with an absorbing interest.

The result was of the highest importance to him.

He had hoped to see Dawes fall before the knife of the Spaniard.

As it was, he did not appear to be any better off than he had been.

Dawes still lived, and he had not forgotten his victim.

With a fiendsh laugh he struck a match.

"I'm coming to attend to you," he exclaimed. "If I've got to die, I shall have the pleasure of your company."

"Have your wounds bound up and you will live," replied Jack. "If I were loose I'd do it for you."

Dawes reflected a moment.

If he released Jack to attend upon him, he could secure him again.

At least, so he argued.

"Very well," he said; "it's a go. I'll undo you for a spell."

With tottering steps he approached Jack.

His knife soon enabled him to cut the rope which confined our hero's hands.

Jack felt like a condemned man reprieved at the foot of the scaffold.

With difficulty he refrained from uttering a cry of exultation.

The revulsion of feeling was so great that his eyes filled with tears, which nearly blinded him.

"Look smart!" cried Dawes; "my head is getting kinder dizzy."

"What shall I use for bandages?" asked Jack.

"Tear the shirt off that greaser, if he's got one."

Jack made an examination.

"It's rather coarse," he remarked.

"I guess it's the one he escaped from prison in. He hasn't had a show to buy another. Rip it."

Seeing the Spaniard's dagger clutched tightly in the dead man's hand, Jack placed himself so that Dawes could not see what he was doing.

He secured the weapon, and put it in his pocket.

All uneasiness vanished from his mind now.

He was on equal terms with the savage Texan, and could show fight if need be.

As rapidly as possible he tore the shirt of the unfortunate Lourada into strips.

With these he skilfully strapped up the gaping wounds on the cowboy's body.

"I've got water, and I've got canned food and biscuits," remarked Dawes; "so if I have to lay up for a week it won't hurt."

He cast a look at the ghastly remains of Lourada.

"Say," he added, "I can't have that carrion lying around."

"What shall I do with him?" Jack enquired.

"Throw the Spanish upstart down the Gap. Fire him out of here, anyway."

Taking hold of the body by the heels, Jack dragged it out of the cave.

Though the sun was shining with its accustomed brilliancy, the chasm looked more black and sombre than ever.

A mephitic odour as of commingled sulphur and pitch arose from its rocky depths.

Jack shivered from head to foot as he pushed the corpse over.

One false step, a crumbling of the soft stone, and he, too, would be engulfed therein.

With a rushing noise the body vanished.

"Come back!" shouted Dawes.

Turning round, Jack favoured him with a look of defiance.

He had made sure that the plank was over the chasm.

There was nothing to prevent him from beating a retreat whenever he liked.

"On the contrary," he replied, "I am

going to wish you a very good morning."

"I'll shoot you like a rabbit, if you attempt to run."

"Do your worst. I defy you!"

Saying this, Jack made for the plank.

With a yell of disappointed spite, Dawes whipped out his revolver.

A mist swam before his eyes, arising from weakness.

He could see Jack, in a blurred kind of manner, crossing the plank.

With a fierce imprecation, he fired.

The bullet whizzed harmlessly past Jack's head.

Dawes endeavoured to run after him, to get another shot on somewhat more favourable terms.

But his legs gave way beneath him.

With a terrible oath, he fell on his knees, and the pistol was discharged in the air.

The ball struck the top of the cave, bringing down a lot of stone and a cloud of dust.

"It's hard to part sometimes, but I must leave you," exclaimed Jack, in a jeering tone.

The almost fainting cowboy foamed at the mouth with impotent rage.

"Why don't you come back?" he yelled. "I—I won't hurt you. Don't you see I'm not well enough to be left alone? I want someone to attend to me."

"I have very pressing business at the ranche which I can't afford to slight," replied Jack. "Shall I give any message to Miss Helen?"

"Fiends seize you! What do you want to make me mad for?"

Dawes stretched out his hand, got the brandy bottle, drank deeply, and rolled onto his back, where he remained, talking to himself in an incoherent manner.

It was a pitiable and degrading spectacle.

Jack walked rapidly away from the cave.

That Dawes would die he did not think.

But whether he lived or not did not matter much to him.

He congratulated himself upon having got so well out of the scrape into which the foul treachery of Felton had betrayed him.

That Osmond would eventually extricate himself from the road-agent's thraldom, he hoped sincerely.

When he reached the spot where he had staked the mustangs, and found them gone, he was not surprised.

It was only natural that Felton should appropriate them to his own use.

Plucking up his courage, Jack started to walk to the spring, for his lips were dry and cracked for want of water.

In due time he arrived at the spring, and drank, then rested himself in the grateful shade of the few trees.

It was a relief to slake his thirst and escape from the heat of the sun, which was almost tropical in its intensity.

The sun had declined a little from the meridian when Jack of Warwick made a fresh start.

He was in high spirits at his escape and the prospect of soon seeing Helen, who would thrill with horror at his adventures.

The walk to the ranche would have been a serious undertaking to any man, but Jack was wonderfully strong and hardy for his age.

Before he had gone very far, he saw a man on horseback coming towards him, riding in a very gingerly manner.

A glance sufficed to show him that it was Mr. Deep, the Austin private detective.

"Ah, cowboy!" exclaimed Mr. Deep, "what's the news?"

"Find out," replied Jack, who did not relish being addressed in this familiar manner.

"My! how uncivil you chaps are. This is my first experience of bull-punchers, and I hope it will be the last. Your colleague, named Warner, last night threw me into a pit, and I had to stay there till morning, when that old compound of Scotch snuff and whisky, MacTavish, got me out."

"Serve you right."

"Hang your confounded impudence!"

The horse began to prance and curvet.

In vain Deep tried to keep in the saddle.

He was thrown off ignominiously, and the mustang trotted off a few yards, and leisurely cropped the grass.

"Hang that beast!" said Deep. "That is the third time he has thrown me since I quitted the ranche to-day. I never saw such a vile screw in all my life. MacTavish would not have lent him to me if he had been of any good."

" Pshaw ! the horse is all right."

" What's the matter, then ? "

" You don't know how to ride him," replied Jack. " What's the use of putting a tailor on horseback ? "

" You are abominably rude. Catch him for me, cowboy."

" Catch him yourself. If you address me in that manner again, I'll treat you to something you won't like."

" Call it square, and I'll give you a dollar."

" Keep your money, catch your horse, and go your way," answered Jack.

" Your rather tough for a cow —"

" Stop it ! " interrupted Jack, with a threatening gesture.

" Beg pardon. Tell me the result of your expedition," said Deep ; adding, as he saw Jack hesitated to speak : " Have a reviver ? "

And he produced a flask, which he handed to the cowboy.

Jack eagerly accepted it.

" Uncommon fine, eh ? " asked the detective.

" Goes down good. You've risen fifty per cent. in my estimation, and if you'll run for Governor of the State next year, I'll get all my friends to cast a vote for you."

" Do better than that."

" How ? " asked Jack.

" Tell me about Felton. Come, there's a good fellow. There's money in it, and I want to land a stake after travelling this distance, being robbed, and losing time and money so far."

" Felton broke his word, and made me a prisoner. He bolted in the night with Osmond."

" Ha, good ! If I can catch the two, I shall get the two rewards. That is splendid ! Which way did they go ? "

" How can I tell ? "

" No, no ; of course not. You were a prisoner. Go on with your story."

" I don't like your interruptions," answered Jack. " However, this is how it was : The Spaniard was asleep. Felton told Dawes he could do what he liked with me. He would have killed me, only he and Lourada quarrelled. They fought. The Spaniard is dead ; Dawes lies in the cave, dangerously wounded ; and I am an escaped prisoner."

This was an extraordinary story.

Deep was of a sceptical nature, and found it rather difficult to believe what our hero said.

" Are you giving me taffy ? " he asked.

" Confound you," replied Jack. " Do you want to insult me ? It's a plain, simple, true tale."

" Humph ! I'm a reader of romance—"

" That will do," said Jack. " You've got the truth. Call it taffy, if you like. I'm off."

" Well, good-bye. Hope to see you again some day," exclaimed Deep. " I'll never rest until I catch the road-agent."

" You talk a lot."

" I'll do a lot, too, sonny. Got any message to send to your chum, Lord Melbury ? "

" Yes."

" What is it ? "

" Tell him that I said the biggest fool that ever walked on two legs was a chap named Deep, from Austin."

" Oh, come, I say ! " remonstrated Mr. Deep, trying to get hold of the horse.

The animal persistently refused to allow himself to be caught.

Perhaps there was something of the manner of a novice in the Austin detective's mode of riding which the horse objected to.

At all events, he had got him off, and he did not mean to allow him to get on again.

" Come to your oats," said Deep, in a coaxing voice. " Poor fellow ! Here ! Oats, oats ! "

The wary mustang would let him come within a yard, and then dash off to a little distance.

" Do catch him for me," cried Deep. " I want to get under weigh quickly, or I sha'n't reach a shelter before nightfall."

The horse knew Jack, who had often fed him in the stables and ridden him to the stock.

When he called him by his name, which was Ranger, the animal trotted up to him.

Seizing the bridle, Jack put his foot in the stirrup, and sprang lightly into the saddle.

He gathered up the reins with a light laugh.

"Hi! Say, you there! What are you doing?" cried Deep.

"I thought I'd ride home, instead of footing it," rejoined Jack.

"But, look here, the horse is lent to me. Mr. MacTavish loaned it to me himself."

"I'll tell him you are a thousand times obliged, and have sent it back."

"I promised to pay him."

"Pshaw! he won't ask for payment. I know him. He'll only be too glad to see the horse again."

"Are you larking with me?" asked Mr. Deep.

"Not the least little bit in the world. Oh, dear, no! I'm solid on having a ride."

"Then I'm to walk, am I? Perhaps get lost on the prairie," cried Deep, furiously.

"That's about what it amounts to."

"Bah! Durn all cowboys, say I. They are a tarnation bad lot. I don't hold with them at all."

"They are as good as detectives," retorted Jack. "If you don't like us, why did you come into our territory?"

"Why, indeed!"

"We didn't ask you, and I guess we shall get on just as well without you as with you. Good-bye."

Giving him this valedictory speech, Jack galloped off at a quick pace.

Mr. Deep shook his fist at him, but was powerless to stop his progress.

It had occurred to Jack that MacTavish was not exactly the kind of generous-hearted person to lend a horse to a stranger.

Nor was it so.

Deep had waited till the cowboys had gone out to their duty, and had then stolen the horse from the stable.

A few hours' hard riding brought our hero to his destination.

Helen was with her father in the garden as he drew rein, and she welcomed him in the most hearty manner.

Their surprise was great when he related his adventures.

"Hech, mon alive!" MacTavish exclaimed, offering his hand; "you'll be wanting a pinch of sneeshin' after that."

"More likely he'll want his dinner," replied Helen.

"I guess that's so, for I'm as hollow as a drum," answered Jack.

"Take the horse to the stable, and I'll set Mauma to work," Helen continued. "In half-an-hour you shall have something very nice, such as I only give my especial favourites."

"Vera good," said MacTavish; "I'm glad to see the cheil back. We'll go up to Snell's, and he can treat me."

"Father, what are you talking about?"

"Aboot a drink; I mean, I'll treat him, and he can treat me after. It comes to the same thing, only a man gets twa drinks instead of one, which is highly beneficial."

Helen could not help laughing as she went indoors to see to Jack's dinner, and when he had put the mustang in the stable, our hero walked up to Snell's with the Scotchman."

The saloon was entirely deserted, though it was expected every hour that the Brazos stage would come into town under an escort of soldiers from the fort near Nacogdochee.

Snell was sitting outside the door, talking to his wife, who stood by his side knitting.

"I saw you ride by," exclaimed Snell; "but you did not stop to talk. Is there anything new?"

"Gi'e us some of your gude stuff, and you'll hear what you will hear," replied MacTavish. "I always hold that the mouth should be filled before the ear."

Laughing at the quaint remark, Snell led the way inside, placed the bottle, water, and glasses on the counter, and listened to the strange story Jack had to tell him.

"It's good to hear that Felton's jumped this claim," he said. "We've no use for him."

"Nor Dawes either," cried MacTavish.

"Sakes alive! the woods are full of better cowboys than he; let him go."

"We may be troubled with him again," observed Jack.

"Why didn't you put an end to his existence when you had the chance?"

"No, Snell," said Jack of Warwick. "I will never take life wantonly; only in self-defence, and then as a last resource."

"Well said, my boy," MacTavish cried. "Human life is sacred. God gave it, and if you take it you can't give it back—no, sir."

Snell acquiesced in this proposition by bowing his head.

"I shouldn't have made the remark I did," he said, "if I hadn't taken a mighty big dislike to that skunk. He's of a revengeful disposition; and I fear you will rue offending him."

"How can he injure me?"

"The evil-minded wait for their opportunities. But, hallo! what's that sound I hear?"

"I reckon it's the stage," MacTavish replied.

They hastened outside, and saw the stage coming up the road.

It was guarded by four soldiers on horseback.

Two on each side, fully armed.

On the box-seat, by the side of the driver, was, as conceited as ever, the very man they had just been talking about.

Mr. Deep, the Austin detective, had struck the Brazos road just at the time the stage was coming along.

The inside was full of passengers, and the colonel commanding at the fort had granted an escort.

This was done at the request of the sheriff, Mr. Prober, who was among the travellers.

He had come to Mowbray's Ranche to see if he could glean any particulars respecting the recent movements of the road-agents.

The stage stopped, the passengers alighted, and were conducted by Snell into the room for refreshments.

Two stayed behind conversing confidentially together.

One was Mr. Deep, and the other Sheriff Prober.

"That's him, Mr. Sheriff," suddenly cried the detective, pointing to Jack of Warwick.

"I must have a sworn information," replied Prober, who was rather a thick-headed individual.

"All right, sir," continued Deep excitedly. "I can solemnly swear that the cowboy before me has within the last twelve hours been in communication with Felton; that he has only just left the cave of the robbers, and that a companion of his named Osmond has actually gone off with Felton."

Jack listened to this indictment with amazement.

It was all perfectly true; but why was he denounced before the sheriff?

He had not long to remain in ignorance of the why and wherefore.

"My lad," said Prober, "this looks very black against you. What have you got to say to the charge?"

"I certainly have seen Felton," Jack replied. "You see, I went to catch him and got caught myself."

"You escaped, I suppose?"

"Yes, sir. I—"

"He did nothing of the kind," cried Deep. "I appeal to Mr. MacTavish. Didn't he ride here in the night and take the other boy back with him to Felton?"

"Dinna appeal to me, you mischief-making loon," said the Scotchman.

"Can you give me an explanation of what is alleged against you?" asked Prober of Jack.

"Full and ample, but it is a romantic story, and, perhaps, you would not believe me."

"He'll tell you a pack of lies," Mr. Sheriff," exclaimed Deep. "Oh, I know him. All cowboys are bad eggs, but he's the worst of the bunch."

"I have heard enough to determine me how to act," replied Prober.

"That's right. You mind your business, and I'll mind mine," said Jack of Warwick.

He strode off, thinking the affair was at an end.

In this belief, however, he was greatly mistaken, for Prober had come to the conclusion that it was his duty to act on the information he had received from Deep.

He knew the detective had offices in Austin, and had ferreted out several cases of much interest to the Texan community.

If he arrested Jack he might be getting hold of a clue to the plans and hiding-place of Felton.

The road-agent had already acquired the title of the Terror of Texas.

No one knew where he would crop up, or what he would do next.

Mr. Sheriff Prober's judicial mind was greatly exercised, and he decided to lay Jack by the heels in gaol.

Unsuspicious of his determination, our hero walked on quickly, seeing Warner and White coming towards him.

Having just returned from the prairie, they were hastening to the saloon to get a cooling drink and see the stage-passengers.

"Are you going to lose your chance?" asked Deep, in an insinuating tone. "I tell you this cowboy is hand and glove with Felton."

"I will arrest him," answered Prober. "Sergeant!"

"Yes; at your service," replied the soldier who was in command of the escort.

"I am about to make an arrest," said Prober. "If I am interfered with in the execution of my duty, I call upon you for protection."

"I'll not see you hurt, sheriff."

"Very good, sergeant; on you I rely, because at this crisis you are a member of the executive."

"If you want protection and will cry out for it, I'll see that you come to no harm," said the sergeant.

"Be sure you holler loud enough. I and my men are going to see if there is any virtue in a little old rye."

The sergeant was as good as his word. He ordered his men to dismount.

They entered the saloon together, their long swords clanking on the floor.

Being soldiers, and especially cavalry, they thought themselves infinitely superior to policemen, and did not care to act under the orders of the sheriff.

It was a duty they considered beneath their dignity, and the sergeant would have allowed Prober to be half killed before he would attempt to rescue him.

"Ha, boys," exclaimed Jack, as he met his companions, "here I am. A bad penny is sure to turn up."

At this moment the sheriff clapped his hand on the cowboy's shoulder.

"I arrest you in the name of the law," he said. "Consider yourself my prisoner."

Jack turned sharply, throwing off the obnoxious grasp.

"What do you mean?" he shouted.

"Stick to him, Mr. Sheriff. Don't let your lawful prey escape; he's in the pay of the road-agents," cried Deep.

Again the sheriff seized Jack, and received a stinging blow in the face for his pains.

He would not leave go.

Deep came to his assistance, striking Jack on the head with a stick.

"Help, boys!" cried Jack of Warwick. "Are you going to see me treated in this way, and not lift a finger in my behalf?"

"Not much," answered Warner. "I'll tackle this bilious-looking chap who is so free with his bit of wood."

"And I'll attend to the grabber," said White, who, though he did not like Jack, was not going to see him imposed upon by a stranger.

By the side of the road was a long deep pond.

It was supplied by two artesian wells worked by windmills.

Sometimes there is no rain for months in Texas, but there is plenty of wind; and whenever the wind blows it works the windmills, and the water is thus pumped up from the earth.

In less than a minute Warner had securely collared his man, and Deep, much to his disgust, found himself being rapidly propelled towards the water.

The pond was called the Cattle Lick; and into it Deep was cast headlong.

"Fire your man into the Lick," cried Warner. "I've dumped mine there, and he's having a cooler."

"Right you are," rejoined Jack, who had succeeded in half choking the sheriff with White's assistance.

Each seized the little man by the collar, and they ran him to the Cattle Lick.

"Murder! Help, sergeant! Help, soldiers! Help! Mur-der! mur-der!" roared the sheriff in an agony of fear.

"Cowboys to the front!" shouted Warner.

The two extra stockmen came out of the yard at hearing the cry.

"In you go," said Jack, giving the sheriff a kick which made him dive like a widgeon.

Prober was a good swimmer. When he came to the surface he began to tread water.

About a dozen yards from him, Deep was occupied in the same interesting pastime.

"Say, sheriff," exclaimed Jack, "how do you like a cooler in the Lick?"

"I'll cool you presently, my joker," replied Prober. "The soldiers are coming."

This was a fact.

The sergeant could not help hearing

the cries of murder, but he had been as leisurely about coming to the rescue as he well could be.

As they walked down the road to the Cattle Lick, the soldiers did not hurry themselves in the least.

They took their cue from the sergeant.

Meanwhile the cowboys were not inactive.

They gathered tufts of grass and clods of earth.

With these they pelted the sheriff and the detective, who had to dive and duck to avoid being hit.

Their heads bobbed up and down like floats when the fish are biting well.

All this time their cries for help and yells of complaint were incessant.

"Well aimed!" said Jack, as he hit the sheriff on the head, and saw him bob under.

"Ditto!" exclaimed Warner, as he performed a similar feat on Deep.

"Look out, Jack!" suddenly cried White. "The boys in blue are coming. Beware of the military escort."

"I think we can manage them," replied Jack. "It's very warm, and they look as if they wanted a bath."

"Going to throw them into the Lick?" asked Warner, with a grin.

"If you fellows will help me."

"With pleasure," cried Warner and White in a breath.

"Three thoroughbred Texas cowboys like us, ought to be a match for those four soldiers," continued Jack.

"Ay, for a dozen!" said White.

There was no time to talk any more.

The sergeant and his three companions approached the cowboys at the double.

Owing to the piteous cries of the half-drowned sheriff and the equally uncomfortable Mr. Deep, they had quickened their pace to a run.

"Surrender!" shouted the sergeant, addressing Jack.

"What for?" demanded our hero.

"I've got the sheriff's orders."

"Is this your first visit among cowboys?" asked Jack.

"Yes; I haven't had any intercourse with you chaps before this."

"What do you think of us?"

"Oh, you are right enough, I reckon, if your fur ain't stroked the wrong way," answered the sergeant.

"That's just it; if we are riled up strong, we're a mighty tough crowd, and don't you forget it," said Jack.

"We're a hard contract for any merchant to take in hand," supplemented Warner, fiercely.

"About as difficult to negotiate as a bogus dollar bill," observed White.

The sergeant looked bewildered.

"What do you mean?" he asked.

"That we're cowboys, and mustn't be interfered with!" returned Jack.

"I ain't going to hurt you. Come quietly, and I'll lock you up in the stable at the saloon till we're ready to start for home."

"Thank you. Aren't you kind? Shake hands."

Unsuspicious that any attack was going to be made upon him, the sergeant extended his hand to Jack.

Instantly he was twisted round, and jerked into the water.

Warner and White served two of the soldiers in the same way, and seeing the fate of his comrades, the fourth took to his heels.

While the soldiers were struggling in the Lick, Deep had made good use of the interval of rest allowed him.

He swam to the shore, and got out.

Jack saw him in a moment.

"There's the mean rascal who is at the bottom of all the mischief!" he cried.

"Let's duck him again!" Warner said.

"We'd best lynch him!" suggested White.

"No, no," replied Jack; "no violence or bloodshed. We'll be satisfied with chasing him out of town."

"Good enough!" shouted White. "After him!"

The three cowboys started after Deep, who began to grow alarmed.

Though he was at the other side of the Lick, he had heard the remarks.

They filled him with dismay.

It was no joke to be driven out onto the prairie.

He had had sufficient experience of that already.

If he could gain the refreshment-saloon, he fancied he would obtain help, and be in comparative safety.

So he began to run like a hare, leaving the sheriff and the soldiers to scramble out of the Cattle Lick as best they could.

Jack saw his manœuvre, and succeeded in heading him off.

Deep was obliged to double, and take the road to MacTavish's, where he had some slight hope that Helen might take his part.

Having the advantage of a few yards' start, he contrived to reach the house before the cowboys.

His heart beat wildly.

He did not know how far their resentment might carry them.

The Texan papers often contained accounts of outrages committed by cowboys.

He recalled a story of an obnoxious person who was bound hand and foot by some cowboys, and then placed before half-a-dozen long-horned bulls.

These were goaded until they gored the unhappy man to death.

What would be his fate if overtaken and caught?

That was the question which agitated Mr. Deep's mind, and it troubled him greatly.

It happened that Helen MacTavish was in the dairy, where a large quantity of milk was stored every day.

Very little butter was made at the ranche, the cream being kept for making cheese, of which commodity large consignments were sent to Galveston every month.

From there the cheeses were shipped to Liverpool, finding a ready sale in that busy port.

Helping Helen was old Mauma.

Hearing the shouting, Helen sent the coloured woman to ascertain the cause of it.

"There's something wrong," remarked the young girl. "We are generally so quiet here. I do hope Felton has not come to terrify us again."

"'Pears to me it's them blessed cowboys," replied Mauma.

"Go and see, won't you, please?"

"I'll go with pleasure to oblige you, missy; but, all the same, I don't see much use of it."

She had scarcely got outside the dairy door, when Deep came rushing along the passage.

He was seeking a hiding-place.

The Austin detective and the coloured woman came into violent collision.

Mr. Deep recoiled, and fell on his back, while Mauma was shot in a tank containing many gallons of milk.

The lacteal fluid dashed up to the ceiling in a shower as the corpulent old negress fell into it.

"Oh, my!" cried Helen. "Where are you going to?"

Mauma sat up, looking the picture of misery and despair.

The milk ran down in streams from her head and shoulders.

"Lord, have mussy, miss!" replied she, "I's in the milk."

"More's the pity; it will be all spoiled."

"No, miss; it will make good cheese all the same. I sha'n't turn it sour. Don't you have any fear, honey."

"Get out at once."

"That's jes' what I'm gwine to do; and if I get hold of that man what sent me here, I'll muss his hair."

"Perhaps he couldn't help it."

"It was done for the purpose to annoy a poor old coloured lady, and I'll have satisfaction out of him!"

Before she could raise herself out of the tank, the cowboys came trooping up the passage in search of the detective.

Owing to the passage being badly lighted, they did not see him.

The consequence was that all three walked over him, and they did not tread very lightly either.

Deep uttered fearful groans and moans, for his internal organisation was seriously interfered with.

He could scarcely draw his breath, and his eyes were nearly starting out of his head with fright.

"Where is the Austin man?" asked Warner. "I've been treading on something soft, and I reckon it is him."

"Yes, yes," replied Deep; "I'm here —that is to say, what is left of me."

"Get up, or I'll make you," cried Jack.

With difficulty the detective rose.

"I've been ducked," he said, "and chivvied, and walked on till I can't stand any more of it."

"It's your own fault," answered Jack.

"I want this thing stopped right here."

"Why don't you let me alone?"

The detective did not make any answer.

"What has he done, Jack?" enquired Helen.

"Denounced me to the sheriff as an accomplice of Felton. They have been trying to arrest me."

"You?"

"Yes. What do you think of that? He's got a grudge against me. But we cowboys showed him what we could do."

"He looks wet," said Helen.

"Good reason why. We threw him into the Lick; the sheriff went with him, and the soldiers after them."

"Give him another turn," exclaimed Warner, with a merry twinkle in his eye.

He pointed to the milk tank, in which Mauma still remained.

Jack of Warwick nodded.

He seized Deep by the waist and lifted him in the air.

"One, two, three!" he cried.

Then came a mighty heave, and away went the detective.

He fell into the milk tank, right on top of Mauma, who was knocked to the bottom.

"Oh, Jack!" cried Helen, "old Mauma is in there. You'll be the death of her."

"I hope not, for I have a great respect for her cooking talents. We couldn't have a better help; her tomato jam and her pumpkin pies are——"

He stopped short.

A tremendous struggle had begun in the milk tank.

Mauma had recognised her enemy, and grappled with him, seizing him by the hair.

Deep retaliated in a similar fashion, and they rolled over and over in the tank.

The milk was scattered in showers on all sides.

At this curious and mirth-provoking sight the cowboys were convulsed with loud laughter.

Even Helen could not help joining in their merriment.

At length Deep managed to release himself from Mauma's vice-like grip, and, with a yell, jumped out onto the floor.

He ducked his head, and very cleverly butted White, after the manner of a goat.

The cowboy sank to the ground with a dismal howl.

This fall made a gap, through which Deep hoped to escape.

He dashed forward and got out of the dairy.

His triumph was short-lived, however.

In the garden he was captured by Jack, who had followed close on his heels.

"Stop!" said Jack. "Are you going to leave this ranche? You have been told to quit."

"I don't want to go," replied the detective.

"When we cowboys give a stranger notice, he's got to quit."

"That's right Jack," Warner chimed in, who had just come up. "Drive the skunk out of camp."

"Hold on," said Deep. "I see you are a hard crowd, and I'll give in to you."

"Isn't it too late, since you have spoken to the sheriff?"

"Not at all."

"How will you fix it?"

"I'll tell him I was mistaken in you. It was another cowboy who was with Felton, not you."

Jack smiled at this.

"Aren't you a cunning fellow?" he exclaimed.

"Why, yes; what I don't know isn't worth knowing," said Deep, with an air of self-complacency.

"You were brought up in a good school!"

"That's so; I forgot twenty years ago as much as most men learn in a lifetime."

"Bully for you! But will the sheriff stand to it?"

"You bet! He's a soft-headed clam, and I can do what I like with him, my boy."

"All right," returned Jack. "I'll take your word for it."

"You won't chase me out of town?"

"Certainly not, if you will keep the soldiers quiet."

"Consider it done," cried Deep. "Say, can you lend me a suit of clothes and a shirt in exchange for what I've got on?"

"We don't keep much clothing in stock."

"You see, I'm all milk and water, with an upper crust of cream."

"Take a walk in the sun and dry yourself," replied Jack.

"My dear fellow, I shall turn sour, and then——"

He paused abruptly, and sniffed the air.

"Well?" enquired Jack.

"Only this : I shall not smell particularly sweet."

"Oh, we don't mind that," laughed Jack. "A cattle ranche isn't a lady's boudoir."

"Why, no; I guess there is more truth than poetry in that remark," responded Deep. "There's a combination of evil smells about a cattle ranche, and each cowboy is a perambulating odour in himself."

"Drop that talk," said Jack. "We do our work faithfully, and do not want to be insulted."

"Not muchly!" exclaimed Warner. "If he insults us, we'll hang him to a sour apple tree."

"Ay, and bury him on the prairie," put in Jack, "and then we'll plough him up."

Mr. Deep smiled in a sickly manner.

"If you did that," he said, "you might fancy yourself at sea."

"Why so? I'm not good at conundrums."

"Because you would be ploughing the deep."

"Oh, I say!" cried Jack, "if you are going to make bad puns, we shall have to kill you on principle."

"That's against my interest."

"Stop it!" exclaimed Jack, laughing.

"Come to the saloon," replied Deep. "I'll set up the drinks and square the sheriff. Be friendly, won't you?"

"I'm agreeable. Come on, Warner," said Jack.

A reconciliation was then effected, and they walked away together.

"White and I will have to ride off!" exclaimed Warner. "Some of the cows want attending to."

"You will have to do without me to-day," answered Jack, "as I am dead tired for sleep."

"That is not to be wondered at."

"When I have had a drink with this merchant," added Jack, "I shall go into the hay-loft and have a sleep."

Warner and White took leave of Jack, thinking that everything was settled in

They did not, however, understand the character of the detective.

He was treacherous to the last degree.

"Let me lean on your arm," Deep said. "I'm rather weak."

"With pleasure," Jack answered.

The detective looked at his hands.

"Your work doesn't make your flesh coarse," he remarked.

"Why should it?" asked Jack.

"They are quite soft and white, like a girl's."

"What are you driving at?" Jack enquired, who knew that his hands were browned by exposure to the sun.

"Nothing. Hold them up, the sun kinder dazzles me, and I can't see them plainly."

Jack did as he was requested, putting his hands together.

In an instant Deep drew a pair of handcuffs from his pocket and slipped them over his wrists.

They closed with a sharp click.

Nothing could open them but the master-key.

This Deep had in his possession.

Then he drew himself up to his full height, and his eyes flashed.

His resentment at the treatment he had received had only been smothered.

"Hallo! What are you up to?" asked Jack.

"Not a word!" replied Deep.

"But——"

"Utter a syllable—cry for help, and I will knock you down."

He raised his fist to give emphasis to his threat.

"You will strike me at your peril," said Jack, his eyes glittering dangerously.

"Texan cowboys are a terror, aren't they?"

"Sometimes they get cornered."

"Thought you were going to have some fusel-oil at my expense—eh?"

"You can taunt me as much as you like, I can stand it."

"Going to lay off in the hay-loft are you?" continued Deep. "Aren't you deceived, my sonny?"

"You have got the best of me, it is true," answered Jack; "but you needn't crow too loud."

"Why shouldn't I?"

"Simply because you may get your comb cut. Now, what are you going to

"Give you to the sheriff as his prisoner, and if he doesn't march you off to Nacogdochee to be tried as an accomplice of Felton, it isn't my fault."

"Prove it."

"I'll swear hard."

"Yes," replied Jack, gloomily, "you would swear black is white; in fact, you'd swear a man's life away."

"It would not be the first time," the detective rejoined. "Put your best foot forward. March!"

Suppressing his rage as well as he could at the clever trick which had been played upon him, Jack started up the road.

Deep laughed aloud at his success.

They came to a small wooden hut, in which garden tools, roots, and seed potatoes were kept.

The door was open, and the key in it.

"Go in there," cried Deep. "That is good enough for you for an hour or two. When I want you, I'll come for you."

He gave him a push, and Jack fell on his back.

With a low laugh, Deep locked the door, and put the key in his pocket.

So far he had triumphed.

Jack of Warwick was his prisoner, and he was having his revenge upon him.

Decidedly he was master of the situation.

CHAPTER XX.

OSMOND GIVES FELTON THE SLIP—HE MEETS WITH FRIENDS UNEXPECTEDLY—THE TRAVELLING SHOW.

FOR two days Felton and Osmond traversed the vast solitude of the prairie.

They avoided houses, and made a circuit of all towns, as Felton was afraid that his description would be telegraphed all over Texas.

If he could succeed in getting into Arkansas, he would feel more at his ease, for that State was known to be a refuge for thieves, broken-down gamblers, and bad characters generally.

He was continually asking Osmond questions about England and his ancestral home, Kenilworth Hall.

On the third day, as they were riding leisurely along, he said—

"We must go to England together, and you will have to introduce me to all the swell folks you are acquainted with."

"I don't know many, but my mother does," replied Osmond.

"It's all the same. You must tell Lady Melbury that I am an American gentleman you have met with, and add that I am wealthy, and own a silver mine in Nevada. That will be sure to fetch them."

"But it is not true."

"Pshaw!" cried Felton. "What does that matter? Who is to prove the contrary, I want to know."

"It is getting into society under false pretences."

"I don't care how it is done so long as I get in. My object will be to marry one of your rich and pretty English girls —a lady of rank, if I can."

"Heaven help the poor victim!" said Osmond.

"Hang your impudence! Ain't I good enough?" cried Felton.

"You're not bad-looking when you are shaved and dressed; but consider what you are—a robber and mur—"

"That will do," interrupted the road-agent, wincing. "I want to forget all that sort of thing."

"You brought the subject up, and I tell you frankly, I do not think you would get any English lady to accept your hand."

"Oh, yes, I should, with a silver mine at my back. They'd snap at that sort of bait. All I want is your introduction."

"I suppose I cannot refuse, though it is rather soon to think of such things; we are a long way off England yet."

"That is true; but I like to build castles in the air."

"There are dangers ahead. You may be caught."

"Stay," exclaimed Felton, "don't talk in that strain. You are a regular Job's comforter! Drop it!"

"I always like to look things straight in the face."

Suddenly Felton's horse put its foot in a hole in the ground, stumbled, and fell, uttering a cry of pain.

Its rider was thrown heavily over its head.

"Confound it!" he said, as he got up and shook himself.

"Are you hurt?" asked Osmond.

"No, only shaken up a bit; but I fear the mustang has sustained a severe injury."

"How is that?"

"It's a dollar to a cent, and that's long odds, that the offside foreleg is broken."

"If so, what will you do?"

"We shall have to ride and tie—that is, you ride a certain distance while I walk; then you walk while I ride. Savvey?"

"Yes; it is awkward, though," said Osmond.

"There is nothing else for it, if it is as I imagine."

Felton advanced to examine the horse.

The poor animal had, in reality, snapped its leg in two places, making a very painful compound fracture.

It stood shivering, as if with fear, and kept up a constant moaning noise.

"As I thought," he exclaimed, "it is a case! Curse the hurt! We are several days' journey yet from the borders of Arkansas."

He took his pistol out of his belt.

Putting the muzzle to the horse's ear, he fired two shots in quick succession.

This was truly a merciful deed.

By so doing, he put the animal out of its misery.

The bullets penetrated the brain, and the horse sank to the ground, convulsed in the throes of death.

When he looked up, he was surprised to find that Osmond had ridden away.

He had halted some yards off.

What did this mean?

Felton was uncomfortably puzzled.

"Where are you off to?" demanded he.

"I don't know," replied Osmond, with an assumed air of bravado; "but I do not intend to travel any more with you."

"What!" yelled Felton.

His face became convulsed with ungovernable rage.

He saw that Osmond had been sensible enough to seize a golden opportunity of giving him the slip.

Mounted on a good horse, it would be impossible to overtake him while the pursuer was on foot.

"Come back," he cried, "or I'll shoot you."

Osmond gave no heed to the threat, but cantered farther off.

Seeing that his prey was really escaping from his clutches, the road-agent discharged his revolver.

He missed his mark, however.

Calling down a million maledictions on his head, Felton gave chase.

But he was, of course, no match for the horse.

Every moment increased the distance between them, until, with a yell of despair, he saw it was a hopeless case.

Felton raved like a madman.

Soon the boy was out of sight of his persecutor, but for some miles he did not relax the speed of his horse.

He dreaded being recaptured.

When he came to reflect on what he had done, he marvelled greatly at his presence of mind.

The idea of running away from Felton had come to him as an inspiration.

He had carried it out with apparent coolness and courage.

In truth, he had been terribly alarmed.

Now he had got away he trembled, and was continually looking back, although his common sense told him the road-agent could not be anywhere near.

In time the nervous dread wore off.

A glorious sense of freedom pervaded his entire being.

It exalted his soul, and throwing aside every vestige of his late thraldom, he was a man again.

With Felton he had always been like a slave, or a cringing, fawning dog afraid of the whip.

Now he could hold his head up, and look anybody in the face.

The tired, careworn, far-away look faded from his features.

Yet his troubles were not nearly over.

Felton had not allowed him to carry a pistol or a knife.

Without any weapon to kill, how was he to get food?

Water was also a consideration, for Felton had the keg in which they carried their scanty supply.

If he could reach a farmhouse, he no doubt would receive hospitality.

Should he reach a town, he intended to sell his horse.

With the proceeds of the sale he could adopt the plan Felton had spoken of—namely, to telegraph to Lady Melbury for money.

This would enable him to return to England, and he did not think for a moment that the robber would follow him.

He was determined to be on the safe side, though.

To be thoroughly secure, he meant to travel on the Continent, and perhaps round the world.

He would not be in one place long.

As the afternoon began to wane, he and his horse showed symptoms of great fatigue.

They could not go much farther without food or water.

As for food, there was plenty of fur and feather, to be sure, but he could do nothing without powder and shot.

The wild turkey and prairie hen were constantly whirring up from the sage bushes.

Antelope and rabbits were quite numerous, and once, to his consternation, he saw a panther.

The savage brute was a good way off.

No doubt it would have attacked him had it not been engaged in tearing the carcass of an antelope to pieces.

Having plenty of food, there was no incentive to it to chase the horse and its rider.

Osmond was beginning to feel very uncomfortable.

Not the slightest sign of any inhabited buildings did he see on any side.

In vain his eye searched the horizon.

Night would be upon him in a few short hours.

The prospect of passing the night without water was a deplorable one.

His spirits had sunk to a very low ebb, when his attention was arrested by a strange object at a distance.

At first he was unable to make it out.

A closer inspection, however, showed him that it was a caravan, such as is used by showmen.

It had been halted by the side of an old waggon-road.

This showed Osmond that he was coming closer to civilisation.

The horse had been taken out of the shafts, and was grazing.

An old man and a girl could be made out, bending over something which was lying on the grass.

Osmond quickened his pace.

He spoke a few encouraging words to the horse, and the jaded animal seemed to understand that it would soon adjourn from labour to refreshment.

The man and the girl saw him coming.

They watched his approach in an interested manner.

Suddenly the horse gave a deep gasp, and sank forward on its knees.

The shock pitched Osmond off, and the animal fell upon its side.

It was exhausted by being ridden hard and kept without water.

Evidently it was in a dying condition.

Recognising this fact, Osmond congratulated himself upon having fallen in with the caravan.

He left the horse to breathe its last, and walked towards the waggon-road.

Written on the caravan he read, "Noah Cobb, Showman. I have the greatest living curiosity—The Talking Ape, or The Man-Monkey. Admission, twenty-five cents each."

The old man was Noah Cobb, and the girl was his daughter.

Her name was Milly, and at the age of sixteen she was remarkably pretty.

She had a small mouth, black hair in curls, and laughing eyes.

Her part in the show was very simple, consisting in playing a pianette.

"Hallo, stranger!" exclaimed the showman. "Where do you hail from, and where are you going?"

"I have been staying with some friends at Mowbray's Ranche. I want to get to Nacogdochee, but I have lost my way, and, as you see, ridden my poor horse to death."

"That's bad. We are bound for Nacogdochee, and maybe it is lucky we have met."

"'THIS IS MY FRIEND, JACK OF WARWICK,' SAID OSMOND."

No. 10.

"Is this the old waggon-road I have heard of?" enquired Osmond.

"That's her. Excuse me for a while, won't you? My daughter Milly and I are in great trouble," said Noah Cobb.

"May I ask what it is?"

"Why, certainly; the talking ape's dead. What I shall do without him I don't know. There has been nothing but bad luck for me lately."

"How is that?" asked Osmond.

"I had a woolly man dressed up in sheepskin; he went off for a higher salary. Then there was my fat lady, a sure draw; she died of Dutch gin; all her salary went in it."

"Is the ape really dead?" continued Osmond, whose curiosity was aroused.

"Next door to it. Ah! he was a good boy."

"A what?"

"A boy. Don't you hear me?"

"I thought you said a monkey," replied Osmond, in perplexity.

"That's what we called him," said Cobb. "Now, ask yourself, did you ever hear a monkey talk?"

"Not I, nor anybody else."

"There's where the curiosity comes in. People are attracted by anything out of the common. We dressed Bill— that's his name—up in a gorilla-skin I bought off of a sailor in 'Frisco."

"Ah! I see," cried Osmond.

"We fixed a hairy kind of mask on his face, and when I spoke to him, asking set questions, he gave me back set answers."

"He drew well, too," said Milly Cobb. First-rate. I've made as much as a hundred dollars a week out of Bill."

"What shall we do without him, father?" asked Milly; "my playing will not keep us."

"We must get another curiosity, my dear girl."

"Of what kind, father?"

"Another talking ape. There is the suit in the van, the props are all there, and I could teach any intelligent boy the patter in a day."

"We've got a supply of provisions, and there are some dollars in my purse," remarked Milly.

"That's good enough; we sha'n't starve for a time. But where are we going to get our new ape?"

Old Noah Cobb's brow became corrugated with thought.

Bill, the talking ape, had been in a faint; Milly dabbed his face with a cloth saturated with water.

All at once he came to himself, and with a strange glare in his eyes, said—

"I'm coming."

Noah Cobb looked curiously at the boy, who was so emaciated that his bones almost protruded through his skin.

"Are you going home, Bill?" asked the showman.

"Yes, boss! I'm on the wing," said the boy.

"I wish you wasn't going to leave me. You've been a draw, Bill. I could give you a good recommend anywhere."

"I'm coming," gasped the boy, in whose throat the death-rattle could be heard.

"Hark at him!" said Cobb. "It's just like a fine piece of acting, ain't it, Milly?"

"There's no acting about that; the boy's dying," answered Milly.

"I know he's kickin' out; there is no denying that; but, lor' sakes! don't he do it well!"

"Hush, father!"

"I never saw a death done better on the stage. Look at his eyes, how he rolls them. Look at him now he's making an effort. It's fine. I tell you he's a born actor."

The boy made a spasmodic jump.

He stood upright for a moment or two, his face upturned to the sky.

"I'm coming," he said in a guttural tone. "Mother, mother, I'm coming!"

These were his last words.

He tumbled in a heap on the ground, and in a brief space the boy was dead.

"His last thoughts were of his mother," observed the showman.

"I have often heard him speak of her in the tenderest terms," sighed Milly. "She died two years ago, and I have no doubt he saw her in the clouds beckoning to him."

"I can only say I'm sorry I have lost him, and pray heaven to be kind to us all," exclaimed the old showman.

He knelt down, kissed the boy's forehead, and closed his eyes.

"We've no spade," he added; "and what I'll do to bury him I don't know."

"He will have to lie where he is,"

replied Milly, " and the coyotes will pick his bones."

" Poor little chap! " sighed Cobb. " He was a small fortune to me—and so clever. I'll never see his like again, mister."

" Call me Osmond."

" Right; I'll not forget. 'Pears to me that you are about the same size and height. Bill's monkey clothes would just about fit you."

" What do you mean? "

" Will you take the place of the dead boy? "

" I—I can't give you an answer right off," said Osmond. " It is such a very queer proposition."

" You shall have good pay, and the same food as me and Milly. We live well, too, don't we, girl? "

" In the towns," rejoined Milly. " When on the road we go short sometimes."

" What will you expect me to do? " enquired Osmond.

" Not much. I shall make you stand up in the van; as many people as it will hold will be admitted; then I ask you how old you are."

" And you will reply, ' A hundred and ninety years,'" said Milly, laughing. " It is all a trick, you know."

" After that," continued Cobb, " I shall ask your name—that is Methusalam —and where you came from."

" Africa, I suppose? "

" Say the great lakes; and there is a lot more patter I will have to teach you. Is it a bargain? "

Osmond hesitated.

To play the part of a monkey in a travelling show seemed rather derogatory to the dignity of Lord Melbury.

Milly looked imploringly at him.

If he consented it would be their salvation.

" Oh, do! " she cried, " and I will love you for ever afterwards."

" Very well," rejoined Osmond, " I can't resist your appeal."

" Will you really do it? "

" Yes; but—"

" What? " she demanded.

" Only for a time."

" I should like you to sign articles for six years, certain," said the showman.

" No," answered Osmond, " I have my own business to attend to; all I can do is to help you over your difficulty until you get another boy."

" I guess that will have to do then. You are my talking-ape until I can suit myself, and in return I'll take you on to Nacogdochee, and give you a handful of dollars into the bargain."

" That's the business."

" And good biz, too, all round. Milly, my dear, get out a can of corned beef and some bread and water," exclaimed Noah Cobb.

Life is full of ups and downs when a boy starts an adventurer's career.

How often lately had Osmond wished he had never run away from home !

He did not like being a rover.

Still, Milly's pretty face and laughing eyes compensated him for what he was to go through.

She had said that she would love him.

He already loved the showman's daughter.

If she really meant what she had said, he felt that he could marry this girl of the prairie.

It was a romantic meeting.

He would make her Lady Melbury, and take her to his ancestral home in Old England.

The old man carried the dead boy to a hollow place, laid him down, and covered him with grass.

It was all he could do.

Milly spread a cloth by the roadside, and displayed her humble fare, which, in his hungry condition, Osmond found excellent.

When it was consumed, Cobb went into the caravan, and produced the gorilla-skin which Bill used to wear.

At his request Osmond put it on.

The fit was as perfect as if it had been made for him.

When he had donned the mask, which went all over his head and neck, Milly brought him a looking-glass.

He could see himself through the eye holes.

" What do you think of yourself? " she asked.

" My best friend and my worst enemy would not know me," he replied.

" Have you an enemy? "

" Yes, and a very cruel one."

" Won't you tell me about him? " continued Milly. " Sit down in your skin, it will enable you to get used to it.

Don't be afraid to speak to me. You are the talking-ape now, you know."

"That is not a nice name to call me," said Osmond, smiling.

"It is your stage name."

"You won't like me in this disguise?"

"What difference will that make? I know you as you are, and I shall always like you for the kindness you have displayed towards us."

Noah Cobb had lighted a pipe.

He was lying on his back under the shadow cast by the waggon, asleep to all appearance.

"Tell me about your enemy," Milly said.

"My story will sound to you like a fairy tale," answered Osmond.

"All the better; I like fairy stories."

How far could he trust this young girl?

He looked at her face, and determined to make her his confidante.

Now he was away from Jack of Warwick, it would be a relief to have someone to talk to about his private affairs.

Before he began, he bound her to the strictest secrecy.

She listened to his story with the greatest interest.

"Now," he said, when he had concluded, "what do you think of my recent adventures in America?"

"They are truly wonderful, my lord," she replied.

It was the first time he had been called by his title.

The name sounded strange to him.

"I want to be always Osmond to you," he exclaimed.

"Fancy my meeting an English lord!" she said. "It does not seem real, especially on the prairie."

"You will not like me the less for that?"

"What woman would? We all worship wealth and rank. But, Osmond, since I may call you so, be careful of this man Felton."

"He is my only dread," answered Osmond.

"There is no telling where he may turn up. You say he has a genius for disguising himself. If you perform in Nacogdochee, we may have him in the audience."

"If so, he would not penetrate my disguise."

"He would recognise your voice. Be careful, I repeat."

"Depend upon it, I will not neglect your advice. That man is the curse of my life," he answered.

"When you come to a town, live in your skin."

"That is an excellent idea."

"Try and change your voice if he should come into the show."

Osmond promised to do as she told him.

He felt as if he had known Milly for years, and could trust her with his life, if need be.

The sun soon sank below the western horizon.

In the van were cubicles, or small beds, railed off, with curtains.

One of them was assigned to Osmond.

It was the one in which the dead boy had slept, and he could not close his eyes for some time for thinking of him.

His was indeed an untimely fate, all the more sad as the poor lad lay unburied on the prairie.

There was no one to mark the spot with a cross; no one to put a wreath of flowers on it.

In the morning Noah Cobb woke early, and breakfast was quickly prepared.

Osmond was very thankful to have met such good friends.

He was equally glad to be on the road again.

His dread of Felton, however, was so great that he kept himself dressed in the gorilla-skin.

It was lucky for him that he did so.

The caravan had not proceeded half-a-dozen miles before they met the famous road-agent.

Cobb and Osmond were walking along together, engaged in conversation.

Milly was sitting on a chair at the rear of the van, sewing some article of feminine attire.

"Say," cried Felton, "where does this road lead to?"

"Nacogdochee," replied Cobb.

Felton, of course, did not recognise Osmond, though he looked at him curiously.

As for Osmond, he was so frightened that he had to put one hand on the wheel to steady himself.

"You're a curiosity-monger, I guess?" continued Felton.

"I used to have a good show, but my people have died or deserted, and I've only this talking-ape left."

"Humbug! Apes don't talk. Your show's a fraud."

"Never mind. It rakes in the dollars and cents."

"Good enough, old man! I've been there, and you can't fool me. Give me a drink of water and something to eat."

"With pleasure."

The showman called to his daughter, who quickly supplied the robber's wants.

"Good morning!" exclaimed Cobb. "I must get under way—time is money."

"All right. Thank you. But, say, have you seen a boy on a horse?"

"No, I haven't."

"Not met anybody?"

"Nary soul. This road is kinder lonely. Two days ago I met an emigrant-waggon, that's all."

Felton gave him a nod, and Cobb started his caravan again.

Then Osmond began to breathe freely once more.

It was a narrow escape.

If Felton had known who the talking-ape really was, he would have committed murder to regain his victim.

Osmond felt faint and ill.

Going to the rear of the caravan, he asked Milly if he might come in.

"Certainly," she replied. "What is the matter with you?"

"Hush!" said Osmond. "The man you fed is no other than Felton."

"Your enemy—the road-agent?"

"Yes. Would you know him again?" asked Osmond. "It is best for all of us to be acquainted with his features."

"I should know him anywhere."

Just then Noah Cobb came behind the van.

He was laughing heartily.

"Look at here," he exclaimed; "you can't call me a bad sort of chap. I did you a turn."

"In what way?" enquired Osmond.

"Why, I knew you stole that hoss."

"Which one?"

"That dapple-grey mustang you were riding. If you hadn't pressed the poor beast so hard it wouldn't have dropped in its tracks."

"You are labouring under a mistake."

"Not me. That man we fed asked about a boy and a horse; but I didn't betray you."

"Why should you?"

"Come, come, you stole that hoss. It is a State prison offence in Texas, and sometimes a lynching matter. You might just as well tell me all about yourself, then I shall know who I am dealing with."

Osmond looked at Milly.

"Speak out," she said. "You can trust father."

"Very well. You shall know all about me, Mr. Cobb, since you desire it; and you will find that I do not belong to the class you intimate."

In a plain straightforward manner he told the showman the same story he had related to Milly.

The old man was as much surprised as she had been.

"I am astonished!" he exclaimed. "It's a wonder that road-agent didn't kill us all!"

"He only commits big robberies. Small people in a small way he lets alone," answered Osmond.

The conversation dropped here.

They pursued their way to Nacogdochee, but it took them a couple of days to get there, as the van could only go at a walking-pace.

Each day Osmond felt happier.

Milly was so kind to him, and he was so much in love with her that he felt as if he were in Paradise.

It was such a change from the nervous, anxious life he had been leading of late.

They intended to pitch their camp on a vacant lot just outside the town.

They had just taken up their place upon it, when Osmond was roused by the sound of horse's hoofs.

He was now wearing his own clothes.

He and Milly had been talking about Mowbray's Ranche, and his chum, Jack of Warwick.

"I should like to see him," exclaimed Milly. "I know I should like him, because he is your friend."

Osmond looked out of the window of the caravan.

He saw, to his astonishment, four cavalry soldiers, between whom walked Jack.

"Good Heavens! there he is," cried Osmond.

Jack had been taken by Deep and the sheriff to the soldiers, who were conveying him to prison.

He looked very dejected.

In the rear of the soldiers came Deep and Sheriff Prober, riding in a buggy.

They seemed to have been enjoying themselves, for they were both laughing heartily.

CHAPTER XXI.

DISCOMFITURE OF DEEP—JACK IS SET FREE—THE VAN ON FIRE—DEATH OF THE OLD SHOWMAN.

OSMOND in a few words explained to Milly that his friend, Jack of Warwick, was evidently in a difficulty.

Why he should be arrested by the soldiers he could not guess.

Surely he could have committed no crime.

To go to his assistance Osmond felt was his duty.

There was no time to be lost.

Perhaps he might do some good for him.

Slipping on his hat, he squeezed Milly's hand.

"I shall be back presently," he said.

"Take care Felton does not see you," she replied.

"Nonsense," said Osmond. "Felton would scarcely dare to venture into a town."

"I know not. You know his talent for disguises."

"Where is he to get a disguise? Besides, there are too many people about for him to hurt me."

He ran nimbly into the road.

In the crowded streets of a busy town he did not feel at all afraid of the road-agent.

It was only in lonely places that the nervous dread came over him, almost paralysing his senses and overcoming his will.

For a long time he had not seen any people such as he had been accustomed to meet at his school and in Warwick.

The street at the top of the vacant lot where the van was standing was pretty well crowded with people.

They stopped and stared at the soldiers and the buggy.

A few yards up the street was the house of a magistrate, or judge, as he is called in the West.

Outside this house the cavalcade halted.

The throng now became denser.

With difficulty Osmond pushed his way through.

The sheriff had got out of the buggy, and had seized Jack by the arm.

Another surprise awaited Osmond.

From the bottom of the buggy Mr. Deep drew the form of a man.

He compelled him to alight.

This man was no other than the Texas cowboy Dawes.

His face was wan and pale; he was very weak, and, indeed, could scarcely stand up.

This is not to be wondered at, when we consider the wounds he had so recently received at the hands of Lourada.

Jack was handcuffed.

There was no necessity for taking this precaution with Dawes.

He was not physically able to run away.

The two prisoners were taken into the house.

It happened that the judge was at home, though he spent most of his time at a saloon round the corner.

This magistrate was a lawyer, and remarkably shrewd, having been educated in New York.

He had a few years back emigrated to Texas, and was growing up with the rising town of Nacogdochee.

The door was shut, and the crowd kept back by the soldiers.

In vain Osmond applied to be admitted.

He was rudely told to stand on one side.

In a private room the judge sat at a desk, which was covered with books and papers.

Jack and Dawes were placed before him.

The sheriff and Deep were sworn, and proceeded to give their evidence.

It appeared that, after locking Jack in the tool-house, Deep refreshed himself, and in the afternoon took him away.

He borrowed MacTavish's buggy for the accommodation of himself and the sheriff.

On the journey to Nacogdochee they determined to visit the cave.

Jack made no objection when asked to show the way.

Here Dawes was easily captured.

Of course no trace of the road-agent could be discovered.

As we know, he was far away by this time.

The judge listened to the evidence attentively, and called upon the prisoners for their defence.

"What have you to say?" he asked, addressing Dawes.

"Nothing," replied the cowboy, sullenly.

"It is alleged that you were one of Felton's band."

"I guess that's about right. You've got me, and it's no use my kickin'."

"What you have confessed will be used against you at your trial."

"I don't care, boss. Everybody always said I should come to a bad end."

"Then you admit the charge?"

"It is true I joined the band. Anything else you will have to prove against me."

"Very well. I shall hold you. Sheriff!"

"Yes, judge," replied Prober, promptly.

"This man stands committed."

Dawes was taken to another part of the room, and given a chair to sit upon.

It was then Jack's turn to be examined.

He was burning to vindicate his character, which had been so foully aspersed by Deep.

"What's your name and profession?" enquired the judge.

"Jack Hardwick, cowboy to Mr. MacTavish, up at Mowbray's Ranche."

"Britisher, I reckon."

"Yes, your honour; and I'm not ashamed of it."

"How about what this Austin man says? I have it on my notes that you were in the cave with Felton."

"The answer is very simple. I went to see if I couldn't capture him, and he captured me."

"Well, what then?"

"I got away," said Jack—"stole off in the night."

He did not enter into the story of Osmond's relations with Felton.

They were so complicated that he was afraid no one would believe him if he did.

"Dawes!" exclaimed the judge, "is this boy one of your gang? Speak up, now."

"No, your honour," replied Dawes. "He never was, either. I guess I'll die, so I may as well speak the truth."

"That will do. Sheriff, what did you arrest this boy for?"

"The Austin detective told me to do so," replied Prober.

"You took the responsibility on yourself on the information you received?"

"I thought it might lead to something, sir," said the sheriff, who began to think he had made a mistake; "but I'll allow that I was hasty, and I conclude that I was wrong, because there's some spite at the bottom of what the Austin man told me. The cowboys had been playing him tricks."

"Humph! Just what I thought. If Jack Hardwick was guilty of belonging to the road-agent's band, he would not have shown you the way to the cave, assisting in the arrest of Dawes, as the latter would have been a strong witness against him."

Jack's face began to brighten.

It seemed as if he were going to get out of the scrape that Deep had dragged him into.

"I leave the case in your hands, judge," said the sheriff.

"What else can you do? You are my help, and have no authority in the matter," was the judicial answer.

"That's so. I take a back seat."

"Do more than that."

"Just say what that is, judge."

"Take off the handcuffs. I release Jack of Warwick, who will leave my court without the slightest stain on his character."

In a moment the handcuffs were unlocked and removed.

Deep was in a high state of excitement.

He did not like his prey to slip through his fingers in this manner.

"Say, judge," he cried, "ain't you going to hold him?"

"You have heard my decision."

"But he's an awful bloodthirsty villain, and I could tell you about his friend Osmond if—"

"I have no person named Osmond charged before me!" interrupted the judge, sharply.

"Wait till I tell you."

"Case dismissed."

"But, judge—"

"Court is closed!" cried the judge.

"This ain't justice if I can't be heard. I'm a detective from Austin, and I want to know—"

Again the judge interposed, looking critically at him.

"Where have I seen you before?" he asked.

"Perfect strangers, your honour," replied Deep. "Never saw you before in my life."

"Hold on!"

"I'm a respectable citizen, and—"

The judge struck the table with his clenched hand.

"I've got it!" he exclaimed.

"Got what, judge?" asked Deep, who appeared fidgety and ill at ease.

"I've placed you. It was five years ago, at Galveston, when—"

"Never been in Galveston in my life, judge."

"Silence! I defended you in a horse case. You were accused of stealing a horse, and I was your counsellor. Your first name is Uriah."

"That's right enough; but—"

"I got an acquittal. You are the man right enough."

"Ah, yes!" said Deep. "I remember now. What a remarkable mem'ry for faces you must have, judge!"

"And facts."

"Well, it wasn't all facts. You see, I'm mighty fond of animals, they all take to me, and that horse I was accused of stealing followed me home. Dear, dear! to think I should have clean forgotten you!"

"I say you stole the horse!"

"The jury said I didn't," answered Deep, with a cunning leer.

"You dare to contradict me!" cried the judge. "That is as much as to say I do not speak the truth, and I call it contempt of court. Fined ten dollars!"

"Thunder! You don't mean it!"

"I do. Pay up!"

"I haven't got over two dollars in my clothes!"

"Can't help that."

"Those tarnation road-agents eased me of my currency when they stopped the darned old stage."

"I shall have to send you up for seven days in the penitentiary. Committed."

"But look at here!"

"Court's closed."

The judge waved his hand; the sheriff handcuffed Deep, who was furious with rage, and marched him and Dawes out of the house.

Jack was about to follow, when the judge said—

"I don't know how you're fixed, but I haven't had my fees."

"Oh, I've got some money," replied Jack. "But I thought I was acquitted of the charge."

"Certainly you are. I'm not saying anything about that, am I? You see, I couldn't get anything out of that fellow from Austin. I've held court, and I ought to have my fees out of someone."

Jack could not see the right of this.

Nevertheless, he felt grateful to the judge.

"How much do you want?" enquired he.

"Make it ten dollars. You've got off well. I'm a little pushed, as rent-time's coming on, and I've a lot of expenses to meet."

Jack handed him a ten-dollar bill, which the judge pocketed with great eagerness.

"Aren't you paid for your services?" asked Jack.

"Yes, after a fashion. We get a bit of a salary, but there isn't much of the fees and fines that go to the country. We keep them. Good day, mister; I hope you find cattle-ranching and stock-raising agreeable in this country."

"I'm doing well," replied Jack, "and have no reason to regret coming here."

"It's a fine country. Good-bye again. Come and see me whenever you are this way."

Jack nodded, and, walking into the passage, let himself out.

With the departure of the sheriff and his two prisoners, the crowd had dispersed quickly.

Only Osmond remained waiting for Jack to come out.

He wondered what had become of him, and was just on the point of knocking at the door to enquire.

Jack was in high spirits. He laughed to himself at the specimen of justice in the Far West to which he had been treated.

Still, he had nothing to complain of.

All he had to do now was to get back to Mowbray's Ranche the best way he could.

He thought he would wait until the stage started, and go by that, as it was less expensive than hiring a horse, and he could not dream of tramping such a long distance.

So absorbed was he that he did not see Osmond.

He would have passed him had not the latter grasped him by the arm.

"Jack!" he cried, "don't you know an old friend?"

"You!" replied Jack. "Gracious heaven! wonders will never cease! Where did you spring from? Give me your hand."

They shook hands in the most cordial manner.

"What does all this mean?" said Osmond.

"I am just as anxious to hear your story as you are mine," replied Jack. "But I am so glad to see you again. I don't know whether to laugh or cry. Let me congratulate you on having got rid of your ghost."

Osmond quickly told him of the clever way in which he had escaped from, and completely baffled, Felton, and joined the caravan.

In return, Jack related the trouble and annoyance he had been put to owing to the vindictive spite of Deep.

"However," he concluded, "he has done himself no good, for I am free, and he has to languish seven days in gaol on bread and water, a not very appetising fare. Talking of food reminds me that I am hungry."

"I could eat a horse, and chase the rider," said Osmond.

They looked around them, and saw a restaurant on the other side of the way.

"There is a shop," exclaimed Jack. "Be my guest; I will treat you to a knife-and-fork breakfast."

"I don't like to trespass on you; it seems like imposing on good-nature. You can't have much money."

That was true; and what he did possess he had to work hard for.

"All I have is at your service," Jack answered. "I'd share my last crust with you."

"My breakfast is waiting for me at the van. I am entitled to it as the talking-ape, you know."

"Surely you don't mean to stick to that?"

"Not since I have met you. I'll go back to the ranche, borrow some money from MacTavish, and start for England at once."

He was always on the point of starting, but as yet he had not taken the initial step.

"I see how it is," laughed Jack, "you have a sweetheart in the person of little Milly."

Osmond blushed like a girl.

"Why not?" he asked. "She is the best and sweetest girl that ever lived, I can assure you."

"Is she fit to adorn an old and wealthy peerage?"

"Yes," replied Osmond, confidently. "You will say so when you see her."

"Postpone the interview till we have had breakfast. Come on. I will take no refusal.

Jack seized his arm, and pulled him across the road.

They went inside the restaurant, and were supplied with all the delicacies the proprietor could boast of.

As they were breakfasting, the door opened, and Noah Cobb entered.

He walked straight up to the table.

His face was red, and his speech husky, and his legs trembled a little, all of which indicated that the showman had been drinking.

"I saw you come in," he exclaimed, "and I waited outside till I got kinder tired."

"Sit down and have something," replied Osmond, good-naturedly, adding: "Jack, this is Mr. Cobb I was telling you about."

"He's welcome," Jack replied.

"No, I ain't, and I can see it," the showman snapped. "You've met with a friend, and you're going to slip me as you did Felton."

"I'll play the talking-ape for to-day for you."

"What's the good of that to me?"

"You can't have me all the time."

"Didn't you promise I should when I picked you up—come, now?"

"Circumstances alter cases. I have made up my mind to go back to England, and, consequently—"

"You're worse than a Philadelphia lawyer. It's true we didn't have any articles of agreement drawn up and signed, but I consider you my hired servant all the same, according to the custom of the profession, which is a week's notice on either side."

"Sit down and make yourself at home," said Jack.

"Not me. I consider he's treated me very shabby," answered Cobb. "I reckoned on him travelling with me to Galveston, and perhaps touring it through Loosyanner."

"Get another boy."

"They ain't so easy got. The boys would come along of me, but the parents won't let them. The law calls it kidnapping if you ain't got the consent of the father and mother."

"Will a five-dollar bill make it up to you?" asked Jack.

"No, nor yet twenty of them."

"Shall I come and perform to-day?" enquired Osmond.

"No; you can stop away altogether. But I'll get level with you."

"How?"

"If I can find Felton—and I think I can—I'll put him on your tracks—cover them up anyhow you like."

"That would be very mean," Osmond said.

He trembled at the threat.

"I'll do it, by Peter!"

"Go back to the van. I'll join you presently, and we'll soon fix things."

"You won't. I ain't done with you yet, you bet!"

"Have sense. I'll—"

"Look at here: I saw Felton jes' now," interrupted the showman, quickly.

"Where?"

"Right here in the town. I'll own up I didn't speak to him; but I will, my boy, next time. I'll have revenge, that I swear."

With this menace, the showman took his departure.

Both boys were somewhat disconcerted, for they did not think Cobb would be offended at the breach of a verbal agreement.

He had taken it very much to heart.

The defection of Osmond meant utter ruin to him, unless he could get another boy directly.

As he had stated, this was an extremely difficult task.

"What is to be done?" Osmond asked.

"We must go to the caravan and reason with him."

"Do you reckon Felton is really in town?"

"No, I don't. Daring and venturesome as he is, I can't believe that he would run the risk of being recognised."

"People don't know him; he always wore a black mask."

"They had him in gaol here, remember."

"He would avoid that locality. Oh, heaven!" sighed Osmond, "I wish he was in the Devil's Gap."

"So do I, for your sake," said Jack. "They'll lynch him if ever he is caught."

"Dawes will be hanged, I suppose."

"No doubt," Jack replied. "Fellows like him are sure to meet with their deserts sooner or later."

Being oppressed at what had happened, they finished their repast in silence, called for the bill, which Jack settled, and went away.

Thinking there was no occasion to hurry back to the caravan, they took a walk round the town.

It was a growing place, but at present its dimensions were not very large.

A few years before it had been nothing but one vast stretch of prairie.

Towns grow like mushrooms in the Western States.

After a couple of hours' stroll and a chat, which they enjoyed, the two friends steered towards the vacant lot.

The van was there, but there was nobody about, except Milly.

She was leaning against one of the wheels, looking very disconsolate.

Something had evidently happened to disturb her mind.

They advanced quickly towards her.

Osmond's heart began to beat rapidly.

"Milly!" he cried.

"Oh, Osmond," she exclaimed, "I am so—so glad you have come!"

She looked enquiringly at Jack.

The latter took off his hat and bowed politely.

She could not help admiring his frank, honest face.

"This is my friend, Jack of Warwick," said Osmond.

She held out her hand, and he noticed that her eyes were full of recent tears.

"I am pleased to know Osmond's friend," she exclaimed, as their hands met in a friendly grasp.

"Pray tell me," said Osmond, "if anything has occurred during my absence to annoy you. I should not have been so long if I had not stayed with Jack, who was brought into town accused ot a false charge, which has been dismissed."

"Have you seen father?" asked she.

"He came into a restaurant where we were having breakfast."

"I thought so. Just now he entered the van, I am sorry to say, dreadfully tipsy."

"He was so when we saw him," observed Osmond.

"Was there any unpleasantness between you?"

"A little. I told him I could not play the ape for more than one day, and he did not like it."

"Just so," said Milly. "He began to vow vengeance against you. In vain I tried to pacify him."

"What did he do?"

"Turned me out of the van, and locked himself in."

"Let him stay there and sleep it off," replied Osmond.

"But he threatened to set the van on fire. Will he do it, think you?"

"Not he. It's his shelter. He's not such a fool."

Milly shook her head gravely.

She knew her father better than he did.

Noah Cobb was very dangerous and quarrelsome when in his cups.

The old showman had done some very queer things when under the debasing influence of drink.

Suddenly the glass in the little window cracked.

In an instant a volume of flame and smoke shot out.

Assuredly he had in a moment of madness carried his threat into execution, not caring for results.

"Oh, heaven!" cried Milly. "My father, my father!"

She wrung her hands wildly.

The woodwork, which was as dry as tinder, began to crackle.

There was no doubt now that the caravan, which had so long been the home of the showman and his daughter, was on fire.

More than that.

It was well alight in the fore part, for another window cracked, letting out the flames.

"Save him!" said Milly in beseeching tones.

"I will, if possible," replied Osmond.

"Heaven give you the strength!"

Osmond and Jack rushed to the door of the caravan, and kicked and knocked against it.

They had no tools with which to attack it.

All they could depend upon was their own strength, and this was of little avail against the bolts and hinges.

Not a sound came from the inside, save the crackling of the timber, and the serpent-like hiss of the fire.

The showman made no sign whatever.

Either he was in a drunken slumber, or he had been already suffocated by the smoke.

Like battering-rams the two boys hurled themselves at the door.

It shook, it quivered, but would not give way.

"What can we do?" exclaimed Osmond.

"No more than we are doing."

"Could I not get in at the window?"

"That would be to court certain death. Hark! a hinge gave way then. Keep it up. Hurrah! We shall do it yet."

A terrible cry was heard from the interior.

It was the cry of a man in mortal agony and fear.

Just such a despairing death-shriek that chills the blood and freezes the marrow in the bones.

The boys' faces went as white as paper.

Noah Cobb had been roused at last, and was burning—choking.

If they had been able to look round the corner, they would have seen his face at the window.

Such an awful face!

Distorted with horror, convulsed with pain.

His hands were trying to tear the wood-work down, and the broken glass cutting his fingers made them stream with blood.

Milly saw it.

It made her reel; she tried to rush to her father's help, but the horror of the thing overcame her.

All the blood left her heart, and she fainted dead away.

The next moment the showman vanished from the window.

That awful face, those bleeding hands, were seen no more.

He had fallen back into the flames, to be burnt alive.

With a crash the roof of the van fell in, and the fire, finding vent, shot swiftly upwards.

"It's no use," said Jack, as he stood still, exhausted by his efforts; "we've done our best, but all is over."

"Keep on trying, for—for her sake," cried Osmond.

"I've been working like a nigger, and am played out. Let us see to your little Milly. She's fatherless now, poor girl!"

Osmond desisted from his efforts.

He saw it was useless to persist any longer.

The old caravan was now one mass of flames.

They went round and discovered Milly lying senseless on the grass, her breathing being scarcely perceptible.

By this time the fire had attracted passers-by and those dwelling in the vicinity.

Men, women, and children came hurrying up.

Seeing the van in flames, Milly in a faint, and the boys standing by, they were inclined to regard Jack of Warwick and his friend as the authors of the fire.

"This is a nice how-d'ye-do!" a big, fierce-looking man exclaimed. "What have yer been up to?"

"The showman got drunk, and set the van on fire," replied Jack.

"What have you to do with it?"

"We are friends of his, that's all."

"Why didn't you get him out?"

"He'd locked himself in. The girl's his daughter; she'll tell you the same as I have."

Osmond took no part in the conversation.

He had knelt down, and placing Milly's head on his knees, was trying to restore her to consciousness.

In a short time he succeeded in doing so.

She was greatly distressed.

The van was now nearly consumed to the wheels.

"Father, where are you?" she asked, with a distracted air.

"We could not break the door in," replied Osmond. "He is—"

"Dead! I know it," cried the girl. "Oh, that last look!"

A woman living close by kindly offered to take Milly in, and, with Osmond's assistance, led her away.

Jack remained to see to the body of the old showman, or what was left of it.

In half-an-hour the fire burned itself out, the floor gave way, and the charred body was visible.

It was a horrible sight, and our hero turned from it, sickened and disgusted.

A bystander, saying that the horse was of no use to the owner, since he was dead, quietly walked him off.

Jack went into the town and found an undertaker, whom he engaged to conduct the funeral of the ill-fated man.

The remains were removed, and Jack paid the bill in advance.

He then joined Osmond, who told him that Milly was calmer, though slightly hysterical, and very weak.

The question that agitated their minds was what they could do for her.

By this calamity she was unexpectedly thrown on the world.

Osmond had asked her if she had any friends, and she had replied sadly in the negative.

Deprived of her only protector, what was she to do for a living?

"Helen MacTavish is in want of a dairy hand," said Jack. "Suppose we take her to the ranche?"

"She cannot milk or churn or make cheese," answered Osmond.

"If not, she can soon learn. Leave her there while you go back to England. You can send for her."

"Of course she could not go with me. But will Helen have her?"

"I'll see to that," rejoined Jack. "Helen will do anything in reason that I ask her."

"Ah, yes! I had forgotten. Helen is to be your wife."

"Some day, and with her capital and my energy, I mean to be one of the first cattle kings in Texas."

"Should you require monetary assistance at any time, write to me. My purse is yours," replied Osmond.

"I shall be all right, without troubling anybody, though I thank you for the offer," said Jack.

It was finally arranged that Milly should be taken to the ranche, and put in charge of Helen.

In her the poor, grief-stricken orphan would have a sincere friend.

Cheerful occupation would drive her sorrow from her mind.

It was useless for her to wait in Nacogdochee for the funeral.

The stage started that afternoon, at five o'clock, for Mowbray's Ranche and Brazos.

Osmond made the proposition to Milly, who, with many thanks, accepted Jack's kind offer.

Our hero booked seats, and at the hour named they took their places, and with lighter hearts started for the ranche.

Nacogdochee was soon left behind.

The prairie was dry and parched with the recent heat, the grass was stunted, and a blue haze hovered over the ground.

In the western sky the sun hung like a ball of fire.

The stage was full of passengers, who were armed to the teeth.

Owing to the recent robberies, and the knowledge that Felton was still at large, no precaution was neglected.

The road-agent had terrified all that part of Texas.

Wild and absurd reports were circulated respecting him, and believed in.

Some said he was at the head of a band of fifty desperadoes.

Others declared that he was playing a loose hand, and lying low, waiting for an opportunity to strike.

The passengers talked about the road-agent and nothing else.

Jack and Osmond did not contribute to the conversation what they knew, deeming it advisable to keep it to themselves.

When about ten miles out of the town, they saw a man coming towards them.

He was alone, looking tired and jaded, covered with dust, and sunburnt.

Getting out of the way of the stage, he turned his head.

Not before Osmond had caught sight of his features.

In a moment the stage had passed, and the man was gone.

Only his back was to be seen.

Jack had been talking to Milly, and though he had seen the man, he took little notice of him.

He deemed him to be a tramp, such as are to be met with on the country roads constantly.

Osmond's face blanched; he trembled violently, and touched Jack's arm.

"What is it?" asked our hero.

"Did you see that man?" Osmond asked, in a whisper.

"Not to notice him. What of it?"

"He is Felton."

"Never! It can't be!"

"I know what I am talking about, and I tell you it is he."

"What shall we do? Stop the stage, and—"

"No, no! He did not see me. For God's sake, let the man-demon go!" replied Osmond.

"Be it so; perhaps it is best," Jack answered.

Nothing was said to the others, though, perhaps, those who talked most boastfully would have drawn in their horns if they had known they were so near the dreaded road-agent.

Presumably he was on his way to Nacogdochee.

The stage changed horses twice at wayside houses, travelling all night by the light of the silvery moon.

It was about eight o'clock in the morning when the coach drew up in front of Snell's.

Jack and Osmond shook hands with the saloon-keeper.

"You two back!" he exclaimed. "Well, I want to know—"

"Not now. We will see you later on, and tell you our adventures, which are very peculiar."

"Do tell! Did you give that skunk Deep the grand shake?"

"Yes. He's got seven days' imprisonment."

"Good. I'd give a sneaking, lying, underhand chap like that six months twice a year to the end of his natural life. Bully for you!"

He looked at Milly.

"Who's the young lady?" continued he.

"That's another thing I'll tell you presently," replied Jack.

"Have they caught Felton?"

"Not yet."

"Confisticate that fellow! He's like an eel! How about Dawes?"

"He's held for trial."

"Good again!" said Snell. "My! Miss Helen has been in a way about you! And MacTavish has drained a bottle of whisky on the strength of your arrest. He couldn't go home last night, and is asleep upstairs in my place now."

Jack hurried off with Osmond and Milly.

Helen was standing on the path near the garden gate, looking up the road at the stage.

The young girl thought she might hear some news of Jack.

She had been crying until the flesh beneath her eyes was red and swollen.

In another minute Jack ran up to her, put his arm round her waist, and was kissing her fondly.

She submitted to his caresses, and returned them lovingly.

When Osmond introduced Milly, and explained the terrible shock she had sustained, Helen received her warmly.

"I will be as a sister to her," she said.

They entered the house, and Mauma placed breakfast on the table.

"Lor' sakes!" she exclaimed, "cowboys is most wonderful creatures. They's got more lives nor a cat."

"Aren't you glad to see me back, aunty?" asked Jack.

"I's real glad."

"That's all right. Give me something to eat, and I will buy you a new cap next time I go to town."

They were a happy party as they sat down to breakfast, all except Milly, whose eyes were kept wet with tears.

She could not forget the awful occurrence in Nacogdochee.

Whatever his faults were, the old showman had always been a good father to her.

He had done all in his power for his child.

Now she was among strangers, who, however, were also friends, and thinking of this she tried to be cheerful.

CHAPTER XXII.

A FRIEND IN NEED—BRIBING THE GAOLER—ESCAPE OF DAWES—FELTON WILL NOT GIVE UP THE GAME.

THE assertion made by Osmond that he had seen Felton was perfectly correct.

That enterprising individual, who had been everything in the criminal grade from a horse-thief to a murderer, was walking towards Nacogdochee.

He was in a desperate frame of mind.

When he saw the stage, he had half a mind to shoot the driver and call upon the passengers to deliver up their valuables.

Another glance convinced him that there were too many of them for him to contend against single-handed.

Osmond did not think the villain had seen him or Jack.

But he had done so.

The man had the eye of an eagle.

"Ha, ha!" he chuckled; "the friends have met, and are going back to Mowbray's Ranche. All the better. I shall know where to find them. Yes, yes! I shall have them—I shall have them yet!"

As he walked on he saw an old man coming towards him with a pack on his back.

This was a Jew pedlar, a Pole by birth, of whom there are many in the States.

The man had a long, white beard, a hooked nose, and a back that was bent with age and toil,

"Good-day, my friend," said Felton, as they met. "What have you got in your pack?"

"Some sheap goods in the jewellery line, ma tear," was the reply. "Should you like to puy anything?"

"How can I tell until I have seen them?"

"Very vell. I show you, for I vant a rest, and if you see anything you like for your girl, I make you a pargain, or my name is not Solomon Moshesh."

He put his pack on the grass by the side of the road, and heaved a big sigh of relief.

In the bag was a polished box, which contained gold and silver plated earrings, brooches, bangles, and bracelets. Underneath was some clothing.

When he displayed his wares, Felton burst out laughing.

"I wouldn't give you five dollars for the whole stock?" he exclaimed; "they are the commonest rubbish. You can't trick me, for I have been in the business."

"Vell," replied the Jew, "if ve can't trade, I vas shorry. They is pretty, if not vorth moch."

"Good enough for servant - girls, that's all. I wouldn't have them at a gift."

"You see, I vas afraid lately of that road-agent they call Felton; they shay he vill spring up from the ground and rob anypody. If I have good goods, and meet him, vere vas I?"

"You're right. I admire your discretion. What have you got in the clothing line?" asked Felton.

"That vas principally an order I got from a shentleman's at a ranche; it is a costume of the theatre. He and his friends vas going to have a stage play, and he order of me a grey wig, a beard, and some old closh. I got them with a great deal of trouble. It vas a pedlar like me he vants to play."

A smile came over Felton's face.

Chance had thrown in his way that of which he was in search.

He wanted to go into Nacogdochee for food, and to hear what was said about him; but to do this, he must have a disguise.

The theatrical costume would suit him admirably.

He determined to have it at all hazards, even though he had to kill the pedlar.

"How old are you?" asked Felton.

"Sixty-five, and I vas fresh as a young boy yet. Look how many miles I valk."

"Don't you think you have lived long enough?"

"Vat an idea!" cried the Jew, holding up his wrinkled hands. "This fall I go back to mine own countree with my hard-earned money, to live with my mother."

"A Jew more or less in the world would not be missed."

"My friend, let me tell you a Jew is as good as a Christian."

"No, he isn't, not by a long shot."

As he spoke, Felton put his hand in his pistol-pocket.

The Jew did not like his conversation or his manner.

They were absolutely alone, and he began to grow seriously alarmed.

"Vel, I vil be going," he said, stooping to pick up his pack.

Rapidly drawing his revolver, Felton shot him in the back.

Falling on his side, the aged Hebrew writhed in agony.

Darting furious glances at his cowardly assassin, he began to curse him, uttering dreadful howls the while.

He would never go to see his old mother in Russia, as he had proposed to himself.

It had been the dream of his life in later years.

And it was never destined to be realised.

The hated road-agent had come across his path like a baneful demon.

"What! will you squeal, you Israelitish dog?" said Felton.

He bent over his victim, and coolly put a bullet in his head.

This finished the business at once, for the Jew kicked out his legs spasmodically and breathed his last in a moment.

"THE MULE TORE UP THE ROAD LIKE A MAD THING."

No. 11

Taking the body by the heels, Felton dragged it into some sage-brush, where it was not likely to be noticed by travellers.

Then he pulled off the Jew's boots.

The right one was empty, but in the left one he discovered a purse made of strong leather.

"Ha! I thought so," he muttered. "These fellows always carry their money in their boots. I wonder how much the old fellow has got. Pshaw! why should I hesitate to rob him? He has made it by cheating."

He opened the purse and uttered a cry of surprise.

All in bills was the large sum of two hundred pounds, or nearly one thousand American dollars.

This was indeed a larger haul than he had expected, and with a smile of satisfaction he put it in his pocket.

He was once more supplied with the sinews of war.

His next care was to rummage in the old man's bag, and find the frugal lunch he carried.

This he leisurely, but with an excellent appetite, disposed of.

The bread and cheese had been wrapped in a newspaper, which he took up casually.

It was a daily journal called the *Nacogdochee Sentinel.*

A paragraph in leaded type attracted his attention.

It was headed as follows—

"Felton the road-agent!
"Arrest of one of the band!
"Dawes, the cowboy, is lodged in gaol, awaiting trial."

Then came an account of the finding of Dawes in the cave, and his arrest. It was further stated that Felton had got away, but was supposed to be in hiding at no great distance from the scene of his exploits.

"Humph!" said Felton. "I will not desert a companion in distress. Dawes must be rescued. But how?"

That was rather a difficult question to answer.

Presently he took the pedlar's costume out of the bag, and discarding his own clothes, which were weather-stained and ragged, put it on.

The things fitted him very well.

He then adjusted the false beard and wig.

There was a shoulder-strap round the box of sham jewellery, and he put it over his head.

This fully equipped him for the part he was going to play. The lines on his face were rugged, and the hard life he had led made him look much older than he really was.

Among the feminine nick-nacks in the bag he found a lady's hand looking-glass.

Holding this up, he surveyed himself, being much gratified by the inspection.

The disguise was certainly complete.

No one could have recognised Felton, the road-agent, in the dress of the ordinary country pedlar.

He stooped his back a little, to counterfeit age.

When he had finished, he hid his clothes and the bag, but did not forget to conceal his revolver about him.

The day was beginning to wane as he stepped out towards Nacogdochee.

He had determined to rescue Dawes, and with his assistance make a final effort to get Osmond in his power.

A dusty walk brought him to the town, which he entered fearlessly, freely mingling with the people, who were returning to their homes after business hours.

He knew his way to the gaol, owing to having been taken there when he was captured; also he was acquainted with the faces of the warders and the head gaoler.

His daring actually induced him to venture to a saloon called "El Paso," which was frequented by these officers.

It stood opposite the prison entrance. He intended to dine there, and bespeak a bed for the night.

For a long time he had not enjoyed the luxury of a bed, but he meant to indulge in one now.

When he entered he made inquiries of the landlord, and was told he could be accommodated. While his dinner was preparing he drank some whisky and looked round the shabby place, into which the setting sun was streaming, showing up the dirt, dust, and cobwebs.

There was only one customer there.

The pretended pedlar had some difficulty in repressing a start.

This man was Barns, the head gaoler, whom he remembered perfectly during his incarceration.

When the escape was made, Lourada had hit him on the head with an iron bar, and his injuries had necessitated his going to the infirmary.

He had only just resumed his duties, and as his pay had been stopped during his illness, he was not in a cheerful mood.

His wife and family were reduced to great distress.

Going up to him, Felton said in a low voice, which he made tremble as if with age—

"Do you want to buy any pretty thing for your wife or your young lady to-day?"

"I shouldn't mind," said the gaoler; "but, unfortunately, I haven't got any money."

"Who are you? I lend money to responsible people in good situations."

"I'm Barns, the gaoler, and I have been sick ever since the prisoners who escaped attacked me. That accursed road-agent, Felton, is the man I blame. If we catch him again he sha'n't get out a second time."

"Ah! I have heard of him," replied Felton calmly. "He is a terrible villain. I would shoot him on sight."

"You are one of the right sort, that's sure."

"I've been peddling amongst the ranches, and the poor cowboys are just scared to death of him."

"He cut up at Mowbray's Ranche, I heard," said the gaoler.

"Ah, and led a poor cowboy, named Dawes, astray."

"Dawes!" echoed the gaoler.

"That's the name; one of the boys on the ranche, and a great friend of mine."

"Of yours?"

"Yes; I've sold him lots of things. Wish I knew what had become of the poor fellow."

"Don't you know?"

"If I did, should I ask? Have a drink at my expense?"

"I don't mind if I do," answered the gaoler.

There was a pause while the drinks were being supplied.

Barns had no suspicion whatever of the pretended pedlar's real character, and was inclined to place confidence in him.

It was quite within the bounds of probability that he had met Dawes in his capacity of a trader and had taken a liking to the cowboy.

"I am sorry for Dawes," continued Felton, "very sorry to think he has joined Felton's band."

"He's in gaol, but there is nothing much against him, as far as I can hear," answered Barns, "except that he was found in Felton's cave, a place in some sand-hills, called the Devil's Gap."

"Did he kill anybody, or commit a robbery?"

"Not that I have heard of; he is charged simply with being a confederate of Felton."

"That doesn't seem to amount to much."

"He is cut about with a knife, though the wounds are not considered serious by the surgeon."

"Who wounded him?" asked Felton, with suppressed eagerness.

"A man named Lourada, who helped Felton to escape. According to his account he was a Spanish marquis. They had a fight in the cave."

"I must repeat that I feel sorry for Dawes; but he should have had more sense than to go with the road-agent."

"He's very much cast down, and don't eat his food."

"That's bad. I'd like to see him free again. Perhaps he'd lead a better life. Say, how much money did you say you wanted?"

"Money! You spoke of it. I didn't mention any sum."

"What do you think of a couple of hundred dollars, repayable so much a month by easy instalments at ten per cent. interest?"

Barns nearly sprang out of his chair.

"Do you really mean it?" he cried.

"Why, certainly. To one in your position it would be a good loan."

"It would be a small fortune to me. I jump at the offer."

"You must see me here to-morrow morning, and we'll complete," replied Felton. "Dear, dear, it's too bad about Dawes! I'm real sorry."

"So am I. But as to the loan?"

"We'll see about that to-morrow.

Dawes saved me from a panther one day on the prairie."

" Is that so ? "

" The beast was just going to spring. Dawes came up on his mustang, fired, and shot him dead."

" That was luck for you."

" Yes, indeed. I never carry a knife or a pistol. Poor Dawes ! If he was to get off at his trial I'd give him a couple of hundred dollars to start in the world again."

" You would ? "

" Yes ; I shouldn't miss it," replied Felton.

Barns paused for a moment.

Then he tapped the supposed pedlar's arm, looked round stealthily, and lowered his voice.

" Why not give it to me ? " he said.

" You ! " uttered Felton with well-simulated astonishment.

" Yes, give it to me, and I will let Dawes out to-night. You take an interest in him, and I want the money."

" How will you do it ? "

" Give him a warder's suit of clothes, and tell him the door will be open. My office is close by. Leave it to me."

Felton was of opinion he could trust the gaoler, but he did not like to part with the money all at once.

He opened his purse, and gave Barns a hundred dollar bill.

" Half down," he said ; " the other half when I see the unfortunate cowboy, whom I love as I would my own son."

" Good. Where shall I meet you ? Here I cannot come," replied the gaoler. " It would draw suspicion upon me."

" Do you know the vacant lot, where I saw a burnt caravan, or, at least, what there is remaining of it ? "

" Yes. Let that be the meeting-place. What shall the signal be ? "

" Pedlar."

The gaoler nodded.

" In one hour the warders will go to supper," he whispered. " Await my coming on the lot. Not a word more."

It was now seven o'clock.

Getting up, the gaoler left the "El Paso" saloon, and the landlord brought in the dinner which the road-agent had ordered.

He fell-to and ate heartily, as he had the appetite of a famished wolf, finishing up with some *aguardiente*, to serve as a stimulant to nerve him for what he had to go through.

Narrowly he watched the clock, as he smoked a fragrant cigar.

" When do you want to go to bed ? " asked the landlord.

" Thank you, not for an hour. I am going to take the air. Will you mind my pack for me ? " replied Felton.

" With all the pleasure in life," cried the landlord. " Are the contents valuable ? "

" Trash to you and me, gold and silver to those who do not know the difference."

" Ha, ha ! you pedlars know how to do it," laughed the landlord.

Felton smiled and went out, muttering—

" The fool can keep the box for the amount of his bill. I have no further use for it."

The hand of the clock marked a quarter to eight.

It was very near the hour appointed by the gaoler.

Would he come with Dawes, or make some treacherous move ?

Felton was determined to sell his life dearly if suspicion had entered the mind of Barns, and he was attacked.

He reached the vacant lot as the clock at the town-hall was striking the hour.

A few stars were shining, but the night was dark, and the lot utterly deserted.

Impatiently, nervously, and on the *qui vive*, Felton waited.

In a few minutes he saw two dim, shadowy forms advancing towards him.

His heart began to beat more quickly.

He did not doubt that they were Barns the gaoler, and Dawes.

The golden key had opened the door of the prison.

Almost anything can be done in the West by the use of money, and Felton knew this fact well.

He was right in his conjecture.

Dawes, looking pale and anxious, was walking by the side of Barns.

There was a puzzled expression on his face, as if he could scarcely believe in his good luck.

Barns had told him that he was to meet a friend in the person of an old pedlar, who had bribed him to let him escape.

He was not aware that he had ever made the acquaintance of a pedlar, except in a casual way of business, when he had bought some trifling article.

Who the mysterious stranger was he could not guess.

Once or twice the suspicion crossed his mind that it might be Felton.

This, however, seemed to him highly improbable, and he dismissed the idea.

When they approached within a few feet of the road-agent, Barns halted.

"Pedlar!" he exclaimed.

"Right," replied Felton, in the disguised tones he had assumed.

Dawes did not recognise the voice, and stood bewildered.

"Now," said Barns, "you two want to clear out of this. I have performed my part of the contract, and must get back to the prison in double-quick time, or I shall be suspected. Give me my money."

"You shall have it," replied Felton.

"Be smart, old man."

Felton put his hand in his pocket, ostensibly to take out his purse.

But he had no intention of doing anything of the kind.

His fertile mind had conceived a diabolical idea.

This was no other than to kill the gaoler and save the money he had promised to part with.

If successful, he could also get back that which he had already given.

He was truly a man of blood, and had committed so many atrocious crimes that he had no compunction.

If he had not required Dawes's services he would not have raised a finger to save him from his fate.

He had not interfered because he liked him, or from any notion of kindness or generosity.

Dawes was wanted to enable him to attack the ranche with a chance of success.

As Felton held out his hand, the eager gaoler stepped forward to receive his pay, as he fondly thought.

It would enable him to place his home in a happy condition again.

He was never more mistaken in his life.

Felton seized him by the wrist, and with a sudden jerk threw him on his back.

Before he could recover from his astonishment, or cry out for assistance, the road-agent fell upon him.

His knife was in his hand.

With the ferocity of a savage, he plunged the deadly weapon into the gaoler's heart. Again and again was the thrust repeated.

"Good Heaven!" gasped Dawes; "It must be Felton!"

The assassin felt in Barns's pocket, and, recovering the hundred-dollar bill he had given him, rose to his feet.

The gaoler would never move or speak again.

"Say, old pard," cried Felton in his natural voice, "that was a smart bit of business."

"Is it really Felton?" asked Dawes.

"Who else do you think would have run the risk and taken the trouble to get you out of gaol?"

"How should I know you under this disguise?"

"It's clever, I'll allow," said Felton. "Come on, we can't stop here; let us talk as we go."

They walked off hastily, and soon gained the outskirts of the town.

The few people they met took no notice of them.

In a short time they were on the prairie, and began to breathe easier.

Quitting the road for fear of pursuit, Felton threw away his false beard and his wig.

"I am myself again now," he cried, "and feel as if I could defy the whole world."

"How can I thank you for what you have done for me?" asked Dawes. "What can I do to prove my gratitude?"

"Help me."

"Tell me in what way, and I will do anything in my power to aid you."

"Good enough, my boy; you can't say more," replied Felton. "Have a drop of this old rye."

He produced a bottle of whisky with which he had provided himself.

"Ah, now you're talking," exclaimed Dawes, smacking his lips. "I began to think I should never touch a drop of the old stuff again."

"Prison diet don't amount to much," remarked Felton.

"You're right; it just keeps body and soul together, that's all. Gruel, black bread, and water isn't very tasty either."

"I've got you out, and you must do what you can for me."

"Put a name to it," rejoined Dawes, handing back the spirit bottle after taking a deep draught.

"I mean having that boy Osmond. If I can get over to England with him I shall be able to play a splendid game."

"Is he rich?"

"Very. He's what they call an English lord."

"What's that?" queried Dawes.

"It's an aristocratic title, and means something very high-toned."

"Like our senators, or members of Congress?" asked Dawes.

"Different from that altogether. We ain't got anything like it in the Republic. The king or queen makes a lord for services rendered."

"That galoot's too young to have done anything deserving of such a distinction."

"True, but the title descends from father to son. That's how this rooster gets his rank. I have influence over him, and I'll make money out of him in lumps."

"Do you know where he is?"

"Why, certainly; I saw him on the stage with Jack of Warwick going to Mowbray's Ranche."

"Is that so?"

"Fact. I never make a mistake."

Dawes ground his teeth savagely.

"Jurush!" he said, "how I hate that fellow, Jack of Warwick. I should not have been captured if he had not shown the detective and the sheriff the way to the cave."

"You shall have your revenge, my boy, before long."

"Promise me that."

"I do."

"Then I will go through fire and water for you; but before we go any farther, tell me how you managed to get over the gaoler."

"I oiled his neck," rejoined Felton, grinning.

"Oh, I see, it was bribery."

"Precisely. Every man has his price,

only some cost more than others. When I saw Barns, I gauged his value. He went cheap, because he was hard pressed and in trouble."

"Let that pass. How do you propose to attack the ranche? The cowboys can fight, and will, too," said Dawes.

"I think I will set fire to Snell's saloon."

"What good will that do?"

"Why, it will bring MacTavish's lot out, and then I can seize Osmond."

"That is an excellent idea. What a head you have got!"

"I should not be of much use if I hadn't. My head is my fortune," cried the road-agent.

"My hands have got me my living," said Dawes. "What shall I do now? I don't know."

"Oh, you will get work anywhere where you are not known. MacTavish isn't the only stock-raiser in Texas."

"I don't want to work any more."

"Why not?"

"Since I joined you, I have got out of the way of it," replied Dawes.

"Bah! Work for your living, my boy," exclaimed Felton. "You are not cut out for a road-agent; you're not smart enough. When we part for ever —as we shall do in a few days' time— hire out."

"I don't want to be anybody's help, I tell you."

"So much the worse for you."

They walked on in silence for several miles, keeping parellel with the road, but at such a distance from it that their faces could not be distinguished by travellers.

The night was far spent before they stopped for the rest they so greatly needed.

Dawes's wounds had left him weak, and ill able to bear prolonged fatigue.

Throwing themselves down on the grass, they were soon fast asleep.

Two days' journey would bring them to Mowbray's Ranche.

Little did Osmond, Lord Melbury, dream of the new danger that menaced him.

His implacable enemy was once more on his track.

CHAPTER XXIII.

AN UNEXPECTED ARRIVAL—COWBOYS' JUSTICE—FIRE! FIRE!—OSMOND'S LUCK—THE
FATE OF DAWES.

IT was a glorious day at Mowbray's Ranche.

But terribly warm, for it was now the middle of summer.

All the cowboys had come in to dinner, it being one o'clock.

Osmond and Jack of Warwick were the first to leave the table, as they wished to have a private conversation.

The young lord was going away the next day to journey alone to England.

It was not likely that Jack would see him again for some time.

They had much to talk about.

"So," said Jack, "MacTavish has lent you money for travelling, and you are off to-morrow?"

"Yes," replied Osmond. "I am sorry to leave you, but I feel I must go. Next year, I want you, old friend, to come and see me, and bring Helen and Milly with you."

"That I will do with pleasure."

"I will prepare Lady Melbury for the reception of Milly. She shall go to school and have some education."

"That will enable her to take a place in society," remarked Jack. "and fit her for the position she will occupy as your wife."

"Have you any message for your father?"

"Tell him I am getting on well, and like the country."

They were joined by Warner, who had finished his dinner, and was smoking a pipe.

"Say, boys," he exclaimed, "the stage is coming into town; let us stroll up and hear the news."

"I'm agreeable," answered Jack; "perhaps Felton has been at work again."

As we know, the arrival of the passenger-stage was pretty nearly the only excitement the inhabitants of the ranche were favoured with.

They walked to Snell's, and in a few minutes the coach drove up.

The driver jumped down from his box, and the passengers alighted.

One, however, remained inside; his hat was pulled over his eyes, and he seemed to be asleep.

Anyhow, he evinced no disposition to move.

"What's new?" asked Snell of the driver.

"We've had a tragedy at Nacogdochee," was the reply.

"Do tell," said Snell, with a Yankee drawl.

"It is suspected that Felton is at the bottom of it."

"I want ter know what it's all about."

"The head gaoler has been found stabbed on a vacant lot, and Dawes, one of your cowboys, has broke prison."

"Is that so? Then you can bet your boots Felton is in it," exclaimed Snell. "I never see such a varmint in all my born days—never."

Osmond began to tremble at hearing this news.

He always shuddered at the mere mention of the dreaded road-agent's name.

"That fellow ought to be lynched," cried Warner. "I'm the boy to do it, too, if ever he falls into my clutches."

"I'll lend you a helping hand," said Snell.

"And I," chimed in Jack.

"Lunch is ready," continued Snell. "Are all the passengers out?"

"All but one, and he seems to be asleep," replied Jack.

"I'll wake him up. Say, stranger—hi, yi!"

There was no reply.

The summons was noisy enough to awaken the Seven Sleepers; but this personage was not in the slightest degree affected by it.

"Get inside, Jack, and hoist him out," added Snell.

Jack opened the door of the coach, and entered.

He touched the somnolent one on the arm.

Only a prolonged snore rewarded this action.

Jack shook him violently, and his soft felt hat tumbled off.

"Confound you!" cried the man. "What did you do that for?"

"Halloa! it is you, is it?" said Jack.

He had, to his surprise, recognised Deep, the detective.

"I—I'm going on to Brazos," remarked Deep. "Let me alone, won't you?"

"How did you get out of prison?"

"A friend paid the fine for me, and, of course, I was let out. Felton is abroad again, and I'm after him, hot foot. He and Dawes have been seen going in a westerly direction."

Jack smiled grimly.

"I don't think you will go on just now," he exclaimed. "I owe you something, and you must have a little more cowboys' justice."

"No, no; I'm on business."

"That does not matter. Come out, or I'll haul you."

"Beware how you assault me! I have a pistol, and know how to use it."

"Thank you for the hint. Hand over your shooting-iron," laughed Jack, "or I'll give you a good old-fashioned knock on the head."

"You—you have no right to rob me," stammered Deep.

"The weapon is confiscated, I tell you. Aren't you a fool to come here? What could you expect but that we should have some fun out of you?"

Reluctantly Deep produced his revolver, and, with a sad sigh, gave it up.

If he had not been so very anxious to run Felton to earth, he would not have ventured among the cowboys.

He knew that they hated him.

Jack of Warwick especially had a deep-rooted grudge against the detective.

There was no help for it now, though. The wily fellow was fairly caught.

Nervously he got up and followed Jack out of the coach.

"My stars! it is the Austin man," said Warner. "Here's a lark!"

"That's what's the matter," replied Jack.

"He shall have a taste of cowboys' justice," continued Warner.

"I'll give you five dollars each to leave me alone," said Deep.

"Not for fifty," rejoined Jack. "You

dragged me into Nacogdochee, a prisoner between four soldiers. I had done nothing wrong; it was to gratify your spite. Now it is my turn."

"If you assault me, an action will lie. I'll have you arrested and cast into prison."

"Very well. You shall have something to go upon. Warner, you are the judge. Will you hear the evidence against the prisoner at the bar?"

"I don't want no evidence," answered Warner, disregarding all rules that govern a court of law.

"But, your honour—"

"Go on. What's the charge?"

"Being an interfering fool, and taking a cowboy off the ranche without any just cause, rhyme, or reason."

"That's a grave accusation," replied Warner. "Now, you are the jury, and it is for you to say whether he is guilty or not guilty."

"We call no witnesses!"

"'Tain't necessary."

"Most decidedly guilty, your honour."

"So say I. The jury is right. He's the biggest blackguard this side of the Rocky Mountains!"

"Pass sentence, judge," cried Jack.

"Haven't we anything else to do? Oughtn't he to be called upon for his defence?" asked Warner.

"He hasn't got any."

"Of course he ain't. I forgot that; but I like to do everything legal. Shall I sentence him to be hanged? Down on your knees, prisoner."

"Oh, pshaw!" replied Deep. "Who are you playing with?"

He was inclined to regard the whole thing as a farce.

In this belief he was greatly mistaken.

The cowboys were very much in earnest, as he was soon destined to find out.

"Silence, prisoner," cried Warner. "Down on your knees, I say."

"Not muchly."

"Knock him down, Jack!"

"If he dares—" began Deep.

Jack cut him short by giving him a blow on the back of the neck.

Deep fell on his knees as if he had been shot.

For a moment he thought he had concussion of the brain.

To this succeeded a feeling like dislocation of the spine.

"That's right," said Warner, with an approving smile; "cowboys' justice! Shall we ride him on a rail?"

"Too good for him," rejoined Jack.

"Suppose we ride him on a mule, strapped flat on its back, like the story of Mazeppa on the fiery, untamed steed of the steppes of Tartary?" suggested Warner.

"Will that meet the case?"

"When the mule once starts, there is no telling where he will fetch up."

"That's true. Osmond, go into the yard and trot out the mule," said Jack.

Deep looked the picture of despair.

He was miserable in the extreme.

"Well!" remarked Snell, who had been an amused spectator of the scene, "if you two aren't the boss jokers!"

"We mean biz all the time, bet your boots," answered Warner. "It's of no consequence whether he lives or dies. This court's found him guilty, and passed sentence. Get up, prisoner."

"It's no concern of mine," observed Snell; "only I thought I should have got the price of a dinner out of him. I must leave you to attend to my customers. As MacTavish says, 'many a mickle makes a muckle.'"

Snell passed into his saloon.

Osmond had gone to fetch the mule, fully entering into the spirit of the joke.

Deep rose to his feet, and tried to look at the affair from a funny point of view.

The pain in his neck was subsiding rapidly.

"Say, boys!" he exclaimed, "you've been playing rather too bad a joke on me. Have you had your fun?"

"Not yet," replied Jack.

"Ain't the joke done, and worked right out?"

"Why, no. We ain't fairly started on you," said Warner.

"Come, come!" exclaimed Mr. Deep, coaxingly. "You are good fellows! None like you! Everyone says MacTavish's cowboys are the best in the country. I've been roughly treated. See what you can do to make it up to me. Stand me something to eat and a drink."

"What a nerve you've got!" cried Warner. "I pay for drinks for friends, but never for rats."

"Get me a drink, won't you? I'm pretty nearly parched. There is a new drink out in Nacogdochee."

"What's that?"

"They call it the 'road-agent.' It was invented by a genius who 'tends a bar in State Street."

"How's it made?"

"Brandy, lemon, iced-water, steel filings, and gunpowder."

"Ha, ha!" said Warner. "You think to have a joke at my expense, do you? If you want a 'road-agent,' you'll have to call for it."

"He had you there," said Jack, laughing.

"Now, boys," continued Deep, "let us be friends all round. I'll set up a dinner and a basket of wine, if you like."

"Can't be done at the price," Warner said.

"You must undergo your sentence. Here's the fiery, untamed steed coming!" exclaimed Jack.

Osmond was approaching with the mule.

It was like most mules—of a vicious disposition.

A halter was round its neck, and it followed Osmond as if it rather expected a feed of corn.

"Keep away from its heels," advised Warner, "or you'll want a new set mighty quick."

"What of?"

"Teeth, stranger. That there mule is a trained kicker; he's taken three prizes for kickin'. Once he kicked a nigger under the chin, and took his head clean off his shoulders."

"Oh, Lord! what will become of me?" groaned Deep.

"Have you made your will?" queried Warner.

"No, indeed. If you'll only let me go back to the town and settle my affairs, I'll return and—"

A roar of laughter interrupted him.

"Too thin," replied Warner.

"You can't deceive us," said Jack.

Warner gave Jack a sign. Between them they seized the detective and put him on the mule's back.

It did not take them long, in spite of

his cries, struggles, and protestations, to lay him flat.

Osmond was ready with a coil of rope, which enabled them to securely fasten him.

His head was towards the animal's tail, and his legs hung over the neck.

"Heaven help me!" moaned the detective. "I wish I was at home."

It was a vain wish, for his home was a long way off.

"Slip the halter," cried Warner.

Osmond took it off, and the mule tore up the road like a mad thing.

When it had started, Warner said—

"Rear rank, take close order, and follow up."

The three placed themselves shoulder to shoulder, and ran after the mule.

When the latter had gone some distance it stopped.

The burden on its back was uncomfortable.

It buck-jumped, trying to cast it off.

Finding its gyrations were of no avail, it started off again on its wild career.

At this moment White, mounted on his mustang, came out of the yard.

He was off to attend to the cattle, which were some miles on the prairie, a good deal of sickness having broken out among them.

"Hallo!" he cried. "What's in the wind now?"

"We've caught that Austin detective," replied Jack, "and given him a ride on the mule."

"Where do you guess he's going to land?"

"Don't know, and don't care."

The mule had passed MacTavish's house, and was careering along like a ship under full sail.

In another minute it would be on the prairie, going due west.

"You're rubbing it in," continued Warner; "but I'm riding that way, and will keep an eye on him."

"When the mule fetches up, you can cut him loose," exclaimed Jack. "I only want to scare him."

"Good."

Waving his hand, White set his horse in motion.

The mule had a fair start, and seemed determined to keep the pace up.

Deep continued to utter doleful cries, which resounded on the crisp, dry air.

Every moment they grew fainter, as the distance increased between him and Mowbray's Ranche.

Of whither he was going, or of what would become of him, he had not the remotest idea.

His cries were echoed by the laughter of the cowboys.

When he was out of sight they did not bestow another thought upon him, for it was time to go to work.

Repairing to the stables, they saddled their horses.

But they were not going in White's direction.

Their herds were grazing in the north-east.

Osmond went into the house, wishing to enjoy a few quiet hours with Milly previous to his departure for the Old Country.

Our business, however, for the present is with White, who kept Mr. Deep in sight.

The cowboys had served the Austin detective a rather dangerous trick.

He was perfectly helpless.

Bound as he was, he could not move hand or foot.

Several buzzards were flying in the air, and hovering over him.

At any moment they might swoop down and pick his flesh.

They were only waiting for the mule to stop, so as to make good their hold.

Deep was in danger of being eaten alive, piecemeal.

It was a terible situation.

After tearing along for about three miles, the mule showed signs of having had enough of it.

His pace slackened.

Foam flecked his sable coat, and his tongue lolled out of his mouth.

There is a limit even to a vicious, evil-disposed, hard-kicking mule's endurance.

It was so in this case.

He came to a full-stop, and rolled on his side, as if he wanted to get rid of his peculiar burden.

There was a danger of his rolling on his back.

If so, the Austin detective would be crushed to death.

White arrived on the scene just in time.

The detective had given himself up for lost.

Hastily dismounting from his mustang, White gave the mule a heavy kick.

"Get up, there!" he exclaimed.

The mule kicked out savagely in return.

"Now, then, you know me," continued White.

Still the obstinate brute would not move.

"What! won't you? Then take this strip of buffalo-hide!"

With his whip he lashed the mule, and compelled it to change its position.

Then, with one hand he grasped its right ear, and with the other cut the rope which bound Deep.

The latter fell off onto the prairie.

With a bound and a joyous bray the mule started for home.

"Air you hurt any, stranger?" asked White.

"Kinder cramped and shook," Deep replied.

"It's a wonder you aren't all broke up."

"So I think. No more cowboys' justice for me!"

"Did they try you?"

"Yes; and carried out the sentence."

"Well, look at here!" said White. "You didn't do the square thing by us chaps, so you ain't got much to kick at."

Deep rose and shook himself.

"To Jericho with cowboys!" he exclaimed. "I don't take much stock in them. They've treated me something cruel. I wish I was at home, and I'd never come on the prairie again!"

"That's what yer oughter done at first," retorted White. "What on airth ever brought you out here?"

"Seeking Felton, the road-agent," replied Deep.

"Pshaw! you might as well hunt a phantom. He's here, there, and everywhere, that man—the devil's imp! I wouldn't mind betting he's hiding in the sage-bush over there."

White pointed to some sage-bush and chaparral which was growing only a few yards off.

He only made the remark as a joke.

Still, there is many a true word spoken in jest.

"Don't say that, for heaven's sake!" exclaimed Deep.

The buzzards had flown away, and there was no sign of life near them.

A blue haze hung over the prairie.

"See here, mister," added White, "I must be going."

"My heartfelt thanks for what you've done for me," answered Deep. "I will retrace my steps to the ranche, and chance it, for I have nowhere else to go."

"Be careful what you do when you get there, or you will be treated worse than you've been treated yet."

Saying this, the cowboy sprang onto his horse, and was about to ride off.

"Ha, ha!" he said, "that was a good joke of mine about Felton."

"A bad one, you mean," replied Deep. "It kinder upset my equilibrium altogether."

"You look scared."

"I'd just as soon see my mother-in-law as I would that darned, forsaken, one-horse road-agent. He don't amount to a row of pins, after all. He ain't worth shucks; but he's made people afraid of him."

"You're one of them."

"No, I'm not," said Deep, who was beginning to regain his courage. "It was only a momentary feeling."

"Bah! you can't deceive me with such talk as that."

"I'm telling you the truth. If I was heeled I wouldn't care."

"Ain't you got no weapon?"

"Nary one. Jack of Warwick and that beautiful cowboy Warner eased me of them."

"I can't help you."

"No matter," valiantly exclaimed Deep. "I'd just like to meet that all-fired road-agent face to face, and if I wouldn't give him Jessie this very moment with Nature's fists, I hope I'll never eat clam chowder again. There, man! What do you think of that?"

"It's a good defy; sounds well," commented White.

"I mean it. I feel it in my bones. Bring on this Felton!" cried Deep, who did a war-dance on the grass. "Let me see him; I'll put the handcuffs on his wrists, and run him all the way to Nacogdoches gaol."

"Ha, ha! you're game."

"To the death. I'm a fighter. Give me a show," exclaimed Deep, "and I'll knock him out in four rounds."

"Ha, ha!" laughed White; "wouldn't I like to see it!"

"Produce him, and, on the word of a man, you shall. I want to kill him and get the reward that's offered for him, dead or alive."

"Good. See you at supper-time. Good-bye."

With these words, White started the mustang.

He had not ridden a dozen yards before a man sprang up from the sage-bush, where he had been hiding.

He levelled a pistol at White.

There was a flash and a report.

The cowbow uttered a loud cry, pressed his hand to his heart, and fell off his horse, dead.

The detective's bronzed cheeks turned white as a sheet of paper.

"Felton, by heaven!" he gasped.

It was, indeed, the dreaded road-agent, who had overheard the conversation between him and the cowboy.

The next moment, Dawes emerged from the sage-bush, and placed himself by the side of the road-agent.

Deep was so dumfounded at being unexpectedly confronted by Felton that he collapsed utterly.

Staggering a few paces he sank upon the ground.

Felton fired straight at his heart.

The detective's eyes rolled, his limbs twitched convulsively, and all was over.

The two men walked away.

They soon found another resting-place, where they hid themselves again.

Here they remained concealed until nightfall.

Felton knew, through information supplied by Dawes, that, as a rule, the lights were all put out, and the people at the ranche in bed, by ten o'clock.

At eleven he arrived with the cowboy at Snell's saloon.

They went to the stable, and getting some bundles of straw, piled them up against the side of the house.

Snell and his wife would be awakened by the smoke, and rush out.

Felton reckoned that they would then raise an alarm of fire.

At this, all in MacTavish's household would rush into the road to render what assistance they could to extinguish the flames.

"I shall wait round by the trees," said Felton, in a hoarse whisper, "and

pounce on Osmond when I see him, retreating behind the clump."

"What am I to do?" asked Dawes.

"In the interval between the first alarm and the coming on the scene of the old Scotchman and his cowboys, you must enter the saloon."

"While it is on fire?"

"Yes, certainly. Snell keeps his cash-box behind the counter."

"I understand," said Dawes.

"Now," continued Felton, "stand on one side while I strike a match, and set a light to the straw."

The straw caught in a moment, and the flames hungrily licked the wood.

In a very short time the house was well alight.

It was not long before Snell and his wife rushed into the open air.

Shouting loudly they ran up the road.

The desperate cowboy did not hesitate to enter the house, though it was full of flame and smoke.

When he was out of sight, Felton retreated to a tree, whose dark shadow hid him effectually.

Dawes walked half way across the room, when he became choked with the dense, suffocating smoke.

Sinking to the floor, he crawled on hands and knees to the counter.

Getting behind, he groped for and found the cash-box.

Putting it under his arm, he began to make his way back to the door.

Of a sudden there was a terrible crash.

The roof had fallen in.

A heavy beam tumbled to the floor, and rested on the cowboy's legs.

It was impossible to extricate himself from his terrible position.

With all his might he shouted for Felton, but the roar of the fire and the noise of falling timbers drowned his cries.

With the utmost anxiety Felton awaited his reappearance.

His attention was presently drawn to the road, up which MacTavish, Jack of Warwick, Warner, and Osmond were running.

Snell and his wife followed.

Their loud cries had roused the house, the inmates of which hastily slipped on their clothes.

The fire illuminated the prairie for some distance.

Finding the heat oppressive, Osmond retreated to the clump of trees.

Felton's basilisk eye was fixed upon him.

Unwittingly the boy came close to the road-agent.

In a moment he felt himself seized from behind.

A stunning blow was given him on the head, which rendered him unconscious.

Felton had secured his victim, and carrying him in his arms like a child, he hurried away across the prairie.

It was not till the morning that Osmond was found to be missing, and the charred remains of Dawes were discovered. Then the cause of the fire was clearly explained.

Everyone recognised the fact that Felton, the road-agent, had been at his dastardly work again.

* * *

The bell was ringing for dinner at Kenilworth Hall in Warwickshire.

Two gentlemen, one young, the other middle-aged, were standing near the fireplace in the historic drawing-room.

These were Osmond and Felton, the road-agent.

They had succeeded in reaching Galveston after the disastrous fire at Mowbray's Ranche, and from there they took ship to England.

Osmond was, as before, under the influence of the road-agent, who had sworn to put a bullet in his heart if he denounced him.

Felton was introduced to Lady Melbury as a rich American gentleman who had been very kind to her son on his travels.

Thus it is that we find him in the luxuriously-furnished room in Kenilworth Hall.

Suddenly the door was flung open, and a figure stepped forward.

It was Jack of Warwick.

A Texan detective accompanied him.

"Seize that man!" cried Jack, pointing to Felton.

The latter turned livid.

He looked round wildly for some means of escape.

There was no outlet save by the door.

Turning savagely towards Osmond, the road-agent put his hand into his pocket and brought out his pistol.

"You first!" he hissed.

But Osmond fell in a swoon, and the bullet passed harmlessly over him.

The next instant, the villain was seized by the detective and Jack, and a terrible struggle ensued between them.

During the contest Felton's revolver exploded.

The muzzle was turned towards his own breast.

A bullet went through his vile heart.

Jack had received a letter from Osmond saying Felton was at the Hall, and had acted on it.

He had secured the services of a clever detective.

They started for England without delay.

Helen and Milly accompanied them on their journey.

The meeting between Osmond and Milly was of the most affectionate kind.

Jack of Warwick and Helen MacTavish returned to Texas, after a stay in England of a few months.

Their marriage took place shortly afterwards.

Milly remained at Kenilworth Hall, and will some day be the wife of the young Lord Melbury, who keeps up a regular correspondence with his foster-brother and dearest of friends—JACK OF WARWICK.